The Wishing-Ring

Judaic Traditions in Literature, Music, and Art
Ken Frieden *and* Harold Bloom, *Series Editors*

THE
Wishing-Ring
A NOVEL

S. Y. Abramovitsh
(Mendele Moykher Sforim)

Translated from the Yiddish by Michael Wex

SYRACUSE UNIVERSITY PRESS

First Edition 2003
03 04 05 06 07 08   6 5 4 3 2 1

This book was first published in Yiddish in 1865 as *Dos vintshfingerl* (The Wishing-Ring).
This translation follows the text of the Warsaw edition of Abramovitsh's complete
Yiddish works published in 1936 by Mendele Farlag.

The paper used in this publication meets the minimum requirements
of American National Standard for Information Sciences—Permanence
of Paper for Printed Library Materials, ANSI Z39.48–1984.∞™

Library of Congress Cataloging-in-Publication Data
Mendele Mokher Sefarim, 1835–1917.
[Vinshfingerl. English]
The wishing-ring / Mendele Moykher Sforim (S. Y. Abramovitsh) ;
Translated from the Yiddish by Michael Wex.— 1st ed.
p. cm.—(Judaic traditions in literature, music, and art)
ISBN 0–8156–3035–2
I. Wex, Michael, 1954– II. Title. III. Series.
PJ5129.A2V513 2003
839'.0933—dc21
2003006720

This translation was undertaken to honor the memory
of my father, Alfred H. Sachs,
and his commitment to Yiddish and Hebrew culture.

— MICHAEL SOLOMON SACHS

S. Y. Abramovitsh (1836–1917) was a Russian Jewish writer whose style set the standard for modern literary Yiddish. Regarded as the founder of modern Jewish prose in both Hebrew and Yiddish, he was termed *der zeyde* (the grandfather) of modern Yiddish narrative literature by Sholem Aleichem. Born as Sholem Yankev Broyde (later changed to Abramovitsh) in Kapulye, Belorussia, Abramovitsh was orphaned at fourteen and spent some time traveling with beggars through Ukraine. He later studied under the daughter of Avrom–Ber Gotlober, a leading figure in the Hebrew Enlightenment, and was strongly influenced by its secularizing trends. Adopting "Mendele Moykher Sforim" (Mendele the book peddler) as his pen name, he originally wrote in Hebrew but switched to Yiddish, the language of the masses, from a desire to be "of use to his people." Combining the spoken Yiddish word with modern literary modes, he is best known for his use of satire and irony. The publication in 1864 of his first Yiddish novel, *Dos kleyne mentshele* (The little man), is seen as the beginning of the modern period in Yiddish literature.

Michael Wex is the author of one novel, *Shlepping the Exile;* five plays; and a forthcoming book about Yiddish. His translation of *The Threepenny Opera* is the only authorized Yiddish version.

Contents

A Note on the Translation

AT ITS BEST, Abramovitsh's style is a marvel of nature, and *The Wishing-Ring*, for all its flaws, is studded with set-pieces that leave the Yiddish reader gasping with admiration and laughter. Although the Yiddish can grow quite complex, mimicking and mocking the speech of "the folk," incorporating various levels of usage into a single run-on sentence, or making puns that secular Yiddish speakers could not understand, it is never "difficult." Any resident of Kaptsansk would have been able to understand it, and I've tried to capture this immediacy in my translation. Abramovitsh himself deleted a large number of Slavic words that struck him as too difficult, quaint, or provincial—too folkish for the folk the next village over. The result is a Yiddish that sounds very much like the small amount of folk-Yiddish still being spoken today. I therefore chose an equivalent English, based on demotic Jewish speech at the turn of the current century. I have tried to represent Abramovitsh's virtuosity without slighting the quality of his humor. Despite its pessimistic theme and the melodramatic, somewhat overwrought treatment of prostitution, much of the book is extremely funny, much of the satire still germane.

With the exception of certain commonly used Yiddish and Hebrew expressions (for example, Chanukah, Bar-mitzvah), the transliteration follows the YIVO system:

ay = long English *I*, as in *mine*
ey = long *a*, as in the Canadian particle *eh*
kh = the first sound in Chanukah

There are no silent letters. *E*s at the end of words are meant to be pronounced.

A glossary of Yiddish and Hebrew terms is found at the end of the book.

Introduction

DOS VINTSHFINGERL, here translated as *The Wishing-Ring*, is quite possibly the most important piece of Yiddish fiction written in the nineteenth century, although its characters are wooden and its plot is haphazard. The book is sometimes presented as the memoirs of its protagonist, Hershele, and at other times as the work of an invisible and omniscient narrator probably to be identified with Mendele Moykher Sforim (Mendele the Bookseller), the pseudonymous author who makes a cameo appearance in the book's final pages. There is a narrative gap of at least two decades, during which the adolescent Hershele leaves Russia for Germany, goes to school, and becomes an educated man of the world while remaining a committed Jew. His clothing is described in greater detail than the *Bildung* of this hidden Bildungsroman.

And yet it doesn't matter. *The Wishing-Ring* remains a seminal novel in nineteenth-century Yiddish literature, a work that fulfills and perhaps even surpasses the ambitions of its author, Sholem Yankev Abramovitsh (1836–1917), who wrote under the name Mendele Moykher Sforim. Disguised as Mendele, Abramovitsh managed to play Chaucer, *mutatis mutandis*, in two separate but related literatures. Both modern Hebrew and modern Yiddish literary prose owe an incalculable debt to Abramovitsh, who perfected what the Hebrew poet H. N. Bialik called the *nusah*, the dominant style or pattern, of both. More remarkably, each *nusah* is discrete and sounds like the work of a different writer, despite the fact that Abramovitsh transferred much of his writing from one language to the other and published both under Mendele's name.

The Wishing-Ring was conceived and originally written in Yiddish; the Hebrew version is called *Emek ha-bakha* (The vale of tears). In its first incarnation in 1865, it was a pamphlet-sized booklet about the benefits of education. Things had changed considerably by 1888, when Abramovitsh decided to revive the title. He described his new project to Sholem Rabinovitsh, better known under his own pseudonym of Sholem Aleichem, who had agreed to publish it in his anthology, *The Jewish Popular Library*:

> Using the title of an old book of mine that was only a few pages long, I've started to write you a brand new book in which I plan to put Jewish life and its most important contemporary issues on display. I want to explain the condition of the Jews in no uncertain terms and point out what must be done in order to improve it. I hope that *The Wishing-Ring* will make a splash, a great impression. . . . It's no mere story like the ones other people are writing today; it's a history of Jewish life. It isn't a dummy to be played with, but a living creature with blood, with a soul, with human feelings and a human face.*

The humanity of face and feeling are matters for the reader to judge, but Abramovitsh's success in capturing the contours and conditions of Jewish life in the Pale of Settlement was acknowledged instantly by the Jews still living there and by the Jews who had managed to get out.

The historian Simon Dubnov called *The Wishing-Ring* "the great epic of Jewish life"—an epic of deprivation in which Kaptsansk (Poorsville) represents virtually any small town in the Pale of Settlement, and Glupsk (a city of fools) stands for Odessa or any other large city. By the book's second page, the status of the Jews in Kaptsansk has been made explicit: they're livestock, nothing but beasts of burden and sources of beef for their slightly more prosperous brethren in Glupsk. Unable to produce anything but children, they have nothing to sell but themselves, and Abramovitsh is not shy about exploring the ramifications of this figure of speech.

There are two sources of evil and folly in *The Wishing-Ring*: Jews and Gentiles. Except for them, everything's hunky-dory. We don't really see the non-Jews, but life in exile among them is the real subject of the book. They oppress the Jews by virtue of their superior numbers and political power; the Jews prey on each other like ravening wolves because there's nothing else for them to eat. By the end of the book, in the aftermath of the pogroms that erupted in 1881 and ended any dreams of Jewish "normalization" in the Russian empire, the two sources of evil finally come together. The book's major female character, Beyle, is delivered safe and sound from

---

* As cited by S. Niger in *Mendele Moykher Sforim* (Chicago: Stein, 1936),220–21.

the hands of the Jewish underworld of Glupsk, only to return to Kaptsansk, marry—and then be raped and murdered by the same Gentiles who rape and murder her daughters. Damned if you do, damned if you don't. The Jews are helpless; Zionism is presented as a possible solution, but it receives a less than ringing endorsement. Jews from the West lack understanding; Jews in the East lack education and power. For all his bitterness and indignation, all his satire and his sympathy, Abramovitsh—clearly no Marxist—had no choice but to end the book with a prayer.

Dovid Frishman, an important Hebrew and Yiddish writer about twenty years Abramovitsh's junior, went so far as to say, "Were a flood to wipe away everything but this book, we could reconstruct the general picture of Jews and Jewish life in the Russian *shtetl* in the first half of the nineteenth century on its basis."* The flood came. It seems that Frishman was right.

* Dovid Frishman, "Mendele Moykher-Storim (Sholem Yankev Abramovitsh): zayn lebn un zayne verk," in *Ale verk fun Mendele Moykher Sforim (S. Y. Abramovitsh)* (Cracow: Farlag "Mendele," 1911), vol. 17, p. 47.

The Wishing-Ring

Book One

Kaptsn means "pauper," the plural's *kaptsonim*,
and our story begins in Kaptsansk

1

SAY WHAT YOU WANT about the Jews of Kaptsansk: they're *not* such big
self-starters, they *don't* pull any major coups in their humdrum little lives
or set the outside world reeling with anything at all. Go ahead and say that
they live from hand to mouth. Say all this, and plenty more. But when it
comes to increasing and multiplying, don't, God forbid, say a word against
them; they're as punctilious as all the other Jews. Not even their enemies
can deny that every Jew in Kaptsansk is weighed down, touch wood, with a
parcel of children, and the benefit that this confers upon the world will be
clearly demonstrated a little below.

The householders of Kaptsansk are what you should never be: absolute paupers without a cent to their names. Kaptsansk itself offers them
no means of earning a living, unless you count round-robin begging at one
another's doors. Let one of them just try to open some kind of business—a
small shop, say—the rest of the place jumps right in and does the same,
until the number of Jews is the same as the number of shops: shopkeepers
like sand on the beach and no one to do any buying.

It's the same in other things, too. They all like to push their way into
someone else's business, step on someone else's toes in the approved Jewish
fashion: If there's two, I'll be three; if three, I'll be four, and so on and so

forth until things get to the point of *ve-KAPTSEYNU yakhad*, gather us together, O Lord, *KAPTSEYNU*, impoverish us, that we might all be *KAPTSONIM* together, and cleave to each other, embrace each other, choke each other in brotherhood, until we all suffocate and drop dead together at one and the same moment.

Such a powerful sense of community—each in the other's pocket, each taking the food from the mouth of the other; this *"Che serà, serà,* nothing for you, nothing for me, as long as we're together" is one of those virtues found only among the Jews of Kaptsansk, by virtue of which it falls to their lot to go begging at each other's doors . . .

Everything they earn comes from elsewhere, especially from Glupsk.* The existence of a Glupsk, where you can still do something to earn a little money, is a miracle for Kaptsansk, which quite naturally sends all sorts of people there: teachers and their helpers, middlemen and marginal men, catch-of-the-day sons-in-law fresh from their in-laws' board as well as sons-in-law who are starting to turn. Jews with this and Jews with that— whatever your heart desires: references, illnesses, prestige, and piles. *Baltfiles* and shofar blowers. And women, all kinds of women: prayer-readers, professional mourners, medicine ladies, who have all passed through the Change; egg-ladies, feather-pluckers, women with Passover goose-fat, all still bearing children. Not to mention an endless jumble of boys, servant-girls, married domestics, and nursemaids.

This livestock is highly prized in Glupsk, and enjoys strong sales; Kaptsansk, in its turn, works joyfully for the common good and continues to manufacture the kind of merchandise that makes the world a better place. It prides itself highly on this very important work, work which makes all Kaptsansker Jews into very important people. Should you ever run into a Jew who's an absolute legend in his own mind, it's a sure sign that he comes from Kaptsansk.

. . . And, uh, the author of *The Wishing-Ring* had the grace to be born in the Holy Congregation of Kaptsansk.

His parents didn't make much of a fuss about his birth. It didn't even occur to them to wonder why *kaptsonim* like them were bringing a living creature into the world, to their chagrin and its own; it never occurred to them to wonder what they could do to make the life that they'd given it

---

* Glupsk means, roughly, Town of Fools.

more pleasant, so that it wouldn't come to them later and complain: *"Gevalt, kaptsonim,* why did you go and have me?"

. . . Go ahead, *ask* a stupid question. His mother did what a mother does: she carried him and bore him and didn't get cute. She was a woman, wasn't she? That's what she was here for, right? Even a hen—I don't mean this personally—even a hen does what God tells her to; she lays eggs and broods and doesn't ask any questions . . .

It didn't interest his father much, either. Somebody else got born? What's it to him? The woman had the cramps, not him, and as long as it's OK by her, it's A-OK with him . . . And you think it matters that he's a *kaptsn,* that he's dimpled all over with poverty, and now has another mouth to feed? Gimme a break—let the rest of the world worry. After all, it was the same faith—first in God and then in man—that got him and his parents and his parents' parents born. A Jew can't wait for a printed invitation, for all the necessities of life to be prepared for him here below. If a Jew doesn't dig in his heels and push, he could wait to be born forever: he isn't such a prize that the world, God forbid, couldn't manage without him. But since he's already pushed his way through and has both feet on the ground, he just keeps pushing, with God's help, pushing and pushing. He pushes and strains with all his might—forward, backward, what's it matter?—through doors and through windows. He pushes his life away and that's all.

But there *was* one thing that gave the boy's parents pause and had them breaking their heads: "Master of the Universe, what kind of name can we give your new creation?" They'd already used up all the names in the family on the children who'd got themselves born before. Starting off with their closer relations, his parents had proceeded systematically to the furthest grafts on the family tree. Each child had two namesakes to look out for it in heaven: one dug up from the father's side, the other from the mother's. That was the deal; every kid got two names: Khatskel-Ben-Tsiyen, Lippe-Todros, Dvosye-Kroyne, Peysakh-Zeylig, Tsippe-Sossye, Stisse-Hinde, Karpl-Faybish, Khune-Leml, Shmerl-Ayzik, Keyle-Rikl. In emergencies, a male did duty for a female, a female for a male, two corpses became a couple and the marriage was made in heaven. Uncle Khayim came out as Khaye, Auntie Brokhe as Borekh; Grunne put forth a Grunem and Nokhem worked things out with Nekhome. But all of a sudden they looked around and—uh-oh, no more relatives, no more names. The boy's parents racked their brains, but all to no avail.

"Listen, Leyzer-Yankl." The new mother finally spoke after a slight hesitation. "Do what I say and call the child Gedalye-Hersh, after Gedalye-Hersh, may he rest in peace."

"Shh, stupid!" The father was incensed. "Your Gedalye-Hersh can like it or lump it—I don't want to hear his name. Got it?"

He was a relative of the mother, Gedalye-Hersh, a nephew of her grandmother Kholtse (the near-eponymous ancestor of Khatskel), and an artisan of diverse skills; he stitched long johns, capotes, caps, skirts, jackets, and skullcaps, and patched the occasional shoe as well—anything, in a word, that he could get. His skill in patching was unmatched in all Kaptsansk, and because patches are more valuable in Kaptsansk than anywhere else, Gedalye-Hersh was the choice of the local beau monde. At the first sign of a rip or tear—straight to Gedalye-Hersh; should a shoe develop a mouth to go along with its tongue, Gedalye-Hersh would stuff it up and warn it in no uncertain terms about ever opening a mouth again. Should the same rip or tear reappear the next day, should the shoe ignore him and dare to reopen its mouth, Gedalye-Hersh was on the job: he patched and patched and patched until the hole bit the dust, along with whatever he was fixing.

Had Gedalye-Hersh ever made it to Paris, he would have been showered in gold and borne upon the shoulders of the multitudes. But in Kaptsansk he was naked and barefoot, carried on people's shoulders only when he'd fallen over from one too many drinks. Not that he couldn't hold it—drinking went with the job; it was a prerequisite for membership in the artisans' association, the Khevre Poyle Tseydek. But even the most powerful drinker can get as drunk as Lot sometimes, and when he sobered up, Gedalye-Hersh had the same excuse as a lot of other drunks: whatever he did wrong, it wasn't his fault—he'd been served from the left hand. And just to prove it, he'd grab a bottle of whiskey with his right and drink it all down in front of a crowd of people without so much as a grimace.

He was always doing these kinds of tricks, to the delight of his Kaptsansker audience. Everyone was charmed, with the exception of Leyzer-Yankl; to him, Gedalye-Hersh and his trade were a slap in the face. Some joke, wasn't it, that he, Reb Leyzer-Yankl, a High Holiday *bal-tfile* at a little synagogue somewhere in Glupsk and a paragon of Judaism the rest of the year, a man who spent his time glancing into religious books and hanging out behind the oven in the *bes-medresh*—some joke that he and that . . .

that *artisan*, that know-nothing, should be relatives. No way would he accept Gedalye-Hersh as family. Leyzer-Yankl looked down on Gedalye-Hersh and never invited him to any family functions. If Gedalye-Hersh turned up anyway, he wouldn't deign to look at him.

Gedalye-Hersh, for his part, wasn't fazed by Leyzer-Yankl's snobbery; *his* teasing was always good-natured. "I don't know what's the big deal with Leyzer-Yankl—you don't need any training to twiddle your thumbs. Let him try and lay a patch like I do, then we'll see. Some big shot—a *beheyme*, that's all he is, nothing more." Gedalye-Hersh always concluded with same line, and waved his hand in dismissal: "May God not punish him for his sins."

He was quite friendly with Mrs. Leyzer-Yankl, and used to patch up her wardrobe, turn out the children's things, and stick patches on her husband's clothes, too, without taking a cent for any of it. Hell, when things were tight, he'd slip her a few groschen on the sly, to help out. People say that he was crazy for her when he was young, and that she was also nuts about him; that everybody was expecting their engagement, when up popped Leyzer-Yankl, the eligible bachelor. Grandmothers and aunts were pressing his case, figuring his falsetto for money in the bank. "A chance like this comes along once in a lifetime."

There was an engagement party, with poor Gedalye-Hersh left outside like a pork chop at a kosher butcher's. People say that he changed then, that he was never quite himself again, as if he were under a spell, God save us. He grew distracted, depressed, tried to drink his troubles away. It's also possible that Leyzer-Yankl's heartfelt hatred didn't help things, either. But be that as it may, one way or the other, Leyzer-Yankl hated him so much that the mere mention of Gedalye-Hersh's name was enough to set him off.

Accustomed as Mrs. Leyzer-Yankl was to her husband's slurs against Gedalye-Hersh, they really hurt her this time, and she dissolved into tears in her childbed. Her husband looked at her with compassion and spoke a little more mildly.

"Don't cry, you fool, you. I'm telling you, a kosher Jewish woman does what her husband tells her. And when her husband says 'No,' it means 'No.' Idiot, just consider who, thank God, your husband is, and who Gedalye-Hersh was."

"Gedalye-Hersh was a kosher Jew, a good soul."

"An artisan a kosher Jew? Don't make me laugh. He wasn't enough of an embarrassment when he was alive, I should go and shame *myself* by naming one of my children for him? Come on—don't talk nonsense."

"But a name, Leyzer-Yankl. Where are you going to get a name? . . . Some father you are."

"A name, yeah, right," he stammered, sinking a little into thought.

"And what, heh-heh, what if I were to tell you that I had a dream?"

"What's with the dreams?" he asked, staring.

"Gedalye-Hersh came to me last night in a dream. '*Mazl tov*, Malke-Toybe!' he said. And then he moaned. 'I can't lie peacefully in my grave because my name has vanished from the earth. Have mercy, Malke-Toybenyu,' he begged, pointing to the baby. 'Now you have the power to put me at ease. I'll intercede for you and your husband at the Throne of Glory, and with God's help your child will turn out to be a good piece of work, as sharp as a tack.' His face lit up as he said this, and then he disappeared. What do you say, Leyzer-Yankl?"

"Nu, nu . . ."

"Stop nu-ing, Leyzer-Yankl. I should see good luck the way I saw *him* . . . He came to me again tonight. Just looked at me and pointed to the child, pointed at the child and looked to me; pointed, looked, pleading at first and then, oy, he opened his eyes wide and came at me with his hands stretched out like he wanted to strangle me. 'If you don't. . . ,' he said angrily."

"And what if you don't? What?" Leyzer-Yankl jumped up in fright and cast a careful eye over the amulets around the bed, the circle of buns from the oven, and the baker's shovel hanging nearby.

"Why are you asking questions, Leyzer-Yankl? . . . *Vey iz mir*, he's playing around with the dead."

"Nu, nu, what do you want then, fool?"

"Have mercy, Leyzer-Yankl. Don't be stubborn."

"All right . . ."

2

THEY DECIDED to call the child Hershl, after the latter part of Gedalye-Hersh, a clever choice in more ways than one. In the first place, his father also had some right to a name. Secondly, it's the Jewish way to make a compromise; as the saying has it, "Let both sides be happy." Thirdly, Hershl is still not Gedalye-Hersh; half-hidden, the disgrace wasn't quite so obvious. Fourthly, Hershl's mother, an accomplished home economist who loved to save for later, thought to herself: "A spare Gedalye around the house could come in handy sometime."

She was dead right, and ended up with just enough names to get by. A little while later she gave birth to another boy, and—long life to Hershl—she called him Gedalye. I say "long life to Hershl" because long life is what his brother Gedalye didn't have. His mother's board didn't agree with him, the milk curdled in his belly. The poor thing suffered plenty, and he took counsel with himself and went off to a better place just as he was starting to teethe.

A number of Hershl's brothers and sisters had had similar brainstorms before he was born—they saw that it was no good to have anything to do with *kaptsonim*, with people whose lives are one long calamity, everlasting trouble, and constant torment. Better to die once and get it over with than to starve to death ten times a day. Rather than grow up poor with cobwebs on your teeth, it's better to get out while you've still got your youth: life without bread makes you envy the dead.

But not everyone is alike. Dvosye-Kroyne and Peysakh-Zeylig made a point of staying alive and tasting the joys of marriage. They were bitterly poor and snowed under with kids. Aside from them, Tsippe-Sossye also slipped through the Angel of Death's fingers. A confirmed spinster, nothing but skin and bones, drawn, hollow-cheeked, with dark circles under her eyes, she'd been a knockout in her youth—bright, lively, charming; a good, honest, kosher soul. But virtues that bring happiness to the rich are usually a disaster for the poor. The misery of her parents' house was a knife in Tsippe-Sossye's heart. It wasn't her own troubles that bothered her, so much as the suffering of the rest of the household, the way innocent little children had to waste away and sputter out like candles. So she decided to go off and earn money as a maid, to repay her parents when they needed it most. She was well aware of her father's opinion of himself, that he'd consider it beneath him to have a daughter in service. That didn't hold her back, though; she was determined to do whatever she had to—no matter what—to get her way.

She picked a time when things were worse than usual. Not a crumb in the house, winter coming on fast, the house cold enough to keep wolves from the door. No smoke from the chimney for weeks on end. Her mother was pregnant with Keyle-Rikl, and having a difficult time of it. Shmerl-Ayzik, RIP, had measles, and one foot in the grave; the rest of the starving, naked children were hiding, hunched in upon themselves in corners, their lips coated with scum. No sound but the occasional moan, a sigh from the depths of a heart. They stared out at nothing from glassy, uncomprehending eyes in which the tears stood frozen.

It was then that Tsippe-Sossye opened her mouth. She cried, she got down on her knees and begged her father to have pity on her mother, on the children, and on her, too, and to let her find herself a place somewhere. She spoke from her soul, a flood of impassioned feelings poured up from the bottom of her heart, and her father, just about crushed to death by their bitter want, finally consented. It broke his heart.

Tsippe-Sossye's departure for Glupsk cost her mother plenty of tears. Her father bade her a sad farewell. A serene, unsullied dove, she left the nest with nothing but the clothes on her back, the blessing of her parents, and the heartfelt bon voyage of her weeping brothers and sisters.

In one of its transports of livestock, Kaptsansk furnished Glupsk with a good-looking young servant-girl.

Tsippe-Sossye found a place in a rich house right away. Everything was fine for the first little while; they were happy with her and her work. She wrote cheery letters home and sent a little money, too. But then things started to happen. The master was giving her the eye, plotting how to get next to her. He was subtle at first, insinuating—take it anyway you like: He was a good man, his money hadn't gone to his head, just a warm, caring person who wanted to be a friend to the poor kid. Why not? Some pretty fine servant-girls had already married their way out of his house—and not too shabbily, either; if she played her cards right, she could be just as well off.

She soon learned the real meaning of this noblesse oblige. A whole new world opened up before her, with new kinds of sorrows, with a Satan and a Hell, fire and brimstone and lust—a world of which she'd never dreamt before. Her life became a battlefield. Weak and poor as she was, she had to arm herself constantly against a mighty Satan, a tub of guts used to getting his way. The thought of her parents' dire straits, of how badly they needed her little bit of help, gave her the strength to endure. She held out for as long as she could, then left the house before it was too late.

She got another position, but only the scenery changed. Everything was fine at first, and then it started, this time with two of them—the master *and* his son . . . Sorrow, heartache, and finally . . . out. Again and again, it was always the same. Nothing, then something, the same old story, a story within a story and the same doleful end to the story. There were downstairs stories, too, stories with the female help: with cooks, peddlers, domestic-agents, and late-blooming old-lady philanthropists, a regular *Thousand and One Nights'* worth of stories. Tsippe-Sossye was the victim of her own beauty.

Being born beautiful brought her nothing but trouble. What business do paupers have being good-looking, when there's no need to give them flowers or candy or worry about their feelings when you tell them what you want or when the way you've used them ruins their life? She's a person, this Tsippe-Sossye? She's a maid! "Your body, baby, *all right.* But what's the rest of you to me? You can drop dead for all I care." And what if Tsippe-Sossye has a mother and father who love her with all their hearts, who'd had plenty of troubles, plenty of worries, took food from their mouths and sat up nights until, with God's help, she grew up? And what if Tsippe-Sossye loves her parents just as much, what if she's working and slaving to support her loved ones, who are all she ever thinks of? *That* never entered anyone's mind. Who is she that anyone should think about her? But Tsippe-Sossye's a human being, too; she thinks, she feels. If you prick her, she bleeds.

"And so," says the author of *The Wishing-Ring* in his writings, *"And so, Tsippe-Sossye couldn't take it anymore. Sick, broken, heavy-hearted, she came back to her parents, a different Tsippe-Sossye from the one who'd gone away. Her mother could feel the bitterness in her daughter's heart, she was dying of pity for her downhearted child."*

"My poor, wretched sister. It was your bad luck that God made you so attractive; your bad luck that your beauty found favor with the fortunate. Poor, unfortunate sister, your world's been destroyed, your life laid waste."

3

RIGHT NOW, our Hershele could take a map showing every city in the world, go over it with a magnifying glass, and still find no sign of Kaptsansk there, though once upon a time, when he was still a kid, he was like a worm in horseradish and thought nothing could be better. Kaptsansk was the capital of the world, its midpoint and very navel. Beyond it, around it: desert, waste, and wild beasts. People in the real sense of the word, the choicest of all God's chosen, lived nowhere but in Kaptsansk. It was for them that the sun shone by day, the moon and stars at night. And God, having nothing else to do, devoted himself to the Jews of Kaptsansk. He gave rain for the sake of their animals—the goats should have food and puddles of water to drink, lest they eat the straw off Jewish roofs and lick the walls of the *bes-medresh*. He sent clear, dry weather to make Friday trips to the market or butcher's a pleasure for the women. He sent bumper crops of potatoes, onions, and garlic, so his poor little Jews should have something to eat. There's nothing else to be said: He that keepeth Israel neither slumbers nor sleeps. He does whatever he can, moves heaven and earth, and all for the sake of the Jews of Kaptsansk.

And the Jews return His favors by blowing Him shofar, singing Him a *Meylekh Elyoyn* and jumping up and down when they say "Holy, holy, holy"; they do him honor with a noodle kugel on Shabbes, with dumplings and pancakes on Passover; with nonstop dancing during the annual parade of Torah scrolls in the synagogue on Simkhes Toyre. On Chanukah they give thanks with a *dreydl*, on Purim with noisemakers, costumes, Purim plays—the whole carnival strictly for the sake of heaven, and for the sake of His holy name . . .

To be perfectly honest, Hershele did know of one other city, which sort of brooded on the face of the earth, aswarm with hosts of angels, adjutants, couriers from the Holy One, blessed be He, to the children of Israel. This was the holy city of Jerusalem, where Jews lay buried in the earth, Holy-Land-of-Israel earth, in a state of suspended animation, neither dying nor decaying; where the Jews get a fig—and olives and dates and pomegranates, and where even the goats feed on carobs.

But Jerusalem today is desolate and waste, and the Jewish world has fallen with it. Jewish life is now in Kaptsansk, that is to say in *goles*, in exile.

At the time of which we're speaking, Hershele's idea of *goles* Kaptsansk consisted of: Gavrilo the Shabbes goy, who put out the candles on Shabbes, took brass candelabra off the tables, and heated the Jewish ovens; Tekla the washerwoman, who also rinsed out the greenish-yellow diapers of Jewish babies and milked the cows; Kondrat the drunk, to whom they used to sell all their *khomets* for a shot of whiskey; the local squire, from whom the Jews leased land and inns with which they fed themselves and their families, and to whom, for the sake of appearances, they were sighingly obliged to pay regular premiums; on whom they were sighingly obliged to depend at *yon-tef*-time for potatoes, turkeys, wheat for their matzohs. And worst of all, Mitka the Christian delinquent and his little dog, Zhukl. Forget little boys: big men in Kaptsansk, Jews with wives and beards, would see Mitka and get the shakes, and go miles out of their way to avoid him.

God only knows where Mitka's bitter *goles* would have led, had it gone on all the time, but miracles do happen—Mitka loved Jewish *khale*. Slip him a piece, and he became as soft as the bread for a while, licking his chops and looking on the Jews more mildly, letting Jewish boys get away with things that he usually forbade . . . Efficient though Jacob's mess of pottage has been, a hunk of real Jewish gefilte fish is a regular magic wand.

This aside, Mitka was just another dopey kid who liked to play tricks and mess around with the rest of the boys, and his thick head led him right into their hands as soon as the games got going. He was born to be a horse; he was strong enough to gallop and rear, and the other kids, the little Jewish brains, used to ride around on him, whacking him on the backside and steering him where they wanted to go. If they were building something—a mill in one of the gutters, for instance—he was no good for anything but bringing the sand, carrying the rocks, digging up the ground, and crawling around in the mud. The Jewish kids used to strain themselves and help him out with instructions: "Work, Mitka, work, that's it, that's the way . . ." And now that Mitka the little *sheygets* has grown into a full-fledged goy, it's possible that he's become a big wheel somewhere by doing just what he did as a kid—taking what he wants at the point of his fist.

Zhukl wasn't such a bad egg either. For a piece of bread, he'd stand on his hind legs, wag his tail, do whatever you wanted. The fact that a piece of bread was worth plenty in Kaptsansk didn't stop anybody from tossing a piece to Zhukl—"It'll at least keep him from barking." Jews with beards would beam with pleasure if Zhukl honored them by taking a bone from their hands. He'd look on them amiably, gnawing at the bone with his canines, while they beamed and stroked their beards, consoling themselves for the waste of food by hoping that, "He isn't dangerous anymore. From now on, we're friends." They'd even pluck up the courage to stroke his head with a fingertip. And just as soon as they'd gained a little *shlep* with the mutt, it was "Go on, boy, bite!"—they tried to sic him on others, as Jews with *shlep* tend to do.

Now that he's grown up, Hershele has realized that Jews are the roosters among the peoples of the earth, forever perched by the domestic hearth, close to their wives and children. A Jew's family is his whole life, as much a part of him as his heart, and Hershele's father was a Jew's Jew and a cock's cock. Today, Hershele knows very well how much his father loved him; it's just that this love was buried deep in his heart, in the traditional Jewish way, and was never to be seen in his face. On the contrary, there was always a dark cloud there, an angry, anxious look, a bitter, sour expression. He was convinced that a father had to act like a father, that it was beneath his dignity to talk or laugh or fool around with his kids. Children were supposed to fear their father and show respect; they weren't to dare raise their voices or, God forbid, laugh in his presence—they had a duty to go around on tiptoe. And any child of *his* who transgressed by laughter, loudness of voice, or unguarded movement was called to account with a paternal look that pierced him straight to the quick.

He scarcely spoke to his wife in front of strangers, or even in front of the family; instead of calling her by her name, he usually just said, "Hey, you," and once in a while, "Idiot." Deep down, he was as fond of her as could be, but he considered it degrading and sappy, un-Jewish, to let it show. He—he's a man, after all, a Jew; and she—is a she: when everything's said and done, nothing more than a female woman . . . And *he* was the rooster of the house, leading the hen and her chicks behind him while he foraged, scratching worms up from under the ground. Any chick who tried to oppose him got a peck in the head: *He* was the cock of the walk, all right, with his chin in the air and sparks in his eyes. And just to prove it, he'd give a clap with his wings and make like a cantor—a loud, drawn-out cock-a-doodle-doo that translated to, "Chickens! Respect! Remember who's boss!"

On certain occasions, however, he could be talkative and gregarious. When a child fell sick, for instance, Hershele's father wouldn't leave the bedside. He'd pet the kid, feel its forehead, comfort it with soft words and promise it presents, as many toys as it wanted—a nice wooden sword dyed with blueberries for Tishe B'Ov; a noisemaker for Purim, a *dreydl* for Chanukah, a flag with a red apple on top for Simkhes Toyre—and he'd make sounds like a noisemaker, spin around and buzz like a *dreydl*, yell out hosannas like a kid marching around the synagogue with an apple-topped flag on Simkhes Toyre. And all to coax the least little smile out of the poor sick kid. If he got one, he was overjoyed.

Likewise when there was some kind of *yontef* or celebration. He was especially affable at the Passover *seyder*, reclining like an aristocrat in his white robe, his wife all in white beside him, the two of them calling each other king and queen. They were radiant, their eyes shone; they looked at each other, at the wineglasses, at the *seyder* plate with everything in its proper place—a real *mekhaye*.

"Nu, Hershele," his father would say, taking him by the cheek, "Nu, Hershele, ask me the *fir kashes*."

Hershele would start to rock back and forth, dipping his thumb in the air, and say loudly in his little falsetto, "Daddy, I'm going to ask you four questions, Daddy," and then rattle them off like gunshots, one right after the other. At the *seyder*, the kids were free to talk and laugh as much as they wanted. It was party time. They would drink themselves silly on full glasses of licorice that their mother used to boil in the big Passover pot and yak away like crazy.

The rest of the time, though, the children's fear of their father was great. At home, Hershele was as quiet as the other kids, as quiet as still water that runs deep. Quietly, the children played tricks on one another, got into fights, made fun of each other with everything but their voices; they gave each other the finger, gave a pinch and a slap, and—shh . . .

Each of them had his own particular nemesis. Hershl's was Khune-Leml. They were like fire and water, those two, as unlike as two people can be. As the elder brother—really almost old enough to be engaged—Khune-Leml wanted Hershele to learn who was boss. It burned him up, the way their father always put Hershele beside him at the Shabbes table and melted with pleasure when Hershele trilled an accompaniment to the songs in his thin, squeaky little voice. So Khune-Leml was always snitching Hershele out to their father and trying to make him look bad; when they were alone together, Khune-Leml used to do mute imitations of Hershele's trilling, bouncing his Adam's apple with a finger, bobbing his head and puffing himself out like a turkey. This made Hershele seethe. He'd stick out his tongue, put up his dukes, and say in a rage, "Get bent, Khune-Leml-loaf!"—but quietly, so that no one else should hear.

At home, where Hershele had to keep everything inside, he was like an overinflated balloon, but as soon as he got outdoors—bang! the balloon burst and everything inside it went flying. He was a ball of fire, an imp, a brat like you wouldn't believe, leaving all the rest of the boys in the dust when it came to throwing stones, holding a goat by the horns and jumping up for a ride, grabbing the community billy-goat's beard and yanking out a handful of hair, sticking pins into a bride and groom under the wedding canopy, chasing a nut-case down the street, grabbing rides off the backs of speeding wagons—with Hershele, these were art-forms. The rest of the kids knew class when they saw it, and they made Hershele number one in all their affairs. Whenever they went to war, he was the general, and wore a large paper grocery bag festooned with feathers on his head. His greatness and valor were manifest in his command to beat without mercy, to execute judgment on everybody for the greater glory of Hershele. And when General Hershele Leyzer-Yankl's gave an order, it was incumbent on all of them, from the biggest on down, to obey without question.

In peacetime, when there was no war on, Hershele and his troops devoted themselves to other matters. On summer days, Hershele took them swimming in the River Kaptsansk, a large sump hole where the local pigs used to wallow, with nothing but their snouts protruding. The march toward it was as lively and boisterous as any other triumphal procession, and nothing they passed remained untouched. Goslings scattered at the sight of them, hopping up and down with the help of their featherless little wings, while the gander snorted through his nostrils, honked, contracted his neck into zig-zags. A calf did itself the trouble of getting up from the grass; it stared hard and stepped back a few paces, tossed its head and bent its brow to the ground, then raised its tail and went sauntering off. The kids undid their clothes while they were still walking, so that they could jump right out of them as soon as they reached the babbling brook.

Between *minkhe* and *mayriv* the kids met in the foyer of the *bes-medresh* for a trade fair. Each had his own line of merchandise, and business was brisk. Here, a crooked old nail was being swapped for a brass button without a hook; there, a whistle made from a nut attracted two strong bidders with bits of mirrored glass and pocketsful of porcelain chunks. The guy with the big green bead was deep in negotiation with a colleague who boasted a needle case, as well as an ear-pick made of tin. Hershele was the official appraiser; his commission came off the top. The fair usually ended in a fight—nobody was satisfied, everybody claimed that he'd been taken.

They'd be on the point of blows; some punk would be trumpeting through the neck of a freshly slaughtered goose, making such a racket that the *shammes* would run out beside himself and shout "*Shkotsim!*" and the board of trade would scatter like mice, each to his own corner.

At Chanukah time, there was a run on *dreydls*; at Purim, on raw material for noisemakers; at Shvues, on hollowed-out eggs to make birds with. Every *yontef* its merchandise. And there was plenty of time for business, thank God, because the *melamed* in Hershele's *talmud-toyre* was just as busy as the kids, touch wood, with all kinds of business of his own. He was a bit of a marriage broker, turned up at every wedding, funeral, and circumcision, and was a standing witness at divorces. And as if that weren't enough, he also had to exorcise evil eyes, check *mezuzes* for wear and tear, and put everything else on hold once a week to collect charity from door to door every Thursday and Friday.

But it can be said to his credit that he relished his pedagogical duties; in the hour or so that he found for teaching, he gave of himself unstintingly. The brief period at his disposal sufficed for him to beat all the students and still have a few minutes left to rest his head on the desk, to relax a little or scratch his beard, groan, yawn, and so on. "Hershele is a scamp," he used to say, "but a nice boy with a good head on his shoulders." Such praise always put Hershele's mother in mind of the dream where Gedalye-Hersh pointed to the infant Hershele and said, "He'll be a good piece of work, as sharp as a tack," and she'd melt with pleasure. Whenever his father, on the other hand, heard tales of Hershele's scampiness, he'd quip, "You-know-who's name and you-know-who's nature—like two peas in a pod. You-know-who, may he rest in peace, spent his whole life futzing around with holes, and this one's also wrapped up in holes. Only instead of fixing them, *he* has to go and make them." His father was alluding to one of Hershele's adventures, which we're going to recount right now.

VA-YEHI HA-YOYM, and it came to pass that a great wonder took place in Kaptsansk. All of a sudden—no one knows quite how—a doctor appeared from out of the blue. Now as a general rule, a Jew has only to hear the word "doctor" for all his ailments to bestir themselves and make their pains felt within him . . . In the days of Yerakhmiel the barber-surgeon and his wife, Yakhne, things always went right in Kaptsansk: illnesses percolated inside the Jews, and the Jews did their best to ignore them. The barber-surgeon did his job; he shaved, sheared, cupped, leeched, tapped veins, and bled the men, while his wife tapped blood from the women. People took sick and died—period—without making any production. It was no big deal. Out of the blue you lay down, and out of the blue you closed your eyes—and you didn't need any drugstores or prescriptions to help you. It's an established fact, it says explicitly in the Psalms, that man lives seventy years—and not even freethinkers can contradict *that*. And if you should die before your time—so what? There's no one to blame. Not Yerakhmiel the barber-surgeon with his instruments nor Yakhne his wife and sure as hell—you'll excuse me—sure as hell not the psalm. No, the fault lies with our sins, the sins of the town. Somebody or other had an itch for something forbidden? For that we've got a rabbi—may he be healthy—and a board of solid citizens to sniff out the problem and bring it to the surface, like oil on water. That's the way it's always been and the way it'll be forever.

But as soon as the doctor turned up in Kaptsansk, illnesses shot up like nettles after the first rain of summer: spasms, stomachaches, lower-back pain, tightness in the pit of the stomach, itchings, pinchings, abscesses, boils, and good old Jewish hemorrhoids. They all came out of hiding and showed themselves in the fullness of their perfection. There wasn't a single sound Jew, no one not somehow afflicted. Young and old ran to the doctor to have their health patched up and mended. Mothers came running, carrying little children with big bellies and skinny legs. It turned out that all of Kaptsansk was one big infirmary where no one was healthy. The living God alone knows *what* would have been had the doctor not up and vanished as quickly as he'd appeared. The Jews forgot their aches and pains again, dragged themselves along as long as their legs could carry them and let the momentum keep them alive. Yerakhmiel the barber-surgeon crept back out like the moon at evening, worked with all his skill, and the Jews died like they were supposed to.

The doctor never left Hershele's thoughts, though. This whole doctor business had a great appeal for him, and he got a yen to be a doctor himself, to do like the real doctor, but with the other kids as his patients. Kids are like apes; they love to mimic everything adult. As the saying has it: Children chew what grown-ups spew. Hershele was crowned with the title of doctor and the game began in earnest. For his own sake, for the sake of his dignity, Hershele became tenderhearted and appeared to worry over the health of his friends, meanwhile hoping from the bottom of his heart: "Master of the Universe, let them be sick, that they might come to me for help."

One Friday morning after his mother had practically given herself an ulcer to get credit for cinnamon, pepper, and flour for Shabbes, Hershele slipped off with a little of each and tiptoed into the empty field behind his house. He sat there by the fence, with a little paper box for which he had paid three buttons plus a leather change-purse in front of him. There were a few vials in the box, for which Hershele had had to trade the lucky two-in-one nut that always helped him skunk the other kids when he put it in his mouth; there was also a beetle with long antennae, tied to a hair from a horse's tail. And so, while the mother was busy at home, breaking her head over how to make something out of her meager supplies, the son was busy with all the stuff he'd nicked, making medicines, waters, and drops in his vials. Once he was finished, he wondered: "Now where am I going to get a patient with a really worthwhile affliction on whom I can prove my mastery of the healing arts?"

And just as he was wondering, he caught sight of Moyshe-Yosse, a ragged and barefoot orphan with no one to look after him, riding around on a stick in the distance. The poor kid was playing all the parts: wagon driver, horse, and wagon. He beat the stick, urging it on with a "giddyup." He lifted his feet, stuck out his belly, threw back his head, and whinnied like a horse; he leapt up and started to gallop. He drummed his puffed-out cheeks with his hands, rattled and squeaked like wagon wheels—snap, crackle, pop. He ran straight for Hershele, neighing as he got closer, then yelling like a horse that's been pulled up, a wagon that's come to a sudden stop, and jumping off the stick.

Moyshe-Yosse's arrival gave Hershele an idea; without stopping long to think, he started to talk to him in Yiddish pig-Latin. "*Soyse-Sosse*, Moyshe-Yosse, *sou sant*, you want, *sue seasick*, to be sick?"

"*So*, no," replied Moyshe-Yosse in the same dialect. "*Sod sorbid*, God forbid!"

"Say yes, dopey. For real. Enough German, let's talk plain Yiddish.

Now say yes. What's it to you? You'll be sick and I'll make you better. Nu, you wanna?"

"I'd rather eat, Hershele."

"Eat? I don't have any food, Moyshe-Yosse, but I can promise you some for later. I'll give you my hand on it. Nu, will you be sick now?"

"But there's nothing wrong with me, Hershele."

"Don't worry, I'll make you sick. I'll give you a little scratch, just one little scratch on the bottom of your foot with this nail. You see?" Hershele took a rusty nail out of his pants pocket.

"But it's gonna hurt, Hershele."

"Just a little scratch, Moyshe-Yosse, I swear. It'll hurt for a little while and then stop right away. *I'll* make you better. I'm doing it for your own good, aren't I? But *you* don't want to understand."

"If it's for my own good, then give me some food. Oy, Hershele, I'm so hungry."

"You and your food!" Hershele was pretending to be angry. "Get outta here! I wanna do him a favor and cure him, and he wants to eat, to stuff himself!"

A few other kids had turned up while they were talking, and were very taken with Hershele's pharmacy and his brilliant idea. They set to work on Moyshe-Yosse.

"You're an idiot, Moyshe-Yosse. If you just let yourself get sick, you'll get a bite right after. You get it?"

They all gave him their hands, holding onto a *tsitse* to make it official. Moyshe-Yosse checked all the *tsitsis* to make sure they were kosher, and once he saw that they all had the requisite four knots and eight threads, he put a finger to his nose and warned them, "Remember, if you don't do what you promised, God will punish you. Say Amen."

Moyshe-Yosse stretched out his foot, the boys holding him tight on either side, and Hershele set to work on his sole with the nail. At first, he went slowly and made a little scratch—Moyshe-Yosse bit his lip and kept quiet; then Hershele dug a little deeper with the nail—Moyshe-Yosse went "Ay-ay-ay" and the gang comforted him. "It's nothing, let it be. You're going to be healed."

Hershele didn't wait. He shoved the nail farther in, the foot was bleeding, Moyshe-Yosse tore himself from the boys' hands and screamed "Gevalt!"

"Ssh, ssh, *Soyse-Sosse!*" A cheerful Hershele tried to appease him in pig-Latin. "I've given you the illness already, now I'll give you the *sure,* the cure."

Hershele took a vial and poured some drops onto Moyshe-Yosse's fresh wound. Moyshe-Yosse screwed his face up horribly and screamed, "It's burning. O God, it's burning," in a voice no longer his own.

Moyshe-Yosse knew why he was yelling. There was too much pepper in the drops and they burned like fire. He quivered, groaned, and burst into tears from the pain.

The kids got scared and took off. Hershele ran a little to the side, where he stood and considered his patient. Moyshe-Yosse rolled around on the ground for a long time, screaming "It's burning" at the top of his lungs. Then he stood up, so to speak, and went on his way, wailing and lamenting, limping badly on his right foot. He arrived in good health and departed an invalid. He arrived hungry, but merry and bright, delighting in the world and the beautiful morning—and the great kindness shown him had left him with a wound.

Moyshe-Yosse lay quite a while with his foot swollen up like a mountain, suffering for Hershele's good turn. When the story got back to Hershele's father—and Khune-Leml didn't skip a single detail—he gave it to Hershele so that he'd never forget, and admonished him in a fatherly way. "Wild man! You wanna do favors? Don't make people sick, and don't do them any favors by curing them. Just you wait, I'll give you favors! Next time, you'll be more careful!"

"And I was the only one?" pleaded Hershele, crying, trying to shift some of the blame to the others. "How come they . . ."

"Shut up, wise guy! They're as bad as you are. You listening, Hershl? You and your friends can take your favors and . . ."

IF IT WEREN'T FOR FOOD, Hershele's childhood in Kaptsansk would have been paradise. He had plenty of time to run around and play; he had a good name among the other children and nothing to complain about in his manifold business and public affairs; he was a general, a merchant, anything you can name that makes little boys feel good. There was only one little problem—food. His tummy kept asking for food. There were times when he came home hungry after a hard day's play, dying for even a few crumbs just so he could have eaten *something*, and—nothing, not a lick of food. He'd cry, tear at his flesh, pull his hair with both hands, and scream until he ran out of strength and fell asleep. Later, once he'd got used to this sort of thing, he'd just move his lips soundlessly. His sister Keyle-Rikl had taught him all about keeping quiet and suffering in silence.

She was sickly and pale as a ghost, her glands were swollen, one ear was clogged and stuffed with cotton. The poor thing used to bear her pain, as well as the hunger and cold, huddled up in a corner like a dove of mildness, looking out with a pair of moist, thoughtful eyes, and never making a sound—unless you count the rattling when she swallowed her saliva. She made strange faces when she swallowed, not out of bitterness or anger at her great suffering—no, her good nature was apparent to all. Her faces meant only that she was struggling to hide her pain by sighing loudly whenever she felt a twitch or pang, and every twist of her features tugged at the heartstrings of anyone who saw her. This kind of rabbi can teach better, do more to make her students good, pious, and submissive than all the ethical treatises and foolish sages with their vinegar-and-molasses words of reproof. Even Vaska, the tomcat in Krylov's *Fables*—a glutton and compulsive snacker whose soul lay in pots full of food—even Vaska would have been moved by such a teacher; he'd have lost his desire for cream and been satisfied with sour milk.

Hershele was a lively, active, carefree kid. He had no sooner stood up on his little feet and taken a look at the world around him, than he decided that he liked it, that he wanted to live and jump around, just like a little bunny. But life looked back at him like a cruel stepmother: "Know your place, kid. A *kaptsn* shouldn't get his hopes up." Life, real life, stopped him before he could get started, taught him the taste of hunger and want, whispered into his ear what kind of a wretch he was, what kind of wretches he came from—a hundred percent *kaptsn*, a hundred percent misfortune—and asked him the first of life's four questions: "Hershele, what are you so happy about?"

Hershele's youth passed swiftly, it bloomed quickly and started to fade, and even as a child he was already a miniature adult: distracted, depressed, with a careworn face and all the mannerisms of an adult Jew with a family to support. All he needed was the beard. A Jew has so many sorrows and sufferings to get through in his little bit of life that there's no time left over for childhood. It shines through very briefly, like the sun on a bleak winter's day, then passes behind a long, dark storm cloud. A boy has scarcely crawled out of his swaddling clothes and started to play when he's lashed to the teacher's pointer. The yoke of the Torah is laid across his neck, and it's "Giddyup, go, little Jew."

O God, just once I'd like to get a look, a distant glimpse, even, of the Jew who grew out of that little boy whom I was fated once to see. He wasn't even two years old then, but I remember his little *peyes* and yarmulke, his coveralls and *tsitsis*, as if it were yesterday. I can see his pallid, gloomy little face as he suddenly emerges from his alcove, disheveled, covered in feathers from the cushions on which he'd been sleeping, drawing himself slowly across to his mother, sitting himself on her knee, removing a breast with his kosher little hands, sweetly making a blessing—"through Whose word everything exists"—and then beginning to suck. "Amen," I replied with fervor, watching the little Jew and his mother with great pleasure, then added, "*Ashreykhem yisroel,* How goodly is your lot, O Israel."

Of course, Hershele was still friendly with the rest of the kids; he kept on playing with them, but it was a different kind of play already, serious and considered: you could rip your torn capote or pull a hair from somebody's *peyes* or God forbid end up with your head uncovered. This kind of play was all about acting like grown-ups. Just talking to a grown-up or going for a bit of a walk with one was naturally considered a great honor among the little child-Jews. The grown-ups were ranked in ascending order: the engaged, the recently married, the established householders, and the clergy, from the beadle right up to the rabbi. Artisans were a different type of grown-up, not quite adults but no longer kids, and they tended to fraternize with the boys and joke around with them. The real grown-ups also looked on them as boys and called the artisans by the same types of names: wise-guys, punks, the fellas, and so on.

Hershele started hanging around the grown-ups, observing their ways and listening in on their conversation. Two Jews had only to stop for a chat and Hershele would spring up beside them like a mushroom, his head tilted upwards, listening with his mouth half-open. If some grown-ups decided to take a little stroll—just like that, you know—Hershele would trot after like a calf behind a cow. A beard was no joke to Hershele—Torah and wisdom clung to every beard, a beard knew everything, understood everything, everything a beard said had been revealed to Moses on Sinai. Whenever Hershele told his friends something unusually outlandish, he always concluded by saying, "Don't laugh, don't laugh. I heard it from a Jew with a beard." And there was no appeal against a lie that came with that sort of proof.

"As a child Hershele considered adults as one world, children as another, and he could see no connection between them. But I later realized that this was a major error. Believe me, it's one big world, with the same behavior, the same way of thinking, the same desires. Big or small, young or old—what does it matter? They're all Children of Israel, and the only difference is that a big child can do what a little one can't. What's labeled wisdom, goodness, and piety among children with beards is foolishness, impudence, kids' stuff for children without."

Hershele started to keep one foot among the little, the other among the big Children of Israel. The foot that stood among his friends was planted firmly on the ground. When little boys play, they play in the world around them and keep their minds on things that they can see and touch. When big children play, they fly so far up into the heavens that they get dizzy. The foot that Hershele kept among the grown-ups sometimes felt the ground dissolve and leave it hanging in mid-air. He was having trouble keeping his balance, but he listened to the grown-ups with both his ears. And if he'd had a few extra, he would still have needed more to catch everything to be heard. Hershele heard plenty about miracles and wonders: tales of the other world, doings in Heaven and in Hell, with every detail filled in as if the tellers had just seen it with their own eyes; tales of reincarnation, of dead people who walk about in our world; tales of good and evil spirits, of angels and of the prophet Elijah—God's messengers—who wander to the ends of the earth and turn up in every corner. Among these was a wonderful story that actually took place in Kaptsansk itself a long, long time ago, a tale that resounded all over the world and is still echoing there today. It goes like this . . .

IN THE DAYS of Reb Shmelke, a great-grandfather of Reb Yudel, the Kaptsansker tycoon, it happened once that the whole town departed to go beg in Glupsk on Purim. Things had been even worse than usual in Kapt-sansk, and Reb Shmelke was the only male to remain in town. Reb Yudel's great-grandfather, Reb Shmelke, of blessed memory, was a good and pious person, perfervidly Jewish, one of the Hasidim of the Old Rebbe. He was also what no Jew should ever be: childless. None of the measures he had taken to get at least one child, a *Kaddish*, had succeeded, and at last he turned his back on wonder-workers, on sorcerers and sorceresses, and began to serve the Lord even more spiritedly and wholeheartedly than be-fore, never loosing the yoke of *yidishkayt* for even a second. And so when all of Kaptsansk had taken off, Reb Shmelke was left in a quandary: How could it be that he wouldn't be able to *daven* and read the *megile* with a *minyen*? To whom would he send *shalakh-mones*? And with whom would he take a drink, in fulfillment of the Lord's command?

Such were his trials on the Fast of Esther, the day before Purim, when all of a sudden the door opened and in walked nine individuals: three grey-beards in mohair jackets, another in a tasseled robe with a disheveled beard and a high, pointy *spodek* on his head. The fifth was wearing a coarse peasant's coat and a money-belt; his face was covered with a forest of hair. The sixth looked half-asleep—he had a thick red nose covered with blisters and pimples, and was having trouble standing straight. The remaining three were dressed like Turks, with spangled bodices in front and short aprons behind—not like men and not like women. They all kissed the *mezuze* as they came in and yelled out, "Good evening, Reb Shmelke. *Gut yontef.*"

Reb Shmelke rose to greet them, giving each of the individuals a warm *sholem aleykhem*, and asked where they were coming from in the time-honored way. He took the Turks for Jerusalemites and welcomed them even more lavishly, thinking, "What fantastic guests. I'll get to hear plenty about the Cave of the Machpelah and Rachel's Tomb, and they might even be able to sell me a little bag of soil from the Land of Israel to sprinkle over me when I'm dead, so the worms won't eat my body."

"Reb Shmelke!" The peasant-coat was speaking. "My merchants want to know if they can celebrate Purim with you. They'll pay you well."

"God forbid," said Reb Shmelke. "Don't even talk about money. You're all very welcome here, believe me; a proper Purim feast with won-derful guests like you is all the reward I need. I've got plenty of wine and whiskey and brandy, and if we run out, we can always break into the *peysakhdike-scilicet* brandy. And you, sir," he addressed the peasant-coat, "You must be the driver. You wouldn't say no to a nice shot of whiskey, would you? I've got some here—ambrosia."

"Whiskey? Did somebody say whiskey?" said Red Nose, coming up a little closer. "I'm the world's leading authority."

"Glad to have you with us—it's written all over your face," said Reb Shmelke. "You look very familiar to me. Aren't you the Hasid that I once spent a *yontef* with at the Rebbe's? You're an authority on whiskey, all right, a real authority, if I say so myself. You understand what I mean when I say authority? The real truth about whiskey and the fire within it isn't as simple as it looks. It can only be understood by fiery, burning Jews like us."

Reb Shmelke took his guests to the synagogue and they *davened mayriv*. One of the greybeards read the *megile* in a sweet and delightful voice. When they reached the part about how Haman was exalted and wanted to exterminate all the Jews through slander and false accusation, the pointy *spodek* started to hop up and down, waving his fist in such fury that Reb Shmelke trembled with fear. The *spodek* grabbed one of the long poles for the wedding canopy and beat the wicked Haman down the steps that led to the reading desk, beat him and beat him, and when the reading got to Haman's downfall, the *spodek* was beaming with joy, leaping and dancing in his happiness. The greybeards bobbed up and down and sang *Shoyshanas Ya'ankoyv* to a sweet tune. Red Nose couldn't hold himself back and said, "What do I care about stories? I only wanna get to the part where we take a drink, and now we're there."

This lit a fire under Reb Shmelke. He ran over to the shammes' cupboard, pulled out a bottle and glasses, and made a *lekhayim* with his guests. The *shammes* himself wasn't there at the time; his contract specified that on Chanukah and Purim he had the right to go begging in Glupsk, just like everyone else. As it also specified that he alone had the right to tend bar in the synagogue and sell liquor there during the year; he also kept a supply of buckwheat cookies, egg bagels, and other snacks on which you say *Shakl* and don't have to wash your hands in order to eat.

Reb Shmelke and his guests celebrated all night. The next morning, when they all went off for a dip in the *mikve*, Red Nose didn't want to go.

"No, *feh*, I hate water."

"Come," said Reb Shmelke, "Don't worry, it's OK. The water in our *mikve* is so thick that you could cut it with a knife."

During the morning reading of the *megile*, the *spodek* and the grey-beards behaved as they had the night before. After the *davening* they had some food and drink, exchanged *shalakh-mones*, then made a benediction and ate Haman-dumplings, hamantaschen, and poppyseed cakes, drank *vishnick*, then made another blessing and sat down to the Purim feast. They ate and drank and fulfilled the commandment to get as drunk as they could get. Red Nose drank more than anybody, matching them ten to one. They fulfilled the commandments of Purim so well that when the citizens of Kaptsansk returned from Glupsk a couple of days later, Reb Shmelke was still dead drunk. When he came to, he was nearly out of his mind with shock—his guests had vanished into thin air, the house looked like a cy-clone had hit it. Nothing was in its place; what he wanted wasn't there; what he needed was nowhere to be found. It was a great wonder, far be-yond his comprehension.

The Old Rebbe, may his memory be a blessing, later revealed the mys-tery to his intimates. They disclosed it to their intimates, and so it went from ear to ear until the whole world knew the secret. Those nine individ-uals were the company of saints, the goodly gang itself! The three grey-beards were the patriarchs; the *spodek* was Mordechai, garbed in royal raiment; the peasant-coat, Elijah the prophet. Red Nose was Lot, the well-known souse, who tagged along after his uncle, Abraham; the three Turks were Mattathias the High Priest and two of his sons, clad in their breast-plates and ephods. The Rebbe said that before the company came to Reb Shmelke, they apprised him of their intention and besought his permis-sion—Reb Shmelke was *his* hasid, and Kaptsansk was part of his demesne. That is, Kaptsansk actually belonged to a nobleman, but the Rebbe made the money from it. That is, the nobleman held the cow by the horns and the Rebbe, you'll excuse me, milked it.

From that time on, Reb Shmelke began to prosper. Serel, his third wife, a hot-blooded young girl whom he had married only for her housekeeping, gave birth to a boy on Chanukah of that year, nine months after these events took place. The Rebbe decreed that he be called Mordkhele-Mattes, after Mordechai and Mattathias. Reb Mordkhele-Mattes was the father of Reb Yankev-Elye, who begat our contemporary, Reb Yudel Kaptsansker.

Kaptsansk takes great pride in this affair—Just look what kind of peo-ple were there once! And don't forget Reb Yudel, who kept his nose in the air and was prouder than hell. A trifle that his grandfather drank up a cellarful of wine and got drunk with Lot? It meant that Reb Yudel could make great marriages for his children.

The story was a big hit when Hershele passed it on to the other boys. Some of them even testified and swore by their lives: They should live to hear the shofar of the Messiah the way they'd heard the very same story from their fathers, and everyone believed them. Two of the boys had an argument over Lot's nose, one of them screaming, "No! My father says that it was red, but without pimples," the other shouting, "No, no, *with* pimples. My father knows better, and he says with." There was a fight about the fathers, about whose father knew better and about where each other's father could go. Other boys mixed in, screaming, "Pimples!" "No pimples!" as if they were dealing with a matter of vital importance, an issue as critical to our lives as those that our scholars debate in their works . . . On account of a nose, noses are pulled; on account of a father, it's "so's your old man." Nor did Hershele emerge unscathed; he took a scratch on the nose for the honor of his own father, for whom he endangered his life. Yet his father showed no appreciation and bawled his devoted son out for the martyr's scratch that he'd received. "*Feh* on the way you behave. Always with the stories, your stupid, little boys' stories!"

7

POVERTY TOOTLED all over Kaptsansk, and the Children of Israel sat with folded arms; there was nothing to do—nothing they *could* do—to drive it away. When people used to get together around the oven in the *bes-medresh*, they'd do nothing but moan and groan: "Things aren't what they used to be, nothing's the same anymore. Once it was *ho-ho-HO*, and now it's nothing but *phnyeh*. What used to be like THIS—today it's like *this*. The same form, but a big difference. Used to be that people were people, Jews were Jews, and business was business. And now, huh, now what are they?" And when the "what" came out, they tended to stare at each other in silence and wait for the question to be answered. One of them would scratch himself, rub his forehead, and mull things over; he'd open his mouth and let out a yawn. Another would hold his beard and shut one eye, then give a wave with his hand and bleat, as if to himself, "E . . . e . . . e, it's all crap." A third would rise from his place, spread his fingers out, and rest both hands on a lectern. He'd rock back and forth and say, *"I'll* tell you, listen. Today— you understand me?—right now it's the messianic era, the end of days."

This was usually enough to satisfy them. Everyone's eyes would light up and they'd throw themselves into a discussion of the messianic era, always beginning with the observation that the current six-thousand-year cycle is God's Friday, that is, it's already past noon on the eve of the Sabbath, and all the signs that the Messiah is coming, that he'll be here soon, are already apparent: the gates of prosperity are locked, the pockets of all are empty; frightening numbers of smart-aleck know-it-alls are abroad among us Jews. Boys consider themselves people of consequence, lords of the manor; a full, fat belly equals wisdom and brooks no opposition to its suppositions; there are troubles and persecutions every day, and the war of Gog and Magog is imminent.

Gog and Magog provoked wider-ranging discussion, and there were all kinds of opinions about them. Somebody took down a copy of the well-known *Avkas Roykhel*, The Peddler's Spice Box (it's a metaphor for a profound scholar), and, pointing the way with his finger, read out the seventh sign, as described therein:

> *The seventh sign: The Holy One, blessed be He, will work a wonder in the world. It is said that there is a marble statue in Rome in the form of a beautiful woman of evil character. This statue is the work of the Lord, He Himself has created it. The evil ones will come to this marble beauty, they will excite her and sleep with her. She becomes pregnant, her womb bursts open and she gives birth to a child named Armilus the Satan, whom the nations of the world call Antichrist. He is huge and ungainly: twelve cubits high and twelve cubits wide. His eyes are red, his hair the color of gold; the soles of his feet are green and he has two heads. This creature presents himself to the world as Messiah, he goes forth and conquers countries.*
>
> *At the same time, Nekhemye ben Khushiel (who is the Messiah of the House of Joseph) will rise against him with thirty thousand mighty men from the tribe of Ephraim. Nekhemye ben Khushiel will be killed in this war, and disasters will increase until the eighth sign.*
>
> *The eighth sign: The angel Michael will arise and blow three blasts on the shofar. At the first blast, the Messiah of the House of David will appear with Eli-*

jah the prophet to take all the righteous, as well as the other Jews who had flocked to the wilderness to wander with them, to Jerusalem. God will rain down fire and sulphur and hail, will kill the wicked Armilus.

The ninth sign: At the second blast of the shofar, the dead will rise from their graves. The Messiah of the House of David will go to gather together the remaining Jews from every corner of the world. Noblemen will carry the Jews on their shoulders and bring them to the land of Israel as a gift for God.

The tenth sign: At the third blast of the shofar, the ten lost tribes, known also as the Children of Moses, also as the Little Red Jews, will be revealed, and all the Jews will sit with their arms folded and with tall spodeks on their heads, beholding and taking pleasure in the radiance of the pure presence of the Lord . . .

The Jews of Kaptsansk melt with pleasure around the oven, their blood is up and pounding, they're ready to grab bow and arrow and run off to the war . . . And don't think they've forgotten about feasting on Leviathan and the giant ox known as the Shor Ha-Bor, or the wine that God made during the six days of creation. The geese of the Talmudic sage Rabba Bar Bar Khune will be served, dripping with fat, on golden platters. The righteous will eat and drink and lick their fingers, and meanwhile the starving Jews of Kaptsansk drool and lick their lips; you can hear their stomachs rumbling, and they scratch themselves, scratch themselves . . .

When it gets too painful to talk about Leviathan, they turn to politics and military strategy—issues on which they're all great experts and subtle scholiasts. They had the whole map of the world laid out on their hands, and while Berl and his company were lining the Austrian troops up on their palms, the Turkish on their fingers, with an ocean or the Prut in between, along the lifeline; while worlds were turning upside down, Leyzer and his company were devoting all their attention to guardian angels in heaven, preferring to base their tactics on Rashi's explicit statement that no earthly empire falls until its guardian angel has fallen in heaven.

Just as Berl was about to close his fingers so that the Turks would fall into the sea and be killed, "No, Berele," screamed Leyzer, "You're wasting your energy, you ignoramus. It's the Guardian of Edom who has to fall, dimwit; that's what stands written. If you don't know, you should keep quiet and not mix in."

Berl was so upset by this that no matter what Leyzer said afterward, he'd scream out the opposite, just to bug him. Like when it came time to count up the treasuries of selected magnates: Leyzer threw himself into it with gusto, rating Reb Itsye Glupsker's fortune at two million rubles in all fairness, and Reb Kalman's at a million and a half; Berele reversed the ratings, more to get at Leyzer than Reb Itsye, and this led to unpleasant results. Some of the company held with Leyzer, some with Berl. They haggled, argued, jibed: "What's the big deal? Money, shmoney." The more sensible among them used to try to make peace: "Listen to us. If you give in to Berl on Reb Kalman, he'll give in to you on Reb Itsye."

"What's all the hubbub?" Someone was ready with a compromise. "Reb Itsye has a million and three-quarters and so does Reb Kalman. This strikes me as fair; both sides can be happy. Leyzer and Berl have to put out for drinks, they owe us all a shot."

"Slit our throats for a penny!" Leyzer and Berl cried out together. "We'll be damned if we've got a cent."

"What does that matter? The *shammes* will give us on credit. Just give him some collateral."

When the discussion turned to Reb Yudel Kaptsansker, they all became very serious. It was their unanimous opinion that Yudel Kaptsansker wasn't so much rich as he was, touch wood, lucky. And why was he more lucky than rich? Here the opinions diverged. Some said that Elijah the prophet had given his ancestor Reb Shmelke a leather purse with a penny inside for *shalakh-mones*, and that the purse could never be emptied. It was always full of as much money as it could hold—no more, no less. Another group said, "No, Elijah the prophet's *shalakh-mones* to Reb Shmelke was a wishing-ring with the Ineffable Name inscribed on it. But he warned him not to wish for more than he needed."

"So?" The others were getting crafty. "So? Even if you're right, then Reb Shmelke could have used the wishing-ring to wish that, since he was already wishing, he could have wished that Elijah the prophet should wish that Reb Shmelke should be able to wish as much as he wished to . . . Oy, oy, if we only had wishing-rings like that, we'd know what to do with them already!"

"Aaach!" they all groaned. "Bad times all around. Some help, a wishing-ring. What are we supposed to do? There's no way to earn a living— you can tear yourself to pieces, it's not going to help. To make a living in these times, to keep body and soul together, you need *real* miracles."

8

OUR HERSHELE already knew the taste of need; his young blood was still burning hot, his prematurely burdened soul struggled like a caged bird to burst its bonds and go free. Hershele grabbed onto the wishing-ring with all his thoughts, absorbed himself in it day and night.

"Master of the Universe," he said to himself, "I mean, really, it's no joke. Why *shouldn't* the Jews have wishing-rings like that? How come once, when you willed it, you gave your Children of Israel manna in the desert and birds, doves, flew straight into their mouths and water flowed from a stone? Imagine—Jews today are also in the desert, among snakes, scorpions, and dragons."

Ah, how beautifully his child's mind envisioned a wishing-ring to which you had only to say, "Ring, I wish for this, I wish for that," and you had it, without any effort or strain. In his storybooks, he'd run across many wonderful things that had been brought about by magic, by divine names and wishing-rings. He'd read, for instance, about somebody who once went flying over mountains and valleys, forests and fields, on a demon's back, until he came to an island somewhere. There was a castle made of jewels on the island, a palace with hundreds of rooms. Upon entering the palace, he saw golden tables set with the most precious service, but no people whatsoever. He took out his wishing-ring and said, "Ring, ring, I want to eat, I want to drink, I want this, I want that, I want, I want, I want." The palace began to fill with princesses, one more beautiful than the next, swimming in pearls, in diamonds, in gold and silver, and they all took hold of the young man. All of a sudden a band struck up and they marched the youth to a marble bath where he rested his weary bones. Afterward they had a meal with chicken soup, and the costliest raisin wine. The youth wasn't slow; he ate and drank and had a good time . . .

The wishing-ring had driven itself into Hershele's head like a nail; he thought about nothing else, he could even see it in his sleep. He was certain that wishing-rings existed, believed in them implicitly, because he'd also heard about them from his father. What else, then? Where else had he heard all those stories about the other world, about everything that happens in Heaven and Hell, about angels, miracle workers, sorcerers, spirits and demons—where else, if not from his father? And had he not believed in these basics, in the fundamental credo of "a father knows," what, God forbid, would have become of his bit of *yidishkayt?*

As long as Hershele was still a boy, he continued to think that if he only had a wishing-ring, he'd wish for a fresh, hot roll with a pot roast and a fat kugel in the middle of the week. At the time, he suffered very often from hunger—from which God spare the Jews—and there are no greater delicacies in the world. He would also have wished that all teachers and Hebrew schools and prayer books should vanish, God help him, like a mist and not leave so much as a trace. Hershele couldn't even look at his school or his teacher, the murderer. As far as music goes, he'd have wished for a good shofar-blower and a hurdy-gurdy; aside from a shofar for the whole month of Elul and a hurdy-gurdy when an organ grinder turned up in town for a few days, he had never heard any music. Later on, when he was older and was starting feel other kinds of needs, he had other kinds of wishes. He would have wished for a princess, a house with furniture and appliances, a few goats and two or three cows.

The princess appeared to Hershele in the guise of Beyle, a short brick backhouse of a girl with full red cheeks, a turned-up nose, and burning black eyes.

Her father, Ben-Tsiyen Tsviyes, was a glazier and a bit of an architect, too—or an architectural critic, at least. He had his own house, though, the third one down from Hershele's, and don't forget that in Jewish towns a close neighbor is a member of the family and counts for more than a blood relative in the big city. Small-town neighbors know the most intimate things about one another: what's being said, what's on the stove, the tiniest details of what goes on in the house. Each keeps an eye on the other, lying in wait like a spy. They quarrel and curse and make up again, only to start fighting anew. Neighbors go into one another's houses for a burning coal, a chopper, a grater, a kosher-stone, a *parve* pot, a soaking-dish, or an egg to put in the *khale;* they consult one another about how many stitches are needed to start a sole and when to give up on the sock; interrogate each other on how to make gooseberry preserves, twist a *koyletch* for Purim, stuff cushions; each comes to the other to show off her hamantasch for Purim, her knishes and pancakes for Shvues; each wishes the other, "May you live to do this again, along with your husband and children," while thinking in her heart, "Get bent, dirt-bag. Go straight to Hell."

Hershele's mother and Beyle's were neighbors of exactly this sort, and Hershele himself was very close to Beyle when they were still little children. They used to run around, play blindman's buff with the other kids, dance and jump barefoot in puddles after a rain, holding each other by the hand and singing a well-known song:

> A sun and a rain,
> The bride's labor pain.
> What did she have?
> A boy.
> What did she call it?
> Moyshele.
> Where did she rock it?
> In a cradle.
> Where did she bury it?
> In a grave.

Sometimes Beyle would say "Hershele" instead of "Moyshele," and Hershele, for his part, would replace the bride with Beyle. Beyle could tell stories about bandits, sorceresses, witches, and rabbis with their wives. Hershele used to listen to her stories, staring into her mouth with pleasure—and nothing more. Beyle was no different to him than Faytl, Mottl, and the rest of his friends. A little later, when Hershele was already learning *Gemore*, he suddenly started to feel shy around her for no good reason, he couldn't figure out how or why. He just felt bashful. But at the same time, he also felt a strong desire to look at her, if only from a distance; whenever he happened to run into her, he'd turn red and stare at his toes. She started to have the same reaction to him, and each tried to avoid the other as much as possible. But the more he avoided her, the more he was drawn to her. Her voice caressed his ears, a word from her mouth, overheard at a distance, melted all through his body. As far as Hershele was concerned, there was nobody better or more beautiful anywhere on earth.

By this time, he'd already learned that it was a great sin to look at or think of a woman. But just because he knew it, he felt he *had* to do it; just because he'd learned that it was a sin, his feelings, as if to spite him, impelled him to look at Beyle. And because his glances were stolen now, not open and free like before, Hershele gave them some thought and grew embarrassed. Anyway, once Hershele had picked up the local habit of wishing, along with the story of the wishing-ring, what did he wish for but a princess, that is, Beyle?

As a means of entertainment and a way to pass the time, wishing was one of the commonest occupations in Kaptsansk. It was an occupation that arose from the constant shortage of the most vital necessities, from sitting around idly with no means of earning a living. It's a fact of human nature that "Since you can't keep your mind off what you haven't got, you'll have to be contented with naught but the thought." "Wishing and hoping is the work of distress, to go out of your mind you first need success." Nowhere else in the world are there such great wishing-experts as the Jews of Kaptsansk: they've got plenty of time to do nothing and they've also, thank God, got no lack of problems—so what kind of a wonder is it that when it comes to wishing, they've attained a higher level than all other people on earth? The simplest conversation immediately turns into a wish. So, to take a random example, if they're talking about the ocean, one will indulge himself and wish, "May I have as much money as there is sand on all its shores." "Eh," says a second, "Let the whole ocean be ink, and give me as many thousand-ruble bank-drafts as that ink would be able to sign." "As for me," wishes a third, sighing and raising his eyes skyward, "Both of you should die, and let me be your sole heir."

You get it? This was how they normally passed the long summer evenings. One such scene will be enough for us here.

No lights burn in the houses. The doors are all open, dinner is being eaten by moonlight, and after supper they spill out of their houses like ants: men in their *tsitsis*, with no capotes; the women unhooked, in nothing but their slips; half-naked children. A mass of neighbors arranges itself outside, young and old, kith and kin, all together. Golden bands of moonlight break through from between the roofs, stretch themselves over the massed heads and feet, creep even farther, dancing across walls, across fences, pointing here to a cat, scratching itself and rummaging on a roof, there to the cows stretched out in the street, chewing their cud, lazily slapping themselves with their tails and panting, rasping heaving sighs all the way up from their bellies.

For the first few minutes, everybody is busy with himself—yawning, hiccuping, waving fleas away and scratching. In the meantime, the women start to discuss their evening meals—this one's *teygelekh* were fit for a king, that one's peas were as soft as marrow, finger-licking good. One expatiates on a stroke of good luck—for a single groschen she got such a bargain, a radish the size of your head, which did her family for a hearty breakfast and for supper, too. And there was still plenty left over for tomorrow, they should live and be healthy.

The women were all speaking loudly, in thin, squeaky voices; the men were still muttering, throwing a word in once in a while only for the sake of form. Finally, they laid themselves on their backs, stared musingly at the starry sky, and began an animated conversation about what was going on up there. The moon was shining over them and each of them exclaimed, "Ay, a nose with eyes," as they beheld the face of the biblical Joshua on its surface. Itsik and Berl, who billed themselves as astronomers, researchers, pointed with their fingers to the Hebrew alphabet formed by the stars and got into an argument about which was *taf* and which was *khes*. Everybody agreed with both of them. No matter which researcher was pointing, they all swore, "Yes, it's really there. I see it, by God, I see it."

"Ay, ay!" one of the Jews burst out in sudden amazement. "So many stars in that milky stream up there, packed together like poppy seeds! I only wish that I had as many rubles . . ."

"Get outta here," says another. "I'll take a lower rate, a kopeck per star."

But there are interested parties ready to go even lower, two, five, ten stars for a groschen. And while they're bargaining, calculating, counting, cutting prices, and casting the courses of the stars, there's a wag sitting off to the side, talking nonstop and cracking wise. The women around him scream, as if to say, *"Feh!* Enough!" and cover their ears, but they're paying close attention and choking with laughter.

The children aren't idle, either. They tickle and slap, flick a nose on the sly. The one with the nose gives a scream, the one from the flick plays dumb, a regular plaster saint, and issues a rebuke: *"Sha, sha."* Mothers curse their children—God should only strike them dumb—and treat them to a passing pinch. The fathers dispense with their bidding and fall suddenly back to earth from the heavens. One of them has a beetle caught in his beard, another in his *peyes;* something was crawling along a third one's back, on the inside of his shirt. A red cow whose giant appetite won't allow her to sleep strays over to our group of Jews while nipping away at the grass. She turns her rear-end toward them and does something that shouldn't be done in public. They give her what-for and drive her away, screaming, *"Haydà! Get going!"* She wriggles swiftly out of Jewish hands and runs off to her resting place.

This incident gives rise to a lengthy conversation. Whose cow? How much milk does she give? What's she worth? "Shut up," one of them adds of a sudden, "And tell me, Jews, what you think the whole Kaptsansker herd is worth, including the goats?" One figures so much, another wishes that he should only have the amount by which the estimate falls short. Each one of them is seized by an itch to wish, and they wish and wish until their tongues grow tired from wishing out loud and they can hear a healthy snoring in the distance. The men try to drive their wives home. "Come to sleep." But the women demur coquettishly. They don't *feel* like going to bed at all, and would rather sleep here, outside, all night long. Of course, one young couple goes home right away; the others haggle and stall until all of a sudden a goat leaps out from a corner. It had been frightened by a couple of kids who'd snuck up on it outside its owner's house, and now it comes running in a big hurry, the kids in hot pursuit behind it, smack into the middle of the mass of Jews. Hubbub, tumult. They all jump up, cursing, and run off quickly, one after the other, without so much as a good night.

Book Two

1

IF THE HOLY TORAH can say, "*Yissoskhor khamoyr,* Issachar is an ass, *gorem,* broad-shouldered, *royvets,* crouching, *beyn ha-mishpesoyim,* between the boundaries," I don't see how anybody can think us out of line if we compare a Jewish bar mitzvah boy with a colt that's being put to work. A young colt runs along behind the wagon that its miserable nag of a mother is breaking her health to pull—she's being beaten from behind to do so. But what's it to him? He runs about as he pleases, races as fast as he can, kicks his feet, dances, skips and leaps for the sheer joy of doing so, waves his tail, and gets some fun out of life. All of a sudden, he's put into a bridle, harnessed to his wretched mother with a rope. "Get going, boy"—there's a whip to give him the right idea—"Get going, boy, you're horse number two." It breaks your heart to see the poor thing's life beaten out of it so young, to see it in its heavy yoke, so sad and dejected, its head already bent to the ground—you could weep for its tender years.

Our Hershele has become bar mitzvah, turned into a colt with a bridle. His little head, his child's arm, are bound, wrapped tight in the straps of his *tefillin.* The first time he pronounces the blessing, he puts all his heart and soul and might into being enslaved, harnessed from this day forth to the worship and service of the Creator: "*Ve-eyrastikh li le-oylom,* And I have betrothed you unto me forever," says Hershele, winding the strap around his finger. He pulls it round a second time and again says, "*Ve-eyrastikh.*" A third time, once more: "*Ve-eyrastikh li be-emuno,* And I have betrothed you

36

unto me in belief, *ve-yodat es ha-Shem*, and you should know what kind of God we've got!"

"Enough being a kid, Hershele." His parents are there, too, with a moral reminder. "You can't do what you want anymore. It's time to start worrying, time to give some thought to your future. Come on, colt, get in behind there; come shlep that yoke, work yourself to death for a piece of bread. Come suffer along with us!"

Mazl tov twice over, you poor Kaptsansker bar mitzvah boy. Once on the yoke of serving the Lord and once on the yoke of spending your wretched life trying to earn a living. Say goodbye to your youth—you're caught now. Be afraid to raise your head freely—it's a sin, it isn't allowed. Worry, sigh, groan—let your brain dry up and wither with care . . .

Because Hershele had a nice, reedy little voice, his father tried to make it a source of income: he'd have Hershele back him up on Rosh Hashana and Yom Kippur in the little synagogue in Glupsk where he had served as *bal-tfile* for a good few years already. Hershele's bar mitzvah came after Shabbes Nakhmu, the Sabbath of Consolation, precisely the time when cantors start preparing for the holidays, when they check their "instrument," testing their throats and examining themselves on the liturgical modes; when the sad and tearful music of bits of the Rosh Hashana *shmin-esre* can be heard in the streets at evening.

The nightingale is a sweet woodland singer, but he's no sweet singer of Israel. Though his lovely spring serenade calls forth feelings of tenderness and love in the hearts of the peoples of the world, it isn't meant for a people that is counting the *oymer*—no way. The Jew's nightingale is the *bal-tfile*, it's he who awakens loving feeling with the sublimity of his *Ato Zoykher*, with the sweet and delightful words of the prophets; a loving feeling so godly and pure—a Jew burns, he's possessed, desire draws all his thoughts to God's holy dwelling in heaven—that it's like God Himself, without any image or form.

"*Koy omar ha-Shem*, Thus saith the Lord," cries the *bal-tfile* in a ringing voice, "I remember the devotion of your youth, your love as a bride, how you followed me in the desert, *be-erets loy zerua*, somewhere out there in the sticks." A scorching pang in the heart of the Jew; he quivers, he shakes, he stretches out his hands in ardent supplication from the depths of his soul. "Ay-ay, Gotenyu, dear, sweet Master of the Universe." And before he

can pull himself back together, the *bal-tfile* works himself up to the breaking point and lets fly with a sweet, moving melody: "Is Ephraim not my
dear son, my darling child? For the more I speak of him, the more I remember him. My heart yearns for him, *rakheym arakhamenu ne'um
ha-Shem*—and may God have mercy on his soul." The Jew's eyes fill with
tears, his heart weeps within him; he crinkles his face like a child and
whimpers, "*Oy, Tatenyu!* Holy, kindhearted, faithful little father!"

And so groups of Jews come together outside the windows of Leyzer-
Yankl's house, like bees at a whiff of honey, to listen to his enthusiastic re-
hearsals of *Unesane Toykef* and other juicy liturgical bits. Leyzer-Yankl
declaims the words, gargling deep in his throat, passing from his chest
voice to a falsetto, and Hershele responds with a tiny peep. They're working like dogs, the sweat pours off them as they run through their repertoire
of vocal stylings: each of them on his own, one following the other in regular succession; both of them mingled together, the voices twining back
and forth with a flourish, Leyzer-Yankl straining downward in supplication, then roaring out a question in his lowest register, Hershele climbing
upwards, squeaking out a coloratura response; their throats bim-bam-
bimming at full capacity, to the delight of the Jews outside.

And so the Kaptsansker nightingale sings his sad, sweet songs at
evening until a couple of days before *slikhes*, the pre-Rosh Hashana penitential prayers, when he falls silent and prepares to depart along with the
swallows and other birds of summer—they to someplace far off and warm,
he and Hershele to the little synagogue in Glupsk.

Slikhes-time in the forest is as deathly quiet as Shabbes afternoon in
Kaptsansk, when the whole town is asleep, but the quiet in the woods is
melancholy. The trees have changed their appearance; they are lost in
thought, worried. The shaking of their branches is a wringing of hands; the
sound of the wind buzzing through them, a bitter lament, a sigh, the groan
of a devoted mother after her children have drifted away. Where a moment
ago there was noise and life, where there was singing and dancing in every
corner, there is now the restful quiet of a graveyard. Everything whispers
of separation and parting. The liveliness, the freshness, the good cheer are
all gone; everything appears somehow angry and ill-humored. The sky is
also unfriendly; it sulks and it pouts. The nest is empty, the birds have
flown. And the forest stands thoughtful and worried, as if the departure of

its songbirds augurs no good. Any minute now it can expect a storm cloud to come up—winter with its bitter frosts—so it's troubled and morose.

And Kaptsansk is now as deathly quiet as the forest. A good half of the town departed with Leyzer-Yankl. The usual transport set off for Glupsk, all sorts of livestock in search of an income.

Kaptsansk had sensed the approaching bitterness—winter was coming, and winter-needs with it: heat, a dress, a shoe, and something to eat, of course. This wasn't summer, when you could get by on whatever came to hand—a radish, a cucumber, an onion, a clove of garlic—anything that would plug up your stomach and let you refute false accusations of neglect . . . And God, the Good and the Almighty, who sustains all His creatures, from the mighty aurochs to the eggs of lice, God tells the summer birds what to do well ahead of time: "Fly and seek your food in warmer lands. And you, Jews of Kaptsansk, drag yourselves elsewhere to seek your livelihood, you poor little Jews. Drag yourselves to Glupsk."

2

YOU HAVE TO KNOW what traveling means to a boy in order to understand Hershele's thoughts on the eve of his departure. He was the happiest person in the world as he prepared for his first trip to another town—and he was going together with his parents. Yes, Mrs. Leyzer-Yankl dragged herself along too, ostensibly to visit the graves of her forebears, but really to do a little business and also, apparently, to check up on a potential groom for Tsippe-Sossye, or maybe for someone else—that was her business and nobody else's. In order to cover their expenses, she also brought along a little merchandise that she could sell for a decent price.

Hershele imagined Glupsk to be somewhere at the end of the world, in the back of beyond where the heavens meet the earth; he figured that the journey there would never really end. Naturally, he didn't sleep a wink the night before; he tossed and turned, thinking all the while of the great happiness in store for him. He could see all of Glupsk looking out for his father, crying in unison, "Where is he, Reb Leyzer-Yankl? When's he coming, Reb Leyzer-Yankl? What could be keeping him? Reb Leyzer-

Yankl still isn't here." And suddenly, joy and exultation. "Reb Leyzer-Yankl's coming. Reb Leyzer-Yankl's already here. And he isn't alone; he's brought his son, the boy wonder, with him." They flock toward them, crowding, fighting over the father and his son, each of them trying to drag them off to his house for lodging, for luncheon, for a party. They get pointed out from a distance: "There they are, here they come, Reb Leyzer-Yankl and his son." And Hershele and his father give them a little taste of a *Na'aritsokh*, they sing a march, a *volekhl*, toss in a beggars' tune from Klivan for a chaser—and the crowd's going wild, jumping out of their skins with joy . . .

Morning had scarcely broken when Hershele jumped out of bed, washed his hands, grabbed the *tefillin*-bag to which he owed this exaltation of his lot, and ran off to the *bes-medresh* to get his *davening* done posthaste. Aside from *davening*, he had some urgent business matters to clear up with his friends before leaving. They were likewise in the *bes-medresh* bright and early because, as everybody knows, the month of Elul is carnival season for boys. They're up to their necks in business, thank God, and don't have to worry about keeping themselves busy for as long as their strength holds out. They have to smuggle the shofar away and try to blow it in the women's section of the synagogue, at the same time as they plan strategy to fend off the *shammes*, who is as furious as ten devils. They also have to go to the cemetery, where there's a tree with late-summer pears, and to the woods with its just-ripened nut trees, where they have to stuff their pockets full. Praise the Lord that at such a time, when there was so much business afoot, they were still free and exempt from their studies. It's the busiest time of year for the teachers; they're like hens in labor, trying to hatch themselves a class for the next semester, butting heads and biting each other's noses over every potential student.

Hershele looked haughtily down at his friends in the anteroom of the *bes-medresh*: "You call these guys people? They're staying here, and me? I'm going on the road." You could have told him that the lord of the local manor had offered him all of Kaptsansk, and his own castle, too, if Hershele would only remain at home—Hershele would have spit on the offer, assuming that he'd even listened.

He said goodbye to his friends and went on his way, all merry and bright.

It was a beautiful day, the kind of present that you sometimes get in

Elul. The sun's shining face emerged very early from her tent in a corner of the sky, gradually driving off the cool mist so she could admire her reflection in the dewdrops, which were sparkling like diamonds in their play of colors. The shadows moved respectfully backward, one step at a time, and the farther they moved, the brighter it got. The sparrows were chirping merrily, hopping around roofs and fences on their thin little legs, running together in a pack to quarrel over a seed or to discuss some vital community matter, running apart to pair off, each one dancing before his intended. They were greeting each other, hugging, kissing, squirming, fluttering their wings—and peck-peck-peck, each on the head of its beloved.

Bleating goats run quickly from every alley to the flock's meeting place, then leave for a day in the meadow. The wild young billy goats, the *shkotsim* of the group, lift up their tails and jump way out in front. Cows move slowly, with unhurried dignity, inclining their heads calmly and quietly, like women of substance—although a few of them do turn their heads backward and let out a hoarse, bovinely-foolish moo, like something from a broken shofar, for no good reason at all—maybe it's a friendly greeting to the whole townful of Jews or a "see you later" to the calves left behind.

Reeling from side to side, the gander leads his whole flock of newly fledged goslings, honking horribly, gobbling, stretching his neck out, turning his head, hurrying to the water with his troops.

The day is as bright and beautiful as Hershele's mood. He had undone his capote while walking, stretched out his hands to grab the long, snow-white threads drifting around in the air like cobwebs; took a good, long look at the doves soaring and spinning with outstretched wings on high— pure and bright, gold and silver—and he enjoyed it, he was feeling somehow lighthearted, feeling all right. This was his lucky day. His business deals had worked out, God be praised, even better than he'd hoped. School's out and he's going away—the whole world's on holiday. "Master of the Universe," he thought, his eyes moist with joy, "I thank You and praise You for all Your loving favors. Nu, let me betake myself to Your service: I'll be pious, I'll study, I'll *daven* with fervor and be a proper Jew."

And as he walked on so cheerfully, so happily, his heart so full of joy, he suddenly caught sight of that image most beloved, the radiant face of Beyle.

Beyle was standing outside her house, putting dishes out to dry and hanging some bits of laundry on the line. She was barefoot, wearing a petticoat that hooked up from behind, still not fully dressed. The sleeves of her blouse were rolled up past the elbows of her thick, ample arms, the bosom a little bit open, exposing, you'll excuse me, the entirety of her throat, and her hair was disheveled, the way it usually is on a hard-working girl in the morning.

Hershele, as happy as on Simkhes Toyre, runs blissfully up to his princess—don't ask *him* how it happened, Satan must have given him a shove from behind. He bids her farewell, shaking her hand like she was a man, and raving on—he couldn't even tell you what he was saying.

Beyle is dumbfounded, has no idea what to do. Once the first flush of excitement is over, Hershele, still somewhat out of his senses, drops her hand and says, with a foolish titter, "Hmm, a girl's hand yet. A woman, eh? See you later."

But soon as he's back to himself, he's speechless. He blushes, turns pale. Beyle has lowered her eyes, quietly chokes with laughter. She slides gradually away from him and Hershele takes off like a thief.

Hershele was on the verge of distraction, full of self-loathing. What on earth had he done? First he promises to serve the Lord and be a real Jew—and all of a sudden a business like this, a stab right in God's back? *Feh!* He spat, scratched his temple in dismay, and said, "Na . . . na!"

3

ARRIVING HOME, Hershele got a bit of a chewing-out for keeping everyone waiting. His father was already in his traveling clothes: a faded calico robe, its sleeves and front skirts covered with hardened grease-spots made of food and greenish tobacco, which shimmered outlandishly in some indescribable color. The back was all worn away, with bits of oakum pushing through in places. On his head was a sort of worn-out, badly crumpled cap. But the torn old traveling shoes with patches that he should have been wearing were not on his feet yet. They'd only just found them and were trying to drag them from under the bed with a poker. The family was dancing around him, packing busily, and he was standing there, saddled up like a horse.

Like a horse, I say, which had to bear a houseful of children. Once a year he had to harness himself up and hit the road, work himself to the limit and tear his health to shreds—the lives of everybody in the family depended on this journey. Which is why the whole house was in motion on the day of his departure; everyone was up and Leyzer-Yankl was standing there, saddled, pale and pensive, a serious look on his face.

Hershele's mother was in her traveling clothes, too, an assortment of ancient rags that made her look thicker and fatter than usual, with a kerchief pushed down on her forehead until it covered her eyes. Hershele was the only one to save himself the trouble of changing—the capote he was wearing was the only one he had. His mother had actually told him to turn it inside out, but Hershele proved conclusively that the lining was hopelessly smudged; it was also in shreds and disintegrating rapidly. He got his way—he could go as he was, but he had to give in to his mother and wear one of his father's old caps, which should have been burnt with the *khomets* a long time before, as well as a cloth belt around his waist.

Now that they were all properly dressed and had grabbed a hasty bite, they bade farewell to the children, grabbed their bundles, and raced right off, breathless, sweating, as dazed as cows in a stampede—the way all Jews prepare for a trip. And way up high on the big wagon were a cage with chickens and a basket of eggs packed in chaff, which Hershele's mother had been sure to put there nice and early.

The wagon was packed with almost a quarter of the population of Kaptsansk—all kinds of Jews, along with girls and women seeking positions as servants and nursemaids: model Jews, kosher Jews, bred-in-the-bone and perfervid Jews, broken Jews, hemorrhoidal Jews, ordinary Jews, regular Jews, and "you-call-these-Jews?" Jews. A mixing together, a tangling up, a transposing of feet—such a crushing together you could die.

Hershele was sweating like crazy, like everyone else inside the wagon; the model Jews were sweating like beavers, their faces stewing like a *tsimmes*. If nobody caught cold, it was only because the wagon was besieged by passengers picked up along the way; they were tottering on their feet, sitting precariously on the back, on the sides, on the coachman's box, and they kept any air from reaching the people within.

The passengers sat angrily at the start of the trip, muttering huffily about the driver; whenever they caught a blow to the small of the back, a press on one of their corns, they'd make horrible faces and bite their lips. "It's nothing. Nu, nu." But soon they were at their ease, they could put this reserve aside, and even apologize to each other: "Shove over!" If you got hit, you screamed. People were unhappy and started to fight. Hershele's mother didn't stop screaming at one of the broken Jews that he shouldn't break her eggs. His father kept his mouth shut; he'd wrapped his throat in squirrel-hide, so as not to lose his voice, God forbid. The horses were starting to get lazy, they shlepped along slowly, waving their meager tails, and the passengers took courage and began to talk among themselves.

The one goy in the wagon finally woke up. A pauper, formerly a steward somewhere, he'd been snoring away, dead to the world, since they got on. Sober now, he looked around at the assembled company in confusion and lent an ear to the conversation—it might as well have been Turkish. He tried to join in with a few words of his own—they were Greek to the Jews. But as long as they caught something, one word out of ten, they'd got the gist and could figure the rest of it out for themselves, and they were racking their brains to come up with some gimmick to get their meaning across to the dumb peasant: a bit in our language, a bit in theirs, a little with the hands, a little by signs, a twist of the finger with the right intonation— what's the difference? They understood each other.

A conversation got going about their way of life and, pardon the proximity, ours. His name, Ivan, was ours; they'd taken it from Yoykhanan. The seven liberal arts had all been taken from us. They elucidated a very nice exemplum from the *Medresh* for him, a witticism out of the *Gemore*, enlightened him as to Jewish customs and the principles underlying them. Ivan appeared to concede—several times he shouted out, "Kugel! *Tsimmes!*" and licked his lips. The women choked with laughter. "Did you hear what he said? Look at him licking his lips. He loves our kugel."

A teenage girl with a married woman's shawl on her head, who was going to look for a position as a nursemaid, was quietly murmuring a sad song to herself:

> The stars are shining in heaven,
> The nightingale sings in the wood;

> The world is pleasant and happy,
> Only I'm not feeling so good.

The goy turned away and started to flirt with the women. The men dismissed him with a wave of their hands: "Once a goy, always a goy."

After they'd gone a fair way on foot, pushing the wagon up a hill, and sat themselves back down again, the passengers gave themselves over to a wide-ranging discussion. They talked about everything that was going on in this world and the next. They talked about business, estimated the fortunes of a number of magnates; the old story about Reb Shmelke also came up, and they decided that Elijah the prophet had left him a wishing-ring. Right away there's groaning, sighing, wishing. One said that if he had a wishing-ring, he'd wish for this; a second, for that; a third, for the other. Everybody wished for something else and alms were dropping like slops— each was showing the other what a good friend he'd be, promising everyone mountains of gold. Feelings of brotherhood increased among the passengers; they felt comforted, not so cast off and alone in the world, and each was very pleased with the other.

And things went on in this way until, with God's help, they finally dragged themselves into Glupsk that evening, more dead than alive.

AND SHE DID NOT do thus to Leyzer-Yankl on his arrival from Kaptsansk—Glupsk did not come out to greet them the way Hershele had imagined at home. No one fought over them, no one tried to drag them off for food or lodging. People walked by indifferently, not even sparing them a glance.

Hershele found this hard to understand at first. Fresh off the wagon, standing on the street with a bundle in his hands, he looked at his father in wordless amazement, as if to say, "What is the meaning of this? There must be some horrible mistake." But after he caught a wagon-shaft in the back and someone shoved his father so hard that he nearly fell on top of the pig that was munching happily away in the gutter (where someone had just dumped a full and fragrant slop pail off a balcony); after the shaft and the shove were topped off with ten different "Up yourses"—Why were they blocking the way like a couple of wooden dummies?—only then did Hershele get the hint that answered all his questions. He hung his head; he understood everything now, and he and his father both slipped a little in his eyes.

As soon as they'd arrived, Leyzer-Yankl consulted with his wife about their things, and whether or not it was already too late for them to go to their acquaintances'. But after the reception he'd received, they both decided to avoid any further delay and just stay the night at the wagon drivers' hostel where they'd been let off.

Hershele received the honor of keeping an eye on the baggage and taking it inside, while his parents rummaged around the chicken cage and negotiated with the coachman; he should please drive into the courtyard so they could leave the cage there overnight.

Let the goyim endure the kind of night that Hershele, hungry, tired, a wreck from his journey, passed in the hostel. It was already pretty late when he pushed his way through the noise and confusion of the people who'd got there before him and threw himself onto a wobbly, splintering plank-bed in a corner, where he finally got his longed-for reception and was welcomed as an honored guest. As all the world knows, the bedbugs of Glupsk welcome their guests gladly and bestow a full range of honors upon them: they hug them, stick to them, crawl under their nails. Hershele's scratching, all his hand signals telling them to keep their honors, availed him nothing. They kept on as they had started, wriggling around, working on their guest with considerable pleasure, until he was forced to tear himself gingerly away and lay himself down on the floor.

And Hershele's lucky day, to which he'd so looked forward in expectation of great happiness, came to an end.

Early the next morning his mother hurried into town to do her business; his father went off a little later. As he was about to leave, he noticed that his pocket was torn. He was in such a rush, though, that he simply grabbed the wallet containing his entire fortune and handed it over to Hershele, who was left by himself near their bundles.

Hershele found a piece of bread, a clove of garlic, and a big yellow cucumber in a bag, and went to town in his own way. He ate with vigor, as if he'd just got up from a sickbed.

Having satisfied one desire, he was seized by a powerful urge to go outside for a bit and take a look at Glupsk.

A whole new world opened up before his eyes, as new to him as if newly created, just now sprung out of the ground. He threw his head back and stood slack-jawed with amazement, not knowing what to look at first. The first thing to meet his eyes was a thick mass of Jews, running and shoving like someone had just shouted fire. Men and women, kith and kin—like a swarm of bees, but dressed in every kind of clothing, from rags and tatters to the most expensive apparel. There were women in satin coats and mud-spattered silken dresses, regular princesses. Had they not been squeaking and blowing their noses, talking in an ear-splitting singsong that could be heard all down the street, Hershele would have thought them aristocrats for sure.

On every side were wagons, pushcarts, cabs, some of them tangled together, snagged on a wheel or a shaft—curses, screams, cries that reached the heavens.

The fact that there were gutters draining through the streets came as no surprise—it was a Jewish city, after all. They had plenty of the same kind of stuff in Kaptsansk, why should it be different here? That's what streets were for—a place to dump your slops. What *did* amaze him were the pointy stones lying around in the streets. Why did they need stones that you could break your back on, when you could fall into the potholes and break your neck very nicely without them? How was Hershele supposed to know that this was pavement, when paved streets were still a mystery to him? He'd never seen them, never heard of such a thing. A little later, when he'd discovered the secret of the stones, it was no more wonder. No wonder, either, were the tightly packed, hunchbacked little houses with broken roofs—that was the way things were supposed to be, that's the way houses looked, or Jewish houses, at any rate. The only thing that really struck him as strange was the two--or three-story brick house in the middle of all this. God Almighty! How does a Jew push himself so high into the sky and risk his life crawling up there on a narrow little ladder outside? Say the *vide*—before you go up that ladder, you have to say the confession before death and kiss your life goodbye.

Hershele's eyes found plenty to look at; his head was thinking and considering, and his feet kept going and going until he suddenly gave a start and—uh-oh, he'd wandered pretty far and was long ago due back.

Only he didn't know the way. He started to ask people how to get to the Kaptsansker hostel. Some of them, running, hurrying, gave him an angry look and didn't say a word; some of them gave him a brief description, in gestures: "Go straight, then left until you come to a lane, then right, then left again. Then ask somebody, and they'll show you."

Did he have any choice? Hershele went wandering through alleys and marshes, jumping over narrow footbridges with plenty of space between the planks and grabbing passing fences as he did so. He seemed to be in the stomach, the very bowels of Glupsk, where the air was close and the stench made you cough. He walked with might and main, drenched in sweat, until he ran into a nice young man who was good enough to pay him a little attention.

"Come," said the young man, looking Hershele up and down with a friendly smile, "Come, I'll take you. I can see you're a real greenie."

Hershele's eyes practically filled with tears as he thanked the young man for his good will.

"It's a *mitsve* to help a stranger," the young man said with a glowing face. "You can't afford to be a rube here in Glupsk. You've got to watch out for your pockets here. You understand me, kid?"

Hershele felt inside his pocket.

"You engaged yet?"

"No," answered Hershele, already growing lighthearted.

"Why not? You'll soon see, we'll have you under the canopy in no time."

Hershele was choking with laughter.

"What? You don't believe me? You'll soon see. Go ahead and laugh—it doesn't matter! Here's a footbridge—go easy, keep your mind on your pocket."

Hershele gave another feel.

"Nu, everything there?"

"Don't be afraid. It's there."

"That's just what happened last year with a boy like you. He kept feeling, he thought his wallet was in his pocket, and what finally turned out in the end? Nothing! The pickpockets, may they burn in Hell, somehow got hold of his wallet, God save you, and replaced his money with toilet paper. You understand? Please, take it out and have a look. You can't afford to be lazy."

Hershele wasn't lazy. He took out his wallet and held it before his eyes. "You see, huh? What'd I tell you?" Those were the young man's last words. He grabbed the wallet from Hershele's hands, made a run for it, and vanished.

Hershele watched this happen with his mouth open and his eyes bugged out, as if he'd just been slapped in the face. He had no idea of where he was or what was going on . . .

The proverb "A guest for a while sees for a mile" was tailor-made for Hershele. On his very first day in Glupsk, the city revealed itself to him in all its glory and splendor: in its winding back streets, its meadows and sands, its gutters and stinking puddles, thick mud and thin mud, cutpurses and thieves. And its self-revelation was a disaster for him.

Smeared, spattered, sporting a fresh-caught Glupsker cold, Hershele came gloomily back to the hostel around *minkhe*-time: no mother, no father, no bundles. He went numb; he was staring like a madman, his heart thumping wildly. Suddenly he realized that someone was bawling him out—"Here he is, the fine young man. Whattaya got to say for yourself?"—and he beheld Reyze the innkeeper before him.

Reyze was a short, thickset woman, well along in years; she had a big belly, a pockmarked face that was always drenched in sweat, a split-level chin, and a string of thin little hairs stretched across her upper lip. The lip itself turned upward onto her right cheek; a red bit of tongue could be seen peeking out from the crevasse once plugged by two teeth. The bottom of her apron was always rolled up, her top buttons always undone. The ends of her kerchief were thrown over her shoulders, and she usually had a ladle in her hand, proof that she was always busy about the stove.

Reyze spoke shrilly, fast and straight from the heart—all in one indignant breath. She always sounded quarrelsome, enraged, even though she was very goodhearted by nature and meant no harm. It was a way of speaking, the result of a lifetime of dealing with wagon drivers. She was always tossing in a "Did you ever hear such a thing? Whattaya got to say for yourself?" loudly and in a singsong. She had one other conversational tic—she often bent her head to the side and ran the tip of her nose down her sleeve, wiping it along the length of her arm.

"Whattaya got to say for yourself?" Reyze was shouting her catchphrase at the unfortunate Hershele and giving her nose a nice trip down her sleeve. "How comes it that a boy should get lost? Who ever heard of such a thing? Just look at him, the fine young man—picks himself up and gets lost."

Hershele was choking on his tears. He bowed his head in silence.

"He's not talking, the fine young man? His parents are dying and he—you ever hear such a thing?—he stands there like a moron and can't open his mouth."

"*Oy vey.*" Hershele gave a cry and burst into sobs, thinking that his parents had really gone on to the next world and that he was now an orphan.

"Nu, stop sobbing, Mr. Lost." Reyze was comforting the orphan. "Just don't do it again. Your mother and father ran their souls out."

"Hic, hic, hic." Hershele was sobbing dejectedly. He wanted to say something, but he was choked up with tears and could barely hic out a few broken syllables. "Moth . . . dead . . . hic . . ."

"*Oy vey iz mir!*" Reyze gave a start. "He thinks dead means they died. It's a figure of speech, you dope . . . Did you ever hear such a thing? Your parents could have died for real, though. Nu, sha, they'll be here soon to find out about you. They took their stuff and moved out while it was still daylight, don't ask me where. They sold the chickens and eggs—I bought some myself. Sha . . . Here, I'll give you some of your mother's eggs. *Vey iz mir*, you ever hear such a thing? He hasn't eaten all day. Go get washed and sit down at the table."

Hershele was back from the dead now, restoring his soul with an omelet that Reyze had hastened to bring to the table, talking all the while in her shrill, angry voice. "Here, eat hearty. Who ever heard of such a thing, fasting the day away?"

He was still eating when his parents ran into the house, frightened half to death. Noise, screaming—joy and anger and scolding all mixed into one. "Praise the Lord!" his mother cried joyously, looking at her son with anger. "You know what you deserve for this?"

"How could you?" rejoiced his father. "How could you do such a thing? You deserve—how could you do it?—you deserve to be ripped apart like a herring!"

"You ever hear such a thing?" Reyze, Hershele's defense lawyer, was running her nose down her sleeve. "Fine parents you are, leaving the child alone to fend for himself. You're yelling? Whattaya got to say for yourself? A kid is a kid, no? So keep quiet!"

"Oy, what a mess you are. You're covered in mud." Hershele's mother was yelling at Hershele and wringing her hands. "You must have all the mud in Glupsk on you."

"Excuse me, what's that you're saying about Glupsk?" asked Reyze, shaking her head. "The princess is displeased with her son's capote, she can't even bear to look at it? It's a capote like every other capote here, and where is it written in the Torah that a Jew has to go around all gussied up? If the mud in Glupsk isn't good enough for the princess, it's no problem, don't worry, Glupsk still looks good to us. We're respectable people, thank God. We've got nothing to hide. The poor kid's tired, he's weak, he didn't eat all day—and what's she worrying about? You should be ashamed of yourself. And you should leave the kid alone."

Reyze's words had the desired effect, and from that time on Hershele loved Reyze from the bottom of his heart.

5

OUR HEROES were staying in separate accommodations. Not that they needed private rooms, God forbid! At an inn, even rich Jews make do with just a bed and stay three and four to a room, just to save some money. A Jew needs to enjoy this world? Foolishness! So what was going on with Hershele's family? They had no other choice.

As usual, his father stayed with the *shammes* of the little synagogue where he led the High Holiday prayers. The *shammes*'s apartment was scarcely big enough for his own family, but what is it that we say? Two's company and so is three.

This precept justifies a Jew's sticking his spoon into another's bowl, shoving in where it's already crowded, putting his foot in someone else's bath, looking on in his *makhzer*, somehow grabbing a nap in his bed when he's already in it, squeezing into a packed wagon, and pushing all his life away. What does it matter, as long as you keep going? As long as you eat your fill, take a nap, and make it through the night; as long as you do what a Jew's got to do to keep himself alive.

And anyway, Leyzer-Yankl thought of himself as a virtual relative of the *shammes*, and it's customary among our people to consider it obligatory to stay with even the most distant relative. The official explanation is that otherwise they'll God forbid offend their kinsman, who might then get mad at them. So if Leyzer-Yankl didn't head straight for the *shammes'* with wife, child, baggage, and chickens, it was firstly because he already knew that it was impossible. And if the *shammes* could be offended? Don't worry—Leyzer-Yankl would explain it to him. And secondly—what do you think?—it was the *shammes'* dumb luck.

Hershele's mother was staying with a woman she knew from Kaptsansk, a cook in a wealthy home where Hershele's mother had sold a few dozen eggs and where she was also expecting twenty geese to pluck over the winter and an order for a couple of dozen stockings. His mother was radiant in her veil, with her Shabbes kerchief on her head. The kitchen seemed to agree with her; she could stretch out and relax. The cook was spoiling her rotten, constantly slipping her food and offering encouragement: "Eat, Malke-Toybenyu. Eat, eat, my dear."

Neither of them shut her mouth. They talked nonstop, making inquiries about all kinds of people, acquaintances as well as complete strangers who had nothing whatever to do with them.

They reminisced about their girlhood. "Remember? Remember, Malke-Toybenyu?" "Remember? Remember, Treyne-Sossenyu?"

They were having the time of their lives. Each looked at the other with shining eyes, each pursed and creased her lips coquettishly, kept saying "darling," "crown," and "may you be healthy." Nor did they forget the most important matter of all: gossip, the best and tastiest spice in every feminine conversation. They fulfilled the customs of backbiting and mockery according to both the letter and the spirit of the law. Treyne-Sossye fulfilled it plainly and simply; she burned with enthusiasm and spoke quickly, rapidly, with relish, the way it should be. Malke-Toybe likewise performed satisfactorily, but with cunning, always shaking her head and piously rolling her eyes as if she were loathe to speak ill of anybody. Inside, though, she was enjoying herself immensely, her mouth was watering with delight, and once in a while she'd make an ambiguous comment, nothing at all on the face of things, but enough to prick Treyne-Sossye's tongue and fire her up to mock even more.

"You should be healthy, Malke-Toybenyu." Treyne-Sossel's tongue was starting to grind out words to dump over her various mistresses. "You have no idea what a pain they are, all the fine boss-ladies today. No matter where I've been, one is always worse than the next. Every damned one of them with her shtik—all they like is to wander back and forth and make a fuss and a racket and jangle their keys and think that they're doing something . . . And you know what it is?"

"What, what?" Malke-Toybe played the innocent and slipped in a word to pull more out of Treyne-Sossye.

"Nothing!" Treyne-Sossye was getting excited. "God only knows what *they* call it—it's a joke, that's what it is. This one's a real homemaker, she's everywhere at once. Yeah, it's true—everywhere but where she should be, like she's playing hide-and-seek. If you look for her here, she's there; if you need her there, ha-ha, she's here. Her husband's looking, the kids are looking, they're calling and calling and she's screaming out from somewhere in a tizzy.

"The other one—*she* should feel all my aches and pains—she doesn't believe in appearances, she has to count the number of grains in the grits. She'd pluck out her eyes rather than lose half a groschen. And how come?"

"She's the boss, isn't she? She wants to save money," said Malke-Toybe, only half-seriously.

"Save money, right!" said Treyne-Sossye, making a face. "She wants to cut a groschen from the food costs, but she'll waste hundreds of her husband's—don't ask *me* on what.

"Another home economist buys up every special in the market. Specials on eggs, specials on butter, specials on shmaltz—everything's heaven-sent. She's got a pantry full of food, and keeps it under lock and key—"

"You don't mean the Mrs. here?" Malke-Toybe blurted out. "She keeps everything under lock and key? Now *that's* a homemaker."

"Tfu, that's a homemaker." Treyne-Sossye echoed Malke-Toybe with an angry laugh, spitting as she did so. "She keeps all her bargains under lock and key until the eggs go rotten, the butter starts to stink, the preserves ferment, and you have to throw everything out . . .

"There's another one, a side of beef who spends her life in the kitchen with her nose in every pot—I need her there like I need something in my eye. She sticks her nose in and balls everything up: the roast gets burned, the soup boils over—a regular blow-up."

"Surrounded by assassins! Let our enemies blow up!" Malke-Toybe said fawningly. "Don't eat your heart out, Treyne-Sossenyu."

"To hell with them!" Treyne-Sossye spat. "What do you know? What do you know about them, Malke-Toybenyu? Not one of them worth a damn. They're a bunch of loafers and lazy slobs. They've got nothing to do, but they act like they're champion housekeepers. Some joke, eh? Like the house would turn upside down without them. You think you know something about it? At first I was stupid, I let it upset me; I used to let them make me suffer. But then I thought it over, and now it's 'Up yours! Curl up and die! Go ahead—poke around, talk, lose your tempers, scream like lunatics—I do what I want and you can get stuffed!'

"So what do you think? Maybe *you* know if I'll still get to heaven? Tell me the truth, my darling dear—aren't I allowed to have something for myself? You understand what I'm saying, Malke-Toybenyu, may you be healthy?"

"May *you* be healthy, Treyne-Sossenyu! What do you think, I don't understand? I understand you perfectly."

"And what, darling? I'm *not* in the right? What do you think, I'm gonna go around dripping in jewels on what I earn from my salary? I'm gonna keep on working forever? You know what they say: Nobody's born with a lifetime guarantee. You've got to live for as long as you're alive, and keep an eye out for the future as well. Strictly between you and me, if I didn't pick up a bit of flour, a bit from the butcher, a bit from the marketing, even my enemies would have to feel sorry for me. Why kid ourselves, Malke-Toybenyu? It's OK, you understand? I've got no claims against God, I can't complain. Bless His Name, I've got what to wear . . . You still haven't seen my wardrobe. Come, I'll show you, darling."

And Treyne-Sossel proceeded to show what she had, laying the merchandise out for inspection: high-button shoes, a dress, another dress with flounces in the latest style, a silken cape with garnet buttons, a jacket, a tasseled burnoose for Shabbes. She stood with her arms akimbo, beaming with pride. Malke-Toybe considered every object with the air of an expert, she felt and appraised, her face glowing as if God's blessings on Treyne-Sossel were a source of great pleasure to her, said "Ach, ach," casting her eyes heavenwards, as if to say, "Praise the Lord, praise His Name!" offering congratulations all the while and reassuring Treyne-Sossel each time that she was as dear to her as her life. And then said, "Can there be another Treyne-Sossye like you on earth? No way." And they're both delighted and swell with the greatness of their pleasure . . .

Let's leave the king and queen for a while—the king with the *shammes*, the queen in the kitchen—and turn our attention to the prince.

Hershele, the prince in question, lay stretched out on a bench in the synagogue like a little aristocrat. It wasn't a bad place for a rest. The bench was twice as long as he was, giving him plenty of room to stretch his legs, and the railing at the end did duty as a pillow. He wasn't at all chary of spending the night there, because he wasn't alone; there were a few other people sleeping in the synagogue with him—beggars, whose company was anything but gloomy. They chatted, told wonder-stories as good as the ones in Kaptsansk—Glupsk didn't lack for anything, don't worry. There were Jews there too, and with the same pretty stories. The path to heaven stood open there, too, and they could wander as far up it as they wished.

Everything was copacetic. Our heroes, praise God, were decently provided for; there was nothing to complain about, and all was well. There was nothing missing but a bit of health. Hershele had had a cold since his first day in Glupsk; he was coughing a little, his voice was strained and slightly hoarse. Nevertheless, he got up in the middle of the night to accompany his father at the first *slikhes*. His coloratura was really pretty spotty, his falsetto more of a grating whistle, but that wasn't really much of a problem. There were plenty of helpers without him; as usual, much of the congregation took up the responses and called out "bim-bam." (There are plenty of Jews anxious to "bim-bam" along with somebody else, whether it's appropriate or not. What does it matter, as long as you get your two cents in and make yourself heard, the somebody else shouldn't think that he's working alone?) And secondly, a strained voice is just what the doctor ordered for *slikhes*. It fits in with the matter at hand, gives you that real *slikhes* feeling: It's pitch black outside, silent, the whole world's asleep. But Jews drag themselves yawning and stretching from their beds; sleep still lies on their breasts, their throats are dry, but they brace themselves and run swooning into the *shul*. They pour their hearts out to the living God in heaven and complain before him in a fainting-roaring-groaning voice, the way a homeless, unfortunate, dejected child complains to his father about the troubles he's endured in his wanderings through the world.

It's this fainting, gratingly languishing voice that touches the heart, that fires it to feelings of pity. The poor, sick child wakes from its fever at night, stretches its hands out pleadingly to its father, groans and howls with pain in a hoarse, dry voice that passes into a cough—it hits you right where you live, tugs at your soul, kicks you straight in the guts.

And when the rooster for *kapores* is taken from his perch in the middle of the night—"Come, be slaughtered for my sins!"—and he trembles and groans in a choked voice—does his grating leave your heart unmoved? Does his wheezing not tear at your soul?

6

MASTER OF THE UNIVERSE! What is it in those hard *bes-medresh* benches of yours that makes anyone who passes a night on one of them, using his fist for a pillow, awaken the next day a new man, as if he had been reborn. It's been happening since Jacob left Beersheba and spent the night on a hard bed of earth in "a certain place," with his head resting on a stone; as soon as he got up in the morning he felt that *"Eyn ze*, this is nothing else, *ki im beys eloykim*, but the house of God—a *bes-medresh*, that is—*ve-ze sha'ar hashomayim*, and here is the gateway to heaven."

Yea, verily, to heaven. For lying on his hard bed in the first *bes-medresh*, which was still without walls or a roof or an oven in the back, Jacob not only saw stars, but the other world as well: fiery angels going up and down a long ladder that reached from earth all the way up to heaven. And Jacob felt himself greatly changed.

Once more: Master of the Universe! What is there in this exile, in this wandering hither and yon all over the world that makes your Children of Israel—who have received this wandering as a gift from you—different from other kinds of people? What gives them a different appearance, a different way of living, a different destiny, a different everything from everybody else? At a time when the rest of the world is still bright, lively, and boyish, fooling around, thinking only of the joys of the here and now, your little Jew is aged, wrinkled, bent, worried, and depressed. His little head never stops working—it thinks and floats and flies, has nothing but goals in mind, things of value and permanence in view: that is, the world to come.

His first couple of days of wandering in the world, not to mention sleeping on the hard synagogue bench, had changed our Hershele so much, transformed him so completely that he was scarcely to be recognized. He never had a cheerful look on his face, was always somewhat sunk in thought, as if the weight of the world were on his shoulders. The words that he'd heard from his parents at his bar mitzvah—"give some thought to your future"—penetrated deep into his heart and were drilling holes in his head. "*Gevalt!* Goals! Ends! And what's the end going to be? A person has to think, has to worry about his future."

So Hershele betook himself to the *Gemore* with alacrity. Where else, according to his mind-set at the time, was he supposed to find the purpose and end of his life, if not in the *Gemore?* It's there that human happiness lies, the best to be attained in this life. A page of *Gemore* with *Toysfes,* the so-called additional commentaries, marks the boundary of human art and science; and if God should help further, if you can figure out a difficulty raised by the Maharam Shiff or explain one of the Maharsho's refutations, you're a made man who can live out the rest of his life in honor and wealth. Real scholars don't grow on trees. *Mi lonu godoyl*—who in all the world is greater, stronger, more influential than a Jew who knows what he's up to, a town rabbi or his second-in-command?

And for Hershele, then, "world" meant "Jews." There just wasn't anything else. Sure there are other people, but they're only nations of the earth, of no concern to anybody. What can they know? If they don't go to *kheyder* like the Jewish children and then claim they don't understand us— nu, what can you expect?

Hershele took the tractate *Bava Kamma* from the bookshelf in the synagogue and set himself to learning *Shoyr she-nogakh es ha-poro,* where Reuben's ox has gored Simeon's cow, intoning it loudly, swaying back and forth and waving his thumb to indicate how the words were to be read.

His brain was pumping, flying high. One thing hooked up to the next until a whole ladder suddenly sprang up, with Mishnaic beginnings, middles, and ends going up and down it in the guise of ill-tempered women who can't get along, and with the Tanna cited first on top of the ladder as king of the heap. Hershele was throwing himself in every direction, flying farther and farther off; a dizziness seized him, his head was spinning, the last thread he was holding onto had just ripped in two—and suddenly he's back to Reuben's ox and Simeon's cow. His head returns to his shoulders, he gives himself a shake and learns on with abandon.

You have to have spent plenty of nights on a rock-hard *bes-medresh* bench if you want to plumb the mystery of such a ladder, feel its real meaning, understand it in the proper spirit. These are no mere things; Reuben's ox and Simeon's cow are not gross, material, day-to-day cows that you can just go ahead and milk. No—they are a horse of a different color, rather like Taurus, Aries, Gemini, and Virgo among the signs of the Zodiac.

Hershele learned with more fervor than ever before, and thus found favor and grace in the eyes of many of the people in the synagogue. "A fine boy," they said. "He's got a real urge to learn."

Hershele's father practically melted with pleasure, and recounted his son's sterling qualities whenever the opportunity arose. "*Oy*," he said, "What you *don't* know about my boy! The *melamdim* in Kaptsansk can't stop praising his good head and his grasp. At twelve years old—would you believe it?—they'd run out of Torah to teach him. They had no answers for his questions, only a couple of ringing slaps, a pinch, a crack in the cheek— a method, you understand, to keep him in his place, he shouldn't think he's some kind of something. It's true, my dear Jews—you can't let a boy have his head; what an adult says, has to go. A boy must know that if an adult says "day," even though it's nighttime, day it is—and no two ways about it. Otherwise, it's gonna go rough for you. Today he asks one kind of question and tomorrow he'll be asking something else. You get me? Pretty soon he won't be satisfied—not with this, not with that, not with all kinds of things . . . I'm saying this for the good of all fathers. Our ancestors understood this better than we do, and that's why things were so good then. But be that as it may, between a slap here and a slap there, my Hershele got through *kheyder* and has started to learn on his own in our *bes-medresh*, under my supervision. Naturally, I give him a hand once in a while. Look at him—small as he is, he already knows all of tractates *Beytso, Kiddushin, Kesubos* and *Nido!*"

Hershele's father would usually conclude in this way, his face glowing, pointing at his son and thinking to himself, "Who knows? Maybe God's out for some matchmaking, and these lies will hatch us a bride."

7

TO TELL HOW HARD Leyzer-Yankl worked at his *davening* on Rosh Hashana would be to fail to do justice to the rest of the congregation. *They* were working, too, shouting along with Leyzer-Yankl in unison. Of course,

Leyzer-Yankl *was* the congregation's emissary, that is to say, the deputy chosen to represent them before the Master of the Universe. But Jews like to mix in everywhere. Give them a deputy with two heads, something really one of a kind—just let him try to open his mouth to say something without all of them barging in, each according to his fashion, in his own personal style, each thinking in his heart: *"Whatever* he might be, I know a thing or two myself, and probably as well as he does. He can call himself my representative because I've given him my authorization, and even if it isn't right to breathe down his neck too much, you've still got to open your mouth and show him sometimes. It's like he's the lawyer, the mediator; you trust him completely, but you have to do something yourself—plead your own case before the Lord up there in the Senate, and also sneak off to beseech the great princes like Petspatsye, the whole parcel of attorneys and secretaries and agents up there in the heavenly court."

And so the Children of Israel labor, and make themselves heard in the seventh heaven. Such uproar, racket, and din that nobody *but* God can understand what His little Jews want, what they're asking for with their screaming.

The assembled Jews shouted well, but Leyzer-Yankl prevailed and outshouted them all; he delivered the *Meylekh Elyoyn* as a lively, crackling march, and Hershele succeeded in making a few resounding squeaks from time to time.

So went the *davening* on the first day of Rosh Hashana. Leyzer-Yankl was on top, he ruled. But the second day went to the congregation. Bits of liturgical poetry and prayers roared and rustled in all sorts of sad voices, like a forest in a storm. Throats cried out, hearts sighed and moaned, hands clapped, fingers cracked, and heads, half-covered heads and heads decked to the waist in prayer-shawls, tossed in every direction and nodded up and down.

The synagogue was packed so tightly that there wasn't room enough for a pin. And hot? Something terrible. Leyzer-Yankl had broken into a sweat; he got caught in a draft and lost his voice. The poor guy was standing there as if he'd been choked. There was only one way to save himself: whenever he was supposed to recite a particularly moving bit, he burst out weeping and let his tears flow free, meanwhile swallowing the words as he rattled them off. The congregation loved it.

Leyzer-Yankl was a world-class crier, his weeping was a delight to the ears. He had a reputation in our part of the world, and was known as The Kaptsansker Master of Weeping. Some even compared him with the famous Lithuanian *khazn* known as "The Lamenting Mother," of whom it is said that he wept divinely, deliciously; always "Mama, mama," pretty as you please, in the real Jewish way.

Looking on at his father, Hershele likewise burst into tears, and his crying gave him considerable pleasure. You have to understand what crying in front of the whole congregation on Rosh Hashana and Yom Kippur means to a boy. They take drastic measures to do so—sniff, God help us, tobacco, pinch themselves in secret, rub their eyes. And Hershele was lucky enough to bring himself to tears without any of these expedients. And so his crying made his heart rejoice; he looked at himself with new respect, looked around to see if people noticed his tears (lest he be crying for nothing), stealthily touching his cheeks to be sure that they were good and wet.

Malke-Toybe went home a couple of days after Rosh Hashana, loaded down with sacks full of feathers that she was taking from several grand houses to pluck over winter; also, a large bundle of thread to be worked into stockings and a little merchandise that she'd picked up on the cheap: soap, starch, calico with red flowers on it for dresses—a really laughable bargain—and the renowned matches of Glupsk, which won't even burn in a fire and are good for extinguishing blazes.

But she was leaving in anger and vexation. She was mad at Treyne-Sossel. After all their intimacy, they'd had a terrible quarrel; their great love turned to nothing.

Nine measures of talk won't last two women more than a couple of days. As long as there was still somebody or something else to talk about, their tongues kept flapping, their jaws kept grinding. But they'd scarcely run out of what to talk about when they started to look each other over for faults to condemn.

Malke-Toybe didn't like the guy who was always coming to call on Treyne-Sossel for a little smooching. And when, yet? At a time when even fish are trembling in the water. She also didn't like the way Treyne-Sossel kept her kerchief pushed back on her head, so that some hair peeked out; or that she slid hoops and a mountain of rags under the back of her dress to make herself look, you'll excuse me, ampler, more thick. Malke-Toybe hinted at her displeasure—"It isn't the way of a Jewish woman"—and on several occasions up and lowered the kerchief with her own kosher hands, gave the back of Treyne-Sossye's dress a feel, then stretched both hands out in front of her in a semicircle, shaking her head and sourly pursing her lips, as if to say, "Oh-oh—you're packing a time bomb back there, God save us."

For Treyne-Sossye's part, having somebody else's eye on her business didn't suit her at all; she didn't need to have a *rebetsin* around. She was also bugged by Malke-Toybe's eating; the woman could pack away enough for ten and still want more, like some kind of locust or something. She blamed Malke-Toybe for a scolding that she got from her mistress; Treyne-Sossel has been framed, and she knew who'd sold her out.

Malke-Toybe and her mistress really did exchange whispers a couple of times, Malke-Toybe rolling her eyes and putting on pious faces, constantly spitting and blowing her nose. And the conversation always ended just as Treyne-Sossel walked in. Malke-Toybe, red as a beet, would scratch herself, twist around, shrug her shoulders, and stand with her back bent like a cat's, a finger pressing on her cheek.

In a word, the erstwhile friends, who'd been as close as heart and soul, started to toss pointed hints back and forth and pass judgment on each other. Each pecked at the other, until they finally unsheathed their tongues and quarreled once and for all.

Enraged as she was with Treyne-Sossel, the departing Malke-Toybe vented her wrath on the whole of Glupsk, and on each individual in it: on the wagon driver, for charging her ten groschen more than everybody else and putting her—somebody should put his soul outside of his body—putting her in a seat low down in the back, between the two rows of passengers; on the travel agent, who wanted three groschen for his trouble and who called her Auntie; on the cow that wandered down the street to the wagon and casually, without any preliminaries, stuck her chin under Malke-Toybe's rear end and pulled out a mouthful of straw—she didn't mean any offense, God forbid, she was just doing what she always did, grabbing a bite off a wagon; and on the young man who bumped into the wagon while twirling his cane and accidentally, unintentionally, without meaning any harm, gave Malke-Toybe such a hit in the face with its knob that he almost knocked her eye out. Anyway, Malke-Toybe was having convulsions, raging indiscriminately at this one, at that one, at everyone in

Glupsk, which, as far as she was concerned, could be swallowed up by the earth, since it was all of their faults that Treyne-Sossel was a vicious bitch, the eleventh of God's ten plagues.

The wagon driver had started to beg his leave of the candidates for the glue factory that the travel agent, the drayman's marriage broker (and like all marriage brokers, a master of exaggeration) had described as lions and eagles; after ten strokes of the whip, these carcasses bestirred themselves, imposed on their old bones to please move from the place where they were, stuck out their tongues and slapped themselves lightly with their thin, patchy tails.

After taking her leave for the tenth time, Malke-Toybe stretched her hands out from the wagon and shouted down the street to her husband: "Leyzer-Yankl, for God's sake don't forget about . . . you-know-what. And bring home a few packs of chicory. Leyzer-Yankl, sweat, for God's sake. Drink a few glasses of dried raspberry. Hershele! Your father's squirrel-hide is tied up with his traveling cap . . . Remember to sweat."

AFTER SEEING his mother off, Hershele returned to his base of operations, the synagogue, where he already felt more or less at home. There were two people who drew him there as if they were magnets, a greybeard called Reb Avrum Mekabel, and Moyshele, a poor boy about the same age as Hershele.

Reb Avrum was one of the high-class *mekablim*—stipendiaries, as we like to call them—whom the Jews group under the heading of clergy and who stand on the second rung, after assistant rabbis. They are usually referred to as *sheyne yidn*, beautiful Jews. Reb Avrum spent the better part of the day bent over a book in the synagogue, but he slept in his own house at night. He was highly respected among the synagogue members, most of whom had first encountered him right after their weddings and were thus quite accustomed to him. It wouldn't be a synagogue without him; there'd be something missing. Reb Avrum had the run of many distinguished houses and he kept company with wealthy people. He sometimes dropped in on them after Shabbes for a chat, a glass of punch, and a good cigar; once in a while, he'd offer to try to arrange a marriage.

The title of "beautiful Jew" fit him perfectly. His capote was always spotless, with nary a rip or tear. He kept a handkerchief in his pocket, never spat, never blew his nose into other people's faces or wiped it on his hem or sleeve the way other people did. His black satin yarmulke was fresh, fine, and all in one piece, not covered with thick flecks of grease or stinking of dried perspiration. His face was spotless, his moderate beard as clean and white as fresh-fallen snow. His thick grey mustache was free of grotesque tobacco stains, and there was always a gentle smile on his lips.

Reb Avrum was always cheerful, his demeanor always happy. The occasional sigh that escaped him had nothing to do with worries or troubles; it was just a plain Jewish sigh, the kind that always goes along with opening a book, making a blessing, taking a glass of wine in your hand, or getting ready to start praying. He liked to talk to people while he sat over his book, listening to whatever news they had to relate and relating something back himself. He used to stroke his forehead when he spoke, raise his yarmulke a little and slowly fan it over his head. Age meant nothing to him—he was happy to talk with everybody and gave everything serious consideration, dismissing nothing on grounds of age: Kids were people too. If he sometimes called a youngster a *shkots*—an active gentile youth, a scampy young fellow—he said it with a smile, as a sign of fondness and deep affection.

Right from day one, Reb Avrum had been observing Hershele's conduct from afar and thinking, "Leyzer-Yankl's son is a good boy, I should get a little closer to him."

One day when Hershele was absorbed in his studies, supporting his head on the lectern with both hands, Reb Avrum stopped beside him, took a look in his *Gemore,* and asked an all-purpose question about what Rashi meant there, what was the Tanna trying to tell us, was the sentence a statement or a question?

Reb Avrum was no big casuist himself, just a simple, lay sort of scholar. Most of his learning consisted of ethical works, *Eyn Yankev* and *Medresh,* books full of wondrous stories and sayings and exempla, of brilliant, beautiful thoughts. He also lapped up the *Zohar* like water, refreshing himself with the words themselves, not pausing to worry about the meaning of the hard ones. From time to time, something would get into him and he'd start to lap up *Zohar* and swallow it thirstily. His eyes flashed, his face was as fiery as if he'd just found love. This tended to happen when he reached those parts where God walks with the righteous in the Garden of Eden, the trees give forth savory scents, sweet smells of spices. Group upon group of angels leaps up to shout "Holy," they praise and extol and adorn His Holy Name in their song. The *shekhine* overflows with ardent, sacred feeling; she groans with longing, moans like a dove for her great love of Israel. Sometimes she laments, weeping for both herself and her beloved nation, which is, alas, so scattered and humiliated in its exile; other times, she comforts her dear beloved, calming it with sweet words and hope for the future: Don't worry—God willing, you'll yet be gathered together and live like no one has ever lived before.

The *Zohar* is a Sinai, a mountain spewing fires of pure, holy love, where heaven betroths itself to earth and seraphs mingle with humans, each kissing feelings of godliness into the other. The *Zohar* is a fiery pillar of love that first appeared to the Jews in the Middle Ages, when they were surrounded by darkness, when hatred, delusion, and savage cruelty imposed horrible sufferings upon them and poisoned their lives; it is the first Jewish romance, the Song of Songs, the Romance of Romances . . .

In his own way, Reb Avrum was—what do you call it?—a poet. He was drawn to the legendary, to the wondrous and beautiful things in the *Zohar*, of which he was, in his way, enamored. The Talmud, by contrast, was a dry thing that nourished the mind without refreshing the heart. Its study was no more than a duty, and he studied no more than he was obliged to. For example, he'd complete a tractate in the nine days before Tishe B'Ov so that people could eat meat, do likewise on the eve of Peysakh so that none of the first-borns he knew would have to fast. He learned a chapter of *Mishne* every day, and said the *Rabbis' Kaddish* for the sake of the souls of the dead whose relatives had hired him to say it. Still, the Talmud was holy to him, and he took great pleasure in others' study of it. Hershele's learning delighted him, and his asking about the Rashi was only a pretext—it was the right thing to say, and he had no intention of engaging Hershele in *pilpul*. It was enough for Hershele to respond, to bob his head and wave his finger. This was the sign of a good boy, a virtuous child, and it brought Reb Avrum to love him.

Moyshele was a swarthy boy, quiet and frail, whose wide, flat face was dotted with pimples. He was the child of poor, honest parents, with whom he had suffered want and deprivation since childhood; he'd never been full in his life. Already as a small child, he'd revealed himself as an intelligent boy with a good head for learning. This was the only comfort in his parents' bitter life. They skimped on the most vital necessities, went without food and drink to pay Moyshele's tuition—as long as he could study, they were full, and very satisfied . . .

Jews—are they human? It's an old question with which the world's been worrying itself forever without coming to any conclusion. But one thing is certain and clear: the Jewish stomach is utterly unlike that of anybody else. Where else is there a stomach that can be filled and satisfied with Torah and learning? What other nation has an expression like "Your Torah is in my guts" in their books? The rest of the world should hear this and consider. Such a divinely powered machine will last forever; no huffing or puffing, no smack with the hand will ever knock it down. A clock that runs on electricity—on the spirit of the *Khumesh*, on God's holy word—is always going to show the right time, and ring out the hours to the world.

Moyshele studied, and his poor, hungry parents were quickened. When he was a little bit older and able to learn a page of Talmud on his own, he left the *kheyder* and went to learn by himself in the synagogue. If he came across a difficulty, he'd ask the adults and they'd help him onto the right track. Shy by nature and with a mild personality—also frail, sickly, and beaten down by want—Moyshele always seemed somewhat distracted. He kept to the sidelines, sat in a corner and studied quietly. He never raised his voice. He was the same way with the boys that he knew, with his friends: he never insulted anybody, never hurt so much as a fly.

Silence had always been his way, but his eyes said what his mouth did not. And God, what eyes he had! A sickly, pale face—and all of a sudden such a pair of eyes! They touched the soul, sometimes tugged at your heart; there was a vast depth behind them, and everything that went on inside him showed up there. Even the biggest troublemaker was helpless when he felt Moyshele's eyes upon him—his heart wouldn't let him lift a finger.

Hershele found fault with Moyshele at first. The way he kept apart in a corner bothered Hershele, who took it to mean that Moyshele was stuck-up. Hershele himself was secretly a little bit vain, and he couldn't stand not to be noticed. He was used to being number one in his *shtetl*, and here was

* Psalm 40:91.

Moyshele, dismissing him out of hand. "No," he thought, "I won't even meet him unless *he* makes the first move."

But after a couple of days without any approach from Moyshele, Hershele couldn't take it anymore. He betook himself to Moyshele in all his glory, intent on teaching him a lesson; he'd challenge him to a duel—Choose your *Gemore*—and they'd see who came out on top. The war between them was begun; each belabored the other with difficult questions. Hershele got worked up, threw himself about, twisting his limbs in every direction. Moyshele, on the other hand, wriggled out of everything, refuted all of Hershele's questions coolly and calmly, and the upshot was: they were friends.

Hershele realized that he'd been all wrong about Moyshele, and he became completely devoted to him. The longer they knew each other, the greater their love, until they finally decided to unite and learn the same tractate. Reb Avrum praised them to their faces for this, smiling and calling each of them *shkots*. A three-way friendship had just been firmed up.

9

LEYZER-YANKL did as his wife had bidden; he drank raspberry tea and sweated before going to bed at night; in the morning he wrapped his neck in the squirrel-hide, which Hershele had indeed found in his travel cap, and sucked down a couple of raw eggs.

None of it helped. He'd apparently caught quite a cold, the second day of Rosh Hashanah. His chest was still congested and whenever he tried his voice, he felt a stitch in his left side.

Nu, a stitch is a stitch, and the stitch on its own wouldn't have worried him too much—a sharp pain is no news to a Jew, he simply ignores it. What worried him, however, was his voice, the sole source of income from which, as it were, he supported his wife and children. Yom Kippur, when his instrument was so necessary, was just around the corner; his voice had so much to do, and here he was, as hoarse as could be. His spirits sank and his anguish was great.

The *shammes'* wife felt his distress and set out to cure him with all the old wives' remedies at her disposal. She gave him a plaster of Spanish fly, made him an ointment to rub under the pit of his stomach. She gave him herbs to drink that she'd got from an old village *goye*, and pickle brine too. She steamed him with feathers, gave him tobacco and burnt coffee grounds to sniff, exorcising an evil eye while she did so, wrapped his neck in one of her thick woolen stockings. Poor Leyzer-Yankl was just like a child: he let her do whatever she wanted, as long as he could get his voice back.

A day passed, two days—and nothing. The morning of the eve of Yom Kippur a sort of voice appeared, but not his real one. In place of his usual instrument, Leyzer-Yankl had a sort of trebly falsetto, somewhat thick in the lower registers, sibilant in the top. He tried it out on the *Yales*. The *shammes'* wife heard him and, shaking her head, with tears in her eyes, exclaimed, "Praised be the blessed-be-He and blessed-be-His-Name! It's delightful; upon my word, even better than before."

That Yom Kippur Leyzer-Yankl performed, so to speak, on his new instrument, using only the thinnest string, in defiance of the well-known proverb "If you can't go over, you've got to go under." With God's help, he got through Yom Kippur safe and sound; he could do without his voice until next year's High Holidays, God willing. It didn't matter so much that he was hoarse now; God would look after him until this time next year.

But as soon as he was able to stop thinking about his voice, the stitch in his side started acting up in a way that he couldn't ignore and which forced him to pay attention. Previously, he'd comforted himself with the hope that "It's all right. It'll go away." He just needed to spend a couple of days in bed. "It's nothing," the *shammes'* wife told him. "It's going around these days."

Only when he could no longer catch his breath and already had one foot in the grave was there any hue and cry. They brought in the healer with all his tools: he cupped, tapped veins, drew plenty of blood, but none of it helped, and Leyzer-Yankl, nearly dead, was wheeled to the infirmary in a cart. He lay critically ill for a number of weeks.

Meanwhile, Sukkes had passed. Hershele's *yontef* had been ruined. His father had taken such a turn for the worse on Simkhes Toyre that it looked as though he were going to die. And so the best and merriest day of the year was a Tishe B'Ov for Hershele. He'd been too upset to eat anything more than the piece of honey cake he got for being called up to the Torah with all the other boys. And was it the same honey cake he'd come to expect? Once upon a time that piece of honey cake would have glowed with the radiance of *yontef* and had a supernal grace, a special taste all its own, with the words *"Simkhes Toyre"* practically inscribed upon it. It virtually called out to you—in words, yet; it had a wonderful aroma, it caused your heart to rejoice, fed and restored your soul—and now it was just a thing, a species of baked goods, cornmeal with honey, which could be purchased in the market for a groschen and to which the blessing of *mezoynes* applied.

Generally speaking, Jews' food on Shabbes and *yontef* has a taste of its own; according to our holy sages of yore, there's a spice in it called *"Shabbes."* This spice, which grows nowhere in this world, which can't be bought for the finest gold and is unknown to all other peoples—every Friday holy angels bring this spice direct from the Garden of Eden to the house of every Jew, where they also, as we say, help cook the *tsholnt*. Others might laugh, but it can be said with certainty that whosoever has never tasted real Jewish *tsholnt* has never really eaten in his life; he has no idea what cooking really means.

Hershele's spirits revived when things started to go a little better with his father. At first, he was so full of joy that he could think of nothing else, and even forgot about himself. But after a bit, his thoughts suddenly began to weigh on him. A deep melancholy came over him, and all he could think of was: Soon he'd be going home—but how could he leave Moyshele and Reb Avrum behind? He'd grown so accustomed to them, his heart drew him to them. Although going home was good—he'd see his mother, his brothers and sisters, everybody else he knew—there was, on the other hand, the question of what point there was to being there. He could picture the misery, the whole family suffering hunger and cold, how he himself used to die many times a day for a piece of bread. A shudder passed through him just thinking about it. But staying in Glupsk never even entered his mind. What stay? Where stay? And how comes it that a boy ups and stays by himself, without his parents? And even if he could, well, uh . . .

These thoughts were flying around in Hershele's head, tearing him apart and making him very gloomy. Reb Avrum noticed that Hershele was looking haggard and proceeded to inquire as to what was wrong. Hershele burst into tears and spilled his whole bitter heart. Reb Avrum patted him on the head and said, "Nu, it's OK. I'll think it over. There's still time. In the meantime, stop your crying and don't be stupid, *shkots.*"

10

HIS FATHER LEFT the infirmary a few days later, so deathly pale that your heart would have broken just looking at him. He'd been through a dangerous illness and had lost so much weight that he was scarcely to be recognized—nothing but skin and bones.

Hershele had never loved his father as much as he did then; never had his father looked on him so lovingly, spoken to him so sweetly and quietly. But his voice was soft and frail. He'd become something of a child himself; his look, his voice, tore at your heart. Behind them lay a sort of quiet, wordless lament for his pain and his miserable life, as well as a plea: "Enough! I've got no more strength to bear it!"

It was plain that Hershele would have covered his father with kisses, if he hadn't been ashamed to do so. But he was ashamed—kissing has no currency among Jews. Where do you get off with this kissing? Out of the blue, you kiss? Especially a child a father?

Reb Avrum took Hershele's father into a corner, and they conferred for quite a while. Then they called Hershele over; his father turned to him and said, "I'm talking to Reb Avrum about your being able to stay here if you want to."

Hershele burst into tears and looked lovingly at his father, too touched to be able to speak. When his father pressed him for an honest answer, all he said was, "No, I can't be without you."

"Ach, Hershele," his father sighed from the depths of his heart. "You're a fool. A child can't stay with his father forever. What can we do? I can feel my strength ebbing away. I've suffered enough in my life. Don't cry, Hershele. What can you do? Sooner or later, we all have to part."

"Daddy, Daddy," wept Hershele imploringly. "Home, Daddy, home."

"Home! A real bowl of cherries at home," sighed his father, turning to Reb Avrum and shaking his head. "You tell him."

"Don't be stubborn, *feh!*" Reb Avrum began mildly. "There's plenty at home without you. Can't you see that your father has no more strength to work? There's hardly anything left of the little bit of money he earned here—it costs to be sick. It's going to be a long winter, a leap year, have mercy on the rest of the kids. You yourself will starve and you'll be taking the last morsel from the mouths of the others."

Reb Avrum's words brought the blood to Hershele's heart, the tears to his eyes. "Thank Reb Avrum," said his father, "Thank him for his kindness in caring for you and looking after you here. Keep to the right path, my son, and obey Reb Avrum as if he were your father. He has only your best interests at heart, may God prolong his years, you hear?"

"Nu, *shkots*," said Reb Avrum with a sweet little smile, clapping Hershele on the shoulder. "Dry your eyes and go over to your friend, the *shkots*, there."

◆   ◆   ◆

Winter came early that year. All of a sudden, before anybody knew it, a cold wind came blowing from the south, a dark, angry cloud loomed up— winter's vanguard of Cossacks, racing ahead with tempestuous huffs: "Tremble, living creatures. Here comes Old Man Winter to rub your noses red." The fields are already buried under a white robe of snow. The trees stand with their heads bowed, stripped of their leaves, their branches fettered in sparkly chains, in bars of ice. No sign of birds or forest animals; it's as if they had all died off. Some are hiding deep in their lairs, others escaped in time and went wherever they wished to go. Everything is deathly quiet, except for the crows circling here and there, busy with their corvine business: weddings, community meetings—the devil only knows what they're cawing and groaning and ripping out their throats about.

Winter has conquered the world on every side; Glupsk alone, the Jewish city, refuses to give in to it. Winter wages bitter war on her, sends cold and frosts, but the puddles in her streets escape unscathed and remain their fluid old selves. Winter rains pellets of snow, but in vain—the mud remains. Glupsker Jews swarm out like ants, trampling it with their feet and making it into soup, a thin, grey-black mire. Winter hoists his white snow banner on the roofs, to show them who's on top; hungry cows, hosts of goats come and pitch it down while they drag off piles of straw to eat. Or else men and women, Jews, come with pots and tubs to fill with snow that they melt for cooking water. There's one other weapon against Winter— fires. The Jewish chimneys get going as soon as he appears, and Glupsk burns. Glupsk sticks a fiery tongue out at Winter. Winter bangs and blows and blusters, and the Jews just blow him off. They go around half-dressed, barefoot, as if the weather's got nothing to do with them or they're doing it just to spite him.

And while Glupsk was waging war with Winter, a wagon was standing near the Kaptsansker hostel, with three skinny, hemorrhoidal, swaybacked, tangle-haired, long-necked, short-tailed horses—you'll pardon the expression—who had to pay for their sins by shlepping a couple of *minyonim* of Jews to Kaptsansk, Leyzer-Yankl among them. The travel agent was rummaging around in the wagon, raking the leftovers—a few stalks of hay—with his whip and bending an eye on one of the horses. He gave it a crack in the chin, just like that, cursing as he did so. "Drop dead, you stinking carcass. He can hardly stand on his feet, but he wants to fly, the beautiful eagle. Ah, you should go flying straight to Hell."

Leyzer-Yankl was rushing up to the wagon, clad in his traveling clothes and with his cap pulled down on his head. Hershele followed with a package which he turned over to the agent, requesting him to make his father a good seat. Then the two of them went into the inn.

Her apron tucked up and a ladle in her hand as always, Reyze was busy settling her accounts with the wagon driver and passengers, thundering her usual reproaches. "Didja ever hear such a thing? Whattaya got to say for yourself?" As soon as she'd done with them and noticed our heroes on the sidelines, she unleashed her tongue on *them*, running her nose the whole length of her sleeve.

"Here he is again, the fine young man. What, you're leaving? Half-dressed and barefoot—didja ever see the like of it, traveling like that in this kind of cold? And what can you say to that over there? A fine father, on my word. He—didja ever see the like of it?—he's in a cap, nicely bundled up, and the kid goes around like it's summer. Whattaya got to say for yourself, I ask you?"

"My son isn't going," said his father.

"Now there's a piece of news! You go and leave your son here, naked, his chest exposed to the weather? Didja ever hear such a thing? Whattaya got to say for yourself? You must have the heart of a Tatar." Looking Hershele up and down, Reyze brought the conversation to an end and went on her way.

The wagon driver was warming up the horses—"Giddyup, go." The passengers standing in the street were pushing to get places in the wagon, throwing their arms and legs here and there, taking their lives in their hands, pushing, squeezing, crowding, crashing.

Poor Leyzer-Yankl was sitting, sort of, in considerable discomfort on top of a bundle, resigned to every shove to his sides. He bade Hershele a sad farewell in a teary, shaking voice.

Hershele took a last look at his father's pale face and melted into hot tears. He was in no shape to utter a word or to watch the wagon depart.

"What's there to cry about?" said Reyze, running up to Hershele after the wagon had left. "Your father's gone away—nu, so what? God forbid, he didn't die. Here," she said, shoving an old jacket into his hand, "Wear it in good health. Don't cry. You want something to eat?"

"No," said Hershele, a little comforted by Reyze's words.

"No, he says," said Reyze. "Didja ever hear such a thing, he says no? Since when is eating a no? Nu, go in good health if it's no. But if you should want, remember, you should come."

11

IT'S WRITTEN in our holy books that in time to come, well on in the future, God willing, after the resurrection of the dead and the final judgment, all humanity will be lined up in a great square and divided into two sections: the righteous on one side, the wicked on the other, and between them, in the middle, the Evil Inclination. To the evil it will appear as thin as a hair, to the righteous, as big as a mountain. Looking at it, all the people on both sides will weep terribly. The evil will lament and scream: "*Gevalt!* So thin a hair on the straight path was too hard for us to get over, and now we've crept along crooked paths all the way to perdition." The righteous will lament and spill tears: "Master of the Universe, we do not understand where we got the iron strength to get over so frightfully high a mountain, to endure so much pain and suffering in our lives."

This wonderfully delineated scene can serve as a fitting introduction to the story of the many sorrows and pains that Hershele has endured in his life. Now, in better times, when Hershele recalls how many mountains of troubles he had to get over until he found his way in life, how many sufferings and afflictions, his heart weeps within him and he marvels that such a

shrimp, a worm, a nothing, was able to bear so much without being trampled. He weeps for himself, and for the many like him among us who are
destined from childhood on to struggle with all sorts of afflictions, to fall
into every pit, to climb the walls and feel the bitter taste of death, just to
reach whatever exalted status hovers before their eyes from afar.

Unhappy Children of Israel! Unhappy even in happiness, so to speak.
Take, for instance, those Jews who have got their status and acquired a certain distinction. Are they up there for good, with both feet firmly planted,
so that the lightest breeze couldn't blow them back down? Does the non-
Jewish world look on them as equals? As human? Is their life really as
happy as it should be? Is this halfway sort of happiness worth so much un-
happiness? A life that you'd wish on your enemies—is it worth this living
death, worth dying of hunger ten times a day?

Yeah, there's still a lot lacking from this resurrection scenario. The
wicked are really here, as is the mountain of sufferings. But the return to
life is all screwed up—there's plenty of people still lying dead, six feet under
the ground. God and His judgment still haven't turned up.

Reb Avrum kept Hershele on his mind, and did whatever he could for
him. He arranged Shabbes meals with one of the householders with whom
he was friendly, and during the week one or another of the *daveners* from
the synagogue would take Hershele home for lunch or supper at Reb
Avrum's request. Half-eating, half-fasting, moving his lips like a hungry
child—that's how Hershele passed his days. He came to understand perfectly why the Hebrew word *vayoykhlu*, so apparently simple and well-
known a word as *vayoykhlu*, which everywhere else means "they ate," is
translated among us Jews as "they acted as if they had eaten."

Yes, many poor people among us come to understand this interpretation. When your heart is faint and you're already wishing that you'd live
just long enough to get something into your mouth—that's when the litany
tends to kick in: Get washed . . . Wait, wait, you've got the wrong dipper
. . . Pass it on to somebody else . . . Nu, excuse me—the towel's over there.
Say the blessing for washing your hands. Make *hamoytse*—don't eat it yet,
we'll get the salt. Stick your spoon in, get a piece of meat. Rinse your hands
before the post-meal blessing. You're given the honor of leading it. Bless
already. "*Raboysay*, Ladies and gentlemen, we're going to make the blessing," which, translated into Stomach, means "Ladies and gentlemen, we
want to eat."

And this was already the high life. More often, *vayoykhlu* had no meaning for Hershele whatsoever, absolutely none, and more than once he dreamt of beggars when he lay himself down at night.

As if it weren't enough that he was wasting away from his eating disorder, his soul had to go ache too—he was terribly homesick at the start. Life at home hadn't been a bowl of cherries, either, but there was still a big difference. It was warmer back there, more satisfying to his soul, like a nest where a baby bird can shelter under the wings of its mother. Back there, he was one of them, everything in his house, in the town, had some connection with him and understood him. Even the animals there, the houses, the air that he breathed, the places where he went walking and played with his friends, all of it somehow spoke to his heart and heard what was in it. Here, though, he was a stranger, alone and out of place; nothing was the way it was supposed to be, everything was different. The sun, the moon, and the stars didn't look as good and friendly as they had in his *shtetl*, and Hershele gazed on them like a divorcé who happens to bump into his ex-wife's relations—they aren't his family anymore, just old acquaintances and sometime kin. Such feelings of longing, which tug and gnaw deep in the heart, and cannot be smoothed over with words—feelings like this cannot be understood by anybody who has not tasted loneliness at least once in his life, a sudden uprooting from his nearest and dearest . . .

Big deal—one little spot, a crumb, in such a great big world. God's great universe stretches itself lengthwise and breadthwise, forever. In the middle of the universe, on the globe of the earth, is a spot as small as a flyspeck: Glupsk. Inside this flyspeck is a dot—a synagogue—and in the dot, a pint-sized point—a bench. And on the pint-sized point is an even tinier point: a species of creature called Hershele. This teeny-tiny creature is like a spider in the middle of its web; long, thin threads extend out of him in every direction, composed of tiny, ethereal points that the eye cannot see—atoms, the philosophers call them. The threads reach beyond the edge of the world to the stars in the sky, to everything in the world around them, and, of course, to Kaptsansk as well. Hershele's soul clambers along these airy threads, drawing all his thoughts homeward. His soul shoots along them like the electricity in a telegraph wire, infecting a tiny part of the long, airy thread with its burning emotions. This part transfers the ardor to the next part, and so on and so forth, until his feelings strike his parents' hearts like lightning; his parents feel Hershele's pain and they hic out a sob.

"Hershele," they say, "is thinking of us." They can picture his situation—alone, away from home—and they melt with pity. But what can such lowly creatures do, when they are in a bad situation themselves, when they are suffering terribly too? His mother toils, ruining her eyesight plucking feathers until late at night, and doesn't earn enough to fill a pot with water. His father hadn't stopped being sick since he came home. He was flickering, guttering out like a candle; he couldn't bear to look on the misery in his house, the sufferings of his hungry, dispirited children. The bitter poverty had become hard for him to bear. He'd suffered enough, he had no more strength. The last drop of sap in his wretched, broken life was hardening. His parents were sighing, moaning and groaning, as they imagined the wretched, uprooted child for whom they longed so, and their bitter feelings were telegraphed through the same airy threads straight back to Hershele's heart. Heart confides in heart, soul whispers to soul, each pours itself out to the other, speaking in wordless quiet.

It seemed to Hershele that his father lay ill, languishing, his eyes as imploring as when they had parted. His father's pale face, the sweet demeanor he'd had at their parting, floated before Hershele's eyes; it upset him, he cried quietly on his hard bed at night, imagining horrible things. This is what the world calls "the speaking heart."

Yes, Hershele's heart spoke, and didn't stop speaking for a good long while, until he got the news from home: "Say *Kaddish* for your father, Hershele. You're an orphan."

Book Three

1

HOMESICKNESS AND HEARTBREAK, his father's death and the suffering it caused his already impoverished mother and family at home; his own particular troubles too—homelessness, loneliness, want—caused Hershele to withdraw into himself like a turtle and lose himself in his thoughts. Thinking became his life. Deep within him was a world in which his soul could spread its wings and fly freely off to the horizon. The practical, workaday world was a cage where want held him captive, pressing his head down, pointing out his weakness and insignificance at every step; a cage that promised him nothing but troubles on top of troubles on top of troubles. So he started to build a wonderful world inside himself, a paradise of flowers and sweet scents, flowing with milk and honey, where the sky was open to heaven and angels peeked their heads out, beckoned with their good, friendly faces while singing sweet songs of hope, comfort, pity, and love. His heart was eased—this life was so good, so pleasant, such a delight.

The raw materials for this world of wonders were the old stories he'd heard once upon a time in Kaptsansk, together with some new ones from Glupsk. The *Gemore* and its dry, serious issues were no longer enough for Hershele; indeed, it was starting to depress him. He learned it only for the sake of form, because he *had* to learn it—if not, he'd lose face with the synagogue's members, along with the meals they gave him. His friend and study partner, Moyshele, kept goading him on—"Learn, learn!"—but opening a *Gemore* made him feel queasy and sick. He had to force himself, sway and rock back and forth, just to gain the needed momentum; it was like getting ready to jump into a cold shower. But artificial momentum is like fireworks—it spends its flame in a few brief seconds.

After a few dips into the "sea of the Talmud," Hershele was feeling chilly, so he hurried out to warm his soul with the legends, stories, and holy books of ethics that he used to perk himself up. He put Reuben's ox and Simeon's cow aside for a time, certain that "It's all right, they're not going anywhere."

Hershele read beautiful stories: about Rabbi Meyer the Miracle Worker; about how the prophet Elijah once took Rabbi Yehoshua ben Levi with him in his wanderings about the world, on condition that Rabbi Yehoshua should look and listen and never utter a word; about the bitterly poor Rabbi Khanina ben Dosa, to whom a heavenly hand gave the golden leg of a golden table. He also read of how once, when Rav Shimen ben Khalafta had no money to make Shabbes, he received a precious gem from out of the sky; how Rabbi Shimen ben Yokhai once took his students into a big valley, said, "Valley, valley! Fill with gold!" and how the valley did so immediately; how Rabbi Yishmoel ben Elisha brought the angel Yufiel, the Guardian of the Torah, all fire and flame, with a face that shone as lightning, down from heaven; and how Elijah the prophet gave fragrant leaves from the Garden of Eden to Rabba bar Rav Khanina, an absolute pauper, who sold them for twelve thousand pieces of gold.

Moyshele was quite dismayed with Hershele's absorption in things of this type, and the two friends often had words about it while sitting in the synagogue with their books lying open before them.

"*Gevalt*, Hershele! Haven't you spent enough time on this stuff already?"

"Huh, what?"

"What about learning, Hershele?"

"But I'm reading a book, Moyshele."

"What good's a book? Look into a *Gemore* instead. Come on, Hershele, start: *Tannu rabonon*, the rabbis taught . . ."

"Ay-ay, it's fantastic! Totally fantastic!"

"What do you mean?" Moyshele was staring at him in amazement. "Nu, come on already. What do you do with the *Toysfes* here? It isn't easy."

"Ah, good. Really good."

"Tell me already what's so good." Moyshele was convinced that Hershele had figured out the *Toysfes*.

"Moyshele, you've got to understand how great Rav Yoysef must have felt when he cut into the fish on Friday night and found a diamond that God had sent him in its belly."

"Eh!" Moyshele shrugged his shoulders and scratched himself in annoyance. "But the *Toysfes*. What problem do they have with Rashi here?"

This was the usual course of their weekday conversations. Moyshele, scratching, urged Hershele on, and Hershele kept finding excuses. But Saturday night, the end of the Sabbath, brought Hershele some relief; he could immerse himself in wonders to his heart's content. Moyshele tended not to study then and didn't pester Hershele about the *Gemore*. And besides, Saturday night somehow lends itself to reflection, to mental journeys to heaven. There's something about it that stirs a Jew up, imbues him with a sadly-sweet melancholy and spins his soul around within him. He becomes pensive, restless, disturbed. "If you want to understand the departure of the Sabbath, take a peek in a Jewish home."

2

SO LET'S LOOK at Moyshele's father's house. Moyshele's father, Shmulik, is an old-clothes man. From morning to night he runs around with his bundles, buying and selling from door to door. He is bowed and bent, pale and wrinkled, aged by trouble and worry. Tired and broken from chasing around like a dog, he comes home to his wretched house—a dog house— with a few groschen sometimes, empty pockets at others, grabs a bite that serves as both lunch and supper, and throws himself down to sleep. He lies there like he's been murdered, without a single sound part to his body. But the dead man is resurrected quite early next morning, to go run and ramble some more. This is the dog's life he leads all week.

Friday night, though, the dog house assumes a different aspect entirely—whitewashed, every corner spic and span. Three scoured brass candlesticks stand on the white tablecloth, along with two fine *khales*, smeared with egg yoke and shining eye-catchingly even from a distance. There's a sweet air of repose, the place is redolent with the aroma of the stewed food warming under a pillow on the oven. Shmulik's wife, smudged and sorrowful all the week long, is aglow in her Shabbes turban; the divine presence shines out from her face. The shoeless little girls, their hair washed and combed, stand together in a corner, with glad expectation all over their faces. Sha . . . footsteps, somebody's coming . . . The door opens. *"Gut Shabbes,"* says Shmulik, home from *shul*. His face shines benevolently as he looks at his wife and children. *"Gut Shabbes,"* says Moyshele loudly, running in as quickly as if he were bearing good news. And, walking about the house, father and son start to sing *Shalom Aleykhem*, the hymn of welcome to the angels sent by God, the King of Kings, the Holy One blessed be He, to escort them home from the synagogue.

Instead of a dog, the old-clothes man is now a prince; it's as if he'd been given a new soul, and a new body to go with it. He makes *kiddesh*, washes, sits down at the table with the princess, his wife, and the children around him. A thrust with fork, with spoon; a piece of fish, a noodle, a bone, a bit of *tsimmes*—food like they haven't laid eyes on all week. Careful not to drop a single crumb, the children eat with a serious demeanor that awakens feelings of pity. They're like squirrels in a tree, cracking their nuts so cutely and seriously.

Shmulik lifts up his voice in *zmires*, in Sabbath song, and gives a rousing rendition of *Mah Yedidus*:

> How delightful your repose,
> Beautiful Princess Shabbes.
> We all run to greet you,
> Saying, "Come, O bride, in your diadem.
> All crafts have been put aside,
> All labor laid to rest.
> We delight ourselves with eating
> Chickens, *khale*, meat and fish."

"Sambatyon, the river of fire, which flows all the week, stands stock still on Shabbes. The cries and screams of those in Gehenna cease when a Jew gives voice to his *zmires*. The terrible river does not get in the way of his songs, the raging waves fall silent. The noise departs and all is quiet . . ."

For twenty-four hours a Jew's heart is merry. "A joy, a celebration, for all the Jews; they are free from care and quite content."

The next day at evening, after the Third Meal, Shmulik sits in the synagogue, dejected. It's dark. There is a hum of people moaning "Blessed are those whose way is blameless," the Hundred and Nineteenth Psalm, which refers to the imminent departure of the Shabbes princess. There's gloom in the air, the scent of pickle brine. The sun has already set, fiery red clouds blaze on the horizon, and the fires of Gehenna loom up before the Jews. The awful decree resounds in their ears: "Let the wicked return to Hell"; those who were allowed to rest on Shabbes and roll on mountains of cooling snow are driven back to their chambers—"Go fry in Hell!" Every Jew sees Angels of Destruction; every Jew sees Hell before him.

Shmulik's wife is at home, sitting on the dairy bench with her arms folded and her legs spread out. It's dark. A ribbon of moonlight shines in through a window, reflecting against the walls and ceiling. Eerie-looking shadows hop and dance, scaring all the children, who crowd together like a herd of frightened sheep, their heads hung down to stop themselves speaking. The house is silent, save for a couple of crickets chirping to each other through the cracks in a corner. Mrs. Shmulik sits pensively, shakes her head, and, yawning, begins to sing morosely: "God of Abraham, now, as the beloved Sabbath departs . . ."

That's it. It's over. She scrapes a match—once, twice, three times. With a stink of sulphury smoke, it bursts angrily into a reddish-blue flame that she has trouble trying to transfer to a cheap tallow candle. Everybody says "A good week" and feels his heart break within him.

"A good week." Shmulik enters the house like a kitten and speaks in a choked voice. He walks around dispiritedly, his eyes darting hither and yon, his face pale and drawn—the transformation is beginning, the metamorphosis from prince back to dog. Shmulik can see the dog's life of the coming week in his mind's eye—the running around, the worries, the shame and indignities of his search for a meager crust of bread—and he is seized with anxiety. But the prince struggles. He won't give up so easily. He's not about to let himself be turned into a dog and dragged off to Hell. He squirms, looks for something to grab onto: There could still be something to hope for, God could still have mercy.

This hope appears in the burning *havdole* candle. Piously, with his eyes a-roll in his head, Shmulik starts to make *havdole*: "*Hiney eyl yeshuosi*, Behold the God of my salvation, *Evtakh ve-loy efkhod*, I shall trust and have no fear." He sniffs the spices to revive himself, drinks from the wineglass, and sprinkles drops from it onto his pockets to assure himself a good and lucky week.

Hope likewise appears to him in the Saturday evening *zmires*. Starting with a soft, sweetly-sad *Hamavdil*, He Who Separates, hope increases in the song *Ish Khosid Hayo*, There Was Once a Pious Man, and flares up in Shmulik's eyes. His face reddens slightly, he looks on his wife and children and, with full faith in God, confidently murmurs the fabulous story of the poverty-stricken believer. "Ach, Gotenyu!" Shmulik finishes *Ish Khosid* with eyes staring upward and starts to cough, quietly humming a high-pitched, sadly Jewish melody. "Ach, make a miracle and help us, Gotenyu, help, help, *vey iz mir.*"

Moyshele comes in and says, "A good week." Hershele has generally come along with him, not to escort Moyshele, but the Sabbath Bride. They both sing *zmires*: *Va-yiten Lekho*, May He Give You, in which everyone is promised the best of everything: herds of cows and sheep; bumper crops of grain; a blessing in their kneading trough, their pantry, and their business; riches, honor, and plenty of more good fortune. They sing until they've finished the song about Elijah the prophet.

A fire burns in the stove. Mrs. Shmulik is busying herself by the oven, the family is at a nearby table, each with a particular task in hand, and one of the two friends, sometimes Moyshele, sometimes Hershele, reads them the story from *Seyfer Ha-Yoshar* about how Joseph was sold by his brothers, or else something equally nice from another holy book.

Meanwhile, a conversation unfolds, everyone has his say. They're off in the stars, no longer in this world—until the borscht with which the Sabbath Queen is led out is ready. The house is a mirror of their moods: half-Shabbes, half ordinary; half sweet, half sour, like the last meal before a welcome guest is seen off. You sip and console yourself: you'll soon see each other again.

All those marvelous stories of miracles befalling ordinary people, of Elijah the prophet sometimes bringing happiness and prosperity to the poor and needy, comforted Hershele and sweetened his bitter life. The old story about Reb Shmelke of Kaptsansk came back to him now. Hershele believed in it religiously and thought that if Elijah had once helped Reb Shmelke, there was a strong possibility that he might help Hershele too: Why not? Just don't ever give up hope; beseech the Lord, *daven* with complete devotion.

Hershele was just entering that stage of life which might be called the springtime of faith, when hope blossoms, the leaves of belief sprout, and a spring of loving feeling starts to flow. The imagination soars up to heaven, nothing is too hard for it, nothing impossible. It hopes and believes, pours prayers out to God from the depths of the heart, and sometimes at night there's a quiet weeping, a sweet, sweet weeping in bed . . .

Of course, this springtime isn't the same for everyone. For some people it's cold and windy, and leaves no mark on their lives. People like Hershele are one-tenth of one percent—spiritual people, God's elect elite.

Hershele started to *daven* with ardor and joy. He *davened* three times a day in the synagogue, like everyone else, and *davened* quietly by himself, whenever the urge came over him. Time was passing, meanwhile. Day, as it does, turned to night, and day also turned to night in Hershele's soul. Feelings of hope and despair alternated regularly within him.

3

THE BLESSING of the new moon, the *Borkhu* prayer and *Kedushe*—the *Sanctus*—exert a magnetic pull on the Jews, drawing them in from afar and bringing them to a halt, no matter how pressed they are for time or how much of a hurry they're in. Say, for instance, you're walking down the street one night in Glupsk, absorbed in thoughts of business. Out of nowhere a *Sholem aleykhem* strikes your ear, and you find yourself in the middle of a circle of Jews, answering each of them with an *Aleykhem sholem*. You give yourself a shake and jump at the moon with them . . . Or you're rushing, running past a synagogue when you hear fingers drumming on the window—"Hurry up, Mister, get in here"—and before you know it you're inside, bowing down for *Borkhu* or jumping up for *Kedushe* with the rest of the Jews in the place.

At such times you no longer belong to yourself, you have no control over your body, just as if you'd been hypnotized. The same thing can happen when you're standing in *shul* in the morning; your stomach is rumbling and there's something you'd like to get done, when suddenly a Jew sidles up, fresh from the toilet, on little cat's feet, and does you the honor of standing beside you. He stoops, rubs his hands, and with a pious expression on his face makes a sweetly enthusiastic start on the morning blessings: "Blessed art Thou . . . who hast given the rooster the understanding to tell the difference between night and day." And you—you have no choice. You respond "Blessed Be His Name" and "Amen," scrunching a serious, sour expression onto your face. He's doing you a favor, drawing out one blessing after the other, and you're standing there and answering like you're chained to the spot, unable to leave, as if you were being milked. And no sooner have you finished with your *Sholem aleykhem*-ing, your *Borkhu*-ing, your *Kedushe*-ing, no sooner paid out all your Amens, than you shrug your shoulders, give a scratch and a good spit, and go back on your way to wherever.

Reb Avrum's finger-drumming on the window at *minkhe*-time got a few passing Jews to drop everything and run into the *shul*. They prayed quickly, in one breath, as it were, jumped breathlessly during the *Kedushe*, and ran right out. Only one stayed behind. He wandered about for a while, looking around; it was clear that he was a stranger. The shine on his long nose was a sign that that nose arrived yesterday or today, fresh from the road, where the wind had tormented it terribly, nipping it and flaying its skin. His grey cat's eyes were moving in opposite directions, as if they were mad at each other—one looked south, while the other looked north.

Beckoning with his hand, Reb Avrum called the man over, motioning him to a place at his side. He swayed nicely during the *davening*, in the real Jewish way, a sign that he was a person of some stature, not a common nobody.

"So you're a stranger here, huh?" Reb Avrum turned to him after the *davening*, looking him over with a friendly expression.

"What else?" As usual, the man answered with a question, delivered in a sort of groaning-hasidic wheeze, while he gave his runny nose a resounding blow.

"If that's the case, then *Sholem aleykhem*, welcome," said Reb Avrum, offering his hand. "Where are you from?"

"Achoo." The man's nose answered in his stead.

"From Yehupetz, maybe? You look like it to me." Reb Avrum reached his conclusion while the nose was still doing its business, and he offered it a sniff of tobacco.

"When do you *daven* in the morning?" asked the man, once he'd finished tending to his nose.

"When? The same time as always. How come?"

"I've got *yortsayt*. The sixth of Tammuz I've got *yortsayt* after my father," he said with a little sigh.

"*Yortsayt?*" asked Reb Avrum, stroking his beard. "You're very welcome here, upon my word. Please be so good as to come here tomorrow at the regular time."

The man sat talking with Reb Avrum a little longer, his eyes leaping in every direction. As he rose from the bench, he scratched the side of his head and made a bit of a face, as if it were difficult for him to leave a house of prayer.

"Looks like quite a Jew to me," Reb Avrum said to himself, as he rose from his own place after the guest had departed. Then turning to Moyshele, who was talking in a corner with Hershele, he said loudly, "Go home, *shkots*. Come on, it's time to rest and get some sleep. And you, *shkots*," he said to Hershele, "Lay down here and sleep. You aren't hungry, are you?"

"No." Hershele answered with his mouth, while his heart was saying, "Oy, food. Oy, would I like something to eat."

But Reb Avrum himself stayed rooted to the spot. He accused himself of being so preoccupied with the stranger that it completely slipped his mind to ask one of the *daveners* to take Hershele home for supper. He knew that Hershele's "no" was no more than courtesy. From one meal a day—if dry bread with garlic can be called a meal—no one gets full, especially not a growing boy with a healthy appetite. Reb Avrum stood there in a quandary, neither here nor there, and, looking confusedly at Moyshele, he asked him, "Nu, how long you gonna stay here? Enough talking already."

"Reb Avrum," said Moyshele, "He's got no supper, Hershele, I mean. I asked him to come home and eat with me. He said it was OK, he doesn't want."

"What? What?" Reb Avrum was so upset that he could hardly speak.

"I asked him: Nu, I'll go home and bring you something back here—he doesn't want that either. Fool," Moyshele turned to Hershele with a plea, "What are you afraid of? There'll still be plenty left for me, no?"

Hershele shook his head and kept silent. His heart was seething like a kettle and the blood was up in his face.

Meanwhile, Reb Avrum hunted around in his pocket and found a three-groschen piece, which he shoved into Hershele's hand, begging him

with all his heart. "Take it, it's all right. You can buy yourself something."
Hershele took the coin and dissolved into tears.

NEXT MORNING, the stranger came to *daven* at precisely "the regular time" and again he sat beside Reb Avrum. His nose was still gleaming, but he wasn't sneezing quite so angrily as the evening before. It was a Thursday, and he was called up to the Torah: "Let Reb Shneur-Zev-Wolf ben Reb Shraga-Faybish come up."

After the *davening*, Reb Avrum learned a chapter of *Mishne* and let Reb Shneur, who had *yortsayt*, have the honor of saying the *Rabbis' Kaddish* afterward. He recited it elegantly, twirling a sidelock as he did so, with his eyes closed and his head shaking in a very respectable manner. Those Jews who usually stick around for leftovers after the *davening*—additional supplications, a look into the anthology *Khoyk Le-Yisroel*—answered his Kaddish with full-throated Amens, the idea here being: a *yortsayt* drink. The idea was manifest on their lips and in their throats; they licked the first, swallowed the saliva with the second. Not because they were so eager for a shot of whiskey—don't get me wrong. To them drunkenness was the worst of sins. But there's something about a *yortsayt* drink that no one can resist; it's got a flavor all its own. So forget about champagne, about the finest wines of the gentiles. The *shammes* brought a quart of strong brandy with cookies and egg bagels, and they all started to make their *lekhayims*.

"*Lekhayim*, Reb Shneur-Wolf," one of them jabbered. "May the blessed Lord grant prosperity to His Jews, simple and easy prosperity."

"*Lekhayim*, Reb . . . Reb . . . what? Shneur! OK, Reb Shneur." Another one forced himself to speak, after he'd sipped a bit from his glass and licked his lips. "Prosperity, sure. But how? That's why God's the Master of the Universe. It'll come one way or the other—do I know?—just so long as He helps you. Are you a businessman of some sort? What kind?" he concluded craftily, just to set things in motion.

"Eh," said Shneur, without adding any real words.

"Get over here, *shkots!*" Reb Avrum called to Hershele, who was sitting in a corner with Moyshele over a *Gemore*. "Here—an egg bagel and a shot for you, and one of each for your friend there."

Reb Shneur's eyes were fixed at one and the same time on Hershele over here and Moyshele over there. Once the crowd had dispersed, Reb Shneur fell into conversation with Reb Avrum about the lot of the Jews. Groaning, he confessed his great envy of those who could sit in the *besmedresh* all day, learning and praying. He tried to get the lay of the land almost in passing, or so it seemed. "Who are those two boys sitting over the *Gemore* there . . . They're fine children."

"As I live and breathe, an expert!" Reb Avrum was smiling proudly, like a father whose children are being praised. "One of them's from here and the other, the one I called over before, comes from a village. He's an orphan who's living here now, a living doll."

"It's written all over his face," said Reb Shneur, looking in Hershele's direction. "Too bad that he has to suffer so much."

"That's for sure," sighed Reb Avrum. "A poor kid, a lonely orphan."

"You know what?" Reb Shneur said after a little thought. His grey eyes were blazing. "You know what just occurred to me?"

"How should I know?" said Reb Avrum with a friendly smile, fanning his head with his yarmulke. "A marriage, maybe?"

"Just as good." Reb Shneur's expression was serious. "Later, in time, he could, God willing, get married out of the deal too. There's a girl involved, if you get my drift. It's like this—just listen."

"Speak, please. I'm all ears."

"To make a long story short," he said, starting to rock back and forth, "My partner is here with me—a very respectable personage, if I may say so, really quite a guy. Now, this partner of mine, if you follow me, has a son and he really wants the boy to get a decent education. The *kheyders* where we are—what can I say? The *melamed* from Brody is an animal, the Litvak is a Litvak, and the rest of them? *Feh.* I was thinking that your orphan could . . . You understand?"

"I understand. You mean he should teach your partner's son."

"A-ha," said Reb Shneur, his eyes flashing. "That's the Scripture I was looking for! Things will go very well for him. He'll get board, shoes, clothing. And as long as he isn't an idiot, he could also get himself a wife. Why not? There's a daughter too. Think it over."

"On the face of it, it looks all right," said Reb Avrum, rubbing his forehead.

"All I want," Reb Shneur explained patiently, "All I want, if you catch my meaning, is to do a *mitsve* and provide for an orphan. It's probably been predestined. Nu, you thought it over yet?"

"Not bad," said Reb Avrum, "But . . ."

"But what?" Reb Shneur jumped up. " 'Not bad,' you say? Try, 'very good.' This always happens with a Jew—don't take it personally. But what? But—I'll tell you. We have to show the boy to my partner. My partner has to like him, that's what. If you want a share of the *mitsve*, don't delay—let the boy go with me to my partner—now! There's no time."

"OK," said Reb Avrum, standing up. "I'll go talk it over with him now."

You could see from their faces that both Hershele and Reb Avrum had certain reservations, even though Reb Avrum had laid the matter out smoothly and Hershele, looking him in the eye, had given a nod of assent.

Reb Shneur marked this well, but assumed an expression of utter indifference. Rising from his seat, he spoke subtly. "There's no time. If he wants to come, he's got to go with me now . . . However you guys want things."

"Just a second," pleaded Reb Avrum. He was encouraging Hershele, who had gone over to Moyshele and was busy rummaging through the lectern with him. "Go on already, Hershele. The man doesn't have all day. Go and come back with an answer. I'll wait for you here."

"I'm gone," said Hershele, departing with Reb Shneur.

5

AS SOON AS Hershele had left, Reb Avrum began an ardent, melodious recitation of the *Zohar*. His eyes blazed, the color rose in his face—he was sipping it up with gusto. It was clear to anybody watching that he got more life and energy out of the *Zohar* than others do from a breakfast of coffee and pastry. Reb Avrum's daily breakfast consisted of a dry piece of *Mishne*, a few tasty legends, a sip of *Zohar* to wash it all down—and this kept him going until lunch time.

Just now, he remained absorbed in his recital for quite a while, flying high into other worlds. Then a change came into his voice, it got lower and lower, as if falling from the highest heavens all the way back to earth. He sighed, stroked his beard, his forehead, and, sitting in his place, looked pensively into the open window directly across from him.

Swallows were floating, hovering up and down in the air, following each other with a whistle into their nests under the synagogue's cornice. "Even the bird finds its home"—the appropriate verse from the Psalms came to Reb Avrum's mind—"And the swallow her nest where she laid her young. O, to be at your altars, O Lord of Hosts," in your holy place, dear father, Gotenyu!

A glance at Moyshele put him in mind of Hershele, too, and he thought: "Dear Jewish children, fledglings from poor families, seeking shelter in synagogues."

"What's going on?" he asked Moyshele without leaving his place. Moyshele was sitting quietly in the corner, resting his head on his *Gemore*. "What's going on, that he isn't back yet?"

"I know?" Moyshele answered in a curt, gloomy voice.

"*Oy vey*, something's wrong, something's wrong," murmured Reb Avrum. "I completely forgot to ask what hostel he's staying in, what's his name, Shneur-Wolf, isn't it?"

"Sounds right," said Moyshele from between clenched teeth.

"Where did he say he comes from, this Shneur-Wolf? I can't for the life of me remember what he said." Reb Avrum's question went unanswered.

He started to dip into a book, but Hershele's prolonged absence had him so disturbed that he was unable to grasp a word—he just stared like a frightened calf. He was starting to have problems with this Shneur-Wolf, something didn't fit. He hadn't really appealed to Reb Avrum from the word go—the way his eyes were always moving, never looking straight into your own—but Reb Avrum's goodness and piety hadn't allowed anything so insubstantial to lead him to think ill of a Jew. So what? It's nothing. A nice Jewish boy. But now that he was ill at ease, his heart began to give vent to its real opinions. Reb Avrum was none too happy with himself, either, or with this whole business—it was moving a little too quickly for him. I mean, he didn't really know where this guy even came from. He was too excited to sit down anymore. He went over to the open window and looked outside.

And beheld a moving scene. A bandit had made his way into a swallow's nest beneath the cornice. A sparrow was sprawling there with its wings outstretched as if it owned the place. The swallows were in turmoil. They came flying from every side. The victimized couple was flying, fluttering back and forth in turn, whistling alarms, taking courage and making attempts to get close to the nest. But the sparrow, angry now, just stuck its head out, opened its mouth, and started to peck.

Reb Avrum felt a pang in his heart. He stepped back from the window, waving his hand as if to drive off some source of trouble, and started to walk up and down the synagogue. In his mind's eye, he could still see the sparrow's head, though; he looked pensively over to Moyshele, stopped near his lectern, and after a few moments of silence said, "Moyshele, maybe you want to jump out and see where he is, the *shkots*? It's almost three o'clock. Run over to the hostels. If he isn't in one, try another—you'll find him in one of them for sure."

"I already had the same idea," said Moyshele, closing his *Gemore* and leaving right away.

Moyshele had been down in the dumps all day because he was going to have to part from Hershele, who had been like a brother to him. They learned together, spent days and nights together, in good times and in bad. Being left alone after having been bound to someone so tightly was worse than death. There was an argument going on inside Moyshele, a bitter dispute among his feelings. His love for Hershele was crying: "Have pity. He's suffering so much here, let him go. The job could be a break for him." But his self-love claimed, "You should have pity on me, too. With him here, life is better, more pleasant, more comfortable." And yet another feeling, hypocritically pious, offered a honeyed compromise: "A pity on the two of us. It's only just that he begin to prosper a little, but if it's the good Lord's will, He can just as easily send him prosperity here."

Hershele's lateness put an end to this dispute. Now all Moyshele could think of was, "Where's Hershele?" Reb Avrum's restlessness had stirred him up even more. He was troubled and didn't know *what* to be afraid of.

Moyshele tried several hostels, and nothing—no one had seen or heard of the man he was looking for. On his way to the rest of the hostels, a thought suddenly hit him like a bullet. "The river. Hershele likes to go swimming and play all kinds of tricks in the water. Maybe he went for a swim and—" Moyshele didn't have the heart to continue his line of thought; he went pale and ran for all he was worth to all the usual swimming spots, but it was a waste of energy, Hershele wasn't there. Willy-nilly, he saw every detail of what had happened: Hershele had sunk into the swampy muck. Crabs were already eating his body, gnawing the marrow from his bones. The river carries off a good seven or so people every summer . . .

Who knows where Moyshele's dire worries and fears would have led, had another thought not struck him. Nu, there's also a Kaptsansker hostel in the world. It's possible, highly possible, that Hershele dropped in there to see some new arrivals from Kaptsansk and pick up regards or a letter from home. Moyshele seized this thought with both hands, amazed that it hadn't occurred to him before, and, strengthened by its hope, went off to the Kaptsansker hostel.

Outside, the hostel was surrounded by wagon drivers holding whips, who were standing around, sitting on benches, scratching their *peyes* ill-temperedly, spitting and cursing and swearing for no apparent reason. There were also travel agents, bargaining with customers and calling all of them uncle and auntie, pointing to wagons at a distance and promising a wonderful trip—fast, quick, and roomy, comfortable as a high-class carriage.

As soon as Moyshele approached, the agents fell upon him like locusts, pulling him, tearing at him. "Over here, young man. Where are you going? Here's a wagon ready to leave right away."

Moyshele barely escaped with his life and ran into the hostel. He went through everybody there, searched every corner with his eyes—no Hershele. He wasn't feeling well, his heart grew dark and bitter. But there was still hope. He tried to get into the courtyard through the back door. Pushing his way through the carts and wagons, through the press of people and horses, whose tails were smacking his face, he saw a familiar face, which gave him a smack in the heart for joy. Shneur-Wolf was standing with someone by a hitched-up wagon, looking worn-out and depressed. Moyshele went up to him quickly and asked breathlessly, "Where's Hershele? Hershele—where is he?"

"Ah," Shneur-Wolf roused himself as if from sleep, giving Moyshele a sharp look. After a few moments' thought, he spoke, a little more lively already. "Just a minute, just a minute. Let me just finish with this fellow here."

Shneur-Wolf called the man aside, and they spoke very quietly, more in gestures than words, for quite a while. The other man got into a wagon and Shneur-Wolf bade him farewell. Coming back to Moyshele, he said with a smile, "Nu, now I can answer you. What was it you were asking?"

"Where's Hershele?"

"Ah, your friend, you mean," as if he'd just guessed. "I'll tell you. Your Hershele is with my partner. I'm staying here in the hostel and my partner's staying with one of his in-laws. I'm going there now myself. If you want to, you can come with me."

Of course, Moyshele was very eager to go and said, "Thank you very much."

Shneur-Wolf led Moyshele through a maze of narrow back alleys and lanes. After they'd gone quite a distance, Moyshele began to slow down. There was an anxious look in his eye, as if to say, "Where is he taking me?"

"He couldn't find anything farther than the end of the world?" muttered Shneur-Wolf as if he were unhappy too, and then, looking at Moyshele's face, said sweetly, "Soon, soon."

"Right," said Moyshele angrily. "Soon we'll be out of town completely. We're already at the cemetery."

"What's it my fault?" Shneur-Wolf calmed Moyshele with soft words. "What does it matter to you if you go for a bit of a walk? Look, there's a green tree, a fragrant lawn. Birds are whistling—whoo, whoo!"

Moyshele broke into a smile and assumed a cheerful demeanor.

"That's it. That's the way I like you," said Shneur-Wolf wheedlingly. "What is it with you, that you never have any time? Nothing but learning! Always with 'Abaye says this, Abaye says that.' You ought to pay some attention to the world around you."

Talking like this, Shneur-Wolf and Moyshele kept going farther and farther until they were way past the cemetery. There was a wagon dragging along there; the Jew inside it was holding the reins loosely, just enough so as not to drop them, relying on the horse's good faith—let it go where it wants to. Shneur-Wolf and the Jew exchanged signals, and before Moyshele knew what was happening, Shneur-Wolf had grabbed him, thrown him into the wagon, and jumped in after. The Jew lashed the horse and off they went.

6

MEANWHILE, Reb Avrum was striding restlessly up and down the synagogue, rubbing his forehead and talking to himself in bewilderment. "Master of the Universe, what's going on here? Where could those kids have got to? One of them is missing, the other one's taking too long—a fine way to take their leave. If *one* goes, he goes—it's nothing. But the other? Where's the other? Something isn't right." He stopped by the window and looked outside, looked and looked, but for nothing. There was nothing to see, nothing to hear. He got himself ready to go, took his stick in his hand, and went out, intending to do something to find out what was going on. One of his closer acquaintances came toward him on the street, a young man of about thirty, well-dressed—half western style, half Jewish—with a small black beard and a sweet, intelligent face. Shocked at Reb Avrum's frantic haste, he stopped him. "Why are you rushing like that? Where to, Reb Avrum? Some kind of business, or what?"

"More like a heartache," answered Reb Avrum, catching his breath. "It's good that you turned up. It reminded me that I have something to talk to you about. But not right now, Reb Refoel."

"Must be about a match for me," smiled Refoel. "But have you heard the news, Reb Avrum? Your pal Gedalye Vintkhapper's gone bankrupt."

"*Oy vey!*" Reb Avrum was astonished. "Just like that, out of the blue? How were His Excellency's relations with him?"

"They were OK," said Refoel, wrinkling his nose. "I'd been expecting it for a while. I discounted the notes that he'd given me by a few percent right away, nothing serious, though. The Lodz manufacturers that I work for aren't going to be angry. But what are *you* in such a tizzy about, Reb Avrum? You know what—come on over to my place, we'll discuss it over a glass of punch. For some reason, I'm in a very good mood today."

"Huh? Yeah, sure." Reb Avrum started as if a thought had just struck him. "I'll take you as far as your room in the courtyard. I'm going to the Kaptsansker hostel there to see about something. Soon as I'm finished, I'll be at your place. Come."

Reb Avrum resumed his earlier pace. Refoel could barely keep up, nor could he divine the meaning of Reb Avrum's haste. "Remember, Reb

Avrum," said Refoel, as they parted in the hostel's courtyard, "Come up as soon as you're done here."

*   *   *

"Good afternoon, Reyze," Reb Avrum said melodiously, walking familiarly into the private alcove, where Reyze had just laid the meat to salt in a soaking dish and was starting on the fish, a good-sized carp and a big pike for Shabbes.

"Ah, company," said Reyze, stopping her work and running her nose along her sleeve. "A long time since I've seen you, Reb Avrum. Is that any way to act? Nu, excuse me, sit down."

Reyze and Reb Avrum had been cordial acquaintances for a good long time. Her husband, RIP, had *davened* in the same synagogue as Reb Avrum, and had got on very well with him. Reyze still used the women's section on the High Holidays—she had her own place. She always relied on Reb Avrum to know when her husband's *yortsayt*, and those of her mother and father, came out. He remembered the dates and took care of the candles, the *Mishne*-learning, getting a *minyen* in the cemetery, and settled with her afterwards. Aside from this, Reb Avrum often used to come to her house for charitable donations or to see an acquaintance who happened to be staying in her hostel, or just to say hello. Reyze always gave him a respectful reception and was eager to talk with him about *yidishkayt* and the way people lived in the old days. "It just isn't the same anymore," she'd groan.

"You're right. It's quite a while since we've seen each other, but I didn't mean it on purpose. I'm here today . . ." Reb Avrum swiveled and sat down on a stool.

"Because a bear took a dump in the woods," joked Reyze.

"I'm here today, "Reb Avrum began, "On account of . . . Reyzenyu, did you see that boy from Kaptsansk here today? You know who I mean, the late cantor's son. He went out for an hour this morning and still hasn't come back."

"God help me!" screamed Reyze, turning away from him.

"What is it?" Reb Avrum started in fright and jumped up from the stool.

"It's the end of his life, his young life is over." Reyze was lamenting as if it were Tishe B'Ov. "I *knew* there was something wrong. Now it's as plain as day—the poor boy's been killed. *They* should be killed without a knife."

"What's wrong with you, Reyze? Who? What?" asked Reb Avrum, turning numb.

" 'Have a dumpling'—you ever hear such a thing?" Reyze bellowed in her normal voice. "All of a sudden he's sitting here between two strangers, the devil only knows who they or their fathers are, eating a dumpling. Where'd they get to be so buddy-buddy with him that they'd give him the food from their mouths? They weren't such nice guys as that; they haggled over the meal with me and put their leftover bread into a doggy-bag. I didn't like it from the start."

"Nu, nu?" Reb Avrum was pushing.

"Nu," said Reyze, her voice dropping a register, "I didn't like it. So what? It's the first time I didn't like something? But still, something drew me to stick, as they say, my nose in, in case I could find something out. What is it that's written somewhere, Reb Avrum? A woman loves to . . ."

"Keep going, dear, please." Reb Avrum was trembling to get to the point.

"What else? A woman is a woman," said Reyze, lowering her voice still further. "I was curious to sniff things out while I was serving them, to get a lick of their conversation while passing them by. Their whispering and the faces they were making, the thieving looks they kept shooting each other, really bothered me. The couple of words I caught made a real impression, and my heart whispered: *Khappers!* All they're out for is to press the orphan into the army with some trick. That's what the dumpling was for. I looked around for the boy, but didn't see him just then. Meanwhile—'what are we, what our lives?'—I'm still a woman with a brain like a sieve, in one ear and out the other: How important can it be, and I've got plenty of other things to do. Now it's all clear." Reyze burst into a falsetto. "They've snatched him for sure, may their lives be snatched away. A terrible pity, *vey iz mir.* Such a good boy . . . Oh, hell! What's the matter, Reb Avrum? Get a hold of yourself!"

Reb Avrum had broken out in a cold sweat, tears stood in his eyes like beans, all his limbs were trembling and he could barely keep his feet. "It's my fault," he groaned, holding his head in his hands. "What have I done? The first time I meet someone, without really knowing who he is or where he comes from, I go and hand the poor orphan over to him."

"What fault is it of yours?" Reyze was comforting Reb Avrum. "It could be the boy's own bad luck, you know. This could have been predestined for him. What do they say? 'His eye is on the sparrow'?"

"Old fool that I am, I deserve to be killed." Reb Avrum hadn't stopped moaning and groaning. "Leyzer-Yankl, RIP, left his son to me and died in the hope that I'd take care of him like a father. Some care! Some father!"

"Nu, what can you do? Didja ever hear such a thing? Sit down, Reb Avrum," begged Reyze with tears in her eyes. She pulled up a stool for him.

"His father won't be able to rest in his grave. 'Where is my child?' he'll cry. 'Is this how you keep your word?' And what'll I tell his mother, the widow, when she comes weeping to me?" Reb Avrum was heartbroken. He threw himself onto the stool, covered his face with both hands, and sat quietly, as silent as the wall.

"You ever hear such a thing?" Reyze was giving moral advice, shaking her head after several minutes of silence. Tears were dripping from her eyes. "How can you take it to heart like this? You, especially, a man, a Jew, a scholar, you know what's written in the holy books. So what's there to say about a woman, then? 'What shall we say, what shall we speak?' By my life— ho! What was that?" She started, hearing a loud bang on the other side of her alcove, as if something had fallen. "The hell with it! Nothing but breaking and falling. It's unbearable what goes on here in the course of a day."

She ran quickly out of the alcove and, in a dark corner not far away, banged into someone or other who had overturned a bench covered with bottles and copperware while he was rummaging around. "Whattaya got to say for yourself? Where'd he drag himself off to with his luggage? You couldn't find anywhere else? Who's there?" In order not to have to wait for an answer, Reyze bent over in all her glory to see who was rummaging around in there. She took one look at his face and gave a scream, in a voice not her own. "Reb Avrum, come quickly. Reb Avrum!"

Reb Avrum awakened from his slumber and flew out of the alcove in haste.

"He's here," Reyze was screaming breathlessly, pointing with all five fingers. "Here he is, him, here."

"Hershele!" said Reb Avrum in a muffled and trembling voice, half out of his mind with amazement.

Hershele was standing with his head hung down, like someone who's done something wrong and senses that he's about to be punished.

"You should *bentsh goymel,* my fine young man, for having come out safe and sound," said Reyze.

"What's it my fault? I didn't knock it over on purpose," Hershele excused himself.

"No, not that," said Reb Avrum, joining in. "Reyze means that you got out of those guys' hands safe and sound . . . What are you looking so shocked for, Hershele?"

"I don't understand what you're talking about," answered Hershele, shrugging his shoulders and starting to gather up the fallen copperware.

"You hear?" Reb Avrum turned to Reyze. "He doesn't understand what I'm talking about. I'm afraid that we cast aspersions on Jews for no reason at all. Let's hope that God doesn't punish us."

"What are you thinking of?" asked Reyze with a little smile. "What about the dumpling? Did I only dream the couple of words that I caught? Nu, ask him where he's been all this time."

"Tell me, *shkots,*" said Reb Avrum, "Where have you been all this time?"

"How come you were rummaging around in these things? And whose things were you rummaging in?" Reyze asked two questions at once, bending over to have a look at a package of stuff.

Hershele stood there in confusion with his eyes cast down and didn't answer a word.

"Have a look how nice," said Reyze, holding a skirt that she'd found in the package. "Whattaya got to say for yourself? Nu, my fine young man, what is the meaning of this girl's skirt?"

"What? What?" Reb Avrum was astonished.

Hershele turned as red as fire. He was too heavy at heart to be able to speak.

"In the meantime, Reb Avrum, you shouldn't be standing. Go into the alcove with him and have something to eat. The boy will eat too. He must be hungry. And while he's eating, he can tell us the whole story."

7

THIS IS THE STORY. Shneur-Wolf took Hershele straight from the synagogue to the Kaptsansker hostel, where he was in fact staying. The hostel sees plenty of action during the week, what with so many people coming and going, and the action is even bigger on Thursdays, when Jews usually start to have no time. Those about to go on a trip start to hurry on account of Shabbes, fearful lest Satan interpose himself: an axle could break in the middle of the road, the wagon could overturn with all the passengers inside or sink into mud past its wheels or—may it never transpire or come to pass—the horses could stop moving and then, God forbid, you'd be late: maybe for your bath, maybe for the roast, or, may it never happen, you could pull up in the wagon in the middle of the Shabbes meal.

In the midst of all this confusion, when everyone was worrying about himself and had no thoughts to spare for others, a little Jew with a red beard was sitting at the end of a corner table, working away at a plate of dumplings from which the steam was rising like smoke. He ate with utter absorption, unhurriedly, chewing everything thoroughly, like a past master of the masticatory arts. Just looking at him could give you a powerful appetite, long after the doctors had given up on your anorexia. The hell with healers, the hell with doctors—a talented glutton is the best appetite stimulant: just look at him, rubbing his hands in selfless devotion . . .

Shneur-Wolf came up to this Jew by himself, and they spoke quietly. The Jew was thinking something over; he laid down his spoon for a while, chewing so slowly that his lips barely moved, and from the glow on his smiling face it was plain that something was giving him a lot of pleasure.

In the meantime, Hershele was standing at the other end of the room, waiting. Shneur-Wolf motioned him over and introduced him to the Jew, who asked him to sit down beside him and said, "I liked you as soon as I laid eyes on you. I hope that my brother-in-law, who's looking for a teacher, will like you too. He's staying kind of far from here. He's very fastidious, careful of his health, and has to have a garden and a little fresh air. We'll go there after we eat; you'll come with, too, so he can get a look at you. The rest is between us. It'll work out, though. Meanwhile, come and eat."

"Bon appétit," said Hershele, as you do when invited to eat.

"No," said the Jew, "I really mean it—eat something." He turned to Shneur-Wolf. "Please tell the innkeeper to give both of you some food."

"Thanks very much, but I'm not hungry." Hershele was being polite, even though it wouldn't have hurt to have a bite.

"Take something at least," said the Jew, slipping a big, black, cheese-filled dumpling into his hand.

"Mrs.! Mrs.!" Shneur-Wolf was calling to Reyze, who was running by with the ladle in her hand and making all kinds of noise.

"Whattaya got to say for yourself?" she asked, breaking off another conversation in order to come over.

"Haven't you got something to eat?" asked Shneur-Wolf.

"Something to eat?" Reyze repeated, drawing out the words. "What's something? Lunch isn't for a little while yet."

"But I'm starving to death."

"You ever hear such a thing? I should cut myself into pieces and cook them? In the meantime, I'll fix you a radish," she said, glancing at the two of them and at Hershele, who was politely eating a dumpling in their company. She gave a little frown and went off.

When Shneur-Wolf received the promised radish from Reyze, he fell upon it hungrily, immersing himself in the plate, and Hershele's finer feelings obliged him to move, as it wasn't polite to watch someone eat.

The door to the hostel never closed. People were always in and out. Catching a shove from behind, Hershele looked around, and who do you think he caught sight of among the new arrivals? Beyle! He felt his heart go thump, a sort of warmth spread over his body, and he felt just as happy, just as well, as if he'd seen his mother or one of his sisters, any of the nearest and dearest whom he'd been missing so badly. His *shtetl*, his house, leapt up before his eyes, and for a moment he wasn't alone. He was so transported with joy that he ran up to Beyle and took her by the hand, completely forgetting that with a girl, a female, you don't shake hands.

Laughing quietly, Beyle slowly pushed his hand away, hinting at Hershele's foolish mistake.

Hershele turned red as a beet; he looked around in embarrassment to make sure that no one had seen him, and muttered something incomprehensible.

"Here, I brought you a present from home," said Beyle, handing Hershele a package. "It's from your mother, and she sends her regards."

The package contained a pair of old, darned stockings and an old patched shirt wrapped up in a little capote, made from the left side of his father's old weekday capote, which his mother had taken in with a pleat.

Hershele loved the shirt and stockings; they were as beautiful to him as could be, they told him stories, spoke in real words. Every patch was a *megile*, an entire history of who had laid it, how and in what frame of mind.

Tears came to his eyes when he looked at the capote. He could see his father's pale face, hear his weak, quiet voice, his sighs at their parting. "Sooner or later, Hershele, everybody has to part." Looking at the capote, he heard a greeting from the other world, a cry of pain from his father. "Ach, I broke my back all my life, and this is all I accomplished. God has taken my soul, the earth my body; you, my son, take my capote, the sum of my possessions, and wear it in good health."

Beyle told Hershele that her parents had sent her to Glupsk to find a place. And seeing as she was a complete stranger, she asked him if he knew where the "slave market" was—the place, so she'd heard, where servants met with agents—and if he could be so good as to take her there.

The prospect of going for a walk with Beyle and being able to interrogate her in detail about everybody back home caused Shneur-Wolf and his partner and the job to drop right out of Hershele's mind . . . What would Shneur-Wolf and his partner think? That the boy is wandering around in the crowd—what else would he be doing? They even looked for him a couple of times—big deal, he'll wait. *He* needed them. And while Shneur-Wolf was wrapped up in his radish and the other Jew sounded the depths of his plate of dumplings in the hope that Reyze would soon bring him something else, our two Kaptsanskers flew from the hostel like a pair of doves and went for a walk through Glupsk.

They were both feeling quite well, enjoying themselves. Reminiscence stoked their minds and opened their mouths: the awkwardness they once felt in Kaptsansk vanished here like smoke. Hershele couldn't get his fill of talking. He made inquiries about every little thing at home, about everything in town, mixing it all together and not even forgetting Shepsl the *melamed*'s goat, Ziml the tavern keeper's new son-in-law, Noyekh the water-carrier's colt, and Anshel the hunchback's calf. Of course, these were all living creatures whose souls had at least some connection with Hershele's. But what did pockmarked Khayim's straw roof, Leybtse-Temtse's bankruptcy and other such dead, inanimate things have to do with him, that simply hearing about them revived him? You have to be alone and away from home, listening closely to your own feelings, to get the sense of this and the answer to the question: That's the way things are! A person's soul is a mirror of the whole world. Thousands of streams within and without a person drain into the sea of his feelings . . .

The slave market to which our youths were bound revealed itself before them in all its nakedness, showing itself for what it was and leaving them no further desire to talk. They beheld a panorama of every sort of look and countenance: long noses, flat noses, swollen noses; lips with cold sores, foreheads glistening with sweat, good-looking, attractive faces grown old and wrinkled before their time; a hodgepodge of rags and tatters, of women with outlandish ideas of style: rags, patches, flashes of skin, naked toes peeking out from decaying shoes; faded, worn-out skirts that tried to pass for stylish, wild hoop-skirts, high-button clodhoppers with crooked buttons; a mixture of voices and tongues to rival the Tower of Babel—thick, thin, hoarse, squeaky, cackling, and singing. The whole Poverty Commando: girls, women, young ones with tiny children, and incompetent, downwardly mobile housewives whom want had driven to market to sell themselves to respectable, wealthy families as cooks, maids, nurses, and nursemaids.

There was plenty of talking and chitchat; sharp tongues were thrusting, motormouths were humming, quarreling, mocking, insulting. Déclassé housewives were moaning and groaning, wiping their noses and rubbing their eyes. Brokers in shawls, in single-sleeved jackets, were wandering around like angels of destruction. One grabs a woman or girl and leads her off like a hen from a cage. Another comes running, madder than hell, very displeased with somebody. A third expostulates, speaks honeyed words to mistresses right there on the spot, praising her merchandise to the nth degree: this one's a mistress of *khale*, that one has golden hands for scouring brass and copper, no matter how fine; another one is a cook beyond compare, the king could eat what she makes—she's never been in service before, her troubles have driven her to it, she was mistress of her own house. Yeah, right—she was the wife of Nakhomtse the Bum.

Our heroes stood awhile in mute amazement, as sick at heart as a pair of lambs. Hershele managed to rouse himself after a while with the thought that it wasn't right to leave Shneur-Wolf waiting so long, but his heart wouldn't let him tear himself from Beyle and he started to look for excuses: She's from the same town, a close neighbor, still a stranger here—it's his duty not to throw her so quickly aside. It even occurred to him that Shneur-Wolf could leave in a huff and that he'd lose his job; but, wonder of wonders, he didn't really care. On the contrary, he had absolutely no desire to leave town precisely when Beyle had just arrived. He really had no desire to do so, but he also had as little desire to admit it to himself. He looked for other reasons, turned tricks in his mind, and finally, as people sometimes do in certain circumstances, fell upon a device to make his pig's foot kosher: It's the will of God! Because he's either destined to get the job, which means that he won't be late, or if he isn't destined to get it, God so arranged matters as to make him want to tarry here, so let Shneur-Wolf leave without him.

With God on his side, Hershele had no need to hurry, and he stayed happily with Beyle, waiting to see what would happen.

Meanwhile, it was getting late. A woman who seemed to be a broker had been watching Beyle from a distance and appeared to like her, as emerged from her sweet, mild words when she approached, telling Beyle that she had a very good place for her, somewhere where she could be comfortable, eat and drink as much as she liked, just as long as she wasn't a *shlimazl.*

Beyle went with the woman, and asked Hershele to please look out for her things, which she'd left in a corner at the hostel. Hershele, of course, wasn't slow to comply, and it was while poking around her things in the corner by Reyze's alcove that he knocked over the copperware and Reyze discovered him.

MEANTIME, Refoel had prepared a regular *seyder* of punch and snacks; it was all laid out on the table, waiting only for the door to open and Refoel to say, "Welcome, Reb Avrum." It was really the perfect time for a *seyder:* God had delivered him miraculously from Gedalye Vintkhapper, who left nothing behind but a flood of debt that washed over the heads of many, drowning them and all their possessions, just like the Egyptians of old. But Refoel had walked through it all dryshod and calm.

Refoel came from a *shtetl* somewhere in Poland and had moved to Glupsk five or six years earlier, working as a commission agent for some big manufacturers in Lodz. Glupsk had long been known as a good trading center, and manufacturers the world over wished to market their merchandise there. Not because it had a port or an exchange or famous banking houses—no! There were no ships on the River Piatagnilevke; no one but the pigs could bathe there in the summer heat, the little water it had wasn't usually enough to put out the fires. It even happened once that Glupsk awakened one morning to find no sign of the river whatever—it had dried up, gone bankrupt. Picked up in the night without so much as a goodbye and vanished into thin air. The news spread everywhere, was trumpeted on the front pages of the newspapers: "The Piatagnilevke Is No More. The Piatagnilevke Has Run Away." A little while after the disappearance, the river turned up again, like every other bankrupt, and once again got credit from the locals: fresh, fragrant slop pails filled with everything good.

Glupsk likewise didn't know from a stock exchange. Jews heaped themselves together on the streets, on the stoops. In place of banking houses, they got by with moneylenders and usurers who were as good at their jobs as plenty of bankers elsewhere, and who calculated their interest simply and straightforwardly according to the weekly portions of the Torah.

So why Glupsk, then? The great value of this town was due entirely to the fact that it was inundated with Jews. Who needs seas, ports, or stock exchanges when you can have a Jewish brain? A Jewish brain is a precision instrument; it can fly high into the sky, spin around and make the world spin with it.

Wherever there are Jews, you'll find the angel Mercury, the guardian of business and trade . . . A Jew tips his hat back, and a plan is born; he furrows his brow, out jumps a bouncing baby deal; and if he should scratch the side of his head, a transport of goods grows out of the ground. And the Glupskers don't fool around: their hats slide halfway down their necks, they're constantly wrinkling their brows, and they scratch the sides of their heads with vigor. If you're not a complete idiot and know enough to watch out for yourself, you can do business in Glupsk. And for the rest, if someone should go bankrupt on you, what's the big deal? Don't ships full of goods sometimes founder at sea? The only difference is that the drowned stay drowned, but the bankrupt goes on paying burial fees to the *makhers* who helped give him his last rites.

The fact that Refoel could maintain his commission in Glupsk for six years without suffering any serious losses proves that he was certainly no fool. He was known in Glupsk as a good, fine, honest young man, even though he had something of the appearance of the "enlightened" members of the new generation. His dealings with merchants in the larger world smoothed this slight fault over, though, and people pretended not to notice. What's the difference? You overlook worse things in a merchant—he's a businessman, he's allowed. Seeing as Refoel was also a widower, a good many people, even the more religious, had set their sights on him for a son-in-law.

He was one of those young people who sprang up among the Jews about forty years ago, who passed from *Tanakh* and *Gemore* to become hidden *maskilim*, secretly "enlightened." These youths, may they rest in peace, didn't cut themselves off from the rest of the community in observance or outward appearance. They washed and said a blessing before eating, *davened* three times a day and studied, just like everybody else. They dressed in Jewish garb, wore *tsitsis*, always kept their heads covered—everything just like everyone, except that they skipped some of the nonobligatory liturgical poems, shortened their capotes a bit to keep them from getting spattered with mud, let their hair grow out a little, shortened their *peyes* slightly, and kept their beards clean and combed. On account of all of which, people used to murmur against them.

They were the *lamed-vovnikes* of worldly education in their time. To all external appearances, there was nothing different about them; they kept their mouths shut and didn't prattle. But good God, what was going on in their hearts! The Jewish spark glowed hot within them, the holy fire of love for all people. The beginning of a new, better, beautiful world floated before their eyes. They hoped and believed that it was about to hatch from its egg to the sunshine—and that life would become a paradise. They lived in quiet fraternity, like Hasidim of the same *rebbe*, only instead of whiskey they gulped down the words of the holy prophets and the modern belle-lettrists, carried poems around with them and also produced their own, or else composed letters, always oohing and aahing over these productions. Should a young man conceive a desire to learn something, to walk on this new path, he was as welcome to them as if he were doing them all a great favor, and they helped him in whatever way they could. This was how these youthful old fools, may they rest in peace, lived. They hadn't quite caught the spirit of education, they didn't know what the wise old children of today do, that the secret of enlightenment is an open, burning mouth, full of sulphur and pitch, and a heart as cold as ice; that the best Torah is business and the finest flower of rhetoric, a coin.

Refoel's surname was Lublinski; but Jews usually just called him Reb

Refoel, a sign of his great popularity. To Reyze, he was the crème de la crème. Right after his arrival in Glupsk, he took an apartment with board in her courtyard, and Reyze took good care of him, taking pains to make sure that his lunch was both tasty and on time.

His acquaintance with Reb Avrum began with a proposition of marriage and grew over time until it became a fervent, reciprocal friendship. There was something in each of them that drew each one's heart to the other. Both of them took great pleasure in spending an hour over a glass of punch or tea, talking warmly and with no ulterior motives.

When the feast was all prepared and Refoel was sitting in his robe and slippers, leaning on an elbow and looking into a book, Reb Avrum came in with a friendly "Good afternoon."

"Ah, welcome." Refoel got up from his stool to meet Reb Avrum and looked him right in the face. "You look like a different person from a little while ago, Reb Avrum. *This* is how I like to see you."

"You see, huh," said Reb Avrum, "how God can turn the bad to good in just one minute. I'm not alone, though. I've brought someone with."

"Where is he then? Invite him in, we'll have a *mezumen*."

Reb Avrum led Hershele in from the vestibule where he'd been waiting and introduced him to Refoel. "The son of a good friend of mine, may he rest in peace. From out of town, he learns in my synagogue. It's because of him that I had such heartache today. Nu, God be praised, it turned out all right. *I* should be buying the drinks."

"*Gut yontef*," Refoel smiled. "It's a happy day for both of us. Come on over to the table and we'll celebrate."

Refoel put a little of everything onto Hershele's plate and urged him to eat and drink and not be shy. The party really looked like a celebration. Small as the crowd was, it was happy and really loved the punch.

Sitting by the open window with Refoel, Reb Avrum told him of the whole affair with Hershele. Refoel looked over to Hershele, who was sitting over a glass of tea at the head of the table, and bethought himself. It was plain from his face that he really liked Hershele and that the boy's bitter misery had touched his heart. "All I'm able to do for the boy right now," he said quietly to Reb Avrum, "is give him a place to sleep here. At least he won't have to lie on a hard bench in the synagogue. Later on, we'll see what else I can do."

"Ach, you're going to get a big *mitsve*," said Reb Avrum, standing up and turning to Hershele. "You hear? From now on, you'll sleep here, at Reb Refoel's. Thank him for his goodness, and let's go."

The proverb, "When does a pauper rejoice? When he finds what he has lost," fit Reb Avrum to a T. He was very cheerful all the way home from Refoel's. Looking at Hershele walking beside him, he felt glad and made jokes the whole way. From time to time an unpleasant thought passed through his mind like a cloud—he had held groundless suspicions about a Jew—but it was only a little summer cloud that floats briefly past the sun and then disappears like smoke.

Hershele, on the other hand, was somewhat distracted; he walked slowly and pensively, unable to put Beyle out of his mind. Did she get a place or was she just wandering around somewhere? And there was also her bundle at the hostel.

"Hurry up a little." Reb Avrum was driving him on. "Why are you going so slowly? Moyshele has to sit there all by himself and he must really be worried about you. Have mercy on him and get a move on."

"Reb Avrum," pleaded Hershele, "Let me run back to the hostel. In all the rush, I forgot to ask Reyze to keep an eye on the things. It's a poor . . . a poor girl's bundle."

"Ta," said Reb Avrum, looking for a while at Hershele, who had stopped walking and was hanging his head. "For God's sake, don't dilly-dally. Come right back. I'll go tell Moyshele myself."

Reb Avrum burst like a bomb into the synagogue's anteroom, so full of the good news about Hershele that he could hardly keep it from blasting out of him right there. At the inner door, though, he ran into a woman. "Where's Moyshele?" she asked in a sad voice.

"Ah, Moyshele's mother," said Reb Avrum.

"This is the second time I've been here already." Her voice was trembling. "Maybe you know, you must know where he is, my son. He hasn't set foot at home all day, or had a spoonful of water in his mouth. I've looked for him everywhere already. *Oy, gevalt!* Tell me where—where is he, my Moyshele?"

"What? Could it really be?" Reb Avrum was astonished and turned as pale as the wall.

❖   ❖   ❖

About seven or eight versts outside of Glupsk, past the oaken inn, a large, pretty forest of pine and oak runs along both sides of the wide, sandy highway to the city. The road is pitted here and there with swampy puddles inhabited by frogs who croak their throats out, spawn, and pass on their legacy of muck and crazy faces from one generation to the next. Because of these little swamps, there are byroads that branch off deep into the woods, where teamsters with their covered wagons and goyim with loads of wood make detours, each in his own way, on his own route. A wagon driver has to be a real pro, a scholar of the road, to negotiate these paths; if not, the wagon will turn over in one of the ditches and he'll end up with a broken back.

At evening, Shmulik the old-clothes man was making his way along a narrow path that ran between fresh young trees at the edge of the forest, his shirt open, his capote unbuttoned, a small cask under his arm. Almost every Thursday, he'd take the cask to the oaken inn and fill it with good, reasonably priced whiskey, which he brought back to his customers in town in plenty of time for Shabbes. Besides the few groschen it earned him, he also got a bit of whiskey for his own *kiddesh*. People who wanted cheap whiskey for themselves, not as a means of earning some money, tended to go on Friday morning, when the road to the inn was often choked with entire families, young and old alike, loaded down with casks and sundry other vessels. This had been the custom from time immemorial, and a Jewish custom overrides a law, even the law of the liquor-licence monopoly, and especially the Glupsker monopoly, which didn't always remit its licence fee.

The sun was at the edge of the sky, large and fiery red. Bidding farewell to the world before going off to its resting place, it cast a look—mild, golden rays—on grass and trees, on hill and dale. The reflection of its shining face was like a friendly smile in the midst of the melancholy shadow that was approaching. It was somehow sad and happy, sweet and bitter at the same time. Nature on a summer evening is a bride who is being veiled; her beauty is unsurpassable, it tugs at the soul of the groom; his imagination is inflamed, he loses himself in contemplation of her face, which is shining out from under its veil, smiling at him, speaking without words and moving him deeply.

Shmulik, the same old-clothes man who chases around the city with his heart and mind focused on nothing but earning money, to whom nothing matters but bread, a goddamned piece of bread; this very Shmulik is reborn here on the green grass, in the fresh air. Noble and godly feelings awaken in him; his eyes look and take pleasure in God's beautiful world; his nose smells the sweet fragrance of thousands of herbs; his ears hearken to the choir of songbirds calling to one another from among the leaves of trees, rhapsodizing and jumping *Kedushe* on their little branches, their throats spilling over with melody, their wings flapping. Shmulik's soul awakes as if from sleep, his face is somehow changed. He looks and thinks, "Oy, it's wonderful"; thinks and feels, "Oy, it's so appealing, it fills your heart with yearning. It gives you a longing, a desire that can't be put into words."

As he was going along the path, he saw an expanse of green in the forest in front of him, wrapped in a dark cloak of shade striped with bright gold lines of light. He threw himself down on it and stretched out on the satin-soft grass.

Shmulik lay staring blankly upward; his limbs felt heavy, as if the earth were drawing him into itself in the same way as it drew the pains from his body. Yet his soul felt light, unbelievably good. A soft blade of grass was petting his nose and cheeks, another tickled him under the collar at the back of his neck, and nearby, somewhere in the grass, a cricket chirped into his ears. It told him a story, sang him a song, rocked him and put him to sleep like a child.

Shmulik lay half-asleep, half-awake, while images coursed through his mind: a trouble-free life, how good it would be to have kasha *and* soup, a house of his own, a small one, with a little garden and a cow, or at least a goat. *That* would be happiness; anything more would be too much. He thought about God. "Oy, Gotenyu, bring me success! Help me, Father in Heaven, show that you can make people prosper. Rescue me, Gotenyu!" And in his head he's already hatching plans for the donations he'll make for the Torah mantle with which, in his goodness and piety, he'll clothe the Lord . . . And then Moyshele came into his mind. A sweetheart, learns like nobody's business—God grant that someone wealthy grab him up for a son-in-law and make him rich. In time, Moyshele could even become rabbi of a big city somewhere, and then . . . then how good it will be for his father, too. He'll live out his golden years in honor and joy. The rabbi's father? No small potatoes.

These waking dreams were interrupted by the pounding of wheels on one of the bypaths in the forest. Shmulik opened his eyes, thinking, "Enough already. It's time to go home." He sat up slowly, yawned, knocked the kinks from his bones, and took up the cask that was lying by his side. A wagon was coming up from behind him, and as soon as it passed, a bitter cry resounded through the forest. "O, Daddy!"

Shmulik looked quickly around in amazement. "Moyshele? What? Where?" Fear and wonder let him stammer nothing else out. His heart told him right away that something was wrong, that Moyshele was in deep trouble.

"Faster, Daddy, save me," Moyshele screamed in a voice full of tears. He looked like a lamb flanked by two fiery-eyed wolves.

It didn't take a second for Shmulik to run up to the wagon and grab hold of it with both hands. But the wolves gnashed their teeth furiously and pushed him away, so that he tumbled head over heels twice along the ground. By the time he came to himself, they were already a good distance away.

Shmulik used all his powers to pull himself together, and he ran after the wagon as fast as he could. He ran, pursuing them, and they beat the horse, and beat it again. The wagon was getting farther away, there it goes, about to disappear. Shmulik was gasping, his heart was pounding. He could scarcely breathe, his eyes were jumping out of his head with anxiety and fear, but he kept up the chase, conscious of nothing but the danger. The wagon was beginning to disappear, and after a little while it was gone.

"Gevalt!" screamed Shmulik, tearing his hair as he ran. He lost his footing and fell to the ground.

This story took place in the days of the *kapore*-chicks—chickens sacrificed for one's own sins—or, as contemporary dirges labeled it, the time "of the hunt, of the game of cat and mouse." That is, the time when Jewish children were let out to play and show their skill in hunting—not with bows and arrows, not as the hunters, but as the prey, as when a cat goes hunting for mice. And everything was fair. A *kapore*-chick or mouse was the name for a kid who left home without a certificate with an eagle on it, a passport, I mean. The cat was allowed to catch him, to say, "This is my exchange, this is my substitute, this is my atonement," and put him into uniform in someone else's place. And there were Jews around who racked their brains to play tricks on other Jews, to take them all the way in and make them into the game.

Goddamned Shneur-Wolf had played his part well and seduced Hershele cleverly. But when Hershele unexpectedly slipped out of his claws and Moyshele turned up in the meantime, Moyshele fell into them in Hershele's place, and bang! he was "caught."

"*Brothers,*" lament the dirges from that time, "*All your hundreds of thousands slaughtered by the wicked Titus at the time of the Temple's destruction; who were killed, burned at the stake in Spain; all other such murder victims combined do not embitter our lives so much as the Jewish noses which the Jews themselves have torn from one another's faces. Yet there is still a consolation: Heroes! They died for their country . . . Martyrs! They were killed in Sanctification of the Name. But* gevalt, *what is the meaning of Jewish lives being ended by Jews? We weep over blows from others and say, 'What matter? The good and the weak often suffer in this world, perhaps the strong will yet have occasion to regret.' But when the beaten beat, the bleeding spill blood, we weep and say, 'Oy, vey.' For there is nothing to say. When we recall the tormented ones whom you yourselves 'caught,' our heart breaks, it weeps and cries out, 'How, oy, how horribly degraded, how sickeningly fallen is the people of Israel.*"

Book Four

1

THE WHOLE WORLD KNOWS that the lion's share of long Jewish noses has fallen to the middlemen of Glupsk. The Lord above has given them the gift of being able to sniff out the least little piece of business from under the ground; it's the only tool they have to feed themselves . . . Whence it's clear how good a God we have, how faithfully He devotes Himself to His little world, graciously endowing all of His creatures, from the eggs of lice, from the tiniest little worm to the Jewish middleman, with the equipment necessary to their sustenance. And Reb Asher, the chief among middlemen, a thin, lively, squirmy little Jew whose hat was always perched far back on his head, who was always twirling his cane, always in and out of all the shops and financial institutions—Reb Asher had been graced with an A-number-one, first-class nose: His soul appeared to have moved out of his head, taking his reason and wisdom with it, and relocated in the neighborhood of his nose. Immediately on Refoel's arrival in Glupsk, it—the nose, that is—sniffed out his commission business with the manufacturers in Lodz and started to drive him crazy with offers of deals. When Refoel wouldn't let himself be moved until he had become properly acquainted with the town and its merchants, Reb Asher was mightily amazed and said, scowling, his nose out of joint, "What? How can it be? A Jew—and he won't let himself do business? No offense, but it can only be because His Excellency has, uh, no feeling for business."

"And where do feelings come to business? For business you need brains, you need to understand what's going on."

"Nonsense," said Reb Asher, turning up his nose and raising his cane.

110

"I mean—you understand me?—I mean passion. You've got to have a passion for business. You've got to burn, burn with passion. Brains are nothing. Excuse me, but take a look at the leading businessmen here. *What*, huh? I'll give you a groschen for all their brains. People do business—what else?—that's why they're people, business people . . . But whether or not they earn money from it, that's all luck—it's God's business. *Mazl makhkim, mazl ma'ashir*—luck makes you smart and luck makes you rich. Riches and intelligence, and everything else—it's all a matter of luck."

"Business that's based on luck, on nothing but taking a gamble, is a card game, Reb Asher, a card—"

"I should know what you're talking about with your card games?" Reb Asher interrupted, turning up his cane and raising his nose. "Cards are cards and business is business. I'm maybe playing here, I'm offering His Excellency a toy? I'm talking business, vital matters of business!"

"Just listen, Reb Asher," rejoindered Refoel, calm and relaxed. "Business, just because it is so great and important—unbinding human hands to labor at good and useful crafts, sweetening this labor by expanding everywhere, bringing distant lands close together; educating and refining, feeding and animating a world of people—just because it is so important, business must be conducted like every other important activity, with calm and consideration, with understanding . . ."

"Tsk-tsk-tsk, His Excellency's off on cloud nine!" said Reb Asher in a bizarre singsong, waving his thumb, fanning his frantically wrinkling nose with it. "I don't know from philosophy. Philosophy, shmilosophy! Take a look—a good head, a brilliant head, a flying head, hoo-ha, hoo-ha! A real head for business, all right."

"A good head for abstraction isn't enough for business. A capital of general knowledge is also required." Refoel stuck to his guns, stinging Reb Asher with every word. "One must study, Reb Asher, study and learn plenty of things that have to be learned. Sharp, calculating Jewish heads without this capital of knowledge give us fraud; from fraud we get bankrupts, and from the bankrupts, poverty and penury. And from all of them together—quarrels, strife, denunciations, hatred from within and without. As long as business isn't based on understanding, on truth—"

"Ay-ay, you're still, uh . . . young yet, you'll excuse me." Reb Asher broke in on Refoel, shaking his head and grinning right into his face, looking at Refoel as if he, Refoel, were nuts. "What, what? Please."

"Just what I said. Indeed, Reb Asher, I'll say it again: Business ought not to exceed the bounds of reason, truth, and justice. There should be only as many factories and stores as the need for merchandise requires; the merchandise itself.shouldn't be counterfeit, adulterated with materials that nature does not use to produce the same articles. Everyone's effort should be honestly rewarded, each should receive his due. And chiefly, there should be a proper and open accounting. So long as this isn't so, I say, there is no hope that all the evils of misery, poverty, hatred, and jealousy—"

"There's nothing to talk about. G'day!" Reb Asher took his leave so as not to have to hear Refoel through to the end. He pushed his hat back, shrugged his shoulders, scratched his temple, scowled, and vanished.

"Good day, goodbye," said Refoel, when Reb Asher was already out the door. "What can you do? I'll just have to get along without Reb Asher's help."

Refoel was not only a scholar in his field, he was also a practical man who was as honest as he was able to be. Before he did anything else, he embarked on a close observation of Glupsk. It struck him as very curious in its houses, streets, lanes, and back alleys; in its Jews, its storekeepers and merchants; in its constant noise and running and haste; curious in all its ways. There was a great lust for business there—Jews did business with each other, drew their livelihoods from one another. A businessman may fall ten times a day and say, "Bankrupt," but he rises again and bargains on. So today, today I say "Bankrupt" to you, and tomorrow you say "Bankrupt" to me. Today this one holds the whip and cracks it, tomorrow that one. And so the wheel goes round, this one up and that one down, then that one's up and this one's down. Their lust warms them up, the Jews take fire, scheme, and do business.

Refoel saw that Glupsk was the place to market his goods. But because it's impossible to market anything without giving credit, and because you've got to be on your guard against bankruptcy, Refoel hugged the ground in his business dealings, and didn't hurry or rush. He sifted his customers carefully, gave credit only to the most reliable. Refoel's rule was: Better to earn less for sure, than a lot on spec; better to go slow and close to the ground than fly and fall down and break your neck. But Reb Asher the middleman didn't agree with Refoel, and he'd bring evidence from the *Medresh*, from proverbs, from the way of the world, to demonstrate the reverse of what Refoel had said.

"As I live and breathe, you're making a mistake," Reb Asher would argue, when Refoel showed no interest in the deals he'd tried to arrange. "His Excellency is living in error. Everything depends on luck. All my life—'I was a youth and now am old,' with a long beard—I've never seen a businessman strike it rich with his brains. Our holy sages tell us that the Lord's blessing is found only in trusting to things that cannot be seen—like buying an *esreg* in a box. And their words are really the sacred truth. Whoever does business on trust, blindly, so to speak, and straightforwardly, without too many deliberations—*Would I, should I, could I*—to him does the Holy One, Blessed Be He, send blessing and success in his dealings. Just be so good as to look at how the world works. Jews, thank God, do business; they buy, sell, take, give, and believe. The merit of their ancestors helps and protects them, and they go on living. Likewise, those storekeepers who want merchandise on credit and whom I've proposed to His Excellency, they're likewise living, thank God, along with their wives and children, married daughters and sons-in-law whom they support. Were there, God forbid, to be a lot of people like His Excellency among the Jews, the world would certainly come to an end. There'd be no trust between people—no more credit, no more business, no more livelihood, and finally, let's *fix* the anti-Semites, we'll all fall down and die. And what else? No one would plough or sow, out of fear that the earth might go bankrupt and produce no crops, not even those that had been put into it already. The Bible talks about this, too. It says explicitly *ha-zoyrim be-dimo*, those who sow with tears, *be-rino yiktsoyru*, will reap with songs of joy. It's true that credit is sown with tears, but whoever takes heart, whoever has faith and grants it, will be reimbursed by the Lord, Blessed Be His Name. And don't forget the proverb: Nothing ventured, nothing gained. The point is that a businessman needs luck, not brains. He needs help from above. You can be as smart as King Solomon, but if you've got no luck, you'll never do anything. Like they say, *eyn eytso ve-eyn tvune*, there's nothing you can do against a bad hand of cards."

These were the sayings and refrains with which Reb Asher was always trying to convince Refoel not to think things over or to deliberate too much, and to make deals with storekeepers through him. He affirmed his *shpil* with oaths and mortal curses: May he not live out his years, may he die a strange and violent death, have no portion in Paradise, not hear the shofar of the Messiah and not merit to lead his daughter to the wedding canopy, if he intended anything but the good of the deal. Simply put, he didn't mean his mediation so much as business itself; he wanted business to prosper and grow. But seeing that he was wasting his breath, that Refoel was not to be swayed, he'd try to convince him by force.

"What can His Excellency be thinking? Does His Excellency think he's the only one, that there's no one else besides him? Ha! Nu, you should know that there's a Moscow and a Leipzig in the world, thank God. And to tell the truth, the Glupsker businessmen are great big fools. What good is His Excellency's merchandise, which costs them so much effort and pain, and high prices, too, when the Russians and Germans in those other cities run out to greet them, tugging at their coats and begging, 'Here, Jews, here! Here's merchandise for you, top quality and super cheap. If you're strapped for cash, we'll arrange terms and you can take it on credit'? And the Jews go there and they take. And if you should sometimes break out in spots, that is, run into a bit of an obstacle and be unable to respond—to pay, I mean—on time, it's no big problem. The Germans and Russians are good people, they keep quiet. His Excellency should know that I'm not recommending those merchants who made their move a long time ago—you understand me?—but those *qui in Moskve numquam fuerunt*. His Excellency understands the meaning of these words? It means that they still haven't been to Moscow, it's still possible for them to go there and get credit and eventually end up with a nice sum of money. And if that's the case, you understand, if that's the case, then they're solid enough right here and right now. A wise man doesn't need any long explanations; one look should be enough."

Sharp words like this didn't help either.

2

REFOEL ADVANCED MERCHANDISE to the storekeepers for several months, according to the custom, but only on the strength of promissory notes from the most reliable people, people whose notes could be easily discounted immediately. Losing a fair percentage thereby didn't bother him, just so long as the money was safe in his pocket and he was able to sleep peacefully. One of the people to whom he discounted his notes was Red-Headed Leybtse, a wealthy Jewish moneylender in Glupsk.

As everybody knows, Red-Headed Leybtse, with his pale face, long nose, and short beard, was the pride of Glupsk, which used to boast of him before the world: "Here, behold my creation, my beauty, the work of my hands."

Leybtse was one of those people who had set his sights on high society, on cracking that exclusive clique that provides the people of Israel with all its officeholders, leaders, busybodies, big shots, activists, toadies, advice-givers, and similar tender souls who confer fabulous benefits upon us poor Jewish children, without our even asking. As a general rule, they're kind-hearted people, who squeeze the life out of others in the friendliest way. A cross word never passes their lips because they're too good to talk to anybody else. Jewish public moneys, which are under their control, are very dear to them, and are not to be spent on any needs but their own. They are happy to dispense with honor, as long as it's somebody else's. When the money comes out of another's pocket, they're big philanthropists; they sigh and moan for the Jewish people—sigh and moan like crazy, but they shouldn't actually spend a cent. *Yidishkayt,* Judaism, sure it's very precious, only slightly less precious than their least little personal interest.

Red-Headed Leybtse aspired to this aristocracy and yearned to get a foot in its door. He was no scholar, but what did that matter? Business made you a *makher,* not learning; learning was usually considered a flaw. "Just *because* you can learn, we can't let you into our club."

Red-Headed Leybtse wasn't burdened with children, two daughters were all he had. Khantse, the eldest, was pretty as a picture and the other one, still just a kid, was ugly. His wife, Yentl, was a big-bellied woman, the absolute ruler of the house. She was always shaking a bundle of keys, had a nice little nest-egg stashed away, and lived a very good life: ate, slept and did as she pleased, and was full-bodied and fat to boot. Even so, a sigh, a groan, would often escape her. She'd complain when she talked to her acquaintances, beat her breast to indicate the wound right there, in her heart. She'd shake her head, roll her eyes skywards, always with complaints against the Master of the Universe. "Oy, for a son, a *kaddish.*"

She'd tried everything already, had run the whole gamut of healers, doctors, and whatever else you want. You want old *shikses*? There were old *shikses.* You want Jewish wonderworkers or, excuse me, gentile magicians? There were Jewish wonderworkers and, excuse me, gentile magicians. And what happened? Nothing. The other women would assume a pitying look, shake their heads along with Yentl, take some of the snacks she'd laid out for them, and chew with languorous grace; they'd console her, and tears would come to their eyes.

"If I myself"—this was the standard form of Yentl's lament—"If I myself, *vey iz mir,* if I myself am so afflicted, so unfortunate, let me at least get some joy from my daughters. Let me be worthy in the eyes of Him Who Lives Forever, Father in Heaven, Merciful and Just, to lead my older daughter to the wedding canopy soon and live to see grandsons from her."

"Amen. Master of the Universe, if You'd only . . ." responded the other women, rolling their eyes and knotting their faces into unusual shapes, as if to say that they'd be more than happy, they'd be literally born again if the Lord would only have mercy on poor Yentele and bless her with some grandsons—and if not, God forbid, they wouldn't be able to endure it.

And so, Khantse was still very young, scarcely out of her baby shoes, when Yentl conceived a strong desire to find her a match. This desire of Yentl's was even stronger than what passes for normal among all women and mothers, for whom the mere idea of weddings, of matchmaking, of marrying off their children is a burning passion. Yentl burned, she worked with might and main and didn't give her husband a minute's peace: *"Gevalt! A groom, a match for our daughter!"*

But Leybtse wasn't in quite the same fever; he was very picky when it came to matchmaking. He wanted a son-in-law who had everything: a silken child from a prominent family, good and pious, with a head on his shoulders and steeped in aristocratic lineage, so that God and man would envy Leybtse alike. A businessman, Leybtse was looking to make a profit in the marriage market, to get his daughter a piece of goods that would benefit them both. Nothing else would do but to unite himself with social lions, become a member of the social register, the crème de la crème. He looked and looked and finally uncovered his treasure; he found himself a Bentsye, a thin, pale little boy with an emaciated face, just now bar mitzvah and already a candidate for hemorrhoids—in short, a jewel, the very thing he'd been hoping for.

Khantse got engaged in an auspicious hour, and became a wife, a Mrs., at fifteen. She and her "old man" lived on her father's board.

The "hubby" was a son-in-law with bells on. He went to the syna-gogue to *daven* every morning, loaded down with a *tallis*-and-*tefillin* bag as big as he was. After *davening*, he came home, kissed the *mezuze*, said "Good morning" to no one in particular, and not another word. He washed, made the blessing, blessed the bread, and ate. Having eaten, he went straight back to the synagogue to study, and came home at noon to eat again. Hav-ing eaten, back to the synagogue, back home at night. He kissed the *mezuze*, said "Good evening" to no one in particular, fulfilled the com-mandment of eating his father-in-law's board, finished eating, said the grace after meals, then the bedtime prayers and straight into bed—to sleep. There was a stale, rotten smell about him, the odor of a young husband out of a textbook, but it delighted Leybtse and Yentl.

Leybtse was enjoying himself, Yentl was delighted, and Khantse, meanwhile, was the same as before—nothing, only now her head was cov-ered. There'd been one little change in her since the wedding, though; she'd become somewhat diffident—she'd lower her eyes whenever she caught sight of her husband. It wasn't so bad in public, but among people she knew, she turned beet-red and tried to escape. Something was making her uncomfortable; what it was, was her secret. Her acquaintances would smile and wink at each other, as if to say, "We get it." Her mother would usually see her off with a mild look when she ran away, smiling and nod-ding her head and melting with pleasure.

Refoel's business used to bring him to Leybtse's house quite often. The first time that Khantse saw him—from a distance, through the open door of her father's room—he struck her as nothing she'd ever seen before: a human being, sure, a nose with eyes, but a different species of human. A different way of talking, a different kind of behavior, different clothing, different everything from anyone she'd ever seen before in Glupsk. She used to cast surreptitious glances at him, not, God forbid, for the sake of pleasure, not to satisfy some desire; no, it was just a little look—she was looking, and he happened to be there.

Her eyes were looking and her head still hadn't formed any definite opinion of him. She might have forgotten about him completely in a little while, were it not for her father, who used to speak of Refoel often, and praise him to the skies.

"You've got to hand it to that young man, I'm telling you. He's a clever one, knows his way around business with all its twists and turns. I'm positive that one day he'll go all the way, all the way, and take himself a bride with a dowry way up in the thousands. Mark my words. But it's a shame, oy," sighed Leybtse, striking his forehead with a finger, "That he's a little . . . what do they call it these days, a little 'fermented,' 'enlightened,' damn it. But beh! It's all right. There's a difference, you know. He isn't one of those penniless sinners. People, you call them? They're paupers! But him? He's a businessman—let those others die so he can live—he knows how to earn a ruble. He's a man, a real man, with a real head for business. You understand? A man like that deserves a bride with a really beautiful dowry!"

These praises went from the father's mouth to the daughter's ears, without the father having any notion of the mess he was making—a complete upheaval in his own home, may it not befall us. Leybtse's praises started Khantse's brain to working. Where things had hitherto been pitch black and peaceful inside her head, dawn started suddenly to break. Her youthful reason awoke from its sleep; her thoughts began to stir and work: she thought about everything, asked what this means, what that means, considered people and their ways, and divided them into those that were beautiful and good and those that were not. Refoel came up; Khantse's thoughts were working, swirling around him, looking over his face, his figure, everything about him. Bentsye also came to mind, just the way he was, with his face, his manners, all of his gestures—and she made a horrible face. Her thoughts went back to Refoel and she thought, "Yes, he *is* handsome. Yes, father, you're definitely right—he's better, he's smarter; there's no comparison." And her thoughts went from her head to her heart. Her feelings awoke, they tugged and tugged, luring her soul onwards. Her heart dropped a hint, and Khantse got a yen to see him again, oy, just to look at him for a while. But instead of "him," who came, as he did every day, but her husband, with his kissing the *mezuze* and his lovely "Good morning." She lowered her eyes when he came in, but no longer out of diffidence, no! This was something else already—he struck her as disgusting, made her feel sick. But she felt an immediate displeasure and considered herself to have done a great wrong. And against her husband, yet—can you believe it? Where does a Jewish woman come to such behavior? She made an effort to smooth her sin over, to take a look at her husband and show him a friendly face. And at the very moment that she'd managed to do so, who should pop into her head, alas, but him, Refoel, as if to spite her? Khantse was upset, she couldn't understand what was going on with her.

She tried to distract herself by working; she took an active part in the housekeeping, threw herself into different kinds of work that she'd never done before. Her mother was delighted; she urged Khantse on, melting with joy. "That's it, daughter. Learn to be a good wife to your husband until you're both a hundred and twenty."

Khantse was home alone one morning, there was nobody there but her. She was wearing a thin, snow-white little cambric jacket, quite close-fitting, with an embroidered collar buttoned tight against a neck as white as ivory. Her young face was charming, apple-cheeked, with a mouth worthy of an artist and moist, burning eyes glowing like a pair of diamonds from under thick brows. On her head was a silken kerchief, pushed back a little so that some hair peeked stealthily out.

She was busy wiping glasses and saucers from which tea had been drunk. As she was going to put them away in the buffet, Refoel came into the house. She turned around, took a look, and fell into confusion; pulled her kerchief down quickly, almost as far as her eyes, and stood silent and bewildered.

Refoel was somehow taken by this. He saw a beauty before him, still only a child, really, and already a wife who had to cover her head. He, too, stood for a while in silent amazement. He soon came to himself, greeted her in the new fashion with great politeness and respect, and inquired after her father. After she replied that her father wasn't home, Refoel asked if he'd be coming soon. She intended to tell him "no," but blurted an unwilling "yes" and offered Refoel a seat. She herself was amazed at what she'd done—why was she detaining him, asking him to sit?—but it was already too late.

It was the same with Refoel. He was sitting before he gave the matter any thought, as hang-dog as if the devil himself had planted him there. A single thought was pounding in his head, "C'mon, boy, get up and go. Don't be a dope." But his heart wouldn't let him: "Sit, sit, it's all right." Meanwhile, his hand moved to his breast pocket of its own accord and started to roll a cigarette.

Khantse was glad to be of some sort of service and brought him a package of matches. Refoel thanked her and tried to find something to talk about. It was difficult at first, short, desultory, disconnected. He kept asking questions. One question, then another, questions straight out of left field, and she kept answering yes or no, or simply nodding her head. But the more they talked, the easier it came. They started to talk about the Glupsker Jews: simple, straightforward Jews who didn't put on any airs; clever, pretentious ones; and so on and so forth. Khantse was interested in knowing whether Refoel was one of the "fermented," the "aristocrats," as they were called, and when she saw him make a face that was worse than the dirtiest curses, she perked up a little. "My father doesn't like them either. He can't even stand to look at them."

"Ah, your father," said Refoel, pursing his lips, as if her words were not to his taste. "His not being able to look at them is something else again."

Khantse stared at him in amazement, as if to demand an explanation. But Refoel saw that this was no time to enter into a deep conversation about things that she wouldn't understand, so he played dumb, pretended not to get her look, and went on to speak of something else.

And as they were sitting there talking, right in the middle of everything, the door opened and they caught sight of a large *tallis*-and-*tefillin* bag made from the skin of an unborn calf and trimmed all round with a strip of blue cloth on which white factory signs of some kind were embroidered, along with numbers to indicate the year. After the bag, a little hand appeared; it gave the *mezuze* a wipe, after the wipe a kiss was heard, and after the kiss there came a pair of little feet, and into the room slid a pale little youth in a capote made of lasting, a meerschaum cane in his hand, and a bizarre "Good morning" on his lips.

Bentsye threw a glance at Khantse, a glance at Refoel. He turned red as a turkey, ran quickly through the room on his little feet and into his alcove, extremely indignant. There was no jealousy, God forbid, in his angry look. Where did he come to jealousy? He didn't even understand the idea, would never have dreamt of such a thing. So what was the problem? What upset him, plain and simple, was her speaking with a male. Sitting unchaperoned with a man was already a sin: *Goye*, it isn't allowed—the law on this point is explicit . . . He'd have been just as angry about a meat pot near a dairy one on the stove; it simply wasn't right, even if the contents never mixed.

Bentsye's entry left Khantse to sit stewing in shame, a whole knot of contradictory feelings tangled up within her. The word *husband* itself, with all its unmentionable implications, was embarrassing enough to her—but when *husband* meant Bentsye? She was ashamed; his entry was a shame to her, his appearance was a shame, everything about him was a shame to her. Did she care what Refoel thought, what opinion he had of her *shlimazl*? But then she got mad at herself—what did she have to do with Refoel, with this perfect stranger? Let him think what he wants— who cares? Moreover, she felt insulted on her husband's behalf; she got angry—why should Refoel think ill of him? He's still hers, after all. Her having kept Refoel there was bothering her. What did she want? What was she after? Meanwhile she felt her heart drawing her, pulling her, dragging her toward him. She was agitated, confused; the blood rose in her face, she changed colors—and she was gorgeous, even more beautiful than before.

Refoel understood her situation and felt obliged to leave immediately. He wanted to go, he tried to go, but in vain—he couldn't tear his eyes from her. The two of them sat silently on tenterhooks.

A loud blowing of the nose, like the sound of a shofar, made itself heard from the other side of the door, heralding the arrival of Leybtse, who rejoiced to see Refoel in his house. He knew that Refoel only came on business, so he was always glad to see him; the more business he did with Refoel, the greater his earnings would be.

"Ah, company! It's so long since you've been here, we should make *shehekheyonu*. What's been with you, Reb Refoel? It's not nice, not nice." Leybtse was knocking his finger against his nose. "Tell me, is this how you treat a friend who really loves you, eh? Honestly! I was worried, I kept trying to figure out what I'd done to offend you. But God is my witness, and my wife and my daughter whom you see before you, that I'm completely innocent. If anything, it's the reverse; I think the world of you. I'm always telling you so, aren't I, Khantse? Nu, it's OK, it doesn't matter. What was, was. Now I'm really glad to see you here—and may God be so helpful to me in *all* my endeavors. So tell me, first off, how's your health, your business health, eh?"

"Good, praise God," said Refoel. "I'm doing plenty of business, and I'm even here on business now."

"Ay, ay. If that's the case, come into my office." Leybtse's face was beaming with pleasure. "Come, please. My daughter will allow herself to be imposed on and bring us a little whiskey and a bite to eat, won't you, Khantse? Or is your husband already home and you want to spend some time with him? Don't be ashamed, Khantse." Leybtse was so happy he was joking; he had one eye on Khantse, who had gone off in great embarrassment, and was winking to Refoel with the other. They went into his office.

3

AT THAT TIME, about forty or fifty years ago, dawn began to break over the long, dark night of Jewish life in our country. A fresh breeze blew in from the west, scattering the dense clouds that hung over the narrow Jewish world so that education, like the star of morn, could send down some of its rays. A small number of Jews rose to study at this dawn, some of whom, their eyes still bleared with sleep and not yet in full possession of their faculties, threw themselves about, rushing in every direction like madmen, breaking, overturning, causing damage in their haste. The rest of the community remained in bed, angry and muttering because its sleep was disturbed.

There were quarrels and heated exchanges between the two sides: one snorted at the other and said they were snoozers—rotten, stale, moldering merchandise. The others sneezed, gasped, yelled: *"Shkotsim!* Libertines!" One group ran farther and farther into the wide world, thinking of the happiness that awaited them there; the group still in bed dismissed them with a wave. "Idiots, you're gonna get hit. You're gonna come back whipped, with your head hanging down." Both sides were arguing, each provoked the other; there was a rift, a collapse . . . hostility.

Young couples were the most seriously affected. This shmeducation was poison to them; it caused trouble, ruined marriages. Young husbands threw their wives away and snuck off somewhere to study. Women started to dislike, to detest their little-boy husbands, to throw off their veils and become "loose." Sons-in-law like Bentsye were dropping like flies, a plague on them and may it not happen here.

Were anyone interested in taking a look at the registry books from that time, they would certainly prove that there had never been so many Jewish divorces as then.

Refoel's visits to Leybtse's introduced this epidemic to the house, and Khantse immediately fell victim. Her head was spinning, her tastes were changing. What once she liked was now *feh;* what used to be good was bad—all the symptoms of that lingering illness, may it not recur today. Bentsye revolted her; she felt sick just looking at him. And Refoel liked Khantse more all the time. He searched out time to see her alone. He was teaching her to think—he spent his time with her in intelligent conversation, and she swallowed his every word. New thoughts, fresh feelings awoke in her—she was stirred up, upset, steaming—steaming for Refoel. Refoel had lit a bright fire in Khantse's heart, and he was burning for her. But for the time being, the fire was hidden; each of them kept it smoldering inside, burning in silence.

Refoel, an upright, intelligent man with some experience of the world, made every effort to still the fire right from the start. He recognized the utter impossibility of realizing his wishes by honest means. Khantse, of course, had a husband; a jerk, to be sure, but still her husband. Jerky husbands aren't so rare as all that. And Refoel did not have it in him to come between them. Besides, there was also a yawning chasm between him and her parents. They were bigoted mouldy-figs from the world of darkness; he was one of the new breed, more or less. What did it matter? The mere fact that they could have a Bentsye for their son-in-law was proof enough of how far they were from a Refoel, as far as the heavens from the earth. Even if Khantse were to be widowed or divorced, would her parents want to marry her to him? And once they said no, it'd really be no. It's the parents who play the lead in putting together a marriage—what do the kids know, what kind of say can they have in such things?

Refoel considered everything carefully and asked himself what he wanted and where all this could lead. But if Refoel did business according to precise calculations that he made in advance, none of his calculations applied to such things as the feelings of his soul. His heart didn't know from accounts, and it didn't want to know; it did what it pleased, drew Refoel farther and farther, until he was past the point of return.

And Khantse? Oy, poor Khantse had trials and tribulations on every side. A good Jewish daughter, she suffered horrible pain at the hands of the Evil Inclination, which set her blood to boiling with sinful thoughts of love and made her feel things that—ay-ay-ay! God forbid they should even be mentioned! And she suffered just as horribly from Bentsye, her *shlimazl*. It was impossible to live with such a person. She hated him, couldn't bear the sight of him. Living—if that's what you want to call it—living together in *mésalliance* is a sin against oneself, against God and man. There was no possibility of getting rid of her *shlimazl*; she was in her parents' hands, they made all her decisions, and in their eyes, little Bentsye was full of grace, the most beautiful thing in the world. What did it matter if she hated, as long as her parents loved? In short, she was damned if she did and damned if she didn't—she couldn't win either way.

Women, may you never be tested thus! May such torments as Khantse's never befall you, O daughters of Israel!

Leybtse exulted in his son-in-law; he bragged and fussed over him in public, praised his wonderful virtues to the skies, and took great delight, whenever the opportunity presented itself, in recounting Bentsye's distinguished lineage, how he came from the crème de la crème on his father's side, and on his mother's from great rabbis, the highest of the high class, all of whom were now Leybtse's relatives by marriage—and that ain't hay. Rov Tsempel, the ornament of Israel, the light of the exile—he was a relative. And Rov, Rov-What's-His-Name, Rov Top-of-the-Heap—he was a relative, too. And so, let the Glupskers know just who Red-Headed Leybtse is!

His wife, Yentl, likewise boasted to her acquaintances of her sweet little son-in-law, Bentsyele, always praising and thanking the Lord for His gift, but usually ending off with a sigh and a sob. "Khantse's still not pregnant. Can you believe it? What is the end going to be?" She'd clutch her heart, tap it with a finger to show that there, right there, was the site of her terrible wound, God damn it.

Her friends were both merciful and talkative, as women tend to be, and each comforted her in her own way. One said, "Yentl, my dear, sha—enough crying. The merit of your son-in-law's holy family will intercede for you before the Throne of Glory, and in a year from now, God willing, your Khantse will give birth to a son." A second told some kind of story about a woman somewhere who didn't conceive for a long time; an expert in these matters came—don't ask *me* what he did—and the woman got pregnant right away: Would that the same should happen to Khantse. Another woman used plain common sense to prove that a little boy, even if he's already married, can't produce children yet: Man or beast, it was all the same. "When your Bentsye is older and grows up a little, God willing, he'll give you what you want—and with interest. Don't be afraid, it's all right."

Sometimes, when Leybtse had made a good discount-deal through Refoel and had taken a pretty penny right off the top, he'd invite Refoel and his closer friends in for an evening glass of tea, and, when they were all relaxed and at ease, he'd encourage his son-in-law, the living doll, to display his learning at the table, winking and blinking to Refoel to pay close attention. "Nu, Bentsye, say something. Short and to the point, something good; nice and clear, the way you can do it." And Bentsye would catch fire; he'd shake his hands and feet back and forth, spew out bits of *Gemore* and make a stew of them.

"Nu?" said Leybtse, whose learning was a little shallow, smiling and beaming, opening one eye wide at Refoel. "The real McCoy, isn't he?"

Refoel would answer with a wordless nod and exchange glances with Khantse, who was changing color from shame, thinking to herself, "Oy, you sure gave *me* the real McCoy, Daddy."

Leybtse did Bentsye in with his boasting. His bitter fate had apparently been inscribed somewhere in heaven: Leybtse himself, by means of his own speech and actions, should unwittingly teach his daughter to hate her husband and fall in love with Refoel. Had Leybtse been aware of this, he would sooner have committed suicide, God forbid, and buried himself six feet in the ground.

Once, when they were all enjoying themselves at the Purim meal to which Refoel and some other guests had been invited, Leybtse got a yen to display all the pomp and splendor of his son-in-law's learning—let everybody hear how nicely he construes a text and see what a jewel he is. "Sha," Leybtse clapped his hand on the table. "My son-in-law will interpret something from the *Megile* for us. Sha, you're gonna hear something now . . . Bentsye, let's go."

And Bentsyele, who had gone overboard in honor of Purim and taken a drop too much, started to speak with real ardor. "On the face of things, there's something the matter here. Why is Mordechai described as 'Mordechai the Jew'? What is the verse trying to teach me? Isn't it obvious, don't we already know by ourselves that Mordechai is undoubtedly a Jew? Mordechai is Mordechai! A Jew! What, they should call Mordechai a goy—put a question mark here—how is it possible? But if we lay even this question aside, along with all kinds of other questions that need asking and on which all the commentators touch, the insoluble old question still remains: Why is it written of Ahasuerus, 'He said,' and of Queen Esther, 'She said'? There has to be some meaning to this. Moreover, there's the matter of the emphasis placed on '*ten* thousand pieces of silver' and the '*ten* sons of Haman'—this is also problematic. Why do the verses go out of their way to stress the number ten in both cases, the *ten* thousand pieces and the *ten* sons, and what difference would it make if it wasn't ten?"

"*Oy vey!*" Leybtse was in seventh heaven. "Have you ever heard *any-body* take hold of a verse like that? Here a twist, there a twist, until he makes it—excuse me—into porridge . . . Is this the real McCoy? Go on, Bentsye, talk, keep talking."

"But everything's OK. The words of the holy Torah are as sweet as sugar." Bentsye let fly again in his sweet little voice. "The plain sense of the verses will give us the answer. As we know, the letter *yud* that was dropped from Sarai's name when the Lord changed it to Sarah, this *yud* wandered around for a long time until Yehoshua, that's Joshua, who was originally called Hoshea, acquired it, entered the land of Israel and subdued the peoples there. The *yud* rested there after the exile in Egypt, it prevailed, as we have already seen. Later, in the Persian exile, Mordechai the Jew (and Jew is *yid*, which is a way of pronouncing the *yud*) the *yud*-Jew Mordechai (and that's Mordechai with a *yud* at the end, not Mordkhe, as you'd say in Yiddish) and the *yud* mentioned in connection with Ahasuerus, which he received at the hands of Queen Esther in the word *vayoymer*, 'he said'—you understand? If *yud* also stands for the number ten in *gematria*, he overcame the *yud*, the ten, from the ten thousands, as well as the *yud*, the ten sons of Haman. Know then, that there are two kinds of *yud*: a *yud* of holiness and a *yud* of impurity . . ."

"Young man!" Refoel couldn't restrain himself any longer and interrupted Bentsye. "What do you want from the poor verse? 'He said' is masculine, 'she said' is feminine."

"I don't know about the feminine gender," screamed Bentsye, flaring into anger. "Only 'Frenchmen,' enlightened types, and scoundrels talk about masculine and feminine genders. *Vayoymer*—he said; *vatoymer*—she said, in all her finery, in the latest fashion."

This was a dig at Refoel and Khantse in the garden, a hint that they often sat and talked without a chaperone. It pricked both their hearts like an arrow. As far as his wife was concerned, Bentsye was dead from that time on; Refoel replaced him in her heart completely.

There were certain times when Khantse was home alone; Refoel knew these times and used to come and keep company with her. He always had some business idea ready, as a cover and excuse for Leybtse and his family in case of emergency.

On one such occasion he found Khantse despondent and weeping. She looked more beautiful than ever, like a rose with dewdrops on a summer morning. He couldn't hold himself back and asked her, in the mild, trembling tones of a devoted father speaking to a beloved, sick child, why she was crying.

Khantse covered her face and cried even more. Refoel thought that the pathos would kill him. He took her hand tightly, begging her, "Tell me, tell me."

Khantse shuddered, went warm and cold at once. The hand that Refoel was holding trembled. Refoel pressed on, begging, swooning until Khantse gave in: It turned out that she and her mother had had a terrible blowup over Bentsye. Coming home from the synagogue as always with his *tallis*-bag, Bentsye, who was very hungry, sat in his room for a long time, waiting for someone to remember him. He still hadn't eaten, there was froth on his lips; he scratched his temple, cracked his fingers, smacked his lips; he sighed and coughed, hiccuped and groaned, until his mother-in-law came looking for him.

"Oy, he still hasn't eaten! Really, it's like cruelty to animals," she blurted, wringing her hands. She ran off and brought her son-in-law his breakfast on a tray: two egg bagels, a pastry, and a cup of chicory. She spoke half in anger, half in sympathy. "Here, eat. Why should you sit quietly, why not tell your wife: Bring me food? *My* husband's no gentleman, I'll tell you. It's a miracle that I noticed you. What would have happened if I didn't? . . . You really hungry?"

"Fine, who cares, it's nothing," stammered Bentsye, screwing his face into a sweet-and-sour smile, and packing his board away with appetite. His mouth wasn't much for talking, but when it came to eating his board Bentsye, touch wood, was a champ, number one in the world.

Once our hero had finished eating and returned to his roost in the synagogue, Yentl went after her daughter, scolding her for the way she treated her husband. "Be aware, daughter, that I have a nose. Ay, do I have a nose! Ay, do I sniff things out . . . And my eyes haven't fallen out of my head yet either, thank God. Don't worry, I see how you behave to your husband. A fine wife you are! You should be bursting with pride, you should be beaming with joy to have such a husband—a blessing from God."

"Let the mother who bore him rejoice," answered Khantse, short and sharp.

"Some way to talk!" said Yentl angrily. "This is the thanks we get. Your parents bang their heads against the wall, for God's sake, plough the earth with their noses to find such a diamond. It's an honor to have a jewel like him in our house. Your father loves him so much . . ."

"He's welcome to keep him," said Khantse with a bitter smile.

"Oy, oy, am I unlucky." Yentl burst out sobbing and beat her breast. "Oy, I've a wound, right here I've got a wound. Since God has punished me, not blessed me with a son, I figured that I'd merit at least to see some happiness from *her*. But no! She doesn't wanna know. Marriage, shmarriage, she thinks; it's a toy, some kind of fiddle or drum, it's playtime—and nothing more . . . Enough acting like a kid, you hear? I'm telling you, you're a married woman. You understand what a married woman is?"

"A married woman is a person like everybody else," Khantse answered calmly, holding back her anger.

"Don't be so proud, Khantse," Yentl flared up, mocking Khantse's words. "A person, she says, a person? You're nothing! You're a female. There's nothing in the world for you except the three women's *mitsves*. *That's* what a woman is. Her womanly intelligence, her own will, are nothing. A kosher, pious Jewish woman is supposed to want to do her husband's will. And that's her womanly intelligence. That's what we were taught when we married. Now do you understand, Khantse?"

"No," Khantse fired back, turning as red as fire. "Where would *I* come to understand what a kosher, pious woman knows?"

"And everything I just said is only barking from a bitch?!" Yentl was shrieking with rage, waving her hand in Khantse's direction. "Just you wait. I'll teach you the meaning of husband, I'll teach you what husband means, I'll . . ." And she ran out in a fury, leaving Khantse to drown in her tears.

Refoel comforted her with sweet, mild words; he pressed and pressed on her hand and, in an access of loving feeling, blurted out, "Darling, soul of mine." Khantse let herself be comforted and looked at Refoel with moist eyes; a lovely, pleasant glance shone out through the tears still standing there—just like a sun shower.

Meanwhile, time was passing and their love grew and sprouted, grew greater and greater as it did so. Refoel sharpened Khantse's mind, taught her of a new kind of life and the means of attaining it: intelligent conversation and worthwhile books that were good for the soul. Khantse soaked up every word; her intelligence quickened, her soul was refined, her feelings became clearer. And Refoel grew more confident, hoping and hoping that everything, God willing, would work out with time. What had looked very difficult before, now looked very easy. Nothing was impossible in this world. Sooner or later, Khantse had to be rid of her *shlimazl*, and Refoel couldn't blame himself for that. It would have happened without him, it *had* to happen. Khantse and Bentsye were not at all well matched, the union was no good from the start. And what about her pious, bigoted parents? They wouldn't want a marriage with someone like him? Don't be stupid—money masks every sin.

Nothing can stand up against money. When there's money at stake, pious posturing and differences in matters of religion grind to a halt. No one Jews it up, no one assumes any airs for the sake of God, except those who figure to profit from it, to grab some coin by doing so. And *they're* just wretched paupers who are forced to make their living that way; if not, things would be so bad with them that they might as well lie down and die in the middle of the street. They're bums, no good for anything else. They're little people—who'd know from them without all this *shtik*, who'd pay them any attention?

This is the origin of the whole comedy of insane piety and goodness, of exaggerated love of "the people," of put-on sighs and groans for the sufferings of the world, of bleeding-heart pity for the poor, as it were, along with hatred, quarreling, intrigues, gossip, slander, and inciting people against one another. Virtually the only means of maintaining peace in the world and contentment among us sinful people who need so many things in order to live—almost the only means of doing so is money.

SINCE THE JEWS' WORLD soured and they became shopkeepers, bankers, moneylenders, usurers, middlemen, old-clothes men, and every other kind of businessman on account of their sins, from that time on the passion for love turned its back on them and the main influence in matters of marriage passed into the hands of the lust for business. Marriage today is also a business. Beauty, piety—these don't matter. The bride can be ugly, as long as she's rich. If a Jew with an eye for beauty should sometimes turn up, it's only proof that he's no real businessman, in the proper sense of the

word. He has something on his mind besides business and finance—nonsense, thoughts with no net worth. As soon as the passion for love catches
sight of an open heart, it rushes in and burns there, and plays its patented
tricks with an acrobat's skill.

This was the story with Refoel. Love, passion, could sense that he was
both a businessman and a man of feeling, and moved into his heart to play
its game. Its tricks conjured up an unbelievably beautiful world, filled with
every temptation and delight. It tickled him, stirred his desire, traced
Khantse's beautiful form from top to bottom—a statue of pure white, each
limb individually worked—and said, "Look how beautiful, son. Look and
dissolve with love." And Refoel's blood came up. He thought continually of
Khantse and vowed to himself that, come what may, he would eventually
uproot all the prickles and thorns that kept him from his rose.

The best thing for Refoel was to go after Leybtse, to court him until
Leybtse became stuck on him and believed in him body and soul. And Refoel knew just how to do it. He had realized that money, a nice little profit,
was the only key to Leybtse's heart, and that he, Refoel, held that key in his
hand. Refoel had been discounting his notes with a number of people besides Leybtse, and even though Leybtse was itching for the business and
kept trying to pry Refoel away from the others, he used to haggle over
every percentage point. It was hard for him not to haggle—what did it hurt
to try? A groschen is money too. But now, on account of Khantse, Refoel
started to shoot Leybtse as many of his bigger deals as possible. He wasn't
as choosy as he used to be—it was also OK to give credit to people whose
ratings were not of the highest; and losing a large percentage on the dis-
count didn't bother him so much anymore, as long as he could keep
Leybtse busy with taking his cut. Leybtse, who thirsted for interest, was
also none too choosy about whose notes he would take; a kopeck of interest was so dear to him that he'd sometimes risk the principal for it. In short,
Refoel made more deals, Leybtse collected more interest, and Reb Asher
the middleman worked happily away. His head was spinning with business,
his hat pushed way back on his head.

"What's the rush, Reb Asher?" He'd be running full speed ahead, the
skirts of his capote flying in all directions. "Stop awhile and tell us what's
new in politics, what's going on in your France."

The phrase "your France" didn't mean that Reb Asher was French or
that he had an estate there which he'd inherited from his parents, God for-

bid! Everybody knew that he was a pauper who had been born in Glupsk, that his parents were paupers and had left him no inheritance, neither here in Glupsk nor there in France. So what was it, then? Easy—whenever Reb Asher used to sit around and talk politics, he'd always refer to "my France," out of his great love for that country. You have to realize that Reb Asher was a walking, breathing newspaper for the Jews of Glupsk. He used to tell them the news: terrible, wonderful doings, wars, miracles that befell the Jews and persecutions visited upon them. People pricked up their ears and dropped their jaws with pleasure, hearing his smooth, sweet words. So, when they saw him charging down the street so quickly, they figured that something terrible must have happened and that Reb Asher was bursting with news.

"No time, I've got no time!" Reb Asher answered, continuing to run and not even looking at his acquaintances, who were standing there in amazement.

Others who met him stared in perplexity. "Reb Asher, your capote's all covered with mud, and the way you're running you don't even notice. It's a shame, good God! Such a nice new capote!"

"It's all right, it's all right," he said breathlessly, nodding his head without breaking his stride.

"*Gevalt*, Reb Asher, what's wrong? More troubles, persecution of the Jews?" Terrified Jews were stretching out their hands to him and screaming.

"Nothing, nothing," he called back from afar, continuing on his way.

"Ah, Reb Asher," said Shmuel the shopkeeper when Reb Asher flew breathlessly into his store. Shmuel spoke with a certain equivocal coldness and looked into his account-book, as if Reb Asher's appearance were less than welcome, despite the fact that Shmuel had been looking forward to seeing him and was really very happy that he had come. "Wait a bit, Reb Asher. Let me finish what I'm doing."

"No time, no time, Reb Shmuel. I've got a very difficult task in hand, a very, very difficult piece of work. You think it's so easy to buy from us, that whoever wants to can come and take merchandise and get credit? No, Reb Shmuel. It isn't like that at all. That Refoel," Reb Asher tapped his forehead with a finger, "that Refoel, I'm telling you, has a head on his shoulders, a first-class brain. How many times do you think he's made me dance around him, and how many more times am I gonna have to dance, until . . ."

"Dance as much as you want and do it in good health, but you don't have to dance around your Refoel on *my* account. And the work isn't as hard as you say," said Reb Shmuel the storekeeper in a wounded tone. He was hoping to increase his own worth and show that he, thank God, was an excellent credit risk, while incidentally reducing Reb Asher's role to keep him from asking for too high a commission. "I've got a Moscow out there, praise God. Moscow is better and safer in every respect—you understand me? But since Poltava's coming up, the fair there is just around the corner and I need merchandise right away—you understand? That's why . . ."

"That's why there's nothing more to talk about. See you later, Reb Shmuel," said Reb Asher, who understood subtle talk himself and was just as sly and clever as Shmuel. He wrinkled his nose, as if withdrawing from the deal, and made as if to leave the store.

"So quick to anger, Reb Asher? Where do you come to such a temper?" Shmuel was trying to keep his bridge unburned. He took Reb Asher by the skirts of his capote and gave him a sweet, shining smile. "Ay, you'll pardon me, but you misunderstood. Wait a minute, Reb Asher, stay here. What I meant when I said 'that's why'—listen, please—is that since Poltava's just around the corner—you understand?—and I need merchandise right away, that's why . . . that's why you should impose upon yourself, Reb Asher, and go quickly and close the deal in a good and auspicious hour . . . And now, enough business and scheming and dancing and jumping. Tell me better, Reb Asher, when you think we'll dance at your daughter's wedding? Maybe you'd like a dress for her, I've got some great stuff here— really exquisite. Take it on credit—eh, it doesn't matter, we'll settle later. It's OK."

Business was booming, in a word. A lot of people wanted merchandise, and Reb Asher was looking respectable in a new capote with a nice long tail to drag through the mud, running like a deer, "his loins girded up," completely absorbed in business—hoo-ha! His forehead was sweating, his nose sniffed and searched, his face shone like that of the High Priest after the Yom Kippur sacrifice. It wasn't so much the money he enjoyed, as the act of making it. He was doing business! Reb Asher was now very pleased with Refoel; he praised him to his face, praised him behind his back, saying, "Refoel has caught on to things, Glupsk has made a man of him. He's got a feel for business now, and there's hope that with time he'll become an important man, a real chamber-of-commerce type."

Refoel's strategy had succeeded. Leybtse fell in love with him, wouldn't let him leave his side. If it wasn't "Please, come over for lunch or tea or *kreplach*," it was "Come on over for a while, what's it to you?" Leybtse's intention was simply to keep an eye on Refoel, he shouldn't do business with anyone but him. As far as he was concerned, Refoel was good and also pious, a model Jewish boy. When others used to demur, pointing to his dress and behavior, which had nothing to do with Glupsk's ideas of proper Jewish conduct, Leybtse would say, "Ay, you fools, you! The Ychupetser *tsaddik*, may his memory be a blessing, said a long time ago that there are many ways of serving the Lord, and that everyone serves Him in his own way. Refoel's behavior is also a way of serving God."

Since Leybtse was treating Refoel like a brother, Mrs. Leybtse was automatically Refoel's sister-in-law; she'd receive him warmly, and always with a tray of preserves for a snack. Yentl was a kosher Jewish woman, and she did her Leybtse's will. Refoel naturally did Leybtse's will; he dropped by the house daily, without even waiting to be asked. As a member of the household, he had frequent opportunities to spend time with Khantse— what did it matter to the rest of the family? They're kids, members of one big family. A little later, Leybtse gave Refoel an opportunity to teach Khantse to write, that is, to read and understand languages, and Refoel was jubilant. It happened like this:

One day, Leybtse ran breathlessly up to Refoel as soon as he'd crossed the threshold, stuck a letter written in goyish, that is, Russian, into his hand, and said, "Here, read. Read it and tell me what it says."

From the expression on Leybtse's face and the way he spoke about the letter, he appeared to consider it a virtue that so fine a Jew as he, a member of the upper classes, should know no Russian. It was as if he were saying, "Here! This sort of, uh, *thing*, is more in your line." Refoel was rather bothered by this and after reading the letter, he said through pursed lips, "Tell me, please, what you would have done if I hadn't come along today?"

"I would have got someone else to read it."

"Oy, it's no good to go to strangers, and have to depend on their kindness," said Refoel, shaking his head. And he suddenly lit up with a great idea. "It's true, of course, Reb Leybtse. I know very well that kosher, pious Jews are wary of learning sciences or outside matters, including languages. But where I come from there's a lot of very scholarly Jews who learn nothing but *Gemore*. Their sons also learn nothing but *Gemore* in *kheyder*. But still, they let their daughters learn to read and write goyish, and nobody takes any notice. There's lots of men like this—they sit and warm the benches in the synagogue all day, while their women earn a living in the market. Women and girls get dressed up and sit in the shops; they pull in customers and sell the merchandise. If a nobleman gets cute with them once in a while, "Khayke, Surke, pretty little girl"—it's no big problem: Is this even a person, that you should take offense? And if he should give a pat or a pinch in the cheek, it doesn't matter either; it's like a cat rubbing against you . . . So you see, girls are allowed. Because according to the law, a woman is exempt from the *mitsves*—she's free to learn goyish. She can look into their books as much as she wants, just as long as she doesn't, God forbid, learn Torah, our holy Jewish Torah. Because the *Gemore* says that whoever teaches his daughter Torah, teaches her to be wanton . . . So let me ask you, Reb Leybtse, why you shouldn't let your daughter learn writing and all the rest of that crap? You're the one who would benefit if she could read and write letters for you in emergencies."

"Yeah, true . . . On the face of things . . ." Leybtse was stammering out disconnected words, wrinkling his brow and tugging at his beard. "You might even be right, but . . ."

"What's the problem?"

"E . . . e . . . listen. If my daughter were still a girl, I would have agreed. 'Go, daughter, to the letter-writer and learn women's sciences with all the other girls.' And I would have, really. But now that she's married, it's a little . . . awkward. Did you ever hear such a thing? A wife, the woman of a man, sitting with little girls! It's as if the *shammes*, for instance, a Jew with a beard and—excuse me—a belly, were to allow himself to be called to the Torah with the kids on Simkhes Toyre."

"Then let the teacher come to you . . . You know what? If you want, Reb Leybtse, *I'll* be the teacher."

"What are you talking about? You, Reb Refoel, a businessman, a respectable person—you want to be a *melamed*, you want to make the kind of living a *melamed* makes?"

"For free, Reb Leybtse. I'll teach your daughter for nothing."

Inwardly, Leybtse agreed to this plan right away, but out of respect, as it were, for Refoel, he vacillated, made sour faces, and told Refoel that he'd have to talk it over with his wife. He did so that night, and they decided to accept: Refoel was one of their own, a close friend, so what difference would it make if he taught Khantse reading and writing while he sat and talked with her? It sure couldn't hurt; on the contrary, it would be very useful for her. She'd learn how to read *tkhines* and to write a letter in her own hand, instead of having to beg for favors from others. It would also be useful to them in business. And what else? It wasn't going to cost them a plugged nickel. So sure, great.

Refoel began to teach Khantse after his fashion, and to tell the truth, he did his job with fervor and devotion. Khantse gulped down her *rebbe*'s Torah and the shopkeepers grabbed up Refoel's wares. Reb Asher the middleman worked and was exalted, and Leybtse took his cut and made money—in short, it was one big party.

5

IT'S LATE AT NIGHT. Glupsk is asleep. But two Jews can't get a wink; they toss from side to side, the beds work beneath them: creaking and groaning, giving a concert in the manner of Jewish beds, which rock, shake, make noise, raise their voices to heaven at the slightest movement. To hear the massed nightly choir of ten beds in a Jewish house is a joy and a privilege. But don't worry—you could get the same effect from this two-man band with its lopsided, unbalanced, humpbacked, worn-out plank-bed and its fold-out cot. Hershele was playing the plank-bed in the vestibule, while Refoel played the fold-out in his alcove. Both of them had too many problems to be able to sleep.

Refoel had kept his word and taken Hershele in as a lodger, just as he had promised. The first time Hershele came in to spend the night, he was as happy as someone whose luck had suddenly changed for the better. The small, low room where he could be alone for awhile, undisturbed by the crowds in the synagogue, looked like a palace to him. He looked at all the things there with a sort of respect, almost afraid to lay a finger on them—he'd tap, but not really touch—and he smiled with pleasure, as if to say, "Hey, pretty good, eh, Hershele? We've sure got one heck of a God!"

The decrepit plank-bed was weak on its feet, worn down, splitting apart, with bits of oakum sticking out of it, and old, greasy patches over the holes—just as it was, the bed was as beautiful to him as anything he'd ever seen. Faded and impoverished as it was, it was still an aristocrat—and with a nice bulging stomach to remind him of its former prosperity.

The first time Hershele climbed into it, the bed reproached him loudly with an offended creak. Holding his breath, biting his lips, Hershele stood on one leg, neither in the bed nor out of it, afraid of raising a hue and cry and of waking Refoel up. But he took a chance, and after begging the bed's permission, slid himself in very slowly, first extending one leg, then the other—and it was fine, everything went well. After a short time, a little rebuke no longer bothered him much, and he eventually got used to the big ones too. The bed could scream, could fight angrily back—Hershele didn't notice. He slept well, he slept through the night like a corpse.

So why then was this night different from all others? Why was Hershele not sleeping this night the way he slept every other night of the year? Was he hungry? Did his empty stomach demand food before it would let him sleep? No! In the first place, the Jewish stomach is not so obsessed with food that it starts to complain as soon as it doesn't get some. Secondly, a stomach isn't so big a deal to the Jews that anyone would listen to its complaints. There are so many laws, old and new, devoted to the stomach, the sinful stomach, devoted to teaching it to eat like a *mentsh:* Don't even *want* this, it's illegal as pig, you're not allowed. *That* you can have, but only a lick, just enough to make yourself *fleyshik*—it's too expensive. There's something else that shouldn't be found within your borders at certain times— you're not even allowed to look at it—and something else again of which you have to eat a piece at least the size of an olive, even though it's unpleasant and bitter . . . And we, the Children of Israel, we and nobody else have plenty more laws of this type, by virtue of which we've managed to keep ourselves alive on the earth.

Where were we? In the third place, Hershele's stomach had nothing to complain about. He'd never gone to bed hungry since he'd started sleeping at Refoel's. There was a glass of tea and a piece of bread for him every night of the year, and on this night there had even been a herring head and a bone with a bit of meat on it, left over from the lunch that Refoel had barely touched. Hershele didn't touch it at all.

Could it have been that Hershele was having trouble with a *Gemore?* Was his brain pounding away at a difficult *Toysfes,* trying to pin down the difficulty that Rashi was anticipating with his "as it is said elsewhere," and come up with a subtle and clever conjecture or else find the proper way of stressing the words? Could this have been keeping him from sleep?

No, again. It had been a long time since Hershele had paid much attention to his studies. When his friend Moyshele was around, he used to spur Hershele on and encourage him to learn with single-minded devotion. But since Moyshele was gone, Hershele's head was always off in the clouds; his studying, such as it was, was as appetizing to him as a plate of warmed-over oakum. Today, though, he really did get lucky—he gave a study like a pro, really got into it, and everything in the *Gemore* finally appeared in all its unearthly clarity: Rashi is not, God forbid, crazy, and the question of the *Toysfes* is still valid, too—they're both right.

So Hershele's insomnia is still a question. What's the story with him today? The story is that he couldn't sleep because of Beyle. "Ay, Master of the Universe, *gevalt*, Father in Heaven, where is Beyle?" These few words were tapping at Hershele's skull, diverting all his thoughts to themselves and occasionally escaping from his mouth with a deep, dire groan.

It was already quite a while since Hershele had parted from Beyle at the slave market, hoping that once she'd set herself up as a maid wherever the agent had taken her, they'd see each other again and resume their discussion of every little thing back home. Miserable and uprooted, Hershele couldn't talk enough at his first meeting with the daughter of a neighbor, practically a relative, a close friend from childhood on. She was redolent of home, of Kaptsansk. Beloved images of days gone by shone out from her eyes. He could feel them in her look, sense them in her voice. He swallowed her every word eagerly, talked enough for ten himself, and had plenty still left to say.

Hershele had looked high and low for her, but no Beyle. Vanished without a trace. At first he comforted himself with the hope that she'd undoubtedly turn up soon. "Why shouldn't she? Maybe she's really busy in this new place of hers. Once she's had a chance to get her bearings, I'm sure she'll go straight to Reyze's. After all, she left all her things there." But after about a month, when she still hadn't turned up, he started to worry for real. It was becoming clear that his interest in Beyle had less to do with her recent arrival from their common hometown than it did with Beyle herself, and with the great pity she deserved: "Who knows what could have happened to her?" Hershele's feeling of pity grew out of another, hidden feeling to which he couldn't put a name—a sort of yearning that had lurked deep in his soul from childhood on. This sort of yearning was starting to make itself felt more strongly, and it finally assumed a name through the constant increase of his pity. These two feelings blossomed and grew and fed off each other. And there was one other factor there, of no small importance: Hershele realized the extent of the danger that he had been in. Had Beyle not shown up, Shneur-Wolf would certainly have put Hershele into uniform and made him into a soldier. God Himself sent her at just the right time to save him from Jewish hands—how many thanks did he owe her for so great a favor? As the saying has it, he should have washed her feet and drunk the water. But what happened instead? She rescues him and he buries her: their quiet exit from the inn to the slave market led him out of, and her into, trouble. Oy, the Angel of Deliverance had disappeared, God knows where. It was a pity, a heartbreak.

This all had a powerful effect on Hershele, calling forth thoughts and burning, unambiguous feelings that had previously been obscure, practically secrets to him. Beyle's image appeared ever more brightly before him, burning him, haunting him, tugging at his soul. He just thought of her, without meaning to; sometimes he'd cry quietly, his heart would soften and he'd let his thoughts carry him off like a baby in its swaddling—and off he'd go, flying to God knows where. Beyle never left his mind, but he couldn't figure any way to find out about her. He could go around and ask? It wasn't fitting for a boy to go asking after a girl. And look at the boy— Hershele, who couldn't even mention the name without blushing. He could see all too clearly that people would have no trouble guessing what was on his mind, or seeing what kind of good boy he really was. And then he'd be exposed in front of everybody, he'd lose both this world and the next. "When had such a thing been heard of among Jews?" It was no joke, not even to think about. Gehenna was punishment enough for such sins, but to fall into Jewish mouths? . . .

Hershele's only consolation was that Beyle might already have gone home. But what about her things? Hadn't she left her bundle at the inn? So she forgot it—anything could have happened. She was in a hurry, in a rush and forgot about it. And since it was a nice warm day, and the sun was shining, he was inclined to soothe himself with this thought. His great joy had him swaying over his *Gemore*, throwing himself into his learning, singing with sweet devotion, and cleverly ironing out all the difficulties in the text.

So what does Satan, the spiteful son of a bitch, go and do? He stands there laughing at Hershele, thinking: "Be happy, be happy, my pretty. Pretty soon I'll have you singing a different tune."

And right in the middle, while Hershele was learning with such light-hearted abandon, Satan's promise was fulfilled. Hershele received a long-awaited letter from home, which he started to read with great eagerness. "*P.S.*," his mother ended,

Unfortunately, I wandered off topic, and on account of all my troubles I forgot to ask after Ben-Tsiyen Tsviyes' daughter, with whom I sent you a pair of darned stockings, a little capote, and a patched shirt—wear them in good health until you're a hundred and twenty. Tsippe-Sossye, may she be well, pulled the stockings from her feet to send you—may God have mercy and send her a husband, it's time already. The poor thing's withering like a leaf, turning yellow and green; she's miserable and I'm unhappy, looking at the bitter sorrows that we both have to face. My eyes are going—may the Jews be spared my fate—from plucking feathers all night. Oy vey iz mir—what a wretched widow I am. It hardly pays at all, not enough for water to boil porridge with—woe unto such a living, such a life. I can barely keep going . . .

Blessed be Esther-Leye, our old dairywoman, who gives me a jug of curds from time to time, and a little milk on credit. Her cow had a calf on the first night of Slikhes; God, may He be blessed, blessed her with a perfect little calf, the best in the world. A calf like this comes along once in a century. You can imagine that Mordkhe the butcher, who isn't such a big giver—he'd let his eyes be plucked out for a groschen—Mordkhe jumped up and gave her ten guilden in cash for it, and let Esther-Leye keep the giblets. People say that he made a fortune off it—six guilden for sure, maybe seven or even eight . . .

Anyway, what I wanted to tell you—my troubles have made me forget already—oh yeah, the girl. A-ha. As if your own troubles aren't enough, there's always somebody else's, as they say. I mean Ben-Tsiyen Tsviyes—he's old, sick, a shell of a man. He has no work and no money. (None of the kaptsonim *in Kapt-sansk can remember poverty like today's. It's a miracle that we're alive, a favor to our virtuous forebears.) And now the Blessed Name has punished him, God forbid, with a new kind of punishment: his daughter, the one with whom I sent you stockings and a little capote cut down from your father's, RIP, capote—there's been no word from his daughter since she went away. He can't take it. It's true, of course, that she doesn't know how to write—writing is no work for a woman—but you can still get a man to do it. What do I do? I impose upon Reb Faybish the teacher, may he be healthy; I tell him what to say, and he writes and writes, adding his own pepper and onions, making my words into fragrant nutmeg, appetizing and delightful. (The rhetorical figures of pepper and onions don't originate with your mother. How could a woman come up with such things? They come from me, Faybish.) Are there no letter-writers, no teachers in so Jewish a town as Glupsk, where the very shabbes goyim who heat the ovens in the synagogue can speak Yiddish and know when you bless the new month and when the new moon falls out? My son! I command you on the authority of "Honor thy father and mother" that, should you see the girl or know aught about her, you should, for God's sake, write; you'll purchase a place in heaven for yourself. Her father, Ben-Tsiyen, doesn't know what could have happened; he's suffering terribly. And Tsviye cries and worries; maybe, God forbid, the girl has died.*

Had Hershele swallowed an olive-sized piece of horseradish all at once, it would not have penetrated his nose and eyes as deeply as his mother's words. Only the reading-stand on which he'd been leaning over tractate *Beytso* in the corner of the *shul* kept him from falling. His heart was full of sorrows that he could not pour out; on the contrary, he kept his pains concealed so that the others in the synagogue wouldn't notice. But when night fell and he went back to Refoel's, where the latter's bed was already creaking and chorusing in its alcove, Hershele flung himself onto his bed and started to think and sigh and groan about Beyle. And the plank-bed played its obbligato, accompanying the fold-away, clinking along in its fashion.

6

SO WHAT IS IT TONIGHT? And why can't Refoel sleep? It's late already, and the fold-away bed croons and creaks beneath him without stopping. It must be trying to tell us something—nothing too welcome.

It had been a day of working and running around the market for Refoel. He had come to terms with quite a few merchants and advanced them as much merchandise as they asked for. He came home in the evening exhausted, just about ready to collapse, but before he'd had a chance to rest or start his accounts or think over what he had to do tomorrow, the mailman came in with a letter. Refoel read it and his heart sank. The factory from which he earned his living was writing in strictest confidence: it was in dire straits, hemorrhaging. Should things, God forbid, continue like this for a little while longer, it was going to—let the hour never come—go under. In the meantime, there was no way that they could send him any merchandise; instead, he should immediately send them as much money as he had. It was a matter of life and death, for God's sakes.

Refoel lay on his bed in terrible misery; his head was splitting, his heart almost burst. He considered his situation from every point of view, went over it again and again: The factory was, God forbid, going bankrupt—this was bad! Goodbye business, he was ruined. The merchants who had taken merchandise on credit would probably do the usual thing and also declare bankruptcy if the factory went under, and not pay their notes at the agreed-upon time. What were they, fools, that they wouldn't make use of another's misfortune, or turn this bankruptcy to their advantage? There were plenty of ways to do so. There was the trick, for instance, of buying up the papers that the factory holds against you for next to nothing, and then using them to cover your debt. "This is my substitute," it's called, and you, go be the *kapore!* Declaring bankruptcy has been a regular practice among business-men from Laban the Swindler to the present day; you need only to know what you're doing, to know the forms and attitudes needed to pull it off like an expert.

And to make matters worse, he'd made deals today that exceeded all reasonable limits. The devil only knows why he'd taken almost all his mer-chandise and more or less tossed it to him, the devil. And now he was stuck—no merchandise, no money. How was he to respond to this urgent request for money? Should he sell the notes from his new accounts, when he knew how great the danger of bankruptcy was? He'd just as soon die— this was theft, pure and simple, picking the pockets of others.

Thinking of these things, he eventually thought of Leybtse—and tossed in the bed, trembling in every limb. Hadn't the better part of his notes gone to Leybtse? And *whose* notes? Not so much those of the better credit risks as those from merchants you put up with only as long as the going was good and there was a surplus of merchandise in the factory: they'd pay on time to start with, just so they could increase their credit later and be able to choose whether or not to pay . . . And why had he gone off on such an ill-considered jag? To rake up big interest, big earnings for Leybtse. And he only did *that* on account of Khantse, his dearly beloved

Khantse. And now it would all come out to nothing. He himself was finished, he had no further function. The merchants would find a way around paying and Leybtse would lose a pile of money because of Refoel—he'd become his blood enemy and not let him cross his threshold. Ay, it was terrible. He'd lost his commission and, *oy vey*, Khantse too . . . Refoel felt a pang in his heart, he gave himself a toss, and the bed creaked and creaked.

His conscience wasn't silent, either; "Swindler! What world were you in, wasting other people's money, squandering it for the sake of your whims, to get what your eyes beheld and your heart desired, what your sinful little being yearned for and what brought you pleasure? Windbag—when it came to preaching, you knew how to talk: truth, justice, consideration, humanity, understanding—beautiful, orotund phrases. Always chastising, always moralizing. You wanted to improve the world, you weren't happy with the one we've got now: Reb Asher the middleman-in-chief was the liar-in-chief; Gershon the shopkeeper, a swindler; Zelig the businessman, a cheat; Reb Nakhmen the congregational treasurer, a devil, and so on and so forth, not a single honest man. And you? Suffer, you swindler, and don't put on any airs!"

His conscience gnawed like a worm. Refoel tossed and the bed creaked. From the other room, the plank-bed was making itself heard, drilling holes in Refoel's skull. It seemed to be creaking with resentment, scolding, upbraiding him on Hershele's behalf: Why had he forgotten about Hershele all this time? Refoel had been very fond of Hershele since his first appearance in his house. He saw a quiet, thoughtful boy, poor and all alone, and felt great pity for him. The boy came home punctually every night, so quiet and calm as not to bother a fly on the wall. He kept his mouth closed, but his eyes spoke for him; his sadly thoughtful look complained of his sufferings in this world. His pale face and ragged clothes, his whole appearance, tore at your heart. From the way he looked at Refoel from a distance, anyone could see how much he loved him, how he clove to him with all his limbs, with body and soul, as if to a father. Refoel felt a certain obligation to do something for the boy, and had made up his mind to devote himself to him and make something out of him. But business and Khantse distracted him so that he had no time left for the kid, and whenever he popped into Refoel's mind, he'd put it off until later, until he forgot about him completely. And now, as he hears the creaking of the plank-bed, he is reminded of Hershele and his heart swells. "Oy, I forgot all about him.

Oy, what a pity. The poor, lost lamb came to my house seeking help, and I didn't pay him any attention."

His conscience was torturing him. "Nice guy! Good, kind and merciful with your mouth, but you don't do a single damned thing. You're all alike, you bleeding hearts, you benefactors and providers. As soon as there's business to be done, you harden your hearts; as soon as it's a matter of your own desires, nobody matters anymore; as soon as it's *your* life, everybody else can drop dead. You're actors, magicians, game-players— wicked people with hearts of stone, eyes of glass, faces of bronze!"

The plank-bed groaned and rebuked him; his conscience pecked. Refoel tossed and his bed creaked.

7

"SHIT ON GLUPSK!" raged Refoel. He awoke terrified and panicky after having dozed off for a bit, and spat in anger. Sounds had reached his ears from the street: a fiddle playing, a flute shrieking, a drum banging like crazy. "Nu, Glupsk—always a racket! Day and night it's all hoo-ha! Cling-clang, fires! Hop, hop—weddings! Stop, stop thief! Not a moment's rest, tfu. Only the wicked should have to endure it."

To be truthful, Refoel was doing Glupsk an injustice. Up until now, its fires and weddings and thefts hadn't bothered him. It could have gone up in flames ten times a night. The alarm bell could have rung, the kettledrum beaten, the robbed could have screamed bloody murder, and he would have gone on sleeping soundly. He was used to it already—madness or disease, it made no difference to him. So what was it, then? He was jumpy, flew into a rage at the least little thing—so he was taking it out on Glupsk. Refoel got out of bed, opened the window, and looked out on the street.

A fresh morning breeze blew into his face, caressing him, kissing his cheeks and eyes, playing with his hair and clearing his head. It was brightening outside, the eastern sky was reddish with a pale dot, the moon, shimmering far off. It was a mixture of day and night, the contention at their meeting. There was a sense that the sun was near—here, you can see her a bit; there she is in all her glory. This is the message of the swallows who, with eyes half-closed, have left their nests to hover and spin through the air with a song. This is also the message of the musicians in the street, as they escort the new parents-in-law home with the melancholy tune known to all of Glupsk as "Day Breaks After the Wedding Feast."

A thin, pale little Jew is walking slowly along with them, one of those Jews who live ten to a room somewhere in a back street—poor and ragged, humiliated, crushed under a mountain of gloom, terrified to lift their heads up. Now, however, the little Jew walks proudly, with pomp, at his ease, in clothes worthy of Shabbes, in shoes and white stockings, his head tilted back, his hands folded behind him under his coat, holding onto its skirts—and he lets himself be honored. Musicians are playing away, little boys in coveralls run ahead, their shirttails sticking out behind them; a woman with her jacket half-off and tucked into her apron, the ends of her kerchief undone, hops about by herself, for herself, waving a handkerchief in the air with her free hand, spinning, reeling, happy and lively. It's nothing? A *kaptsn* and his wife, two fine new in-laws, are being escorted home with a march through all the main streets—let Glupsk not sleep, let it not be slow to awaken and see!

Refoel turned his nose up with a sour expression; he didn't seem too pleased with all the hullabaloo. For his money, it wouldn't have been such a tragedy if the in-laws would have walked home on their own little feet without the help of an orchestra.

Refoel turned away from them and looked into the street, where Glupsk, the great beauty, revealed herself before him in all her morning—you'll excuse me—nakedness. The gutters, the "fragrant perfumes" poured out of the houses last night, were scenting the air; the houses, their shutters still closed tight, looked like giant garbage cans, with all sorts of good things lying in front of their doors: bones, crumbs, all sorts of household goods. Pigs, the tycoons of the animal world who always earn more than a living wherever they happen to be, were eating what had been prepared for them, absorbed in activity and munching with pleasure. Dogs—jobless paupers with no means of earning a living, dying of hunger—skinny greyhounds, cripples, ragamuffins of every type, were rummaging in every corner, begging, looking for a piece of bread. A dog sticks his nose into the workplace of a pig, giving him a bite in the ear as he does so; the pig takes it badly and gives a grunt, the dog opens his mouth with an arrogant bark, a pack of dogs comes running and a battle ensues over a bone—tearing, biting, each one snatching it from the mouth of another. Crows were wandering around there, too; thieves, rascals intent on getting hold of something for themselves. One of them was standing on a pig's back, craning its neck and watching slyly out of the corner of one eye as the pig busied itself in a pile of trash; no sooner had it found something than the crow jumped down, grabbed it, and flew quickly away. The cows rose at the crack of dawn from where they had been lying in the street, licked themselves from front to back with their tongues or else scratched themselves, rubbing against a wall, and went off like good housewives to sniff out bargains in the market. Whatever God sent was fine—a straw or piece of hay was a good enough find.

At that time of the morning, the Glupsk market with its various four-footed creatures and their customs, their chasing after a profit, looked the same to Refoel as the fairs of the sinful two-legged creatures with their swindles, tricks, and cheating. He stood distracted, lost in thought: outlandish creatures, two--and four-footed, kept spinning around him, exchanging faces, all of them blending together.

A bang from the vestibule brought him back to reality. He lent an ear and Hershele came into his mind. "O, Hershele," he thought with great pity, "He must be awake. Just like me—he didn't close his eyes all night. What could it be? Maybe he's sick or maybe his heart is telling him that it's pointless to rely on me. Who knows where I'm going to end up, and he'll lose his place to sleep. Poor kid—his happiness lies in that broken-down bed. So who's to say then what's good and what's bad? Everyone is made from the same stuff, yet how different they are in their needs. The biggest palace is too small for one, a space to lay his head is enough for another. All the leaves on a tree are the same—but these are fresh and firm, those yellow and dry, they fall and the wind blows them sadly around. Oh, you poor orphan, you wandering child!"

While Refoel was thinking, he heard another bang, louder than the first, stronger, as if a window were being opened in a hurry. And then he heard Hershele's breathless scream, "Her! It's her!" And when Refoel burst into the vestibule, terrified, Hershele was already gone—through the window and into the street. Refoel saw him from a distance, chasing after the in-laws and disappearing with them down a side street.

8

THE AGENT who had taken Beyle from the slave market took her to her own place, a broken-down little house in a far-off side street, on the pretext of "Stay here for a while and I'll go off and check things out with the Mrs. who has the place for you. Stay here and rest—just looking at you, anyone can see that you're tired from your trip. You come, I think you said, from Kaptsansk?"

"That's right," answered Beyle. "I just got here today."

"A complete stranger here, for sure. No friends or relatives, eh?"

"That's right. As lonely as a stone."

"You see how Hodel the agent can guess? Some have beauty but I've got brains. What'd I tell you, huh! Nu, believe me now that God's going to help. If it's His will, your luck will shine like the morning star, you'll live in great happiness and pleasure, Amen, Master of the Universe! Girls from Kaptsansk do very well here. As long as they aren't idiots, they can make something of themselves . . . Uh, what was I saying? My memory's going a bit—may you be spared the same—in my old age: in one ear and out the other. Yeah, now I've got it. Remind me, I wanted to say, what you said your name was."

"Beyle."

"Beyle, Beyle, Beyle. You're pretty, Beyle, knock wood; you'll certainly do. And there's no rule that says you have to be a fool," said Hodel, looking Beyle up and down with a shining face and giving her a pinch in the cheek. "Goods! . . . I could swear that you're hungry, Beylenyu. Just look how pale she is—it hurts me to see it. Hungry, yes? Tell me, dearie, tell me, tell me."

Beyle hadn't had a bite to eat since early in the morning, when she arrived in Glupsk, but she was embarrassed to say "yes" and so said nothing.

"Silence is also an answer. O, Hodel knows, all right, knows everybody's secret thoughts. I know girls, all right. Jewish girls are bashful, especially the ones from small towns, but their bashfulness is a kind of stubbornness, too. *Feh!* A terrible thing, stubbornness. If you want to taste some living in life, the first thing to do is get rid of your stubbornness. Remember my words, daughter; you'll bless me for them one day . . . Now

I'll just jump out and buy you something. It's still a long time till we eat. My husband wanders around the market all day, trying to make a living, the boys sit in *kheyder* from morning to night. My two daughters are working, one for a milliner, the other for a seamstress. If only you have their luck! Pretty, nice, they get along with everybody, not a speck of stubbornness in them. People are crazy about them—they're just like their mother at their age . . . So, we don't eat until nighttime. So I'll jump out . . ." And Hodel disappeared.

"A saint this Hodel, by my life," thought Beyle. "You can see from her house that she's poor herself, yet she worries about me like a mother. She's a good, tenderhearted jewel. May the Lord repay her for her kindness."

And while Beyle was thinking and looking over everything in the house, thanking and praising the Lord for His great goodness to a wretch like her, for being so merciful as to send such a good, kosher soul her way, Hodel came in and laid a whole package of food in front of Beyle on the table, saying sweetly, "Eat, Beylenyu! Here's a garlic clove for you, and a radish and a green cucumber. Eat, dearie, be healthy. From the bottom of my heart I want you to eat and look good. A girl has to allow herself some indulgences, she has to get some fun out of life. As a girl, I never refused myself anything my heart desired. Ay, did I live it up! Be happy, Beylenyu, and don't worry! Don't let yourself worry! Eat!"

"Why should you put yourself out like this?" said Beyle, hesitating to touch the food in front of her. "I'm not so hungry. And why should you spend so much on me?"

"Please, don't talk nonsense. A girl has to eat, I'm telling you, she has to put some meat on her bones and look her best, otherwise she can't show herself in public. And besides, I'm not spending anything on you, you aren't eating my food, the way you think. First it's God's and then it's yours. With God's help, when you slip into the place that I've got for you, you can pay me back with gratitude. Don't make me ask you again, just eat. Enough complaining, there's no more time. I have to go now—on your account. So wish me luck."

Hodel left right away and Beyle started to eat with appetite, very happy that her luck had led her to meet such a kindhearted woman, who treated her like her only child, as soon as she had arrived. The only thing to mar her joy was that her mother didn't know and was certainly afraid for her, the devil only knows about what. Remembering everybody back home, she felt a pang in her heart and sighingly thought, "Oy, what are they doing there? How are they?"

She pictured the hard, bitter life at home to herself. Her mother was bent over with age well before her time; she harnessed herself from morning to night, led a life of need and want, had yet to have a single hour of contentment. Her father toiled, broke his back for a piece of dry bread. He was happy with a meager porridge or a pot of potatoes for all his effort; sometimes he came home heavyhearted and empty-handed, and they didn't even have that. He'd grown emaciated lately, as if he'd shrunk; he was sick, broken, barely alive. And oy, the children! Their lives ravaged, their youth embittered! They never ate their fill, not an ounce of flesh on them, only skin and bones. "Oy, what are they doing there? How are they?"

She also pictured her departure from home. How sad her mother was to part from her child. Her mother trembled and quaked, her whole body shuddered. It was hard for her to hold herself back—she poured out the accumulated sorrows of a lifetime in hot, steaming tears. Her old, broken father plucked up his courage, so to speak, and said goodbye to her quickly and quietly, while what blood he had left boiled over within him. He was pale, terribly upset. Her departure was a heartbreak for the entire family. Beyle saw this before her, felt her heart go out to all her loved ones. "Oy, what are they doing there? How are they?"

Apparently, poor people have souls too. Parents and children, children and parents, the entire household, all feel love for one another, maybe more than the well-off sometimes do.

A cloud of melancholy passed over Beyle. She felt that her heart was about to break and a flood of tears rained down. But hope, like a beam of light, shone forth from a corner of her soul, pushed its way through the thick clouds of melancholy and whispered good tidings: joy and pleasure later, God willing, when God helps her land a good position through Hodel the agent, that kosher soul. She'd work for a while and scrape up a few groschen and send it all home. Or she'd go back home herself, with presents for everybody, and help her mother at home and live happily with her parents, may they be healthy.

Hope rocked her to sleep with these consolations. Beyle's eyes closed; she lay down on a hard plank-bed, dozed off, and dreamt of bedding. A double feather bed, a tower of large and small pillows. A beautiful wardrobe, too—she must have got married. But who's the groom? Where is he? She didn't have the vaguest idea, but there was foot-stomping and crowding, pushing on every side, and everyone was saying, *"Mazl tov, Beyle, mazl tov."*

The sun had set, the house was dark, and Beyle was sleeping comfortably. There was a fire burning on the oven, a couple of damp wood chips cracked and smoked and popped; a flame, a pop, another flame, a giant pop. Long fiery tongues kept licking a pot; it whispered, jabbering something in pot-talk. Hodel was skimming it from above with a wooden spoon and speaking quietly with her husband, who stood bent over at her side; whenever he spoke, she put a finger to his lips.

"Sha! Burn like a fire, with your lisp! Here he comes already, Mr. Handsome and his silver tongue." Hodel, very angry, scolded her husband quietly, imitating his lisp. "You sick? You got no strength to talk a little quieter instead of whistling and waking her up. You hear, *shmendrik?*"

"Some question, do I hear? What else? But what for? Tell me why we're farting around; why didn't we take her there right away?" Mendye whispered in Hodel's ear, bending way down and speaking as quietly as he could. Unfortunately for him, sounds like "sh" came out of his mouth with a whistle. He was missing a couple of front teeth, without which these sounds *have* to be whistled out. And it was his bad luck that these were the sounds that were always on his lips. As the saying has it, "If God wants to punish an ignoramus, He puts a Bible verse in his mouth"; that is, an ignoramus spews verses, but they come out hash.

"Ay, the hell with you and your whistling and whispering." Hodel whispered her curses quietly, biting her lip with all her strength, her eyes turning red. "Why, you ask, didn't we take her there today? Idiot! You still don't know that bitch—she'd poke out her eyes for a groschen. Well, her eyes can crawl out of her head before she'll see me bring this bit of goods to her. This time, I won't take any crap. Sha—don't interrupt me. What, dummy—what are you looking at me like an idiot for? Listen instead, *shmendrik*, and keep quiet."

"Be quiet, be quiet—that's all I know how to do. What's the point of all this muffling?" Mendye whispered into his wife's ear. His tongue stumbled, though, from too much care, and he confused "s" with "sh," "sh" with "s," and was whistling worse than ever.

"Tfu!" spat Hodel, waving her spoon at her husband. "Some whistle.

Someone should whistle *you*, by God. Nu, *shmendrik*, you hear? The girl's sleeping, so be quiet. We don't want her to wake up and hear . . . I've got another reason for not hurrying: let her stay here two or three days, pamper herself a little bit, put on a bit of weight—when you stuff a goose, you get *shmaltz*. So there's two reasons, two plagues on you. And the third reason outweighs all the others, a third big plague on you for having a brain like a cat and forgetting what Nakhmen-Traytl wrote in his letter. He wants good merchandise. And since he'll be coming any day now, I want to have everything ready, so that all he'll have to do is take a look and write out an engagement contract without having to hang around too long, and then take his blushing bride to where he takes them every year and makes a nice piece of change. You know that Nakhmen-Traytl always pays his matchmakers good money. I was at all the hostels today, looking to see if he was here yet. Tomorrow you'll go look for him, sniff him out like a bloodhound. Now do you understand, moron?"

"What's not to understand? Why didn't you say so to start with?" Mendye concluded with a lengthy whistle.

"And now, you can curl up and die, *shmendrik*, you can be the sacrifice for all of Israel—she's up," said Hodel, making an angry face at her husband, then running over to Beyle, utterly transformed, her face happy and beaming, a sweet smile on her lips.

"A happy awakening, Beylenyu! Did you sleep well? Nu, enough sleeping, it's time to eat. Mendye!" Hodel spoke to her husband amiably and pleasantly, "Go call the children in, Mendye dear. Be a husband, Mendenyu—get the herring ready and cut the bread, and meanwhile I'll go over to the pot for a second to keep things from burning—I wouldn't want you, God forbid, to divorce me."

Hodel urged Beyle on at the table. "Don't wait to be asked, enjoy yourself!"—and gave her great hopes that, with God's help, she'd soon be raking it in, in a good position on easy street. Beyle let herself go at the table and went to sleep with an easy mind.

Book Five

1

"YOU GIVE HIM"—good old man, the jewel of God's little world—"dominion over the work of your hands." So goes the verse in Psalms, and goes on to list all the creatures subordinate to man: all the sheep and cattle, even the beasts in the woods, birds in the air, and fish in the sea. But catching fish and birds in nets, ruling over animals isn't such a novelty—they're animals, after all, beings without a shred of sense. It's more of a novelty the way good old man racks his brains to get his peers, his brothers and sisters, his own flesh and blood, onto the end of his fishing rod.

This art, this uncanny human cleverness, comes to mind when one walks on the Jurdike, a back street in Glupsk, and takes a look at the house of Levi Bokher.

It's one of those houses that are a blot on the people of Israel and that blacken its face to the world. Good, kosher Jews pass it by; they spit and keep silent—it's nothing. They're silent, all right, but Satan screams at the top of his lungs. And the thousands of unfortunate souls who keep falling into the hands of the wicked—the traffickers in human livestock—they are screaming too, and their bitter cries, their bloody tears, go all the way up to the highest of heavens. The kosher Jews might turn away and spit, but it's precisely that spit that produces this stinking muck in the life of the Jews. Outsiders, members of other nations, grab their noses and cry, "Ay-ay-ay, there's a stench coming out of you, Children of Israel."

It's already noon and the shutters of this house are still down. In a little room that looks out to a garden in back, a couple of elderly ladies were sitting over coffee and pastries. The first was stout, big-bellied, and thick; a short woman, poured straight out from top to bottom in one broad mass without any sign of a neck. The lower part of her face was bulky and wide, with a two-story double chin and a pair of fat cheeks that drooped like pancakes. They were dappled with yellow spots that were joined to each other by thin reddish capillaries, all of it crowned by a small, narrow star on her forehead, beneath which lurked a pair of lustrous, moist grey eyes. All in all, she looked like a loaf of sugar, wide on the bottom and tapering all the way up to her head. The angel responsible for her birth seemed to have been as diligent as a first-rate grocery clerk—he packed up her soul and sent this piece of goods into the world wrapped up in a funnel-shaped bag. In her day, this baggage had been a bestseller; now, in old age, she was Levi Bokher's and went by the name of Auntie Sheyntse.

The second woman, in contrast, was tall and skinny, with sunken cheeks and thin, colorless lips, a thin, pointy nose, and piercing blue eyes in which a fire could now and then be seen. She must have been pretty in her youth, but now she was faded and wrinkled, and looked like a whacked-out willow twig: Hodel the agent in all her glory.

Auntie Sheyntse was packing food away with both hands and urging Hodel to join in. "You should be healthy, Hodel, but you eat like a kid—slowly, bit by bit, you hardly need to chew it. Here, darling; please, take a real piece and eat it all at once. My pastries came out really good this time—it's Khane's recipe, you know. I put in plenty of eggs and cinnamon and butter, and I didn't forget about the ginger, either. Here's one that's nicely burned—take it, please, and eat."

"You should be healthy, Sheyntsenyu, my darling dear," Hodel said graciously, drawing her lips together into a long, narrow beak and taking a birdlike sip of her coffee. "What else am I doing but eating? Your pastries came out great, fit for a king. My luck, by God, should be as great as your skill in homemaking, Sheyntsenyu."

And so the two of them sat pleasant and easy, talking about all kinds of things, reminiscing about their youth, the old days. They'd had the same profession as girls, come up in the same establishment; once they'd passed their prime, both suddenly took the veil—got married, that is. Luck was with Sheyntse, and with time she became madam of her own establishment. She had a reputation in the city, her house was patronized by the most respectable people, and she was living out her days in wealth and respect. Sheyntse observed the Jewish rituals and was very punctilious in the three women's *mitsves*. Shabbes and *yontef* she went to *shul* to grab herself a "Blessed Be He and Blessed Be His Name"; when she saw the other women jump *Kedushe*, she jumped too; when she heard them crying and lamenting over the *tkhines*, she cried and lamented too. She wore a kerchief on her head, pulled nearly down to her eyes, so that not a single strand of hair should God forbid peek out. This kerchief was her passport to respectability, and she was very proud of it—it masked her shame and proved to the world that she had taken herself a man according to the laws of Moses and Israel. Old women, the kind who occupy themselves with good works, often came to her for donations; she'd give them a few groschen, sometimes an old dress, a pair of worn-out stockings. She'd also offer them honey cake with whiskey; they'd dunk, make a blessing, pull a face when they swallowed, and wish her success in this world and a seat in Paradise in the next. Sheyntse had been blessed with good luck and money; she wanted for nothing but children—she had none, and this cast a pall on her life. "Go ask God questions," she'd complain, touching her head as she spoke. "What does it help? Already married, thank God, and still nothing, just the same as before. Maybe it's right, maybe it has to be that way on account of our sins."

Such beautiful words, just like a regular saint.

Hodel, on the other hand, had no luck at all. She did have children—a great wonder in itself—but she was a terrible pauper, God preserve us. She had as good a head for business as Sheyntse, and maybe ten times better; she'd already worshipped, as they say, every false God of commerce, stretched herself in every direction, but all in vain. She wasn't destined to be a madam with her own establishment; she had to become an agent and wait attendance on Sheyntse. It was like a stab from a knife; in her heart, she was Sheyntse's mortal enemy. Talking to Sheyntse, Hodel was sugar-sweet, her mouth stretched into a smile, her eyes shining as if she could finally die happy because of her great joy at Sheyntse's position and good fortune. But in the middle of a conversation, she'd give Sheyntse a jab, stick her with a pin, a sharp word that she pretended to deliver in all innocence. "Oy, Sheyntsenyu love, soul of mine, sitting with you is all I live for. I swell with joy just looking at you. Today you're a countess, no evil eye. And once? You remember? Who would have expected it then? You give me such pleasure—the Lord should only find me worthy to live to see you have children . . . Don't moan, Sheyntsenyu, don't grieve. I know how bad, how bitter it is without children. I mean, what was the point of getting married?"

"Sinful flesh does what it can. Beyond that—do I know? Go ask God questions. Some he gives money, others children. It's also miserable and bitter without money." Auntie Sheyntse could give as good as she got.

"My children are my only consolation, more precious than fine gold . . . It's OK, Sheyntsenyu, don't give in to your grief . . . I've been sitting here long enough; I'd better go."

"What's the rush, Hodel? You're longing for your old man at home? It's no small thing—an hour already since you've seen him."

"You should know, Sheyntsenyu, that I wish all my friends the same luck. What a Mendye my Mendye is! A jewel! If only he could get a break . . . You'll thank me for the girl. A piece of goods, eh, Sheyntsenyu? It's true that you screwed me a little on the price, but—pssh—you got yourself a bargain. It's your good luck that Nakhmen-Traytl was held up somewhere on the way and didn't get here like he'd written . . . Sha, let me at least tell you what I heard. Now, just between us, he got married four times this year, got the goods safely across the border, and unloaded them at a good price, real good deals. Luck's on his side, that Traytl; he's making money hand over fist. Mark my words, give him a little time, he'll grow into a great big Reb Traytl, rolling in dough . . . Where is the girl, anyway?"

"In her room. I told her to wash herself with soap and water and get rid of her *shmattes*. That's what comes of them," Auntie Sheyntse sighed. "You wash them, clean them up, give them shoes and clothing, and as soon as they've got enough . . . they turn into princesses, nothing's good enough, like you were trying to kill them or something. Oy, the times! The times!"

"Nu, what can you do? Buy a cow, have a row." Hodel comforted Auntie Sheyntse with a sweetly roguish smile. "Of course, things were better in our day. You remember, Sheyntsenyu? Nu, time for me to go. Let me at least take a couple of pastries for the kids, they should know . . ."

"Wait a bit, Hodel. I'll give you some honey cake for them, too . . . Ay, did my honey cake turn out today—a wonder . . . And while we're on the subject, maybe you'd like to dunk a bit in some whiskey. If you ask me nicely, I'll pour myself a shot too and make a *lekhayim* with you."

"If you like," said Hodel craftily, a fire lighting up in her eyes.

Both of them were very cheerful and happy, very garrulous by the time they said goodbye. Hodel congratulated Auntie Sheyntse as if she were taking her leave of a new mother, wishing that she might raise the girl up and get a lot of joy from her. And they should both be healthy and visit each other further for similar celebrations, God willing.

Still in the house, Hodel encountered Beyle, washed, shampooed, nicely dressed; shining, beaming, utterly transformed. "Such a stroke of luck for your mother!" said Hodel in a strange voice. "You shine like the morning star. Just don't be a fool. Do what Auntie Sheyntse tells you, and everything will be fine."

2

BEYLE'S ENTRY into her new place was like stepping into another world. Everything seemed somewhat strange to her: the people, their behavior— she even struck herself as strange. Looking into the mirror on the wall of her room, she failed to recognize herself: it didn't look like her, but it couldn't have been anyone else. It was as if she'd changed her skin. She felt her finely combed hair, which had been smeared with almond oil, marveled at her bare neck, her soap-washed hands, the fashionable, nicely trimmed dress, and practically fainted with pleasure. She was enjoying herself. Why should she feel suspicious? This was probably the way it was supposed to be, it must be standard Glupsker practice to trick servant-girls out like dolls. You have to remember that Beyle was still a kid, maybe fifteen, sixteen years old, and where had she been born? In Kaptsansk, outside of which she'd never set foot until now, never seen anything of the world. She'd only heard that somewhere far beyond the gates of Kaptsansk lay a big city called Glupsk, the best on earth. And why? Because it was inhabited exclusively by Jews. It was like a hundred Kaptsansks—and did they know how to live there? Ay-ay-ay! She was certain that the Glupskers were all kosher, kindhearted, nice, fine people, and the proof was before her eyes: first Hodel the agent and now Auntie Sheyntse. The world didn't call her Auntie for nothing—she must have earned the title through her good works. A woman who is everybody's Auntie is usually a modest, pious Jewess . . . And let's not forget all the other people here, likewise good and merry and friendly. "So many daughters!" she thought to herself. "A-ha, I get it—they're boarding. Now it makes sense. They stay home while their husbands study . . . Auntie Sheyntse has been blessed by God!" Beyle interpreted everything after her own understanding, according to the way she'd lived in Kaptsansk. It was the only way she knew, nothing else made any sense to her. The next morning, when she asked Sheyntse, "Mrs., tell me what to do," and Sheyntse answered with a smile, like a real, pious Jewess, "Don't be in such a rush, daughter. Your time will come," Beyle took it at face value: it must be the way here to love your servants, to break them in slowly and mercifully.

Beyle remained firm in her judgment that good old Glupsk was a real Jewish city, that its citizens were saints, very fine people with very good habits.

Her only regret was that her mother wasn't there to see how well her daughter was doing. She should have got some pleasure after all her grief in childrearing. Since Beyle was sitting idle and alone in her room, longing for her loved ones, her emotions went to work, and she began to frame a letter home. But that's easier said than done. Even Jews with beards, unusually clever and experienced people, world-class experts at finding fault with others, at holding forth on everything under the sun—even they can feel the hand of death upon them when they have to write a letter. They scribble and scrawl with their pens, strain and rub their foreheads—but it doesn't work, one word doesn't go with the next, they can't write any better than animals.

So what do you expect from Beyle, a little girl from Kaptsansk, who isn't such an expert, isn't such a brain-trust as they are? But maybe just because she wasn't such a brain-trust, a few words strung themselves together in her mind, in the well-known "breviary" style; senseless non sequiturs seasoned with Kaptsansker German, the German, that is, which the Children of Israel slip into their documents, their teachers into the Bible, and their women into their prayers, because nothing else will do, there's no other way to say some things. Go tell a dog, for example, "Please depart" instead of "Get out," or speak Yiddish, not goyish, with a cow or calf . . .

Since the main point of Beyle's letter was praise of the Lord, she began it in the following manner: "*Praised and thanked be the Living Father in Heaven, for He is with the solitary, guards the wanderer, raises up the fallen. His grace has made itself manifest in the great wonders worked with me, in His lead-*

ing me on the proper path and delivering me now into a place of goodness." And
so on.

Having laid the letter out in her mind, Beyle was confronted with another problem: How does the cat get over the river, how does she get it
down in black and white? She herself didn't know how to write, nor was it
appropriate for her to ask one of Sheyntse's daughters or sons-in-law.
What could she do, then? She thought and thought, and suddenly it came
to her: Hershele. "Yeah, Hershele, he'll write it for me . . . What is it, anyway, that I always want to see him, and when I do, my heart starts to
thump? What is he, my brother? No. My fiancé? No. So what then? It
makes me blush and giggle. A fine laughter, huh? Maybe it's a sin to think
that way? But what can I do, it happens on its own. Maybe I shouldn't want
. . . Not want to see him? But *vey iz mir*, I want to, and now more than ever.
Master of the Universe, I confess. Master of the Universe, do all girls sin
like this in their hearts, or am I the only one?" And tears came to Beyle's
eyes.

◆   ◆   ◆

Sheyntse and her husband Levi were the perfect couple, a real match made
in heaven. They were both involved in the business, and each one demonstrated a peculiar expertise. When Sheyntse earned the title of Auntie, Levi
was likewise deservedly crowned with the name of Bokher—youth, bachelor, it also sounds like the Hebrew for "to choose"—and there was no one
so expert in "merchandise," no such master among all his companions,
who often used to consult him on difficult matters. He would adjudicate
their questions and solve their dilemmas. And don't forget, these white
slavers were clever bastards, dandies who knew their stuff. They messed
with people's heads, deluded and seduced hundreds of creatures with gim-
micks of every kind. There were all sorts of actors and sleight-of-hand
artists among them, who put on a show, disguised themselves as fiancés,
business-owners, agents, nice, good kosher Jews—among other things, according to the circumstances—in order to lead girls astray. So, if these
kinds of people had respect for Levi, thought as highly of him as of a *rebbe*,
Levi Bokher must really have been one hell of a *bokher*.

Levi Bokher wasn't home when Beyle came into his house; he'd gone
somewhere to clear a difficult issue up for his comrades. Auntie Sheyntse,

who held her husband in high regard and didn't make a move without him, kept Beyle in a room of her own, separated insofar as possible from the rest of the household, giving her a bit of work simply for appearances' sake—patching shirts, sewing buttons, darning stockings—and telling her that she'd have plenty to do once the master of the house returned. Auntie Sheyntse treated her very well; she pampered her so that she'd look good, so that Levi would be pleased when he saw her and know that his wife was a person to be relied upon.

When Levi came home and saw Beyle, he liked her so much that he started to tremble for joy. "Listen, wife," he said to Sheyntse, "This is a beautiful piece of goods. She's still raw, a little sharp yet, but with time she'll grow into something of value. It's very possible that she could end up somewhere far, far away, with 'Uncle Ishmael,' for example. We'll be able to get a fortune for her. In the meantime though, before we can find someone who'll really appreciate her, we've got to teach her good manners, how to behave like a *mentsh* and how to please."

Beyle's first teacher was one of the "daughters," a quick, clever girl who started to teach her the basics. Beyle was stupid, though, and didn't understand a word. She was also shamefast, and a little obstinate too. But the "daughter's" instruction was only a way of killing time, more in the spirit of fun—Levi took over a little later and began to teach Beyle according to his own system. And it must be said to his credit that Levi Bokher was devoted to the education of his "apprentices," as he called them; he behaved like a good *melamed*, using every means at his disposal to banish their small-town savagery, their stupid, religious-fanatic obstinacy. At first, he was nice about it, and tendered moral advice; and when that didn't work, he used his hands, a stick, a strap. If a hair was out of place—slaps and blows until the message was clear. Sometimes he'd shut his students up in a cellar with no food or drink until they'd learned to be good.

On one occasion, Levi brought one of his pals to Beyle's room to get his opinion of her and of how much he thought she'd bring. As they came in, Levi said with a sweet smile, "Daughter, I've brought you a fiancé, a regular pearl of a fiancé." The fiancé wasn't shy, of course, and started to kid around with her as if he were already her lover. Seeing that Beyle kept her head silently lowered, he took her by her bare neck, petting her, poking her, to get at least one look, one word, out of her. Beyle, red as fire, pushed him away. This only incited him the more; he hugged her and tried to give her a kiss. Beyle gave him a couple of stinging slaps, tore herself out of his arms, and ran off. Her fiancé was dumbfounded.

Beyle had committed a serious offense, and Levi executed judgment with a strap the very same day, admonishing her as he did so. "Here's your just desserts, you delinquent, you! Here—this is so you'll remember, so you should keep your behavior in mind and know better the next time. Here, here! A girl should be quiet and nice, should like people, be kind to them, show them a friendly face. She should beat all that religious-fanatic crap and crazy superstition right out of her skull. A girl has to have re-spect—respect above everything else!"

Now Beyle knows where she is, who Hodel the agent and Auntie Sheyntse really are. Now that their "grace has made itself manifest in the great wonders worked with her," in the goodness and piety of these two lovely souls, Beyle frames another letter home, filled with dirges and laments this time—and not in Kaptsansker German, not in "breviary" style, but in plain Yiddish, the language of her broken heart and despairing thoughts.

You could hardly recognize her in all her fine new array: her thick black hair had been trimmed all the way up to her ear-lobes, her embroi-dered white dress was cut low in the front, there was a narrow red ribbon around her neck and her sleeves scarcely came to her elbows. She looked like a real lady, one who lacked for nothing and had nothing to complain about. But may the Daughters of Israel never feel the bitterness in her heart! And this bitterness could be seen in Beyle's pale cheeks, in the black circles under her swollen, burning eyes, in her whole demeanor. She had aged ten years, changed completely.

As she was sitting once in her room, desolate and alone, Auntie Sheyntse glided in as quietly as a cat. Beyle began to tremble with fear and lowered her eyes. "I've missed you terribly," said Auntie Sheyntse, coming closer to Beyle. "My Levi was on his way to you just now, but I said, 'No, let *me* go.' You see how much I love you. What else should I do? I'm telling you, just take a look at yourself in the mirror, how pretty you are. Such a neck on you, *I* should have such luck. Gorgeous hands, as I am a Jew. So sweet, so lovely—the rest of them here can go burst with envy. This is the kind of beauty I was, daughter, when I was your age. They hung themselves for me. Oy, did I set the world on fire? Yes, I did. It's still a pleasure for me to think back on all those good, happy times. Now I'm old, of course. But look at me, right here and now." Auntie Sheyntse smiled and pulled herself up to her full height, throwing her head back, grabbing her sides with both hands, her belly sticking out in front, "Look at me and tell me if Sheyntse isn't still all right! What I'm saying is, don't be an idiot—do what you're told . . . You're not saying anything?"

"What should I say?" Beyle wouldn't look at Auntie Sheyntse. "I don't know what you want from me."

"What are you talking, what do we want from you? Your own good, that's what we want. We want you to like your fiancé. He's dying for you, for a word, a glance. He's ready to go to the devil, he's so crazy for you. 'Here,' he says, 'Here's presents for you, darling—a bracelet, coral earrings, a ring, a gold chain'—God only knows what else, and you, you're like a rock. Go do you favors! *Feh!* It's a shame, a scandal!"

"Why does anybody need to watch out for me? I've got a mother and father."

"I've heard all this nonsense before. What am I, a fool, that I'll stand here and argue with you? I'm asking you for the last time: Yes?"

"No."

"The same old shit," Auntie Sheyntse was beside herself, shaking her head, little red veins popping out on her fat, greasy cheeks. "Who do you think you are, Beyltse. You're gonna eat my food, wear my clothes for nothing? You think you're something? That we're just waiting for you to say yes? Don't get me wrong, Beyltse. Who's gonna hear you? You're nothing more than a dummy, a hunk of flesh, a piece of slut-meat . . . This whole matter is up in the air yet, we still haven't agreed on a price. Now do you understand what we're telling you, Beyltse?"

"Merciful God!" Beyle burst into tears and wrung her hands. "Master of the Universe, save me, deliver me from Jewish hands."

"Shut up, bitch. Just wait, Miss Big Mouth—Levi's gonna come and show you who's boss. He'll put you back in the cellar where you can starve and howl like a dog. Mice and worms will eat your flesh, the devil will carry you off pretty quick." Auntie Sheyntse departed in a rage. Beyle grabbed her hair with both hands and threw herself weeping onto the sofa.

3

AMONG THE "DAUGHTERS" at Levi Bokher's, there were some who were kindhearted and decent, for whose fate one could justly sigh and groan: "Oy, diamonds in the mud! Low as the world has brought them, tender, merciful hearts still beat within them."

The best of them was the Turk. This Turk, whose name was Gitl, was a *melamed*'s daughter from Dalfenivke, a poor *shtetl* full of purebred *kaptsonim*—kosher, straight-ahead, truly pious, mean-what-they-say kind of Jews. So Satan had to bring them a *shlimazl*, a clever young bastard, to make the following proclamation: Any poor girl from Dalfenivke who wants to prosper, see the world, and live happily from the work of her hands should come with him to his home in Constantinople . . . Some small potatoes, Constantinople; when a Jew hears Constantinople, he catches a whiff of the land of Israel, and sees strange pictures in his head: Turk and Jerusalemite, turban and *shtrayml* all mix together. So Jews naturally flocked to him from all sides, each of them begging, "Take my daughter, merciful sir."

The merciful sir lived up to his name, picked out several pretty girls—among them Gitl, the prettiest of all—and took these happy souls away with him. The upshot was that after all kinds of comings and goings, Gitl came to Levi Bokher's and became a Turk, without ever having seen one.

During the time that the Beyle affair was unfolding, an episode also took place with the most senior of the girls, whom everyone called the Captain, an episode so tragic and frightening that it touched all her comrades to the quick—because it showed plainly how dire their condition really was, how woeful and lost their lives. This episode made the Turk even kinder to Beyle; she loved her and hugged her, cried when she looked at her, the way a devoted elder sister hugs and kisses her orphaned little sister.

The Captain came from a far-off *shtetl* somewhere in Poland. Her parents, impoverished members of the middle class, were of high social rank, among the most prominent people in the *shtetl*. They lived poorly, had to count every cent, never allowed themselves any luxury, but their poverty neither coarsened nor abased them, didn't make them vicious, as it does to so many others. They lived in peace and love, truly blessed by heaven; one was ready to give the other the last bit of food from his mouth—let what may, come, as long as they were together. Many wealthy people, people who bathed in milk and butter but were at loggerheads with each other, could well have envied them.

The darling of the household was Eydl, the eldest daughter. She was esteemed by all, everybody hastened to do her will. And Eydl came by it honestly, she was really someone to love. She was beautiful, like something in a picture. God, that master craftsman, the greatest painter there is, used the finest materials at His disposal—the white of the lily for her cheeks, the red of coral for her lips, the blue of the sky for her eyes, the black of the raven for her hair—added the purest essence of charm, waved his hand and *voilà*, a perfectly beautiful Eydl. She was well-grown, with cascading silken locks, like a tall, many-branched young tree. She was kind and tender-hearted, a housekeeper beyond compare. Every corner of the house bore witness to her skill, from the pots of fresh flowers to the embroidered silvery curtains on the windows to the shining brass and copperware, which sparkled and caught the eye. She sewed, washed, embroidered, did everything around the house, wouldn't even let her mother bend over. She also sewed and embroidered for others, to bring in a little money.

One day a fine, respectably dressed young man named Shmerl appeared in the *shtetl* as if he'd dropped straight down from heaven. That is, he'd come from very far off to do business with the local gentry. The *shtetl* Jews, chronically unemployed, idle twenty-four hours out of every day, had nothing else to do but talk, sniff around, feel things out, and attend to the business of others. Now, thank God, they had something new to talk about, a new field of display for their intelligence and groundless suppositions. New dispatches went out about him daily: Shmerl is a VIP in high society, Shmerl is as rich as Koyrekh, Shmerl is a *makher* by the most powerful noblemen, Shmerl this and Shmerl that, Shmerl isn't married, and if he isn't, why keep it a secret? . . . Respectable people came up to shake his hand; those who lived on handouts stood on their heads to beg for a donation; marriage brokers ran around like chickens with their heads cut off to find him a wife. But Shmerl was the kind of guy who cared about beauty, not money—he was interested in the bride, not her family or her dowry, and he liked Eydl more than all the other girls, not one of whom came up to her little finger. The marriage brokers didn't hesitate; they grabbed the skirts of their capotes and ran hell for leather to Eydl's parents, spewing out talk, praising Shmerl to the skies, saying, "There is none like unto Shmerl! There is none better for your daughter than Shmerl, Reb Shmerl, for he is such and also such, the picture of perfection and a storehouse of virtues. Just think, Shmerl—of course, it's really Reb Shmerl, but it's so easy just to call him Shmerl—Reb Shmerl, nu, you could search the world over, with a candle, yet; you'd find his equal as soon as you'd find pork in your mouth. The whole matter, from start to finish, from Reb Shmerl's arrival till now, is a miracle and a wonder, incontrovertible proof that the match was made in heaven. Forty days before Eydl was born, it was already announced up there. You understand? How could it be otherwise? To tell God what to do, to oppose this match is to mix into things that are none of your business, and stick your nose into the order of the world—*feh*, awful, what kind of Jew could do it? And besides what a Jew can and can't do, questions and complaints won't help you either, don't make me laugh. You understand? And so, we've got to hurry and grab the bargain with both hands before someone else comes along and beats us to it."

Her father had accepted the offer inwardly—"Sure, why not?"—but hemmed and hawed as if he wanted to think it over, a vacillation for the sake of form. Her mother, however, a garden-variety Jewish woman with a burning passion to marry off her children, leapt immediately at the match with body and soul, and Eydl was engaged. Her fiancé really *didn't* ask for any dowry, but her parents still undertook to provide whatever they could afford and to give their daughter suitably sumptuous outfits for Shabbes and *yontef*. Simply disposing of their eldest, best-beloved child was beneath them; her husband should never be able to throw it up to her that "I took you out of a barn, out of your father's penniless house; you were naked, barefoot and I was the one who clothed you and made you respectable."

"Take when you can get," thought her groom with a smile. He did them a favor and took.

The groom hastened to hold the wedding as quickly as possible after the engagement. Business, he explained, demanded a rapid return home. Difficult as it was to part from their dearly beloved daughter, to let go of the ornament of their house, her parents accepted it gracefully, consoling themselves with the thought that their daughter, thank God, was provided for, that she had met up with someone who knew how to appreciate her.

They took pains to pay off the dowry, packed up Eydl's wardrobe, and escorted her with tears in their eyes, with blessings and good wishes beyond number.

The young couple departed and stopped over in Glupsk, not because it was on their way, but because business, according to Shmerl, demanded a short detour there. And since they were still on their honeymoon, Shmerl, the loving and devoted husband, did his best to make things pleasant for his bride. He found them a place to stay removed from all the noise and bustle of the city center, a calm, peaceful inn amid meadows and trees, where songbirds could be heard. Shmerl didn't skimp; he took a three-room suite, as befit a man of his stature.

The innkeeper, a lively, busy Jew with a big belly and a yellow beard, greeted Shmerl with a heartfelt "Welcome," as if they'd been friends for years. This didn't mean much, though. Anyone who travels knows that most innkeepers have shining faces and sweetly smiling lips; that they're mild, gentle souls who rejoice and are as glad to encounter newly arrived guests as they would be to meet members of their immediate family. But be that as it may, Shmerl really was a welcome guest. The innkeeper laid a hand over his heart, nodded his yellow-bearded head, and swore by his Jewishness that they would be able to rest at their ease, that everything would be in order. And when he stole a look at the good-looking woman and cunningly managed to find out that she was Shmerl's wife, fresh from the wedding, he gave them a hearty Jewish *mazl tov*, with a roguish gleam in his eye, and demanded a piece of the wedding cake with a mocking, somewhat insolent smile.

Eydl's first encounter at the inn was with a tall, thin woman who burst into her room like a bomb immediately after their arrival, casting her eyes on Eydl, on Shmerl, with a joy that was unconfined, as if they were her long-lost brother and sister. Coming up to Shmerl, she opened her mouth to speak, but he cut her off angrily, and she was left standing as if she'd been strangled. Shmerl sent her to Hell, and she ran out as quickly as she'd run in.

"There you have it, my love," Shmerl smiled sweetly at his slack-jawed wife, "Glupsk and its unbelievable, world-famous *kaptsonim*. And *that* was the genuine article—they don't make them like that anywhere else. A Glupsker *kaptsn* will force his way into someone's house with just that kind of insolence. If he can't find the master in one room, he looks for him in a second, a third, even in his bedroom; if he should happen to be sleeping, the *kaptsn* coughs and clears his throat until he's woken him up. It's all right, though—since when do Jews stand on ceremony about things like this? To you, my love, it's news, but I already know the Glupsker *kaptsonim* and their ways. Here, darling, spit seven times—keep the evil eye away!"

After all the hoopla at home and on the road, Eydl slept very well and rested up at the inn. Nobody bothered her, there were no other guests just then. It was quiet and peaceful, everything was running smoothly, and Eydl was happy.

Shmerl was often visited at the inn by a lively, pockmarked little man with a cataract, a white spot, in his open but sightless right eye. This eye was never still; whatever the seeing eye did, it did too, as if seconding the other's motions. If the good eye rolled and looked angry, the blind one with the white spot rolled too, and assumed an angry mien. If the good one winked cunningly, shone merrily, the blind one, winking just as cunningly, wasn't slow to do its stuff, as if to say, "Make way for an expert," thus lending so weird and repulsive an aspect to his face that it would have been better for him and for everybody else if the eye had dribbled out and disappeared completely.

Eydl couldn't abide this man, she recoiled whenever he came into their suite; but for the sake of her husband, who spent plenty of time with him, mostly away from the inn, doing business, she forced herself to receive him pleasantly.

Eydl likewise took Shmerl's disappearances into the city for hours on end, his agitation and constant distraction, as proof that he was a big businessman with a good business, thank God. Much as she would have loved to have her husband sit by her side or go for walks with her, she let it pass; she felt great joy in her heart that the Lord had blessed her with a husband, a go-getter, with whom it was to be hoped that things would go very well for her, God willing.

One time Shmerl came running in, breathless and distracted, with the little one-eyed man hurrying after. Shmerl took his wife off to a corner, where he whispered short, staccato words, quickly and pleadingly into her ear. "Eydele, darling! A deal, there's a deal going down, but I don't have enough right now . . . not enough . . . a few hundred . . . What'll I do? . . . This man here will lend it, but it depends a little on you . . . He, you understand, he's demanding my wife's signature . . . your signature on the note . . . Oy, help, darling . . . right away . . . there's no time . . . every minute a gold piece . . . Here, lovey, here."

And at that very instant, a promissory note appeared before Eydl. She signed without any complaint. On the contrary, the respect shown her and the opportunity to be of use to her husband gave her great pleasure, a feeling of "It looks like I'm also a bit of a somebody, thank God; my signature is worth something too. I can also do business."

The little man took the note, inspecting the signature carefully with his good eye, while the blind one apparently followed it and did the same. The good eye gleamed, gave a cunning wink, and so did the bad one. Having looked his fill, he folded the note quite leisurely, stuck it safely into his pocket, and made a hasty exit along with Shmerl.

It was a good day, a happy day for Eydl. Going over everything that had happened to her in the last little while, the sudden transformation of her life, she lifted her hands to heaven in thanks for such good fortune, for so dear a husband—for so unexpected a gift. In her great joy, she took paper and pen and sat down to write a letter home. She reconsidered immediately, though, and postponed the writing until later, when she should have arrived safely home with her husband and had a chance to look around and see everything there—all the goodness and good fortune that had come her way—with her own two eyes. Then she'd send her parents a long letter, describing everything clearly and in detail; they'd rejoice in her good news, as well as in the gifts she'd send to her mother, her father, and the rest of the family. And God willing, she'd be able to do so in a short time; from today's deal, which had been settled and arranged with the help of God, it looked to her as if her husband had nothing more to do there— finished, the end, soon they'd leave and she would come to her resting place. She'd discuss it with her Shmerl today, and inquire about the deal by the way—why not? She also had some part in it, she had signed the note.

And as Eydl was sitting so cheerfully, picturing her happy life in her mind's eye, the innkeeper came quietly into her room. His face shining, he bowed, looking at her without speaking and blinking his eyes oddly. "You're here all alone?" he asked after a moment's silence, smiling sweetly and rubbing his hands as if to give her a sign.

"What's wrong?" Eydl started and gave him a sharp look.

"Nothing," he smiled affably. "You don't understand what I want? What do I want? What an innkeeper always wants—money."

"Oh, that," said Eydl lightly. "My husband will give it to you when he comes."

"No good, no good. Right now, you understand, right this minute I have to go away for a few days, and I absolutely need, need," he stretched out his hands and rubbed them, "The dough, I mean. I've got to go right away, so what can I do? It's quite possible that you won't be here when I get back, that you'll be at your own place—I'm sure they're expecting you already. Oy, a pretty pickle we're in. You know what? Excuse me, just sign this bill, and we'll have everything settled before I go. Don't worry—I know you're good for the money . . . Take care now, and give my regards to Reb Shmerl. You have no idea what a Reb Shmerl you've got—a Reb Shmerl of silver and gold. You'll soon find out, though, just what your Reb Shmerl is made of."

Eydl signed the bill, of course, and bade the innkeeper a hearty farewell, very pleased that he had so high an opinion of her husband as to praise him to the skies. She assured him that the money would be paid, and accompanied by a nice present to boot.

Shmerl came home rather late that night, very merry and red-faced. He hugged his wife, stammering disconnected phrases, just like a drunk. "Finished . . . John Hancock . . . Sprinkled with whiskey, let it arise and blossom, break plates . . . Let it arise, rise like in a baking trough, and blossom, the way a garden, gard . . ."

"*Feh!* What kind of talk is this?" said Eydl in astonishment, tearing herself from her husband's arms.

"Ay-ay-ay—Look who's so holy, just look at Miss Religion there . . . 'Don't touch me.' What, you don't like it? You think I care? Don't make me laugh! *Yibone ha-mikdosh*, may the Temple be rebuilt . . . You know what *yibone* means in Russian?" Shmerl flew into a rage, looked at his wife angrily, and ended with a whistle.

"Nu, enough, enough. Go to sleep already." Eydl swallowed his terrible words and tried to pacify him with nice ones. She took him under the arms and lay him in the bed, telling him to go to sleep.

Eydl lay in her own bed, unable to sleep. Her husband's behavior made her feel sick—*feh*, she'd never heard such crudeness. There were nothing but evil thoughts in her mind: "Do I know where he was, or whom he met there? Men, who knows what they get up to?" Her head was splitting from all her thinking and reconsidering, her eyes ran with tears of resentment.

"No, no," she gave herself her word, "This will never happen again. From now on, I'll be smarter. He's got to be taken in hand. Not a step without me, not a millimeter. A wife needs to know everything, everything."

And so Eydl pledged herself to behave like this in future, to take her husband firmly in hand for both their sakes. This comforted her a little, and she finally fell asleep.

EYDL WOKE UP late the next morning and lay in bed, devising a plan to conquer her husband and put the fear of God into him. All she could come up with was to get angry. Getting angry is a wife's best defense in any battle against her husband, especially for the first little while after the wedding. Not even the strongest man can hold out for more than a few days against an angry wife. He then has to lay down his arms in shame and disgrace, plead for mercy, and become a good little boy—until the next altercation.

Eydl readied herself to enter the lists fully armed that very day. She rehearsed her angry look—contorting her face, throwing her nose out of joint, bugging her eyes—and was ready, loaded, waiting: as soon as her husband showed himself with a "Good morning," she'd commence firing. But all her waiting was in vain—just to spite her, he didn't turn up. This made her even madder, she was seething like a kettle, didn't know what to do anymore. Stay in bed and wait—what was the point, how long can you wait? There's no choice; she decided to get up and go into his room. "Never, not under any circumstances." She wandered around her room, still not properly dressed, on fire with rage—"Me go to him? No, no"—meanwhile putting her ear to the wall and hearing nothing, becoming curious—as women do—and slowly, carefully, opening the door a crack. Not a rustle. She couldn't stand it anymore; she flung the door all the way open, looked inside, and he wasn't there. Eydl burst. It was too hard to hold herself back any longer, and with a heavy heart she said, "That's it! This is the last time. He goes off somewhere with his pals, passes his time with God knows who and forgets that he has a wife. Some way he talked to me last night. Ha! And I should let it pass? Never!" Suddenly, she caught herself. "What's wrong with me? Where do I get off with such horrible thoughts,

with thinking about him like that? Did we come here to play? He has business! Yesterday he was . . . well, what of it? It happens when businessmen
finish a deal. What's it to me? Oy, my heart, my heart . . . Let me at least
get dressed."

She went into the alcove in Shmerl's room and ran out again, terrified,
pale, breathless.

"What's the matter, Madame? *Vey iz mir,* you look like you've seen a
ghost." Brush in hand, the chambermaid had come in to clean the room.

"My things. Where's the chest, the things, my things?" screamed Eydl,
trembling.

"Ah, your things?" said the maid in a foolish singsong, giggling and
stretching out the words. "Not to worry. Sha—it's all right, Madame,
he-he-he. Real early this morning, before our goat went to the meadow
with the flock, your husband took your things and told me, he-he-he, he
told me . . ."

"Nu, come on already. Talk! What did he say?"

"What did he say?" asked the maid sheepishly, displaying two rows of
white teeth. "Wait, wait. Let me try to remember. What, what . . . yeah,
that's it. He said that he'd be back in an hour to take you away."

"Where away?"

"What do you mean, where away?" wondered the maid, shrugging her
shoulders. "Away is away. You probably know where. What, I should
know?"

"What time is it now?" Eydl was still quite upset.

"You wanna know the time?" asked the maid, screwing her face up
charmingly. "Way past noon. Lunch time already, he-he-he . . . I must
have come to check on you a hundred times already, and you were sleeping
like a log, like you'd just come out of the bath. Why are you so pale? You
want me to run down and get your breakfast?"

"No. Get out of here, leave me alone," and Eydl shooed the maid from
her room.

Eydl passed the day in terrible turmoil, looking closely for the first
time at everything that had happened to her. When she began to consider
things carefully and dissect them in her mind, this whole affair with Shmerl
suddenly struck her as very strange, the beginning even more so than the
end. All of a sudden some Shmerl or other pops up like he's just dropped
down from heaven. Shmerl who, Shmerl what? Where does he come from,

this Shmerl? Nobody knows who he is; he's just plain Shmerl, a Jew, a male, a young male—and that's enough. There's a wedding with music, a cele-bration, a party, dancing, jumping. She went to the canopy like a kosher Jewish daughter, relying on her parents, who certainly knew what they were doing and to whom they were marrying her. Could it be otherwise? Her parents, in turn, relied on the marriage brokers, honest Jews who could never tell a lie. And the marriage brokers brokered the marriage on the basis of rumors and reports in the town; where there's smoke, there's fire, a general rumor is an oracle from heaven. An angel, so they said, had long since announced this marriage in heaven. The real marriage broker, so to speak, was God, and they, the marriage brokers, were nothing more than His messengers.

For the first time her eyes opened, and she beheld error in all its folly and repulsiveness. She finally saw the disgrace of marrying a man before knowing him, before knowing who and what he is. For the first time, she awoke to the truth: "*Gevalt*, Master of the Universe! How foolish we Jews are, how badly we act by letting ourselves be persuaded, deluded into mar-riages by liars who misuse the phrase 'made in heaven' in order to make themselves a living. No matter how bad a match might be, they always haul out the same old phrase, their all-purpose answer to every objection. They even use it to justify the objections: If this isn't right and that doesn't fit, if the match isn't even or it's totally odd—that's their final proof that God's behind it all, that even though it doesn't look right at first glance, it's going to come out just fine . . . And the fools believe them and never think to ask how these liars know what's been proclaimed in heaven, how they know the will of God. Did He tell them? And if these liars really are the messengers they say they are, then all their marriages would last forever. So then why do we see so many unhappy couples, so much weeping and tears, hatred and strife, so many desertions and divorces among us?

"Oy," a sigh escaped Eydl from the depths of her heart. "It's all a racket. This whole deal with marriages is nothing but foolishness, decep-tion, and deceit." That much seemed clear to her; you didn't need to be terribly bright to understand it, the simplest of women could figure it out. It was obvious to her now, but where were her brains before? Where were her parents' brains, that they didn't consider things thoroughly? What was the point of this passion for marriage, for pairing off children as quickly as possible? Master of the Universe! People, aside from being either male or female, are also human beings with souls, with free will, humanity, feel-ings—and they shouldn't be mated like animals. And now it turned out that ill-considered hurry and haste had led her into the teeth of calamity, into the hands of God knows who. She had nothing but the calico dress she was wearing, not a cent to her name. She was far from home, alone as a stone. What would come of her here, what would come of her parents at home, once they got the terrible news about their ill-starred daughter? Such mis-fortune, such disgrace! Outward shame, inward pain.

Things looked dark and bitter enough, yet suddenly—go riddle the human heart—a ray of hope shone through. "No!" she said, reconsidering, "It isn't possible. Let's not get carried away with suspicion for nothing. It could turn out to be nothing . . . I need to be patient and wait. And keep quiet in the meantime. It's a good thing that the innkeeper's gone for a cou-ple of days. It's better he doesn't know, better to keep quiet in the meantime."

She went to take a look out the window; she looked and looked—and nothing. She passed the day in suffering and anguish, looking, not taking a single bite to eat. She fell to her bed that night like a corpse.

The little one-eyed Jew came in next morning. The sight of a familiar face—even one she'd never before thought much of—brought Eydl back to life again, and she ran toward him without thinking, greeting him warmly. "Oy, a very welcome guest indeed. If I knew where you lived, I would have gone to you yesterday . . . Have you heard? . . . Do you know anything? Do you know, maybe, where he is?" Eydl spoke, Eydl asked breathlessly, choking on her tears, not taking her eyes from the little man.

"I heard alright," he said angrily, waving his thumb back and forth. "He should know from his life—the bastard, the robber—like I know where he's buggered off to. You hear, that's why I came. Maybe you know?"

"You're asking me?" said Eydl, making a face and jumping a few steps back, as if the man had burned her.

"He's cost me enough time, enough money, the son of a bitch. A-a, let him croak, wherever he is. Let no good come to him, 'cause he's living off my money. Ay, if I knew where he was, heh-heh, I'd send him—and his grandfather—straight to Hell."

Eydl covered her face with both hands, sobbing and weeping, her shoulders, her whole body trembling. The man watched her in silence, his good eye taking her in from head to foot while the bad one followed suit and rolled itself up and down.

"Please don't cry. Don't waste your beautiful eyes," begged the Jew, apparently moved to the point of heartbreak. "Do me this one favor. Have mercy on yourself and stop crying. Let's not kid ourselves. You're a smart girl, let's consider the situation calmly and see things as they are. You haven't really lost a thing. On the contrary—you should be healthy—on the contrary, the hell with that . . . that . . . You should raise up your hands to Him Who Lives Forever and make the blessing, 'Who hast freed me,' and that's all."

"Oy, I'm ruined!" wailed Eydl, drying her eyes. "What you see is all I've got. Nothing more than the dress I'm wearing—my entire fortune. What can I do now? Where should I go, where should I turn?"

"Dear, dear, by my life," the Jew comforted her. "Don't be crazy, you're with Jews here. Not in a forest with robbers or way out in the sticks, in a desert, with wild animals, God forbid. Please, don't lose hope."

"But things are so bad now, so bitter and bleak." Eydl turned to the little man, whose sweet, truly Jewish words of comfort were beginning to overcome her earlier hostility, and poured her heart out to him. "It's awful. Not a cent to my name, and I owe, yet. Besides deserting me, he took off and left me here as collateral. I owe for the rooms; they've already asked for the money, and I signed the bill. And then, I owe you, too. You've got a note from me . . ."

"Nu, so what? Should I go and rip out your soul? Should you tear yourself apart, take it too much to heart and God forbid die or commit suicide? What's the point? Very clever, by my life . . . On the contrary, just because you owe others, you have a duty to guard your health, to cherish your pretty eyes, your body, and everything else, so you can work and earn money, both for yourself and for your creditors, and gradually pay them off. Don't worry—this isn't the first time this has happened. You aren't the first and you won't be the last . . . For my part, I'm ready to wait. As long as you're healthy, your credit's good with me. And nu, what—it's such a disaster to be healthy? And as far as being a deserted wife goes, don't worry. It's just more foolishness. With God's help, we'll find a way around that, too, for sure."

Eydl was deeply moved by these life-giving words, and didn't know how to thank the little man for standing by her in her time of need. She was completely reconciled with him in her heart, and she gave him a wordless look of friendship that spoke louder than any speech.

"You know what," said the Jew in a begging tone, clutching at his heart, "In the meantime, for the present, I'd like to invite you to come stay with me. I've got a big house with enough rooms for me and my wife and plenty of others. We can find a room for you too. Whaddya say?"

Eydl hesitated silently. It would be a little awkward to say yes—how would it look to his wife? But saying no would be even worse, she had no floor underneath her, no roof above her head. The Jew, though, seemed to see right into her heart, and slipped her some words to convince her.

"Your coming will be very welcome to my wife. I should only be as happy as she's going to be with you. She's a very good person, more hospitable than anybody I've ever seen. She loves everybody. All women should have a reputation like hers . . . And don't worry, you'll earn some money. I'll come up with something . . . So what's there to talk about? Nothing. God willing, we'll still settle our account; just stay healthy . . . Now I'll go pay your bill for the inn."

"Who can measure a Jewish soul?" thought Eydl after the man had gone. "To look at him, you wouldn't think much, but what a good heart he has. A Jew really stays a Jew. No matter how ugly he is on the outside, that's how beautiful and pure he is within. Jews really are, as it's written, the merciful children of the merciful. May God not punish me for not seeing this before and for not being able to stand him."

While Eydl was still regretting her groundless hatred for so kosher a soul, the little man came back and took Eydl from the inn to his house, and to his wife, Sheyntse.

Naturally, if Sheyntse is his wife, the little Jew with the bad eye is her husband, none other than Levi Bokher himself.

Shmerl, the so-called husband, and Levi Bokher had been working hand-in-glove in this whole affair with Eydl. The innkeeper, a sharpie from way back, a former clerk, a broker who knew how to do business, also joined in the dance. The three of them played a scene right out of the theater. Each played his role like a master. Hodel the agent, whose modus operandi consisted of running around, sniffing things out, opening her mouth and throwing herself into the middle, whether she'd been invited or not, Hodel also snuck into the play through the back door, like a process server. She sniffed Shmerl out as soon as he arrived with Eydl; it was she who burst in on them like a bomb the minute they arrived at the inn. Her joy so confused her that her mouth opened and she came within a hair's

breadth of calling Shmerl by his real name, Nakhmen-Traytl. She would
have made a real mess of things, and opened Eydl's eyes before it was time.
Nakh . . . Nakh . . . the beginning of Nakhmen was already rolling out of
her throat. Good thing that Shmerl twigged in time, yelled at her and
threw her out.

5

A NEW WORLD opened up for Eydl in Levi Bokher's house, a new world
with new troubles, beside which her earlier troubles were a piece of cake,
the introduction to a story that was just getting going, an utterly terrible
but all too usual story. A story that takes place nearly every day with many
other unfortunate Jewish girls who are tricked into a snare like Eydl. A
story that has long since stolen in among us Jews like a long-drawn-out disease, as if to spite so kosher a nation, one so careful of sin as the people of
Israel. And we haven't been able to get rid of it yet.

The essence, the content of this story is nearly always the same, and
there's no further need to go into detail. It starts off nicely and then goes
awry. It has every kind of flavor—sour and bitter, cold and warm, pricks of
conscience with physical suffering and pain. On the one side there are vex-
ations deep within the soul, the feeling of a duty to maintain one's self-
respect, one's honor and dignity as a human being, the fear of sin, of shame
before God and man, which is rooted in the human heart. And on the other
side, the sufferings inflicted, severe sufferings—pain, duress, blows,
hunger, and afflictions of every kind: promissory notes obtained by fraud,
creditors, nuisances, troublemakers, foul temptations that irritate and ex-
cite the blood—they all cause storms, upsets, struggles within; a long, hard
war that sinful humanity, mere flesh and blood, cannot endure—and so
falls.

And Eydl, poor Eydl, fell. She fought for her life against all the bitter
torments inflicted upon her, renewing her strength and convincing herself
of miracles and wonders—maybe her steaming tears would soften the
hearts of her tormentors and they'd let her go, or maybe a miracle would
allow her to escape unnoticed—but time proved that she was dreaming. It
was easier to melt a stone than the stopped-up hearts of those evildoers;

sneaking quietly away was no solution, it would only insure her misfortune and bring more troubles upon her and her loved ones. "Now," she considered, "I'm the only one who is unhappy. Who knows me, who knows who I am? At least my shame is covered. There's still hope that I can buy my way out of here one day and be free. But if I sneak away—even if it's possible—they'll find me for sure wherever I am. They'll find their way to my home, present the notes I signed, and reveal the kind of house that I'm in. My parents would be ashamed to be seen, the pain would kill them. My sisters would sit on the shelf, they'd never be able to get married—the whole family would be destroyed." There was no way out. Eydl suffered and struggled until her strength gave out. Then she fell.

Yes, Eydl fell indeed, but she didn't sink too deeply. Her body was taken, but her soul, a gift from God—no one could take her soul. Feelings of goodness and mercy beat within her tender heart. She felt the sufferings of many of her unfortunate comrades, and was there to help them in their emergencies; at times of anger and quarrels, she served as their advocate, intervened for them with Levi and Auntie Sheyntse, disregarding the torments, the hatred and misery that this would often bring her way.

Eydl's comrades loved her. She was their chief. Malvinke, a buxom girl, clever, lively, cheerful, with a broad face and upturned nose, crowned Eydl with the title of Captain—and everyone took up the name. Even the Turk, who had been head-girl before her, voluntarily relinquished her position and became more attached to Eydl than anybody.

Auntie Sheyntse alone hated Eydl from the bottom of her heart. "Deserted wife" was the only name Sheyntse ever used for her, just to get a jab in. It's well known that Auntie Sheyntse ruled her house with an iron hand, that she wanted no one but herself to be allowed to lift up her head or have a will of her own. She was always complaining about modern times and modern people. "Things," she would groan, "Ain't what they used to be. A madam used to be a madam—everyone in the house killed themselves working for her. And now? Now 'they' want their say too—as if they were somebody."

It bothered her greatly if one of the girls should be unusually pretty, and Auntie Sheyntse would arrange an interview and tell her of her own good years, how beautiful she had been, how they used to just hang themselves over her, but that it never went to her head and she had been scared stiff of her madam.

The only words Auntie Sheyntse had for a girl whose behavior displeased her were: "You're a person, you impudent slut? You're a dummy, a painted dummy, a hunk of meat, a piece of goods, and that's all!"

Auntie Sheyntse was thus a blood enemy to Eydl, both because of her beauty and because of the impudence she displayed in retaining her human dignity and teaching the other girls that they were people too—in contrast to Sheyntse's Torah. She'd complain at every opportunity that Eydl had forgotten all the good they'd done her when her husband ran off and left her starving, naked, and sunk in debt. Were it not for Levi and her, Auntie Sheyntse, that is, where would Eydl be now? Auntie Sheyntse's education and way of thinking made such remarks entirely plausible, and she generally concluded her list of benefactions with a complaint: "Master of the Universe, what's the world coming to? What kind of people are these today?"

The thought that God knows a person's heart, that a pure, unspotted soul is what really matters to Him, gave Eydl the strength to endure her bitter torments and foul condition. Women of great saintliness and chastity had also, as the books write, been captured on occasion, tortured and forced as she had been—and God had forgiven their sins on account of their purity of soul. He saw their pain and eventually helped them out of it. Eydl likewise hoped to be delivered from her captivity. She hoped and hoped . . .

And ended up like all her fellow unfortunates: with a scourge of an illness that finally began to consume her. She lay a long while in an isolation room in the hospital, shut off from the world, forgotten, cast off like a withered flower, a broken vessel, a potsherd of no further use, a thing to be avoided and only looked at unwillingly.

Auntie Sheyntse didn't visit her even once; she forbade the other girls to set foot in the hospital, and took care against their doing so. Only rarely and with great effort did they succeed in sending some preserves with Malvinke, who would risk her own neck to steal off to Eydl with the package of contraband.

Once, after Hodel the agent had sat with Sheyntse in her room for a couple of hours; when she'd had enough talk about the corruption of the modern world and the evils of modern times; once she'd already fulfilled the commandment of dunking a piece of honey cake and taking a shot of whiskey, and was getting ready to leave, she suddenly caught herself, as if she'd just remembered something very important.

"Oy, Sheyntsenyu, it's a good thing that I remembered—I could have left without saying a word. You listening, Sheyntsenyu? Yesterday I was passing right by the hospital, so I thought to myself, 'Hmm, why don't I go in to see that beauty of yours, the deserted wife, as you call her, and find out how she's doing?' Oy, what should I tell you, darling? God, our enemies should be in her shoes, everyone who wishes us ill. She's so changed that you wouldn't know her. The flesh, the beauty—nothing left, God save us, but skin and bones. I should live to see as many good things as I had tears in my eyes and breaks in my heart when I saw her lying on her cot there, weak and broken. She looked at me with a pair of dull, swollen eyes; she sighed but never spoke. She looked and looked, the tears drip-dripping. I consoled her, encouraged her with my words—the usual stuff—but in my heart I knew that it was all for nothing—she's an empty shell. May God forgive me, but for His sake I told a lie; I told her that you sent her your warmest regards and wanted to know how she was doing. As soon as she heard this, her whole body began to tremble. She was burning with the fires of Hell. Her eyes were blazing, pitch and sulphur came out of her mouth: fierce, quiet curses. May they hurt you as little as you heard them. May they fall on the heads of our enemies, on mad dogs, O Master of the Universe."

"Amen!" Sheyntse let fly at the top of her lungs, jumping out of her seat as if she'd been bitten by a snake. "Nu, I'm asking you—what's the world coming to? Here's the thanks we get for doing her a favor. My husband stood by her in her time of trouble, when she had been abandoned and left naked, lonely as a stone—she might as well have drowned herself. It isn't enough that my husband didn't ask her for his own money—and it was a considerable amount—he paid off what she owed to others! We took her into our house, a lost and hopeless girl. 'Here, here's everything you need.' She ate our food, she wore our clothes. Maybe you know what was missing? She ate, drank, dolled herself up, lived and had fun and all at our expense. Sure, she's got what to complain about! But these things happen, God save us. But what? Who's to blame for that? How, I ask you, am I supposed to keep from blowing up when I hear that such a . . . such a . . . you'll excuse me, such a—"

"Sheyntsenyu, darling, please, don't eat your heart out. Think of your health. Idle curses vanish like smoke in empty fields and deserted forests. I swear to you, Sheyntsenyu, you should have as much life and health as I have remorse and anger at myself, for having said anything. Nu, do you need any further proof of how much I regret it? Dear heart, sweet soul, don't take it so to heart. Sha, calm down a little, if not for my sake, then for your own, for the sake of your health. Think of your health."

Hodel delivered this speech through tightly stretched lips and in a tone of prayerful supplication. She got up from her seat and cast a subtle eye on a large round bottle of *vishnick* that was standing in a corner.

"You know what, Sheyntsenyu?" she asked. "I don't think it'd hurt if you took a little *vishnick* to calm yourself."

"What do you think? I'll do as you say," Auntie Sheyntse answered, puffing like a goose and nearly melting from fatness, "But only if you join me and have some too. Very good *vishnick*."

"Ach, for the sake of your health, I'll drink as much as I can." Hodel let herself be talked into it and helped Sheyntse lift up the bottle.

When Hodel left, she was happy and feeling no pain. Auntie Sheyntse's face was flushed. She lay herself down to sleep, forgetting all about Eydl and not even seeing her in her dreams.

Some time later Eydl came out of the hospital, a different person from the one who'd gone in. Frail, broken, yellow as wax, emaciated, dried out. Her hair was falling out and she was wearing a faded old dress. Having nowhere to lay her head, she came to Levi Bokher's house at evening, naked, hungry, faint. Seeing her from afar, Auntie Sheyntse barred the door before her. Eydl was stupefied, and had no idea where she could go to pass the night.

At first that night seemed to be one of those beautiful summer nights, dark and comely with a sky-blue veil and a kerchief of stars that shone like diamonds; a mild, lovely, friendly night, bringing scents of herbs and grass to every nose, giving everyone a free concert by that world-renowned singer, the nightingale. Everything looked fine and beautiful, a positive delight. And all of a sudden, it changed completely, as if a fit of madness had come over it. A dark, black cloud was approaching, the face of the night became clouded, its form wild and strange. No more loveliness, no more mildness; it was cold—ice. All its lights went out at once, it started blowing, acting crazy, storming and making an uproar. The darkness grew deeper and deeper; howling, whistling demons were jumping, dancing, spinning about. The nightingale went mute and hid among leaves and branches; the concertgoers scattered, making quickly for home, certain that somewhere in the forest a sorcerer had hung himself that night.

The next morning they found Eydl hanging from a tree in Levi Bokher's garden.

Who would miss a person like Eydl, if she went and hung herself? Let them all perish thus! Is such a person worth speaking about or even mentioning? Of course not—so good riddance. Nobody cared but the other girls, the same kind of goods as she was. Her life and its bitter end touched them to the quick and gave them a powerful hint of how utterly unfortunate, how deeply degraded they were. And they thought it over carefully.

Eydl was taken just as she was, without any big, long ceremonies, thrown into a garbage cart, and wheeled to the cemetery, where she was buried behind the fence like a dog. Malvinke and the Turk stood over the fresh grave with lowered heads, wailing and lamenting bitterly.

"It's no use," said Malvinke, wiping her eyes and waving her hand. "Bite your lips and be quiet, sister."

"Oy, my heart's boiling and seething, overflowing with pain; hot, bitter tears are spilling out of me all by themselves," said the Turk, grabbing her breast. "Woe to our lives and woe to our death. Here you have us—under the ground and over the ground."

"Over the ground, you say!" asked Malvinke, feigning incomprehension. "I see spider webs over there, with sucked-out fly carcasses in them."

"It's you, sister, and me, and all of us," said the Turk, fixing Malvinke with her red, tear-swollen eyes. "You said it—spider webs, spiders. Our spiders tangle us up in their webs and suck away at us, suck out the last drop of our blood and then go their way, looking for fresh new victims, while we sucked-out flies hang there and rot. Oy, it's a heartbreak!" The Turk burst into tears and beat her breast. "Let me at least say what's on my mind. Can you believe it? The people who torture and seduce and suck, they're the respectable ones; and the ones who are tortured, seduced, and sucked dry, you know what they are? A shame, a disgrace even to mention. Those exalted respectable people are on top of the world when they're living, and on top of the cemetery when they're dead. Just look at their gravestones, with dirges and praises engraved all over them, and Eydl, good, dear Eydl whose world they destroyed, whose life they poisoned—Eydl lies buried behind the fence like a dog. Her parents—God only knows where they are—can't even hope to come weep at their daughter's grave sometime. Poor Eydl, what have people brought you to? Oy, God full of mercy, where are you?"

"What good is mourning, what good is crying, when it doesn't change a thing? Sha, sister, sha." Malvinke tried to stop the Turk's crying, and burst into tears herself.

"I was somebody's child too," the Turk overflowed with a new flood of tears. "A tender, beloved child. My mother took plenty of trouble with me from the time I was born. Gradually, a little at a time, I grew up, and every day that I grew took its toll on her health. She stayed up over me at night, took food and drink from her own mouth, and after a few years had passed, finally saw her child grown into a flourishing rose. Suddenly people, heartless people, came to her carefully tended rose and uprooted it, trampled it ... Let's at least cry ourselves out now. Let my tears soak down to Eydl through her grave, so she'll know that she's being mourned by her devoted sister, who is as unhappy and unfortunate as she was."

AT THE BEGINNING of her fall, the Turk, like all similar unfortunates, felt herself sinking ever lower into the depths of filth. But sin was a boa, as big and long as a rafter; and the sinner was the victim who, transfixed by its gaze, approaches nearer instead of running away, and gives herself over into the jaws of the destroyer. The same power of enchantment seems to lie in the eyes of Satan, the serpent. No sooner does a person stray from the proper path and enter the devil's domain than she is drawn by this power, dragged like a splinter in a whirlpool until she loses her reason and plunges down to the depths of Hell. She needs plenty of courage and outside help to pull herself out and regain her former state. Let the fortunate, whose path through life has been happier, who have sailed the stormy seas of life without suffering any shipwreck—let them not lord their virtue over those unfortunates whom ill-luck has dragged off and tossed down to the depths of a boiling abyss. Let them not, if they have the slightest sense of mercy, let them not point at their misled brothers and sisters, or shame and insult them with complacent mockery. Neither curse the errant nor push the fallen away, but seek out a means and lend a hand to help raise the sinners from their sin.

When sins are concealed, there will be no more sinners. If you are in no position to help, if the fallen one remains a lost sheep forever, at least place your hands upon this sacrifice and confess the sins of your house and of all of Israel . . .

It's true that at first the Turk felt that she had taken an ugly fall into the web and that it was no good to stay there. But she'd become so entangled that she couldn't make a move. The web-spinners devised ways to deal with her, tangled her up so that she could never get out of their hands. She wanted to escape, but lacked the strength to do so. It was as if the lines of command between body and brain had been cut. But at the very beginning she still had some small hope of doing something to save herself. She delayed it, though, until later. Meanwhile, time passed and she became ever more entangled. Her will began to weaken, she would have lost her reason and been lost forever herself, had an unexpected turn of events not come to her aid—the violent death of the Captain revived her, shook her unconscious soul awake. The voice of Eydl's blood cried out to her from the ground: "Master of the Universe, why was I tormented, why were my years cut needlessly short? Oy, to what did people reduce me with their wickedness? Wake up, sister! Gird up your loins and escape from the hands of the evildoers!"

The belief in reincarnation, that is, that the human soul migrates into some other creature after death, seems at first sight to be foolish, irrational. Properly considered, however, it isn't so foolish at all—there's a good deal of truth to it. How else can you explain the voice that kept ringing in the Turk's ears, rousing her constantly? Or the image, the image of Eydl, which appeared in her mind and stood before her eyes, whether she was awake or asleep? How can we explain the spirit that beat in her heart, admonishing her, teaching her decency and piety, forcing her to escape and climb back to the proper path? It was Eydl—in the Turk's heart, in her head, in all her members. Eydl's spirit breathed within the Turk, and was her life. Eydl's sterling character served her as a model and illuminated her way; only through Eydl did she gain courage, did her enfeebled will become fresher and stronger. Eydl's voice screamed loudly within her: "Wake up, wake up, my sister. Strengthen yourself and escape from the hands of the evildoers."

The Turk took it upon herself to do everything she could to get herself out of the web. And just as she was thinking of finding a way out, a new carcass fell squirming into the web beside her—Beyle, a child. Seeing her, the Turk felt her pity awaken, and from that moment on she was very devoted to Beyle, looking after her as if Beyle were her younger, orphaned sister, and looking for ways to get the two of them out of there. But this was only possible so long as she and Beyle remained together in Levi Bokher's house—and what would happen if Beyle were sold to someplace far away? The Turk would never see her again. This fear cast a pall over the Turk's whole life, and she began to pay close attention to Levi, to see what he was planning to do with her beloved Beyle.

7

"WHERE CAN HE BE RUNNING so fast, so early in the morning? Something isn't right." Refoel was looking out of the open window of his vestibule, watching in amazement as Hershele ran breathlessly down the street. Wasting no time, Refoel got dressed and went out to discover the meaning of Hershele's hurry.

This has been the Glupsker way from time immemorial: Let just one of them stir, the domino effect kicks in; one after the other, an entire community stirs with him. You almost never see a Jew by himself—they come only in tens, a *minyen* at a time. Not because single units are so cheap, ten for a groschen like cucumbers or radishes, but just because Jewish souls like to stick to each other like sardines, and are just as hard to separate. If one of them does something or other, the next one senses it immediately. One has scarcely opened his mouth to speak, when another jumps in and interrupts him. If Grunem wants to take a step, Gimpl gets between his feet; let Berl go hide himself in a corner, up springs Yankl-Shmerl like a mushroom.

Refoel's leaving the house so early in the morning had been anticipated by others who were rushing breathlessly down the street, still not properly dressed: one in slippers, no stockings, running and poking his hand into the slightly tangled sleeve of his capote; a second was hurrying along, dealing with the buttons on his fly, which, just to spite him, didn't want to stay closed; a third couldn't allow himself time to stop, and held his nose be-tween his fingers, ready to blow it at the first opportunity; and a fourth col-lided with a Jew running in the opposite direction and both fell flat on their faces. Glupsk was on the move.

"Mister, mister, what's the rush?" someone shouted from a distance and started to run.

"Excuse me, mister. Why are you rushing, where are you rushing? Mister, mister!" Refoel, quite uneasy by now, was also shouting to this one and that one.

Scream bloody murder, you won't get an answer. Jews don't have the time. They communicated with him by gestures: there, there, to the back street. One of them, more settled than the others, answered curtly and sharply: "People are running, so I'm running too."

At the entry to the back street, Refoel bumped into a myopic, wrinkled woman who was wringing her hands and shaking her head, complaining to herself in a weepy singsong, as if lamenting someone's death. "Woe is me. A terrible misfortune has befallen us. Woe, woe is me."

"Huh? What's wrong?" asked Refoel, beside himself with fear. "What happened? Who was hurt?"

"I should know? Everybody was running, so . . ." The woman stared, shrugged her shoulders, and went her way.

The little street was bustling. Jews in *tsitsis* without their capotes, with pillow feathers on their yarmulkes, half-asleep, not yet "ready," stood in their doorways, their pointy-bearded heads thrown back, looking out with one hand over their eyes. Female heads were sticking out of the windows on either side of the street, sweaty faces just out from under the covers, yelling back and forth to each other, wheezing from lungs that hadn't yet been cleared. A crowd of Jews was running back and forth, amid much talk-ing and hand-waving, quarreling and telling-off. Everyone had something to say.

"Some drunks got into a fight. Punches were flying like on Simkhes Toyre."

"Where's the fire? Tell me where it is. Why hasn't the alarm-bell rung?"

"A cut-purse took something. Oy, did he make out? Plenty of store-keepers should do as well."

"Dear wedding-guests! Paupers! You've got all the escorting you're gonna get for three rubles. *Feierabend,* we're going home." The musicians had stopped in the middle of the street and were screaming.

"Oy, they're making a funeral for that punk there, and they're making a good one . . . The angels of destruction, the cops, have already come."

From everything that was being said, Refoel deduced that there must be some kind of trouble in which Hershele was involved, and he made hurriedly for the crowd at the end of the street, where the real action was. He pushed his way through, exploding into the center of the circle like a bomb, and beheld a terrible sight. Hershele, beaten and battered, with a lump on his forehead, was holding tightly to the skirts of a woman's dress with both hands. A policeman was holding Hershele by the collar, hitting him on the back of the neck. Hershele argued, begged, took a vow with a bitter lament, and the woman—it was the same new in-law who had been hopping along the street not long before—the woman was cursing him with machine-like precision, throwing her hands in all directions.

"What's the meaning of this?" asked Refoel furiously, placing himself directly across from Hershele.

"Oy, Reb Refoel!" screamed Hershele, as a new flood of tears poured out of his eyes. "Do a *mitsve. Gevalt,* let her tell . . ."

"What are you listening to this thief for?" the woman screamed in a high-pitched voice. She turned here to Refoel, there to the policeman, again to the crowd, and spewed out a mixture of Yiddish and Russian, as the situation seemed to demand. "Screw the kid, Master of the Universe. From my pocket, he picked my pocket. Father in Heaven, I want he should get as many beatings as where my wallet is. I'm a woman, a poor, *vey iz mir* . . . What are you so quiet for, asshole?" She rallied her husband, who was standing at her side, giving him a poke with her elbow to get him talking. "You'll hear, what my husband he'll tell you. Talk, you son of a bitch. Screw you and get loquacious with the be-foreskinned, tell him, shit-for-brains, what you saw, that you saw this *sheygets* . . ."

"Whattaya got to say for yourself?" said Reyze, pushing her way into the middle of the crowd with the help of a basketful of food that she'd just picked up at the market. "A fine boy, by my life. Have you ever seen such a business?"

". . . saw this *sheygets khap* by me my wallet," concluded the woman with a loud, outlandish squeak, calling her husband to witness and giving him a good pinch in the behind as she did so.

"Oy, have mercy," gasped Hershele, drawing Reyze's attention pleadingly to the woman. "She's inventing all this for a reason. I recognized her; let her tell me, that's all I want, let her tell me where she led her off to. Her."

"I can't make out a word," said Refoel, shrugging his shoulders in amazement.

"Her, Reyze! You remember her. She once left her things with you. You remember her?"

"Oy, I'll be damned," said Reyze, shaking her head. "Now I get it. I understand. Now it makes sense. Of course, it's Hodel, good old Hodel. Don't ask, Reb Refoel; trust me. I'll tell you later. But now, let's take her to the police station."

"To the police station, to the police station," cried voices from the crowd.

"Jewish justice, all right! Just like Sodom." The woman spewed her words out breathlessly, mustering all her powers of persuasion. "If it's lies that I'm telling, Master of the Universe, it should dry up, my tongue. What am I, a bitch instead of a Jewish woman, that I should lie here and bark? Let my husband bear witness. Mendik—enemies, your bones should rot inside you—Mendik, what are you so quiet for? Get loquacious with him, asshole! . . . You hear, sir? I'm going along on my way, I—how do you say it?—I'm an in-law now, I just married off my daughter, wish me *mazl tov*, here's for you a piece of honey cake. So I'm going my way, I'm hopping nice and Jewish, and my husband, Mendye, he's going too. The music's playing, a *mekhaye*. And meanwhile, from the devil comes this fine young man . . ."

"You ever hear such a jaw-concerto?" Reyze cut Hodel off in midspeech. "Whattaya got to say for yourself? We don't know her, alas? We don't know who she is?"

The policeman saw that there were two sides to the story, so he stood there, looking silently from one side to the other and waiting.

"Make him *treyf!*" said a voice from the crowd.

Refoel did what had to be done, and the in-laws and Hershele were immediately taken to the police station together.

Hodel's eldest daughter, Tsippe, had already been engaged twice, and both engagements had been canceled as a result of Hodel's failure to pay off the promised dowry. The present groom had likewise dug in his heels;

he'd settle for nothing less than the whole of the dowry—cold, hard cash down to the last penny. He wouldn't agree to any form of security at all—not to a promissory note, not even to a contract promising Tsippe, and hence him, a half of everything Hodel had, just as if her daughter were her son, after Hodel's death. He still said no—a wife with one of those contracts wouldn't do; all he wanted was the dowry he'd been promised.

Poor, saintly Hodel was very anxious. Woe unto her life—the third fiancé would also call off the wedding, and her daughter could stay single until her hair turned grey. Hodel would vent her grief on her husband, Mendye—it was all his fault, the idiot, the moron, the fool—nor did she forebear the occasional slap. And Mendye, to give him his due, put up with it all, submitted without a word.

At times she didn't show much respect for the Master of the Universe, either, and accused Him (and this is only a quotation) of not running His world with justice: He was with the rich, the satisfied, the strong. The rich have this world as well as the next, the strong are always on top; money goes to money and the poor have children whom they can't marry off.

And at just that time, in an evil hour, during this business with her daughter's fiancé, while Hodel was worrying herself sick, she transformed herself into a brigand, into a wild animal whose children were starving, and went out intent on hunting, of doing everything possible to find some prey. Luck was on her side; she found some immediately. In a single month, she used her lying ways to marry two newly-arrived, pretty, kosher, and innocent girls to two members of the fraternity of pimps. These fine young men immediately took their merchandise out of the country and gave Hodel a nice piece of change for her services as marriage broker. And there was a third merchant, a good friend of hers, whom she was trying to match up with Beyle, so that he'd buy her and take her off Levi's hands. It was still up in the air, not entirely settled, but chances looked, God willing, pretty good—Hodel would make a nice fat profit.

Hodel raised her eyes in praise and thanksgiving to the Lord, blessed be He and blessed be His Name, for His great wonders, for the grace that He hath manifested toward her and her daughter. She paid off the dowry, made a nice wardrobe for the bride, a new jacket for herself, and a capote for Mendye, and had the honor of leading Tsippe under the canopy to the beat of the kettledrum. Levi Bokher and Auntie Sheyntse escorted the bridal pair to the canopy, and everybody danced and partied all night long.

In the early morning Hodel the agent and her husband were hopping along the street to a march. Had Hershele not recognized her immediately and grabbed the skirts of her dress with a scream, Glupsk would have slept through the celebration and not come running to honor so dear a mother-in-law, one of its leading citizens.

LEVI BOKHER'S CELLAR was a deep, dark pit, and when headstrong girls with ugly, small-town ways—as, for instance, shame, standoffishness, not letting anyone get too palsy-walsy—when such girls went down there, their souls were purified, they became better, friendlier, more malleable, and emerged as fully-fledged social beings. This cellar was truly a hell, and the Angel of Destruction, with his thousands of eyes, was nothing in comparison with Levi Bokher and his one blind eye. He had thousands of demons within him, and his bad eye, with its constant movement, was as terrifying as a corpse that walks among the living.

There are many like him wandering God's world in human form; drinking, reproducing, stuffing themselves to bursting, they appear to be people. But in reality they are demons of the lowest sort, who have made a furtive escape from under the ground and come here to deceive, delude, and visit troubles on people. And they are not to be got rid of. They are not to be smoked out with incense or ink, which frighten even Satan and his gang. The Gehenna-police don't pursue these deserters too hard, the devil doesn't want to take them back to Hell. On the contrary, he bids them good riddance, let them go to some other hell, these filthy, foul, corrupted demons.

Therefore, Auntie Sheyntse had only to mention Levi's name and say that he'd throw her into the cellar, to set Beyle's every limb to trembling. Lying terrified on the sofa in her room, Beyle passed some difficult moments. Her situation was like that of a freshly buried corpse expecting, according to what is written, the imminent appearance of the horrible Angel of Silence, who would beat him with fiery rods of iron. But this is only a parable; Beyle felt far worse than the corpse. There was no comparison. A corpse *has* to suffer; it died so worms could eat its body, and the Angel has been appointed to flog it and take it in hand. Beyle was a living creature, though, with no obligation to let herself be tortured. She didn't understand what they wanted from her. What right did these "worms" have to her body and soul? Worms that knew nothing of her previous life, that hadn't felt her mother's pain during pregnancy or her bellyache at the birth, her heartache during the upbringing, her suffering, worry, vexation and hardship until the child had had smallpox, measles, all the childhood diseases, and finally stood on its own two feet. The worms' first glimpse of her was as grown, beautiful, lovely, as if she'd just appeared that way from out of the blue. A man plants a tree in his garden, tends it, spares himself no effort, devotes himself to it for a number of years until he lives to see ripe fruit— and someone else comes along, the devil knows from where, and tears the fruit off. How does anybody have the heart to rob parents of a child, the dearest and best that they have, which has cost them so much trouble and health; to embitter feelings of sweetness, extinguish the light of hope, to ruin a life and ravage a pure and innocent soul? And who are we talking about? Jews!

Beyle lay in terror. At the slightest rustle, her heart would pound, she would tremble and shake. Here comes her Angel of Destruction to inflict terrible, frightening torment upon her.

She heard steps, the door opened; a cold, shaky hand laid itself from behind on Beyle's bare shoulder. Her whole body went cold, she sat up quickly in great fright, her eyes like those of a lunatic.

"What are you so scared for, baby? Didn't you recognize me?"

Beyle, very upset, took a look and saw her "fiancé" before her. This fellow, who was always being presented to Beyle as a husband, was a fine piece of work. His face, with its rosy cheeks, thick lips, fleshy nose, and flaring nostrils, not to mention his rounded belly, bespoke a delicate nature that liked to indulge itself in pleasure. He was one of those refined people who'd send the whole world to Hell for the sake of his soul's delight. People matter to them only insofar as they are or can be useful or amusing. Others might suffer terribly, toil until the sweat drips off them, take food from their mouths, lose sleep; it can cost them their honor, their health, and their life, but as soon as the business is finished, they're thrown away like a pair of old boots. The sufferings of those who afford them some pleasure don't move this sort of person any more than the suffering of a fresh-caught fish squirming under the knife; on the contrary, the more it squirms, the more it tosses about, the greater their pleasure. A good name, learning, grey hair are no protection against such as these; they rob the most intelligent, the most distinguished of his dignity—to them he's a nobody, as if he weren't even there. Nothing is sacred to them, they have no feelings, no mercy. The sorrows and pains of others are nothing but novelties to tickle them; if someone falls and breaks his neck, they choke with laughter: "Look how nicely he stretches himself!" If a grieving, downhearted woman should be crying, they like to watch the color rise in her cheeks and say, "Ah, how pretty. Her tears make her really gorgeous." It gives them pleasure when somebody climbs and clambers up the walls, dances on a tightrope to get his daily bread, when a barefoot pauper runs hopping through a scorching winter frost; when ten paupers fight like dogs over a bone that's been thrown them. They are a kind of creature that was laid aside for a while by the Master of the Universe, the great artificer, before He had fully completed them; the devil snatched them up and hurriedly put a stone inside them instead of a heart, a dog's soul instead of a man's, and unleashed them to make trouble in the world.

"Baby," he mewed, approaching Beyle like a cat, "You're so beautiful when you pout and make faces like that. I like you so much."

"Go, go!" said Beyle, drawing a little farther back.

"I'm going, I'm going," he said, sliding closer.

"Not like that, a little farther, if you please." Beyle drew herself back again.

"But first we've got to say goodbye," he said, stretching his arms out to give Beyle a hug.

"By us, we don't use hands," Beyle pulled herself farther back.

"By us where? In Kaptsansk, you mean? Well, you're not in Kaptsansk anymore. You're here now, understand?"

"What have you got against a poor, lonely girl like me? I'll yell for help. Where am I, in a forest or among Jews?" Beyle spoke with feeling and wept hot tears.

"You're even more beautiful when you cry, like a rose with splashes of dewdrops on it. Stop it—I won't be able to control myself."

"Have mercy, I beg you, have mercy on me and my tender years."

"Sweet as sugar," he mewed with an unpleasant smile, putting his hand in his breast pocket.

"Have mercy on my mother and father, if not on me. They're old and broken. If you knew how much they loved me, how hard it was for them to part from me. But want forced us, oy, want, want."

"Here, baby, here," he said cold-bloodedly, taking a golden bracelet from his breast pocket and twirling it right before Beyle's eyes.

"Get out of here, you bandit," she screamed, pushing him so hard that he flew to the door and dropped the bracelet. And as soon as he was out, Levi Bokher came in with fire in his eyes, the bad eye rolling something awful. Beyle trembled and went white as a sheet.

"So, mademoiselle, you're going to play the queen in my house? You think that there's no law, no order in the world?" asked Levi Bokher with quiet fury, taking Beyle by both arms, clamping them so tightly that she lost her breath and bit her lip from the pain. "You were joking, weren't you, my little bird? Answer me, dear heart, weren't you?"

"Oy, I don't feel well. Let me catch my breath," sighed Beyle, changing color with fear, like a trembling chick in the claws of a hawk.

"So I'm right, eh? You *were* joking." Levi had a strange, sweet expression on his face that was worse than the most violent curses. "Come on and answer—right now."

"Answer what?" stammered Beyle, bowing her head.

"Yes or no. Straight to the point. I want to know."

Beyle stood in terrified silence. Suddenly, the Captain came to her mind and seemed to be there before her in the lamentable state in which she'd returned from the hospital—weak, broken, grieving, and pining. She seemed to be pointing to the tree on which she'd hung herself. "Rather than end up on the tree in a few years, after a life of torment and ruin, it's better to die a pure death right now," thought Beyle. Raising her head, she said "No!" boldly and sharply.

"Aha! So I guess you want to discuss it with me in the cellar," said Levi, his fury mounting, his blind eye going into action. "Yes or no? You've still got time. One, two, three . . ." Foaming quietly at the mouth, Levi threw himself onto Beyle like a mad dog. As he was grabbing her hair to drag her from the room, Auntie Sheyntse ran in, frantic, very upset, her kerchief askew, her hand on her heart, scarcely able to catch her breath. She took

Levi by the shoulder and whispered something in his ear. At once, he was standing helpless, as if he'd been given a slap in the face.

"Beylenyu, darling, what's the matter? *Vey iz mir,* you're not looking well at all." Auntie Sheyntse spoke as sympathetically as a devoted mother. "Go into the garden, daughter, take a little fresh air."

Beyle stood in mortal terror for a while, then came to herself and left in a hurry.

"Oy, send her father to Hell and let her burn there, that slut Hodel, together with her Mendrik!" Auntie Sheyntse erupted into curses after Beyle had left. "She must be sitting there right now, and God in heaven knows what kind of mess that slut, that cat, can make us with her evil tongue. Master of the Universe, let her tongue wither away! You don't know the kind of bitch she is already? When things get tight, she always finds a way to wiggle herself out—and wiggle someone else in to take the fall. 'Where is the girl? Where is she?' they're asking. And they want to know. People are taking her side, moving heaven and earth for her. It's terrible. You understand?"

"Who told you the secret about what's going on there?" asked Levi in astonishment.

"Who? Itsik Faktor, who hangs around the big shots there and cocks an ear to everything that happens. And if you're wondering why this time it's worse than before—before, we used to . . ."

"What good to me are stories about before," interrupted Levi. "What's the situation today?"

"Not what it used to be," sighed Sheyntse deeply. "Times have changed. And so has the governor. There's a new one, just arrived; he doesn't know us and we don't know him. They say that he's untouchable, on the level. You can't pay him off. Understand? It's a bad business."

"Unbelievable," said Levi. "And unbelievable means give them this," he shook a finger at his wife. "Nothing, not here. If, may the hour never come, they should turn up asking for her, answer two words: Not here. You listening? Not here, not here, not here."

"Sure, as long as they're idiots and believe us and don't make a search. Some excuse."

"Stupid woman! We've got to get the *khomets* out of the house in time, I mean, take her away to our friend Fayvl, nice and quiet, without anybody noticing. You understand?"

And that very night, the rattle of wheels was heard in Levi Bokher's courtyard. Auntie Sheyntse and Beyle were on their way, on the pretext of going for a little drive so that Beyle could get some air and have a few moments' pleasure. After everything was said and done, Auntie Sheyntse was still *Auntie* Sheyntse—a dear, kindly soul.

Book Six

1

ALTHOUGH REFOEL'S BUSINESS AFFAIRS were driving him to meet with his bosses, the distressed manufacturers, in Lodz, he postponed his trip for awhile because of the many important matters that needed his attention in Glupsk, and, indeed, a little on account of Hershele too. Now that Refoel knew the meaning of Hershele's attack on Hodel the agent, he understood full well that this Hodel, over whom everybody was making such a fuss, had committed a heinous crime against a Jewish girl, which could by no means be allowed to pass unchallenged. He used every means at his disposal, left no stone unturned, to get to the truth of what had become of the poor girl, and to make sure that Hershele, who was still in jail with Hodel on account of her false accusation, should emerge spotless and free.

But more than anything, it was Khantse who kept him in Glupsk. Since he'd heard the bad news about the factory in Lodz, and foreseen how much money Leybtse was going to lose because of him, he had been avoiding Leybtse's house. His heart longed for Khantse and the pleasure of her company, but it was too difficult for him to go to her: how was he supposed to look Leybtse in the eye while he cheated and deceived him with his tongue? . . . And bad as things already were for Refoel, what with not knowing what to do, his conscience had to go and open its mouth inside him.

"Corrupted being," it exclaimed. "You feel like seeing her? Why? For your own sake, your own enjoyment, your own desire. As long as you can get a look every once in a while and take your pleasure from her beauty, you can go away—and God knows when you're going to come back—without thinking about her, without considering that she's going to turn her brain inside-out trying to figure out what your sudden disappearance could mean. She can't even begin to understand it . . . She was a simple little wife, given away without too much thinking or choosing, like every other Jewish girl in Glupsk. She was satisfied with the way things were; all was right with the world, it was running like it was supposed to. And then you come along, wonderful you, and light a devil of a fire inside her—you teach her to comprehend things. Her previous life, the world around her, *they're* no good anymore; *you're* her whole world now—and suddenly you go away, without even a veiled explanation to keep her from feeling insulted and cast off; to leave her a hope that you'll return, so she won't sputter out like a candle from heartache and resentment."

So Refoel decided not to budge from Glupsk until he'd fulfilled his obligation to speak with Khantse and to give her a frank explanation of everything. It cost him plenty of pain to drag himself off to her. He stood distractedly at the door for a while, his eyes cast down as if he'd come to rob the place—going into Leybtse's house was as easy for him as dying. His only hope was that he'd get lucky and Leybtse wouldn't be home. This emboldened him a little, and he took his heavy heart into the house. The first person to greet him was Leybtse.

"Welcome!" he said, tapping his nose with a finger and nodding his head. "Ay-ay-ay, so long that you've been missing! It wasn't very nice of you, on my word. I never expected, I didn't believe you could do such a thing."

Refoel was upset; he muttered quietly, as if to excuse himself. Leybtse was walking up and down the house, tugging at his beard and rubbing his forehead, also quite upset; his face was fiery red. Bentsye was huddled in a corner, wearing a housecoat and a cap with earflaps; he was as pale as the wall, his face covered with large drops of sweat—altogether, he looked like a drowned rat. In the middle of the room lay a large leather suitcase, already packed and swelling in the middle, not yet fastened with the cord that was tangled around it. All was quiet for a while, they were as silent as if their tongues had been frozen, but you could see that Leybtse's blood was boiling.

Finally, he spoke distractedly—"That's the way things go"—stopping in front of Refoel and looking at him sharply. "It's very nice of you at least to have come. Is that any way to behave? Is that how people act? Nu, anyway—how's, uh, business?"

"Beh," bleated Refoel, mumbling anything just to wriggle out of an answer, and thinking to himself, *"Feh,* Leybtse must have figured it out already. He knows all about my troubles."

"That's what you say—beh?" said Leybtse with a frown, not taking his eyes from Refoel, and thinking to himself: "Heh, heh. He knows everything already. That 'beh' must mean that he's already figured out what's going on here."

"But why are you staring like that, Reb Refoel? Why aren't you talking?"

"I'm looking at the suitcase is all. Who's getting ready to go away, Reb Leybtse?"

"Come on now, you know. And don't worry—it's good that you know," answered Leybtse, assuming the air of a clever person who takes everything in at a glance. Then turning to his son-in-law, he said, "You might as well go to the synagogue for a while, Bentsye. Nothing's going to change for the moment."

"Should I go like this, in my housecoat, or get my capote from the suitcase?"

"It's OK the way you are. What's wrong with a housecoat? You've gone to the synagogue in your housecoat before."

"Oy vey, my walking stick! We packed my walking stick," Bentsye said to himself in dismay, letting his feet carry him to the door, where he kissed the *mezuze* and left the house as quietly as a kitten.

"Now we can speak freely," said Leybtse, grabbing hold of his beard and fixing Refoel with one eye. "Why kid each other? There are no secrets in the world. So here's the story. Their life, understand me, is ruined. You know him, my son-in-law, so please, tell me, what's the problem? A fine young man from a fine family, an absolute delight. For my own part, I love him. In my eyes he's as good as you can get. I'm happy with him. So you'd think everything's fine. But what good is any of this when his wife is an idiot? You understand? She—it's like some kind of farce, I'm telling you— she isn't happ ..." Instead of finishing the word, Leybtse, straining and making faces like a woman in labor, waited for Refoel to deliver it from his mouth.

"Isn't happy." Refoel got the idea and uttered the entire word, feeling a load slide off of him as he did so: it turned out that Leybtse wasn't upset over his business dealings with Refoel, but over something entirely different.

"She isn't happy. She says she doesn't love him," Leybtse said, spitting three times. *"Feh!* I haven't recognized my daughter for a while now, she's changed so much. She talks in a way that people like us, people in our position, simply don't. Have you ever heard such a thing, to hate a husband? And who, yet? It's a joke, I tell you, such a . . . excuse me, such a . . . it's like some kind of spell, a trick of some sort. Maybe you don't want to put up with this, maybe it's unpleasant for you to hear it? Please, tell me; I beg your pardon, tell me."

"This is why he's mad at me, thought Refoel, breaking out in a cold sweat. "It looks like Leybtse's figured everything out. He thinks it's all my doing and he's daring me to explain myself. A nasty business."

"Aha! You're silent. You've got nothing to say to me? Nu, hear me out then. So what, you say, that my daughter hates him. Nu, go ahead and hate him and keep it to yourself. Whose business is it to know what you like? Love, shmove; hate, shmate—foolishness! Crap like this between husband and wife—it isn't worth mentioning, so why bother to mention it? Just keep quiet. But the goddamned spell is so powerful that—no! 'I can't live in the same house with him,' she says. 'To live with a man whom you hate,' she says, 'Is a sin. Don't bring me,' she says, 'into transgression . . . I'm not an animal,' she says, 'I'm a human being, a human being with a will, with a mind of my own.' You hear how such a . . . such a—pardon me—talks. In short, what with one thing and another, things have got to the point of having to take the poor little husband, with his bag and baggage, his kit and caboodle, and send all of it back home to his parents.

"Oy, what a day they gave me today, my daughter and her mother, hot and cold . . . You know what?" Leybtse concluded with an entreaty. "We don't have to be ashamed with you, Reb Refoel. You're one of us, a good friend, so come on, let's go pay a visit on Khantse, she's sitting in her room in a funk. Bawl her out a little, you know what I mean, let her understand that she's an idiot, a foolish little woman who doesn't know what she really wants. Believe me, it'll have an effect on her. As far as she's concerned—and this is just between the two of us—you're a very important person. Besides, you'll also be fulfilling the *mitsve* of trying to bring peace to a husband and wife, of bringing a couple together. So come on, then, let's go."

Leybtse dragged Refoel forward by the hand. And poor Refoel, what could he do but let himself be led unwillingly down the long corridor, dragging after Leybtse like a calf behind a cow?

As the door to Khantse's room opened, they could hear the voice of Yentl, part hard-cop, part soft-cop, who was standing and arguing with her daughter, who sat at a table in the corner with her head in her hands. Leybtse and Refoel had scarcely entered when the conversation was broken off.

"It's OK, Yentl. It's only us. Reb Refoel has a few words to say to Khantse," said Leybtse, winking at his wife to tell her, "You can go now."

But Yentl didn't want to take the hint. She stood in astonishment, shrugging her shoulders and looking sourly at her husband, as if to say, "Who told you to come in here, you moron?"

"Nu, sit down, please," said Leybtse, sliding Refoel a chair directly opposite Khantse. Pleased as punch with what he'd managed to accomplish, he went over to his wife, whispered something in her ear, and the two of them went out.

Clearly, it had been Leybtse's evil destiny to assist his daughter in everything he didn't want her to do, right from the very beginning. It must have been written in heaven that he himself, his strange ways, should make a mess of his own household, that he himself should cause things to turn out exactly opposite to what he wanted. Ill-starred Leybtse! Are there other such *shlimazl*-fathers among the Jews? It would be worthwhile to find out.

Refoel and Khantse sat and gazed at each other in amazement for a number of minutes, not saying a word. Refoel spoke first, with a bitter little smile. "You know why your father brought me here, Khanele? He wants me to restore your husband to your good graces and also bawl you out a little."

"So you're working for my father? Nu, bawl me out, if that's what you said you'd do," said Khantse, somewhat vexed.

"No, Khanele, I'm the one who needs bawling out, not you," sighed Refoel.

"So you're insinuating," said Khantse, reddening like fire, "That what's between me and my husband is your fault, and now you're sighing about it?"

"Don't torture me, I beg you. Ay, if you only knew what's in my heart."

"And what would happen if I did? Would I take pleasure in your devotion and beg your pardon for what I just said?"

Refoel had no ready answer for her. He knew that if Khantse knew his heart, knew why he had come, she wouldn't have found it too pleasurable, and would certainly have had no need to beg his pardon.

"Or maybe you think that you deserve to be bawled out because you're feeling guilty for not having come to visit for so long?" Khantse tossed him a further barb.

Refoel was quite upset. He looked at Khantse lovingly, pleadingly, and kept silent.

"Silence also speaks," said Khantse, so moved by Refoel's look that her heart broke and tears came to her eyes. "Don't be angry, I beg you. Don't be offended if I got a little worked up just now. What should I do? I've had such a day today, oy, such a day—let me only be able to get through it."

"Dear, dear Khanele," said Refoel, so moved that he rose from his seat and went to take Khantse by the hand in order to pour out his feelings to her. He didn't notice that Yentl had come into the room, as if she were looking for something.

"Mama!" exclaimed Khantse, so that Refoel would know who was there. "What are you looking for?"

"Nothing, nothing! There's a knitting needle missing from the stocking—I looked for it in here, didn't find it. I'll have to go look somewhere else," answered Yentl, taking a look around and going unwillingly on her way.

Yentl's real intention had been to keep an eye on her daughter, who was sitting with a young man, unchaperoned. Women are usually more sensible than men: as long as Khantse and her husband had been man and wife, Yentl wasn't bothered by her sitting alone with Refoel in her room. Now, however, that Khantse could take it into her head to say that she didn't like her husband, "Heh, heh," thought Yentl, "We need to keep an eye on you." Yentl's heart was telling her something, but she didn't know what. The knitting needle was only an excuse.

Khantse understood what her mother was doing and Refoel also knew the meaning of the needle. Both of them had a lot to tell each other, and both of them realized that this was neither the time nor the place to do so.

"Ay, Khanele, I've got so much to say, but . . ."

"Oy, Refoel, I've got so much to tell you, but let's wait. I'll let you know when to come."

"So," said Refoel with a bitter smile, "I'll go now and tell them how I scolded you."

"And that it didn't help."

As he was leaving, Refoel bumped into Yentl at the door. She was running to tell her daughter the good news that the knitting needle, praise God, had been found.

2

REB ASHER THE MIDDLEMAN had been rather displeased with Refoel of late. Everybody knows that Reb Asher was anything but puffed-up; he didn't stand on his dignity and could swallow a sharp word without taking any offense. It didn't matter if someone thought him a liar; when necessary, he could make himself blind, deaf, and ignorant, and carry on doing business. And as a supplement to all these sterling qualities, he also had no fear of using his feet—a hundred times a day wasn't enough to make him tired of running to someone with a deal, no matter how vigorously that someone refused it. If the door was barred before him, he'd push his way in through the window. This way, that way—what was the difference, as long as he got in? . . . Which led to the general opinion of Reb Asher as a ball of fire, a man with an iron character. He crawls! Once he starts something, he works, he crawls, he pushes until he gets what he wants.

Nevertheless, Reb Asher's crawling to Refoel had been of no avail lately; his words impressed Refoel like a chickpea impresses a wall. On one occasion, Refoel got angry with him and showed him the door with such a scream that even a person like Reb Asher, no stickler for respect, grew enraged. Madder than hell, he ran quickly out to the street and vented his wrath at Refoel in front of all the people there.

"Jews! Have you ever heard of a Jew with no faith, who won't let you speculate or do business? We'd have a fine commerce if all the highways had to lead to iron bridges. It's like he's picked my pocket with his obstinacy . . . I'm telling you, brothers, none of these 'fermented' types, these deep thinkers—you can't depend on any of them. At first sight, he looks like a regular businessman—comes up with schemes, does business, does it pretty well—but the devil finally reveals himself: 'Whoa, hold back!' These people have no faith, they don't trust a single Jew, not Gedalye the mercer, not Faytl the haberdasher, not even Reb Yidl the moneychanger—not to mention God Himself. You understand? It's really a matter of 'none who go to her come back'—once a man's been infected with these ideas, the curse is on him for life: he'll never be a businessman. He has no faith, a Jew's word is nothing to him; you could lie down and die in front of him, he wouldn't give you credit unless you could pay him back on the spot. To him, a Jew's draft or note is a pawn ticket for the world to come—and for people like him, this world is all that there is, simple materiality, cash on the line. The world to come is nothing. No angels, demons, and evil spirits, nothing but delusions. And in case you think I'm joking, I've sworn to him a thousand times on my portion of the world to come, and it made no more difference to him than . . . Moscow can believe, Leipzig likewise believes a Jew. And if once in a while there's a bankruptcy, nu, what's the big deal? Moscow doesn't turn upside down, the Germans go on believing and lend even more. *Feh* on that deep thinker; *feh*, I tell you, Jews . . ."

The black morning when Reb Asher jumped out of his skin with anger occurred a couple of days after Refoel's encounter in Leybtse's house. Refoel was sitting at home, distraughtly pondering his situation. His business affairs demanded that he leave, yet he was unable to move. He had to talk to Khantse and tell her the whole truth about his pain and suffering, but he had to wait for the right time, until she wrote to him as they had agreed. And now, after what had happened between her and her husband, he was ten times more obliged to speak to her. But *what* to say, and what would come out of it? He didn't know himself; the situation was so tortuous now, even more tangled up than before. He felt, though, that he couldn't just leave things as they were; and he would also be very sorry to leave poor Hershele in the lurch. Things were bad. He was in a real fix, his head was splitting from thinking about it, and all of a sudden—haul out the welcome mat, here comes a guest! Reb Asher is here with his projects! It goes without saying that Reb Asher got what was coming to him and went away like he'd just been scalded. Rid of his guest, Refoel returned to his thoughts, languishing in them so deeply that he didn't notice Reb Avrum come in.

"Good day," said Reb Avrum, after standing in the doorway for a couple of minutes without Refoel's seeing him.

"Huh, what?" Refoel was too startled to look around.

"Nothing. I said good day. Don't be offended that I've disturbed you."

"A-ah, Reb Avrum!"

"I would never have bothered you, only . . . I promised. I've come here with a request."

"*You* bother *me*, Reb Avrum? No, never! Please, take a seat and let's hear your request."

"Reyze's going out of her mind. She's got a complaint against you, Reb Refoel. It's been a while already, she says, that you haven't been eating, haven't been drinking. No matter what she puts on the table, it comes back to her almost untouched. She says that she's breaking her head trying to figure out what's going on. Maybe you don't like the food? But she spares no effort, she says, does everything possible to make the food as good as can be. She doesn't scrimp on eggs or fat, she looks out for all kinds of new dishes, whatever is available: pot roast, sauerbraten, meatballs, a *tsimmes* with a chicken neck stuffed with *farfl* or kasha, stewed goose cracklings, browned till they're fit for a king. Maybe, she says, you're God forbid not well? If so, Leyb the barber-surgeon is still walking the earth. What do other people do? If there's no doctor or healer, there's always an exorcist. Seeing the way you've been looking the last little while, she says you're not healthy. She asked me just a little while ago, 'Go in to him and find out. You're a man,' she said, 'aren't you? So go and take a look at what's going on with him.' Nu, Reb Refoel, really, eh? What *is* the matter, anyway?"

"Eh, it happens sometimes. Who doesn't have problems from time to time?"

"Maybe you're taking this stuff with the orphan too much to heart? Sure, sure it's a problem, it's causing me trouble, too. Leyzer-Yankl, RIP, left him in my care. But still . . . though now that we're talking about it, let me ask you what's going on with him now, with the *shkots?*"

"The same as before. Hershele won't budge: let the woman say where the girl is. And she won't budge either: when the *sheygets* learns how to pick a pocket properly, maybe she'll know what he's talking about. In the meantime, things are bad."

"Isn't there any way around it, a charitable donation, for instance, if you know what I mean? How would that work?"

"I've already tried it. But it looks like somebody we didn't know about from the woman's side got there ahead of me. The situation now is like this: either they both sit in jail or it all gets smoothed over and they both go free."

"So let her go then, whatever her name is. Why be vindictive? Let both of them out of jail, and an end to it."

"It isn't a matter of vindictiveness, Reb Avrum, it's a matter of mercy for a human being, a Jewish girl. It's certain that this Hodel has shipped her off somewhere."

"Even so, I ask you, nu-nu-nu? I don't understand the danger in shipping her off. She isn't going to be eaten, God forbid. Among Jews, she won't disappear; someone'll find her for sure."

"Ay, Reb Avrum—how to tell you? We're dealing with things that aren't . . . clean. Hodel, understand me, Hodel's reputation isn't so good."

"What do you mean by that, Reb Refoel? I don't catch your drift."

"The drift is that this is mixed up with something terrible."

"Ay, ay, what's the matter with you? I don't understand what this can all be mixed up with. Let it be, they've been in jail long enough. I'm sorry for the *shkots*."

"And do you think, Reb Avrum, that this *shkots* of yours will want to be freed without bringing things to a close, without finding out where the girl is? You should see how he's sacrificing himself for her. At first sight he looks quiet and bashful; but what courage, what strength he has to be so unbending in the pursuit of what's right. He's really risen in my estimation, as high as anyone can go. I love him from the bottom of my heart. No, Reb Avrum, he's no *nebbish*, no *shlimazl* of a bench warmer or yeshiva-boy. He's going to grow into a man . . . Shh! Someone seems to be knocking at the door." Refoel pulled himself up to listen. "Come in, come in."

A beautiful, well-dressed young lady entered. Pausing at the threshold, she cast her glance first on one, then on the other of the two men, not knowing to whom to address herself. Reb Avrum followed the Jewish custom on beholding a woman: he became a little embarrassed and turned his face to the side. Refoel rose and approached his guest with a friendly demeanor.

"I'm looking for Reb Refoel. I have something to talk to him about," said the lady, sizing Refoel up with her eyes.

"At your service," said Refoel with a bow.

"What I have to say is strictly for the two of us."

Refoel invited the unknown woman into another room, winking to Reb Avrum to stay put.

Reb Avrum sat all alone for quite a long time, while strange thoughts moved into his head as if it were an open field. There was a Hodel spinning around in there, revealing herself disgustingly. Hershele and his Kaptsansker maiden were also spinning around. Reb Avrum gave a start, slapped his forehead and said "A-ha!," as if he had just figured out the difficulty Rashi was anticipating with his "as it is said." "A-ha, now I understand what Refoel's getting at, what 'shipped off somewhere' means. *Feh, feh,*" he said, lifting up his yarmulke and fanning his head with it, as if he were driving off flies. But the flies didn't give up; thoughts crept in, pecked at his head—this unknown beauty jumped right into the middle. In his mind's eye he beheld a beautiful figure, a radiant face, shining eyes; a delightful warmth spread over him, and his godlier side felt sick . . . Reb Avrum wrestled with his thoughts, strove to occupy himself with serious matters: a chapter of *Mishne*, a difficult *Bartenura*, a nice piece of *Zohar,* but all in vain. Thoughts attacked him like locusts; there was nothing for him to catch them with. Go pound Torah into your head, when it's swarming with something else! He was imagining, thinking of God knows what. Reb Avrum started sighing very Jewishly, while tracing the words of *Pittum Haketoyres* onto the table with his finger. *Pittum Haketoyres* once, twice—he didn't know what he was writing, didn't know that he was writing.

"Ach, don't be offended, Reb Avrum." Reb Refoel had come in very upset and hurried over to the wardrobe to change.

"I see that you're in a big hurry. It's time for me to go, too," said Reb Avrum, rising from his seat and going over to the door.

"There isn't a moment to lose. I have to run. Come back later today. Remember, *today,* Reb Avrum."

"Something isn't right," thought Reb Avrum as he left Refoel's. "Who could this beauty be? A relative? Why is he so upset? Hmm, his wife maybe? But what? Isn't he a widower? . . . You can never tell with a Litvak." Reb Avrum regretted these thoughts immediately and grew angry that it had even occurred to him to think such things of Refoel. Refoel—such a decent, honest man, with such a good heart. He shook his head in vexation, took hold of his beard, and quickly went off.

3

WANTING, AS SHE SAID, to give Beyle a little pleasure, Auntie Sheyntse
went out for a drive with her in the evening, to get a little fresh air. Two of
them left the house and one came back—Auntie Sheyntse, all alone. The
Turk was completely out of her mind with worry over Beyle, with not
knowing what had happened to her or where she was. She was too worried
to be able to sit still and she went in and out, from the house to the garden,
from the garden to the house, watching everywhere, rummaging about in
case she could turn something up.

She was sitting dejectedly among the dense branches in the garden in
back of the house, on an evening when the sky was a mirror of her heart—
gloomy, covered with dark black clouds. Tishe B'Ov was in the air. The
greenery was thin, faded; trees rustled, lamenting for their leaves, which
were starting to turn yellow, and for their balding crowns; they threw
themselves in whatever direction the wind blew them. Birds stood sad and
preoccupied, each on its twig, each on its branch, scratching themselves
under the wings with their beaks, casting an eye out here and there, shaking their feathers, yawning, then straight into their nests to sleep, without
singing as they do before sunset. Even the randy rooster had lost any desire
to fool around with his wives. His posture, his crow, weren't what they
should be; the crowing was more of a whistle, like something from a
cracked shofar. He stood distractedly, stretching out his neck, blinking his
eyes, twisting his head to the right and the left, looking altogether idiotic.
All of a sudden he shuffled his feet, moved himself to the side, scratched
the ground with a downcast wing, gathered all his wives and—good
night—went off with them to his home. A quiet sadness, a melancholy,
hovered round and round in the air . . . Hearts turned sour and bitter.
There was a longing, a dreaming, a yearning to go elsewhere—and souls
wept silently, poured themselves wordlessly out.

And so the Turk was sitting gloomily among the branches, sunk in
thought. Night began to fall, the darkness increased. The trees appeared
somewhat awkward, took on strangely altered aspects, and the conjuring
imagination dazzled the eyes with fanciful tricks. In the darkness, at a distance, the Turk thought that she saw Eydl hanging from a tree, signaling to

her as she swung: "Come, sister, come swing with me on the tree." The Turk started with fright. Before she could move from her spot, she heard footsteps, and Auntie Sheyntse came into view, standing in the garden with Itsik Faktor, a sort of creature graced by God with a very flexible back for bowing and bending over; with a brazen face, a pair of thieving eyes, and hands perfectly fitted to his work. This creature kneeled, bent, crawled, pushed his way through holes and cracks, sniffing, feeling, eavesdropping on what was going on in official circles. He'd grab a word and drag it off, cat-like, from one place to another, toying with it and stealthily taking a bite.

Auntie Sheyntse was carrying on a conversation with this creature, and the Turk could catch every tenth word: "In prison . . . Hodel . . . Where's the girl? . . . Bad . . . He's working, Refoel the commission agent . . . Money, tithes, endowments, donations"; this was Itsik's part. Auntie Sheyntse argued, rolling her eyes skyward, and pressed something into Itsik's hand. Then the two of them disappeared.

The Turk absorbed every word she heard. She figured that something wasn't right, that there was some sort of problem—if Itsik Faktor was there, there was trouble—and it suddenly occurred to her that Auntie Sheyntse's talk with Itsik Faktor had some connection with Beyle. The more she ruminated on what she had heard, the clearer it was to her that they'd been speaking of Beyle. It appeared that someone with some power and influence was working on her behalf, and that Hodel had in the meantime been called to account for it. That explained why she hadn't been seen at the Auntie's for several days now. The Auntie had hurried to hide the contraband before it was too late—*that* was the meaning of her drive with Beyle.

The Turk was positively dying of pity for Beyle, and she swore to avenge her in any way she could. She left the garden and stumbled around the courtyard in a frightful rage. As she was standing by the gate, she saw a phaeton pass by in the street, and recognized it as the one that the Auntie had taken with Beyle the day before. Her feet began to move of their own accord, and she jumped into the phaeton.

"Where to?" asked the driver.

"Where to?" The Turk thought it over. "There, where you went last night. Now you know where to?"

"Some question, do I know? My head's still between my shoulders, thank God. I know, I know where I took the Auntie and somebody else last night. Maybe you're really the Auntie herself. Your shawl is pulled so far over your head that I can't see your face."

The phaeton drove to a house in a remote area on the very outskirts of the city.

"Whoa!" The driver stopped his horses, speaking as if to himself. "Now, eh, you see that I know. Big surprise—I've been a driver all my life and I shouldn't know where Little Fayvl lives? Don't make me laugh. I'm like a rabbi, I can feel my way through the hard parts in the dark. And my horses are very learned, too . . . A question she asks me, do I know where Little Fayvl lives? Behold the house of Fayvl the Little or Fayvl Yoktan, as he's known among us!" The driver was talking to himself. He put the fare in his pocket and drove back to town.

The gate to Yoktan's house was locked, a circumstance that didn't much bother the Turk. Had it been open, she still would not have gone in; it could have raised suspicions and ruined her plan. She knew who Little Fayvl was, that he was one of Levi Bokher's gang, a depraved bastard, just like Levi Bokher.

It was now clear to her that the Auntie had hidden Beyle in his house until the heat was off. It was enough for the Turk to know where Beyle was, now she had to figure out what to do next.

She didn't sleep all night for thinking of where to start and what to do. Finally, Refoel the commission agent, whom Itsik Faktor had mentioned, came into her mind. She paused and thought, "That's who's been working so hard." The next day she enquired after Refoel, arrived while he was talking to Reb Avrum, and told him the whole story in secret.

ANYONE WHO THINKS that Reb Asher the middleman stayed angry with Refoel for his bad treatment of him is, you'll excuse me, greatly mistaken. After everything is said and done, Reb Asher was first and foremost a Jew, to whom the trivialities of honor do not matter, who can take a slap once in a while without, God forbid, making a fuss about it. Had Refoel been a nobleman, you can be sure that it would never have occurred to Reb Asher to take offense, not even if he, the nobleman, that is, had given him one right in the neck and shoved him down a flight of stairs. He, Reb Asher that is, would have stood up with God's help (as long as he hadn't broken his neck), shaken off his garments, made a bit of a face, and gone straight back up to the nobleman, bowed respectfully, and tried once again to creep in with a bit of business—maybe this time he'd have mercy.

Had Refoel, on the other hand, been a Jew, a real, hundred percent Jewish person, Reb Asher would have talked to him Jew to Jew without any ceremonies or b.s., given him hell good and proper—on the spot, as it were—and gone off calm and collected, planning to return the next day to discuss the matter with him again.

But Refoel was neither the one nor the other; or better, he was and was not the one, was and was not the other. To talk to him like you talk to a Jew—I shove you, you shove me; I grab your beard and wave my thumb in your face, you grab my beard and do the same—was absolutely impossible. Sure, of course, he was part of the Community of Israel, but there was something in his dress, in his manner, that wasn't quite . . . Jewish. God forbid you should act like yourself, act familiar, act like a Jew, with him. But what else are you supposed to do? To treat him with respect, to swallow his insults and stand before him like a slave, or like a Jew before a nobleman—basically, he's still a Jew. If not a hundred percent, he's at least a Jew in part.

It was therefore no wonder that so unpleasant an encounter as Reb Asher's with Refoel—something Reb Asher could neither swallow nor respond to—had left him completely perplexed, his heart bursting with anger. Even a middleman who was also an angel would not have been able to take it, and would also have blown up. Reb Asher did the right thing by leaving quickly. As soon as he got to the street, he vented his wrath behind Refoel's back. And he was right. Even a dog who's been caught in a door and managed to escape to the street, stops, lifts up his tail, and barks from afar. It was also very nice of Reb Asher to confine his actions to his mouth; sometimes in such cases, a Jew doesn't hesitate to use his pen and send a secret denunciation to the proper authorities in black and white. But as soon as Reb Asher had poured out his heart, spoken out in front of people, his anger departed and he cooled down.

"As I'm a Jew," thought Reb Asher, making up with Refoel in his heart, "If he said this and that, bawled me out with such and such words—so what? It's nothing, vanity of vanities. All the vainglory of honor isn't worth a single groschen, and what does this foolishness have to do with business? A real businessman doesn't chase after honor. He looks out for a profit . . . After all his raging that I'm this and that, I'm still not going to give up on the deal. Today or tomorrow he'll accept it, with God's help. He can get angry, turn his back on me as often as he wants. What kind of way is that to talk—'I don't want.' *He* doesn't want—and what about me? I'm nothing, what I want doesn't matter? In a day from now, a few days from now, we'll see whose will is stronger. It doesn't even begin to worry me. Ay-ay-ay," Reb Asher gave himself a sudden shake, scratched a temple, and sighed. "It doesn't begin to worry me, I tell you. What worries me, and plenty, is that today, *oy vey*, is Thursday."

Thursday is a rough day for a Jew. On Thursday his wife wants money for Shabbes. On Thursday a poor Jew is like a late-summer fly that won't go away. He creeps, searches, rummages, sticks his nose into everything, even at the risk of his life. Despite all of Reb Asher the middleman's strenuous exertions, his running around in a tizzy day and night, he lived in want, and, like all the other Jewish poor, his soul used to perish every Thursday, until he succeeded in hitting up an acquaintance for a few *guilden*, interest-free.

The Thursday in question was even worse than usual, as there was nobody left to borrow from. And then it came to him—Refoel! He'd hit Refoel for a loan. This thought helped him to make up with Refoel and forgive him his trespass "A Jew is not allowed to be angry," thought Reb Asher to himself, imagining the clever conversation he was going to have with Refoel. It would start off just like that, not about anything in particular, then roll inexorably on until it finally struck pay dirt. He stroked his beard with unaccustomed pleasure, as if a stuffed carp lay before him on a plate and the fragrance of Shabbes delicacies was rising into his nose. And as he stretched his foot out to start on his way, he caught sight of Refoel driving by in the distance; from the expression on his face, it was evident that he was very preoccupied, that he was hurrying to conclude a deal. Reb Asher felt a blow to his heart. He stood slack-jawed, his mouth wide open and his nose thrust out.

"This is no regular ride he's taking," reckoned Reb Asher. "Oy, I understand. I understand all right why he's in such a hurry—it's not so easy to fool me. He's running to make the deal without me. Oy, how can I keep from losing my mind when I see all my efforts, all my work, go for nothing?

I propose the deal, I work, I do, I crawl out of my skin, I talk and talk until I could burst with talking, and *he* thinks I'm a kid, an absolute beginner that he can do whatever he wants with. No sirree! I've got a nose and I can smell, I can smell what's happening even from a distance."

And Reb Asher's nose wrinkled up. Great as his wrath was, today was still Thursday. His empty pocket, his bitter want, reminded Reb Asher that a *kaptsn* has no right to be angry, that he has to take a slap with a smile. No matter how much others might wrong him or rob him of what was rightfully his, he has to bear his pain in silence, grovel at the feet of those fine people and even give them his blessing—long may they live—praise them to the skies with a smile, so to speak, on his face. So Reb Asher restrained his anger, put his nose back in joint, stuck a smile onto his beaming face and went round to Refoel's a couple of hours later to ask for a loan for the Sabbath. But woe unto him and his terrible luck, Refoel wasn't at home. He persevered and went back a couple more times, and still no Refoel. The living God alone knows the heaviness of Reb Asher's heart; and since he had passed the day in travail, he did a little dancing that night . . .

A hot time for the Jews—a celebration, joy to the Jewish world. At the beginning of the month of Ov, when the new moon was supposed to appear, the weather underwent a sudden change, in complete contradiction to the almanac. There it said beautiful, clear days (as you'd expect in July or August), but it had turned as cold and rainy as autumn. Jews were sinking up to their necks, crawling through the Glupsker muck in their shoes and stockings, the women in their silken dresses and golden bracelets. Of course, they weren't so upset that their clothes were spattered and covered with mud—why else were they so long and awkward, if not to serve as mud-flaps? The pain was in the Jews' hearts, on account of the moon. There was none. Jews were pining to see her radiant face, if only for a single minute, long enough to make *Kiddesh Levone*, to perform the ceremony of the Sanctification of the New Moon. The first quarter had already passed, she was physically mature, full-grown in every respect, fit to be blessed—but go sanctify her according to the laws of Moses and Israel, the way Jews do it, when she's hiding like a bashful bride . . . Then suddenly on Thursday evening the cocks began to crow, a breeze came blowing, the clouds scattered, and a lovely, clear moon, like a fresh-coiffed bride in her finery, proudly appeared, escorted by her jubilant relatives, the Star family, decked out in gold and jewels. The face of Glupsk began to shine with all its puddles—everything was a-sparkle. Jews raced with the good news, urging each other on: Faster, Faytl. Over here, Zeyrekh, Grunem, Sender, Fishl! Berl the shoemaker leaps quickly from his bench, Shmerl the tailor puts his work to the side, sticks his needle in his lapel, and they run out to look into the shining face of the moon. The whole crowd started swaying, yelling in all sorts of voices; you could hear little boys' thin falsettos, the deeper voices of adolescents, the thick, hoarse, strained basses of old, aged, grey, nasal, long-nosed, big-bellied grown-ups. The moon went her way and the Jews hopped and leapt at her, in accordance with the terms of the ceremony, in a happy, lively way.

Reb Asher was likewise hopping on tiptoe in the midst of the crowd. Catching sight of Reb Avrum nearby, he bowed weirdly in his direction and sang out "*Sholem Aleykhem*" three times.

"*Sholem aleykhem, aleykhem sholem*," responded Reb Avrum, interrupting the flow of his prayer. A minute later, the shoe was on the other foot. Reb Avrum turned his face, said three *Sholem Aleykhems* while bowing to Reb Asher, and Reb Asher responded with *Aleykhem Sholem* while he danced around and recited "Just as I dance toward you" to the moon.

As the two of them were dancing, bowing, and *Sholem aleykhem*ing each other, a phaeton with three people inside drove by quickly. Reb Asher immediately recognized Refoel as one of them, and his whole body began to tremble. His voice changed, went from low to high, as if a bone had caught in his throat, and he ended his *davening* with a weeping squeak. His soul wept within him; he was pained and vexed at Refoel's deceit, at his sneaking around to make deals without him. He cast an eye on Reb Avrum, looking at him sharply and thinking, "You've got to be squeezed, old man, and I'm just the guy to get it out of you. From you, I'll find out everything."

The Jews finish their *davening* and spit, then scatter in the directions of their homes. Reb Avrum had spat and wanted to go on his way, but Reb Asher grabbed him by his jacket and said, "What's your rush, Reb Avrum? If you please to wait a minute, we can go together. You're going home, of course?"

"I'm very sorry, but this time we aren't headed in the same direction," said Reb Avrum. "I'm going to Refoel's now."

"Oh, very good," said Reb Asher, snorting with pleasure. "If so, I'll keep you company. There's something I'd like to discuss with you while we're walking."

"OK. If you want to put yourself out."

"What shall I say, what shall I speak?" Reb Asher, walking, began his entrapment. "Our meeting here today was arranged in heaven, Reb Avrum, it really comes from God. Running into a man like you right after *Kiddesh Levone* is a good sign that the month ahead will be a fortunate one, Amen. Aren't I always saying everywhere—in the market, in the brokerage houses—I'm always saying, 'There's only one man who's a man of truth, justice, righteousness, and real Jewishness. And who? Reb Avrum!' Oy, Reb Avrum, Reb Avrum, the times we're living in. What do you know of these things? You know your *bes-medresh*, you spend your life in study and worship, you learn, you pray, how happy you are. Oy, if you only knew our business people, our storekeepers, our marketeers—God shouldn't punish me for what I'm about to say—there's nothing they won't do. There's no honor among them; yes isn't yes, no isn't no, an oath is not an oath. 'And he said'—by them it means, 'he barked'; 'and he spoke'—swindles, thieves' cant, everything backwards and behind-hand. Each thinks only of himself, of his own good; the whole world was created only for him. Take a quick glance at them, they look like everybody else, skillful people, leaders . . . What's the point of talking? Vanity of vanities, absolutely nothing. Do you really think—sure, anybody could think it—that he, your Refoel, for example . . ." stammered Reb Asher, not finishing his sentence and quietly fixing his eyes on Reb Avrum to see whether he took the hint and, if it met with his approval, whether he could be spoken to bluntly.

"What about him? What about my Refoel, for instance?" Reb Avrum asked angrily. "What, Refoel isn't an honorable man?"

"Yes, yes, Reb Avrum! I beg your pardon, but you've misunderstood me. On the contrary, I meant the opposite. The meaning of my words is, could you think that Refoel, your Reb Refoel, for instance, is like those people I was talking about? God forbid, don't get me wrong. He's a model of rectitude, I'm telling you. Justice can be found among those deep thinkers, too. Their word is their bond. I love him, truly love him. For his sake, I'm ready to go through fire and water. And you can tell him I said so—no one could call it tale-bearing. Yes, but . . ." Reb Asher paused and sighed, as if what was coming was hard for him to say, "But it pains me to have to say that he, your Reb Refoel, isn't really treating me right."

"How isn't he treating you right? Take the mush out of your mouth, Reb Asher, and come to the point."

"Since you want me to, I'll tell you, Reb Avrum." Reb Asher frowned, as if he were speaking against his will. "Whom should I tell if not you, Reb Avrum? What, I beg you, would His Excellency do, if His Excellency, by which I mean you, were to propose good, doable deals to a man, were to labor and walk and talk yourself hoarse, only to have him go quietly off in the end and make the deal on his own? Now, of course, you understand what I'm getting at."

"You're wrong, Reb Asher. Refoel is not the man to do that. No."

"And if yes, as I've said—then what?"

"I'll pay the fine myself, as much as you want."

"Then let His Excellency take the trouble to find out where he was rushing around to so distractedly, so breathlessly, all day. But quiet—keep it between the two of us. Will you give me your word on this, Reb Avrum, your word of honor?"

"I give you my word of honor. Nu, here we are, Reb Asher. Good night."

"What do you think, Reb Avrum? Maybe I should go in, too, since I'm already here."

"OK by me, if you want to. Who's stopping you? Come on."

Reb Asher followed Reb Avrum anxiously, and gave him the honor of opening the door.

"Locked!" said Reb Avrum. "Refoel isn't home."

"Oy vey," groaned Reb Asher, cursing his luck in his heart. "What do we do now?"

"Nothing," answered Reb Avrum like a simpleton. "Now we go home to sleep. To rest after the day's work. I still have to go somewhere, so I'll cut across the courtyard here to the next street. Good night."

"Wait, please, wait a bit," said Reb Asher, scratching his temple and trying not to say what he meant. "It's bad. Shabbes eve . . . you understand. I can't go home, oy vey . . . Perhaps you've got a little money?

"My whole fortune amounts to a pittance. I can lend it to you, if you want," said Reb Avrum, putting a hand into his pocket.

The moon in heaven witnessed this gloomy scene and could testify as to how Jews supported themselves; how Reb Asher, the town's leading broker, who was forever occupied with business, put the loan that Reb Avrum had given him for Shabbes into his pocket with a bitter sigh. After so much work, so much running around all day like a dog, he came home to his wife and children tired, broken, with a few groschen that were not even his.

The moon beheld this Jew, beheld his worry and want and bitter misery, and went on her way, thoughtful and sad. And down below, a dog was barking.

5

GOING OUT INTO THE STREET on the other side of the courtyard, Reb Avrum saw Refoel talking with the woman who had come to see him that afternoon. In the darkness of the night, the shine of her face in the moonlight looked like a white picture painted on a black background, and the contrast lent it even greater charm. Reb Avrum looked at her, and the beautiful Shulamite appeared in his mind, along with all the verses, all the praises of her in the Song of Songs; not, this time, as an allegory of the Community of Israel, but simply as a good-looking woman. Reb Avrum lowered his eyes and kept his distance, trying not to be noticed, but Refoel caught sight of him and came over, handing him his key and saying, "Here. Let yourself in. I'll be right there."

The moon peeked through the window and into the room, reaching Reb Avrum in a broad band of spangles as soon as he opened the door. The golden spangles danced, clambered up his chest and neck, into his beard, onto his head. And strange thoughts forced their way into his heart, led it astray like scoffing companions. His good inclination wrestled with them, tried to drive them out, but in vain: the Shulamite did not leave his heart.

"Why are you sitting in the dark, Reb Avrum?" Refoel asked when he came in. "Why didn't you light a candle?"

"I'm fine without one, just me and the moonlight."

"I enjoy sitting in the moonlight too, sometimes," said Refoel, sitting down by Reb Avrum. "That band of light seems to me like a bright ladder from the earth up to heaven, and my thoughts clamber up and down it like angels. My heart seems to hear a distant greeting from its primeval birthplace. It dreams of misty, unclear things, old things, forgotten with the passage of years. It yearns and longs without knowing for what . . . You, of course, understand the depths of these things that words cannot express, Reb Avrum. I always say that you are a poet and that your Hasidism is a divine poetry. Real, pure Hasidism exalts the human spirit, warms it, lends it fire, ardor, like a fine old wine, and carries the soul far off to the higher spheres, to those holy worlds of comfort, rest, and eternal peace . . . It is all very beautiful, but we still need to light a candle."

"If you want," said Reb Avrum, starting as if he'd just awakened.

"Now we're back here, in this world," Refoel said, lighting a candle. "And there's news, Reb Avrum. The orphan has been freed."

"Who, the *shkots?*"

"The *shkots.* And the girl has been found."

"Where was she?"

"In a place where the righteous never go. It took plenty of effort to free her from Jewish hands. It's a miracle that that young lady turned up. *She* saved the girl."

"She! The one who came to see you today? I knew in my heart that she hadn't come for nothing. I confess that she hasn't been out of my mind from the time that I saw her. She's done a great *mitsve,* 'may my portion be with her'—I should get a portion in Paradise like the one she's just earned."

"If you want to share her portion in the world to come, Reb Avrum, you must at least know about her portion in this world, and how bitter it is." And Refoel began to tell Reb Avrum the story of Beyle and of the Turk, through whom Beyle was found at Little Fayvl's, where Auntie Sheyntse had hidden her. He concluded his sad story in great anger and with barbed words. "There's your nice little Jews for you. Pretty stories, like we were living in Sodom."

Reb Avrum was as shocked as if he'd just burned himself. He waved his yarmulke over his head and looked strangely at Refoel.

"What's the matter, Reb Avrum? You don't like what I said about Sodom?"

"Right, right. Instead you should say, 'Like we were living in *goles.*' There's a big difference. Like it says in the Bible, the people in Sodom were evil and sinful by nature. But in *goles,* good people are made bad, pious people sinful. Our sages say that want compels a man to act against both God and reason. Want, as the proverb has it, can break iron."

"Whatever. But a sin stays a sin. And meanwhile the Jewish people is distinguished for its foulness.

"And *that's* the problem. Once somebody or other commits a sin, it's already the whole Jewish people. What did *the Jewish people* do?"

"Its sin is what it didn't do, that it didn't think of doing anything and takes no steps against the awful things that are happening within it."

"Ay, as I live and breathe," said Reb Avrum, frowning. "Is that to say that you want rabbis and rabbinic judges and other kosher, respectable people to go to a Levi Bokher or a Little Fayvl and punish them in their whorehouses, degrade themselves with an Auntie Sheyntse, a Hodel the agent, and other such impudent sluts whom it's a shame even to mention? And forget about honor—if you admonished them, would it help?"

"Like cups on a corpse. Admonishing them is only a distraction, it's as useful as exorcising an evil eye," said Refoel, growing excited and standing up. "Oy, the admonishers, the admonishers. I know them, our admonishers. They can't bear to look on the sins of others, which are like a hair, but don't see their own, which are as thick as beams. We've got enough, more than enough admonishers among us. They aren't what we need, we have no need of open mouths. It's the one kind of merchandise, practically the only one, with which we're well-stocked, thank God. What we need is doers, workers, practical, intelligent people who won't allow these crimes, who will take steps against the dealers in human flesh who lead Jewish girls astray. They're reptiles who swarm in the filth, in cesspools made by Jews and gentiles. They are the maggots in our wounds, in our broken body, our rent limbs, our rotting bones. Jews, unfortunate souls cry out to you from these places—Jewish girls, your sisters, prisoners lured into a net. Seduced! Sacrifices that the full allow to be taken from the hungry, the coddled from the poor and needy. Do something for your trapped, unfortunate sisters, Jews!"

"Easy to say. What can a beaten-down and degraded people do? Our sages tell us that a prisoner can't free himself from his prison."

"That isn't a rule and it isn't a law. The opposite happens often. Want endows a person with the strength and intelligence to do what he has to, to be free of it. How many prisoners, for example, loose their own shackles and go free? Anyone who sits with his arms folded, waiting for help, isn't worth helping. Justice, pity—these are sparks that fly from hard flint when it is struck with steel . . . Come, Reb Avrum. Come see the children."

"Where are they?" asked Reb Avrum, rising quickly.

"I took them to Reyze's to have something to eat and a little rest."

A hand holding a letter reached in through the open door. Refoel took the letter and read it, and the color rose in his face. It was from Khantse, who gave him to understand that her mother had left today to go see the Tuneyadevker Rebbe, may he live and be well, so that he could effect a reconciliation, restore marital harmony between her and Bentsye. Her father was accompanying her mother on the first half of her journey. So this was a good opportunity for them to talk. She would expect him, she wrote, that night.

Refoel went with Reb Avrum as far as the door of Reyze's house, where he parted from him and went on his way.

Beyle was sitting at the table as ravaged and apprehensive as someone who had just risen from bed after a dangerous illness. She sat quiet and feeble in an outlandish dress, her arms bare, her face clouded and sad, as if to tell of the pain and tribulation she had experienced—not with anger or sharp words, but with an entreaty, a plea for mercy. She took a taste of Reyze's soup the way a sick child takes a spoonful of medicine for its mother's sake. Hershele stood opposite and looked at her lovingly, unable to understand the real meaning of the pain that showed on her face and lips, or of what really lay behind the tears that dripped into her spoon whenever she raised it to her mouth. He felt drawn to her with all his strength, he wanted to hug her, caress her, pour out his tears together with her. Had he been told, "Give her a kiss and then die!" he would have done so willingly and very happily. But shame kept him at an immovable distance. The sense of shame is so strong among Jews, it makes them so obstinate, that they would sooner die than give an open display of love. Hershele stood shamefast, grabbing the occasional furtive glance. Reyze and Reb Avrum stood apart in a corner, she beating her breast and wiping her nose on her sleeve, he rubbing his tear-filled eyes. They were both shaking their heads, now at Beyle, now at Hershl. Reb Avrum stroked his beard and rubbed his forehead, while his heart wept and screamed within him. "*Oy vey*, Master of the Universe. Look, and see our disgrace, the disgrace of Thy people Israel!"

Book Seven

1

A BEAUTIFUL FRIDAY MORNING. Light, warm, a shining sky. The night's thunderstorm had refreshed all the plants, which were beginning to yellow in the June-July heat of Tammuz, and brought them back to life, as green as they had been before. Toward day a breeze came up and scattered the clouds. The sun came out, the world was bathed in light.

Creatures of field and forest awaken, delighted with the lovely world before them—the grass fresh, the trees newly shampooed, dewdrops sparkling on the leaves like diamonds. All living things, from the smallest worm to the birds of the air, go out to their work, hissing, whistling, jumping and flying, creeping and climbing. And the people of Glupsk rise early—boys and girls, kith and kin leave the city with all sorts of receptacles in their hands and go to the Red Inn to buy cheap whiskey for Shabbes, as they have done since time immemorial.

And hard by the forest, at the side of the road that leads from Glupsk to the inn, there was a party going on. Mikhai the Shabbes goy, who lit Jewish stoves and put out the candles on Shabbes, who bought the whole town's *khomets* every Peysakh, Mikhai was whooping it up with Gavrilo, who shepherded the Jewish-owned animals, and the two of them were high and happy, joyously singing well-known Russian words to a drunken tune, dancing excitedly to the beat of Stempenyu's fiddle.

Nothing about Stempenyu was like anybody else—not his face, not his movements, nothing in his whole appearance. Every person has a permanent image, a particular face of his own, though certain features might

217

change. With Stempenyu, though, it was hard to say what his face really looked like, because it changed from minute to minute, depending on what he was thinking or saying, according to the gestures he happened to make. No ape could hold a candle to the faces that he made, and he could make more than one at a time; sometimes each half of his face was doing something different. When one side was sad, the other was happy; one eye wept while the other one laughed. It was dangerous for pregnant women to look at him then, in case the shock should make them miscarry.

Stempenyu was never seen in *shul*, neither during the week nor on Shabbes and *yontef*. No one ever saw him observe any Jewish ritual. Still, it didn't bother anyone, nobody paid him much mind; it was as if he had no connection with them—he could do what he wanted, they weren't responsible. Stempenyu knew spells for fever, toothache, and other infirmities. He had love-potions so powerful that a single drop on the clothing of a man or woman was enough to kindle a burning passion in their hearts. He had many avid customers for these drops, which were marketed under his name.

Stempenyu had a sort of fiddle that he played, as it were, in the forests and villages and inns—anywhere where *shkotsim* and *shikses* used to dance on their holidays. He would also entertain the crowd with sleight of hand and magic tricks: he'd eat fire and pull long ribbons from his mouth; break eggs into his hat and then set doves flying out of it. He'd take a coin from someone and blow on it. It would disappear, and he'd find it in someone else's pocket. If he wanted to, he could conjure a lock up from nowhere and hang it on somebody's mouth.

Stempenyu didn't stay in any one place, but was always wandering from one to the next. Wherever there was a crowd, that's where he was . . .

Now he was playing for Mikhai and Gavrilo. He scraped the fiddle, they leapt and danced. Anybody passing them stopped, and a large circle of Glupsker Jews had gathered round to watch them celebrate and wonder what kind of holiday, what kind of big celebration, it was. And in the middle of all this merriment a woman leapt out of the crowd, weeping and lamenting, wringing her hands and screaming, "Oy, killers, murderers!" before collapsing in a faint.

Tumult, turmoil, terror—and no more party. Stempenyu wasn't playing, Mikhai and Gavrilo were scared sober, their faces as white as sheets.

"Who is that? Who? What?" people were asking each other in amazement.

"It's Basye, Shmuel the old-clothes man's wife." It was the same Basye who had gone to the *bes-medresh* the day before to find out why her Moyshele hadn't come home, even though he hadn't eaten all day. And where was he? When she didn't find him there and Reb Avrum couldn't tell her where he was, she left with a broken heart.

The sun had already set. It was getting dark and Basye was sitting in her house, dejected and worried about her darling son, her pride and joy, who was a blessing from God. She was sunk in her troubles, her household duties forgotten. She forgot that her little daughters were hungry, that it was time to light a candle, heat the oven, and put the supper pot on to cook. The little children were sad too; they were huddled in a corner like sheep, sighing quietly with their heads hung down.

Who knows how long Basye would have sat this way, were it not for the cat, which awakened from a nap on the oven and leapt onto her, curling itself and rubbing lovingly against her. Basye came to herself, recalled that she had a house and children to look after. She also remembered how her Shmulik spent all day pursuing his hard-won livelihood, passing through every street, every house and courtyard. He came home at night tired and hungry—she should see to getting something ready for supper.

While she was thinking about her husband, it occurred to her that he might have taken Moyshele away with him. It was Thursday, after all, when Shmuel always took his cask to the Red Inn to get whiskey for his customers. It had been a bright, shining day with a warm breeze blowing through God's little world. The fields of vegetables and grain were positively edenic, the odors of fragrant herbs delightful—so maybe Shmuel had decided to give Moyshele a treat, maybe he went and got him from the *bes-medresh* and took him for a walk in the countryside. "Why am I saying maybe? That's for sure what Shmuel did, and he was right. Our Moyshele, our gift from God, knows nothing but the *bes-medresh*, where he spends all his days learning Torah. The poor boy is weak, thin, nothing but skin and bones, let *me* suffer for his sins. And what kind of pleasure, what kind of treats, do his poor parents give him? Treats—some joke, treats. Where do we come to treats? God above, Heavenly Father, if we could only be sure of always being able to give him the bare necessities! It makes me so unhappy.

And he, the dear child, does he ask us for luxuries? A piece of dry bread is enough for him when he's hungry; if his shoe should rip so that his toes stick out, it's all right with him, he doesn't complain. We can't even give him enough air—only a low, tiny, crowded apartment where we have to sit on each other's heads. It just kills me to hear him coughing sometimes at night. Shmuel really did the right thing to take Moyshele away from his *Gemore* for a while to go for a walk in the country. It's a big *mitsve:* let Moyshele stretch his legs and breathe some fresh air; let him have a little pleasure in his life."

These thoughts calmed Basye down immediately. She stood up and lit a candle, then went cheerfully to work. This had its effect on the children, who started to help their mother eagerly. One peeled potatoes, another brought a jug of water, a third jumped up to get some kindling, a fourth put it into the stove and Basye lit it, blowing on it to make the fire, and then put the pot on top. The splinters cracked, sparks flew, the flame surrounded the pot, and the children's hearts were gay. The cat sat on its behind, warming itself by the fire, licking its paws and enjoying itself.

"If a cat washes itself, it means that we're going to have guests," said the eldest girl.

"Daddy will soon be here with Moyshele," said Basye with a happy smile.

One girl, the youngest of the children, jumped up full of joy, clapping her hands and singing:

> Pi-pi-pi
> Where's daddy?
> He isn't here.
> When will he come?
> Tomorrow morning.
> What will he bring?
> A glass of beer.
> Where will he put it?
> Under the door.
> How will he cover it?
> With a piece of paper.
> Who will drink it?
> You and me.

"We'll all drink it!" the children yelled, asking their mother, "All of us, right, mama?"

"All of you," Basye reassured them. "Your father will be here soon with money. I'll buy flour to make *khale* for Shabbes, I'll buy fish, make kugel— and everything will be nice.

> Hop, hop, hop,
> Everyone get happy.
> Mama's baking *khale*,
> Hop, hop, hop.
> Dad brings money,
> Mom calls him honey.
> Kids, come eat.
> Here's a bowl of soup,
> A chicken foot,
> A herring's head
> And an apple kugel.
> Hop, hop, hop,
> Khane, Leye, Tsipoyre,
> Hop, hop, hop,
> Esther, Sore, Dvoyre.

This was sung by a cute, clever, barefoot little girl, wearing only a skirt, who was jumping and dancing for joy. With every couplet, she grabbed the cat by the ears, and the cat responded with a meow.

Nothing can so soften the heart, so imbue it with feelings of holiness, as poverty, provided that it is pure and modest, not sordid and filthy. Poverty breeds intelligence, poverty ennobles the heart with fine feelings and good morals. Poverty breeds domestic happiness—intimacy between parents and children. How many wild delights must be invented to satisfy wealthy children who bathe in luxury and have everything that they want; how many steps must be taken to blow a spark of mercy and human feeling into their souls, sunk as they are in the muck of coarse passions?

But the souls of the poor can be moved by the smallest trifle and filled with sweet, godly feelings. The smallest good thing in their lives makes them joyous and cheerful. A new capote, for example, new shoes are a great pleasure; if you make *kreplakh* or some other such dish once in a while, it's a major *yontef*. The domestic lives of decent, refined poor people are filled with poetry. Show respect for the children of *kaptsonim*—the greater number of poets comes out of them!

A long time had passed, meanwhile, without Shmulik and Moyshele coming home. The fire on the oven was slowly going out, the pot of porridge seethed, cooking more and more quietly. The candle flickered, the house became darker, and so did Basye's heart. Her melancholy returned, at first only inwardly. "Shh, not a word. Don't upset the children." A little later, she gave voice to the words. Basye's pain was now doubled; she was worried for her husband and also for her son. Shmulik's usual way during the week was to come home in the evening, a little earlier on Thursday so he could give her the money for Shabbes in time. And now it was already midnight, the cocks were crowing and he wasn't home. Something wasn't right, something must be wrong—but what? Basye's imagination began to soar; she worried about terrible, frightening things until her buried melancholy leapt from her heart and poured itself out in tears and bitter sighs. Seeing their mother crying and sighing, the children went sadly off to a corner, where they huddled dejectedly, their heads hung low. The candle was about to go out, the last bit of tallow had drained from the holder; there wasn't so much as a spark on the oven, the pot was cold as ice, but no one was thinking of food. They were too depressed. Even the cat folded up its tail, went petulantly off and stretched itself out on the oven to nap. The kneading trough for the Shabbes *khale* stood in a corner, empty, looking desolate and abandoned. The cricket that usually started to chirp when the household went to sleep at night stuck its head out of its hole, looked around like an idiot, and didn't make a peep. Only one big fly, holding onto the ceiling with its feet, let itself part from its sleeping fellows as if sleepwalking, to go bother people with its silly antics: it spun and flew back and forth as quick as you please, banging into the window, into a pot, dancing past an ear and buzzing incomprehensibly.

Basye's thoughts were leaping just like the fly, exciting her mind. She felt shut in and wanted to go out on the street and search for her loved ones, inquire after her husband at the houses where he delivered the whiskey. But she realized that all the houses were long since closed up, that everybody was sleeping. She took a look at her poor little children, lying cuddled together, bearing their pain in silence. A life—if you could even call it a life—a life composed solely of troubles. No, her heart wouldn't let her leave them alone at night.

In the midst of her reflections, a dog turned up outside the window, its tail cast down, its head stretched upward, and commenced a fearful howl. The dog's howling, which, as they say, betokens no good, just about pushed Basye over the edge. Terrified, upset, she grabbed a poker, raced outside, and drove the dog off, unloading her feelings onto it with vicious curses. The dog ran off, stopped some distance away, and started to bark in its regular voice, as if it were arguing with Basye like Balaam's ass, asking her, "What did I do to you, that you should beat me with a stick? Foolish woman! Don't you know that a dog's howling has no meaning? Only fools are frightened by it."

The sky had been clear at the beginning of the evening. A quarter-moon was visible in the midst of the great crowd of twinkling stars that were standing on guard. Soon, though, a dark company of clouds appeared from out of nowhere. They grew gradually wilder and wilder, raging until they stirred up trouble, a storm, and everything went black. There was thunder and lightning; tears, whole rivers of water, poured from heaven. The city slept, with no idea what was going on outside; the only witnesses were Basye and her children, whose troubles had kept them awake.

The next morning, after telling Tsipoyre, the oldest girl, to keep an eye on the other children, Basye went off to the Red Inn to get some information about her husband. God's blessing was everywhere—bumper crops in the fields, song, fragrance, life—but Basye was too sad and worried to notice the world around her.

At the Red Inn they told her that Shmulik had been there as usual the day before, taken his cask of whiskey, and gone back to town. But it was easy to see from the faces of the inn people that Shmulik's disappearance was a source of great wonder. Their mouths said, "It's nothing," in order to comfort Basye and keep her from crying and grieving; but their hearts thought that something was wrong, that there was some kind of foulness at play. Basye left the inn, unable to think for heartache. She walked by the edge of the forest, rummaging through it with her eyes and imagining terrible scenes—bandits, wild animals, all the evils that can befall a person in the woods—and suddenly caught sight of a circle of people in front of her. Stempenyu was playing his fiddle, Mikhai and Gavrilo were dancing, making occasional recourse to a keg of whiskey lying under a tree with the rest of their things. Basye pushed her way into the crowd, took a look—*Oy vey*, it was her husband's cask. She threw herself on the two goyim with a cry, shrieking as if at murderers; her grief was too great to let her finish speaking, and she fell into a faint.

That Shabbes was Shabbes Petrikhe and Aleksei in Glupsk—that is, the Shabbes of the two persons who received promotions that day. When Mikhai and Gavrilo were put into prison on suspicion of having murdered Shmulik and his son, Jewish Glupsk was left like a widow. The Jews were screwed. What would they do without a Shabbes goy? Who would put out their candles and do whatever had to be done around the house? How was it possible for the Jews to get by without goyim? So instead of Mikhai the Shabbes goy, they got by for the time being with Petrikhe, a woman who used to milk Jewish cows on holidays. And into the shoes of Gavrilo, the shepherd-in-chief, stepped his disciple, Aleksei, a little *sheygets*. But neither of them was fit for the job. As a woman, Petrikhe lacked the masculine strength to hold all the shots of whiskey she received for putting the candles out. By the fourth shot, she was flat on her back drunk. A lot of unsnuffed candles melted down in many a house, giving off smoke and fumes, and the Jews—may it never happen again—got headaches. And what else? The cows weren't milked until late, around noon, because Petrikhe lay in a drunken stupor from which she couldn't be roused.

Things didn't go so well with Aleksei either. No sooner had the little goy become a prince among the animals, than it went to his head: the whip was in his hand, to use where and when he pleased. And it had to happen: he raised his whip at boys who were playing peacefully on the street. There was a row, a brawl, screams; the animals remained unsupervised and scattered in every direction.

2

THE MOMENT when the wagon with the *khappers* disappeared was one of indescribable horror for Shmulik. There are no words for the pain of a devoted father who sees his beloved child in the hands of bandits and is helpless to come to its rescue. The tongue freezes; there are no words, no wails, no laments. Shmulik let out a scream and fell to the ground . . .

So what finally happened to him? Did he go mad with heartache, or just fall down and die? God forbid! Madness is for the wealthy, for pampered little people who can't bear suffering. The slightest fright scrambles their brains, the least little grief drives them out of their minds. This is hardly the case with *kaptsonim*. *Kaptsonim* are made of iron; no bullet can stop them, no cold, no hunger, no suffering or want, plague or affliction, because that's what they were born for—to suffer, to undergo, to endure their whole life long. And the Master of the Universe gives them a full measure of suffering, as well as the iron strength to bear their troubles without going mad or dying.

Have no doubt about it. Shmulik suffered greatly because of his kidnapped son; he was bleak and bitter, but how many other broken hearts and bitter spirits there were among the Jews in that terrible time! Master of the Universe, how many rivers of tears were poured into your wineskin then, tears of poverty-stricken parents whose children were taken away as they slept in their little beds, beholding pleasant dreams; tears of mothers whose only sons were taken; tears of desolate widows who mourned for their kidnapped orphans, their sole comfort, their sole support in life. Many nests were ravaged, many children stolen, the hearts of many parents were torn to pieces—but people still endured. Praised be His Great Name, *shehekheyonu*, who allowed these *kaptsonim* of ours to live, *vekimonu vehigianu*, and let them live to see newer and worse times, see their remaining children taken away too.

Shmulik screamed, but did not go mad; he fell, but his soul stayed within him. Hell opened up beneath him, angels of destruction tore at his heart, but he kept his wits about him; he knew that his Moyshele had been caught and that he had to hurry to rescue him. It never occurred to him to consider whether his feet would serve for the chase. An old-clothes man who wanders from early morning till night through every courtyard and street, who climbs up and down hundreds of stairs every day—why should he think of his feet? Who considers the feet of a *kaptsn*, who asks him whether or not he wants to run an errand? And aside from the fact that Shmulik was an old-clothes man, he was also a Jew, and walking isn't the same for a Jew as it is for regular people—the Jew's head is in the clouds, flying in front like a locomotive while his feet drag after, like train cars, on the ground.

Shmulik's heart was seething like a cauldron, his thoughts were rustling, banging, lifting him up from the ground, moving and driving his quickly running feet.

The path that the *khappers* had taken was a narrow one, off the main highway. It stretched like a ribbon between grasses and crops, wandered off into puddles, lost itself going down a valley and reappeared, snaking its way up a mountain.

Shmulik ran with all his strength, looking and listening all around him. But all for nothing—everything was silent. He heard nothing but the rustle of his steps, saw nothing but his own shadow dancing beside him in the light of the newborn moon, which seemed to be swimming high in the sky like a little silver boat. At times his shadow stretched itself out on the ground at double Shmulik's length, at others it climbed up grain stalks and trees, twisting, bending itself out of shape like an acrobat.

Twice he thought that he heard a voice in the distance. The first time, it was the footsteps of a hare that had been frightened by a crawling worm or the rustle of a falling leaf and jumped past him, flying as fast as it could, straight into the grain fields. The second time, it was his own voice that he heard, a sigh that escaped him when his hope of chasing down the wagon was beginning to flag. Is it really possible for a man, no matter how light on his feet, to compete with a horse, especially when the horse is being driven with whips? "Oy, it's impossible," thought Shmulik gloomily, beating his breast and waving his hand, as if to say, "It's hopeless." But he kept running nevertheless, uphill and downhill, as if he were being pushed from behind, driven onward by force.

It took a long time, but Shmulik got tired. He was tripping over his feet; he ran, fell, stood up and fell back down. The fire within him was growing weaker and weaker, no longer driving him so powerfully as before. Shmulik fell like a leaking balloon that hops along the ground until the gas has all escaped and it finally comes to rest. He stretched himself out in a daze.

He saw business, the things he thought about all the time. He saw *shmattes*. A whole pile of *shmattes* appeared before him, *shmattes* of every kind: the noble, silken *shmattes* of the city's hoi polloi, and the coarse, filthy *shmattes* of that other hoi polloi; pants, breeches, underwear, *tsitsis* and waistcoats, capotes and frock coats, *spodeks* and derbies, one *shmatte* no better than the next, and all of them pretty good *shmattes* . . . Plenty of merchandise, plenty of *shmattes*, thank God, in the world. But what good did it do him, if the *shmatte* business was so bad these days? The *shmattes* you tried to buy were too expensive; for the ones you were selling, they wanted ten for a groschen. All day today he'd walked his feet off, yelling in every courtyard, "*Shmattes!* Come out with your *shmattes.*" He was hoarse from screaming, the *shmattes* seemed to be laughing at him. As he mounted a steep flight of stairs to go into a house, a pair of torn pants came charging at him, huffing and puffing until Shmulik was nauseous and tumbled down all the stairs to the ground and broke his back and didn't know what world he was in.

Coming to himself a little while later and opening his eyes, Shmulik beheld the moon and the stars, a forest, a field planted with grain. He recalled the horrible business with his son, jumped up, and started running quickly, bugging his eyes out to search—but no wagon. He tore at his head and wept without tears while running uphill. Suddenly, merciful God, the wagon appeared before him—in a ditch near a bridge across a stream, where it had turned over while speeding downhill and broken an axle, which its owners were working on.

Shmulik threw himself onto them like a wounded animal that throws herself onto the hunters who have stolen her beloved child without shooting her quite to death, and a bloody battle began. While one of the *khappers* hurried to harness the wagon, Shmulik bit into the legs of the other like a leech, while pulling Moyshele toward him with his hands. Love for his child, the horrible misfortune, the burning desire for vengeance—these three things together turned the feeble Shmulik into a Samson. But not even the strength of Samson is a match for *Jewish* Philistines. Four hands, along with feet and teeth, tore into him until he could take no more. Moyshele received his own portion, got what he deserved for not keeping still while they were taking care of his father.

"Reb Hersh-Ber," said one of the *khappers* to the other, "What's the point of messing around with this Jewboy? He's stubborn, he holds onto the wagon tightly and doesn't want to let go—nu, OK, it's good. Let him stay here in the wagon and it'll come out just like the verse in the Bible, 'Him and his son,' the father and the son together. It's nothing new. Such things have been seen and heard of before."

"You're absolutely right, Reb Shneur-Wolf. Two is better. Just be so kind as to help me tie this ram up." And Reb Shneur-Wolf wasn't slow about it. He worked with gusto, tied Shmulik up in accordance with all the laws for binding a sacrifice, paying no attention to his trembling, groaning, and screaming. The horse was harnessed, the wagon ready. A lash, a poke, "Giddyup, ha!" and the father and son were carried off to the *akeyde*, the binding, to be offered up in place of others on one and the same day.

A bitter scream drifted far into the deep silence of the night; the scream of the captured, the imprisoned, rent the heavens, rose up to God with a lament: "Woe, Master of the Universe, woe to Thy people Israel."

The nightingale stood on its branch as if strangled, the frogs in the brook went mute and hid themselves in the water, hearing the screams and laments of the unfortunate. How horrible, how horrible does such weeping sound in the silence of the night.

And a voice was heard. "Giddyup, giddyup, giddyup."

The young moon, only one week old, went off to bed early, like a child. And wherever she passed, the sky covered itself with dark clouds. There was thunder and lightning. Suddenly a rattle of wheels was heard. A carriage pulled up in short order, men jumped out to find the source of the screams. They took a look and were astounded. There was clamor, uproar, cursing. Hands stretched out, fists appeared; Shneur-Wolf and his partner understood what these hands meant, and came up with the idea of getting out of there quickly, before they were beaten. The dark clouds came to their aid, and they disappeared into the blackness.

3

THE CITY OF ZHITOMIR, the capital of Volhynia, is beautiful. She has no pretty palaces, no lofty towers, no highly ornamented buildings, but is beautiful nevertheless. She nestles among mountains, forests, flowing rivers, and valleys; has gardens and boulevards, and these are her adornment and beauty. Driving into her on the Glupsker road on a bright summer's night, when the neat houses with their closed shutters can be seen among the trees and a quiet peace prevails, one cannot get enough of looking at her; the city is as beautiful as an enchanted, sleeping princess in a fairy tale. The night covers her with a dark-blue shawl specked with golden stars, and the moon, a past-mistress of flirtation, stares at her with a sweetly shining face. Blooming acacias and fragrant herbs bring her the fragrance of spices. A crystal-clear stream, flowing out from a rock, murmurs quietly, accompanied by the nightingale's love song . . . And the city sleeps and dreams.

And on the night when the events with Shmulik took place, when this beautiful princess, having rinsed herself in the downpour, was sleeping as soundly as if she had just had a bath, a carriage drove into the city, its horses flecked with sweat, its wheels rattling so hard on the stones of the paved Glupsker road that sparks were flying. It came to a halt by the gate to a courtyard. The driver crawled down from the box, as did the two people who had shared it with him. These latter were both clean-shaven and dressed in western style. The driver, a healthy, strapping fellow, went up to the gate and knocked with all his strength.

"Who's knocking like a bandit and making the walls shake?" said an angry male voice from within the courtyard. "No peace, not by day and not by night."

"Shut up and stop your barking, dog-face!" The coachman gave it to him in an ear-splitting voice. "Open the gate—now. You hear?"

"No mercy even for the sick. They knock and they yell. They never stop yelling. Would you like to know where you can go?" mumbled the doorman, spitting with anger. He put the key into the lock and turned it with a show of painful effort, cursing a blue streak as he did so. As soon as he opened the gate and saw the carriage and its passengers, the doorman was transformed. He doffed his cap quickly with a sweet expression on his face and stood reverently, like a serf before a nobleman.

"Go," they told him, "Go wake up the supervisor of the infirmary. The manager of the *aktsiz* wants him. He's sitting in the carriage."

"With pleasure, Meine Herren," said the doorman unctuously, pretending to talk to himself as he put his foot forward to go. "How could one not obey such great, good people as the Herr liquor-tax-owners. They don't bother people for nothing . . . and a bucket of whiskey is also nothing to them."

"I have to thank you, Rochlin, for the respect tendered me here by the doorman," joked the younger of the two men after the doorman had gone. "Just because he saw me standing with you, the idiot thought that I was an *aktsiznik*, too, and looked at me with respect. If he knew that I was only a regular person, just another student, he would have talked to me differently. Really, the prestige of you *aktsiznikes* is a big help to us poor *maskilim* these days. Nothing is forbidden to you; you do what you want, everyone approves and gives you respect. Quite a life, isn't it? You have all the pleasures of this world, and we—if it weren't for you, we'd be finished, God forbid."

"Don't complain, Rivkin," Rochlin consoled him in the same joking way. "That's why you *maskilim* will inherit the world to come and merit to feast on Leviathan."

"If you want, I'll make a deal with you right here and now, Rochlin. We'll give you a good portion of Leviathan, of the *Shor ha-Bor* and the wine from the six days of creation, if you'll give us meat, fish, whiskey, and a little something else from your share of this world."

"Ah, but first we have to make inquiries at the stock exchange, to see if there's any demand for your notes and shares in the world to come. For my part, I'm quite doubtful that any real merchant, not even one of the most devout, would give a plugged nickel for any of it. Faith is one of those things that has more to do with your mouth than your pocket. When it comes to denying and avoiding spirituality, there is no greater heretic than the pockets of the wealthy. I'll prove it to you, and even name names. But this isn't the time or place. Here comes the supervisor."

The eastern edge of the sky was starting to lighten. Someone still not fully dressed hurried out and stopped by the carriage.

"Herr Supervisor," said a soft voice from inside, "Is there space in the hospital for two more patients?"

"There isn't a single empty bed right now. You know very well, Mein Herr, that the infirmary isn't very big in comparison with the number of Jews here, which keeps growing and growing since those two new sources of Torah and prosperity, I mean the government Rabbinical Seminary and the head office of the *aktsiz,* opened here. Really, the number of people of every sort who turn up here! The city fathers are always holding meetings about the infirmary; they talk, they yell, they deliberate—and nothing."

"Nu?!"

This "nu" had a number of meanings. It could be construed as a question: "Nu, when are you going to stop your babbling?" Or as anger: "Nu, you *sheygets,* you!" Or as many another thing. The supervisor, who really was a chatterbox and owed his position to the manager, felt all the meanings, all the interpretations of this "nu" at one and the same time, and thus rushed to cover his mistake.

"Everything I said was only by the by. It can't hurt for you to know what's going on here, if you understand me. So far as your request goes, I'll fulfil it tomorrow with the greatest of pleasure. Your wish is my command."

"Thank you very much. But this can't wait until tomorrow. Take a look—the patients are here in the carriage."

"Strike me pink! In the wagon, and *I* didn't notice . . . Now I see, oh yes. There's hardly a sign of life on them. Tsk, tsk."

"That's why I'm asking you to admit them right away, without any delays."

"Hey, Ivan!" The supervisor called the doorman. "Get a move on and get the men and things here to move these patients."

"Rivkin!" said the manager, getting out of the carriage. "Here's my card to give to the doctor. Please, go get him right away in my carriage. I'll walk home. Don't worry—a bit of a walk will be nice after sitting for so long. And you, Herr Rochlin," he said amiably, turning his face to Rochlin, "Please don't leave here until the patients have been delivered to their place and received the proper treatment."

Meanwhile, day was breaking, the sky was reddening in the east, and Shmulik and Moyshele, father and son, lay on the same bed in the ante-room until a place was made ready for them. Bruised and beaten, they both lay in a daze, as white as sheets.

SHMULIK'S WAS A GENERATION of *maskilim*—deep thinkers—and *aktsiznikes*. The Jews at the time had no desire whatever to accept the *Haskole* that had been prescribed "from on high" as a cure for all their ills. They dug in their heels and said, "*Shkoles ni zhelayes*, We don't want any schools." The world at large didn't take well to their attitude, fearful lest it, the world, should God forbid come to an end on account of the foolish people of Israel, which did not want to be educated. And God only knows how the world would have ended up, Jews and—I beg your pardon—goyim alike, had the Angel of Prosperity not turned up out of the blue to help in this evil hour (may we be preserved from such today). This same Angel of Prosperity, who has turned the wheel of Jewish fortune, along with the whole life history of the Jews, from Egypt on up to the present; who lavishes honor upon the wealthy and wisdom upon full, capacious pockets—this Angel made a thorough investigation of all those means of livelihood that had succeeded in leading Jews from the paths of righteousness at various times, and found no better way of tangling them up in the *Haskole* than the liquor-licence monopoly. It had the power to extend its domain to wherever Jews were living; to employ thousands of people from the upper and lower classes in various positions that would in turn bring prosperity to tavern-keepers, innkeepers, workers, craftsmen, storekeepers, and regular house-holders, not to mention charity cases, clergy, idlers, and *kaptsonim*. Moreover, the *aktsiz* in and of itself, whiskey, that is, has the power to com-mand the human soul. Nothing in the world is stronger than liquor. It takes a man's money, heart, and brain away, makes the permitted forbidden and the forbidden permitted.

And because of all these qualities—those listed above as well as those not mentioned—the ways of the *aktsiznikes*, the whiskey deacons, almost none of whom would be too fervently religious, wouldn't bother the Jews so much; all their sins against God and man would be forgiven, even those that dare not be mentioned. And if once a blind eye is turned to the great, the little will follow their example. Youthful, green *maskilim* will start to sprout like grass in towns and villages, will look at and study forbidden books. Secretly at first, in attics, cellars, the women's section of the syna-gogue, or in the bathhouse; then go openly to schools, gymnasia, universi-ties and wear uniforms with brass buttons. There will be light and joy for the Jews, and the world, the goyim, will squeal in delight.

And that's exactly what happened! In those evil times, when everything was bitter and dark, the wheel gave a sudden spin—Jews took over the *akt-siz*, the monopoly on liquor licences, *aktsiznikes* made their appearance in Jewish life, and a fresh invigorating breeze blew through the tents of Jacob.

There were *aktsiznikes* of various sorts, every type of person. The mid-dling type, the ordinary *aktsiznik*, deserves to be introduced first and in most detail.

The ordinary *aktsiznik* was usually a native of a small Jewish town. His father, Elyakim-Getsl, a *kaptsn*, a respectable and distinguished pauper, named him Faybish and raised him in the traditional ways of study and marriage. As a child he learned Torah in *kheyder*; later in a yeshiva; some-where along the way he got married, and after that . . . left or ran away from his town, his family, and his ball and chain—his wife, that is—either for a while or else forever. Now he dresses in the latest western style, with white linen collars or maybe paper ones, two for a groschen. His jacket, a true source of delight to him, is so short that it barely covers half his rear-end, just to spite the capote, RIP, which had formerly dragged all the way to his heels. He'd done the same thing with his *peyes*; heaven forfend that Faybish ben Elyakim-Getsl should leave even a trace of them behind. In their place, he grew a long forelock at the front of his head. He did plenty of work on his beard and mustache, at first trimming the beard with scissors, then shaving it off completely and sending it to Hell. He oils his hair with enough pomade to keep it shiny, and sprays his clothes with perfume before the least social gathering to make them smell nice. Going bare-headed is very important to him. No sooner is he inside than his head is bare, even before he takes off his coat and galoshes. And not only when he goes into a house with people, but any structure at all, a shed, a stall, and so forth.

In short, Faybish observed all the *goyishe* customs he'd adopted far more rigorously than the goyim themselves; not only is a new thing an important thing, but more than that, there's a special taste to the forbidden. A cigar, for instance, is a real treat for a religious Jew on *yontef*, because it's a kind of novelty: smoking at the same time as you make *kiddesh* and eat fish, soup, and *tsimmes*. And a cigar on Shabbes is a real treat for the nonobservant, because smoking is forbidden on the Sabbath. Faybish was ashamed to speak Yiddish, and prattled away so mercilessly in Russian as to torture himself and make anyone listening feel ill. Nothing came out of him with fluency but curse words and *aktsiz*-terminology, *otnoshenye* and *rasporazh-nye*, for example, "official letter" and "orders." Faybish is *feh* to him—he calls himself Pavnutye Akimovitch and rejoices to hear that the image of God, his Jewish look and demeanor, has fallen away from him. Such praise spurs him to put even more pomade on his head, to spend even more time looking into the mirror to learn how to hold his nose at such an angle as not to betray his origins. In the town or village where he happens to live, he hangs around with the local officials and gentry; he is drawn to sit at their green baize card tables and dinner tables as well. In the event of one of their holidays or a birthday, he decks himself out in his best, not sparing the perfume and pomade, and comes to wish them a good *yontef* or a *mazl tov*, bowing and bearing a gift. And if luck is with him and he's invited to stay for a meal, he mixes meat with dairy, kolbassa with cheese, chomps away for all he's worth, just to let everybody see that he isn't one of those fanatics who believe in superstition. From his flaming cheeks and his eyes, which cast about in every direction as he chews, he appears to think that he's doing his companions a favor that they'll never forget. And when, as usual, they make fun of the Jews or even of himself, in a supposed spirit of camaraderie, he either keeps silent and pretends to ignore it, or else laughs along for harmony's sake. First thing in the morning, before washing his hands or rinsing his mouth, he hurries to eat, even though he doesn't feel like it, just to fulfil the transgression of eating instead of *davening*.

Still, he wasn't so ill-disposed toward God as he looked. In his heart he was a penitent and asked the Lord's forgiveness. Some of his sins he confessed to Him; for some of them, he adduced permission from various books or passages where these were permitted, or else proved to Him that these prohibitions had only been instituted to guard against real transgressions. He ate *goyishe* food in the open, but when he occasionally chanced to eat Jewish dishes, he did so with appetite and in transports of pleasure.

He wasn't so bad to people, either. He was very good to Jewish girls; he didn't behave stiffly or keep his distance like a stranger, but was as friendly and loving to them as if they were his sisters. He was on intimate terms with all of them and said exactly what was on his mind, not making any distinction, God forbid, between a servant or the daughter of a prominent family; on the contrary, it was a *mitsve* to befriend a poor girl and be even nicer to her. He once had a spot of trouble with his landlord's daughter, a married woman who lived in a *shtetl* somewhere and had come home to see her family. It was like a party—everyone in the house hugged and kissed her, and she hugged and kissed them in return. And Faybish was right in the middle. The two of them, he and she, embraced and kissed each other breathlessly on both cheeks. Once the initial excitement had passed and everyone had cooled down a little, the woman started to look at her relatives, asking them one after the other how they were and what they were doing. And when she got to Faybish, staring at him in amazement, he rushed in before her, saying in a tone of like amazement, "What do you mean, you don't know who I am? It's obvious—I'm the local *aktsiznik*."

And an *aktsiznik* really was a very important person in his town—a lot of people depended on him, especially the tavern keepers, who were considered prominent, respectable citizens and played almost as great a role in town as the moneylenders. They were completely in the hands of the *akt-siznik* and were scared to death of him.

Tailors, wedding-jesters, and other such artisans, the folk poets who wrote songs about all the evils and disasters of their times, songs later sung by Jews everywhere, wrote the following about Faybish's brand of *aktsiznik:*

> The young *aktsizniks*
> Are all no-goodniks.
> They shave with blades
> And ride on jades,
> Wear galoshes,
> To eat—none washes.
> They go into restaurants
> For a spot of tea—
> Don't envy the lives
> Of their poor little wives.

Not even this one little poem ever spread among the people; unlike so much other poetry of its type, it was never taken up to be sung. Which proves how powerful an influence money is, how it atones for every sin.

A step lower than these middle-class *aktsiznikes* were the people employed in distilleries, storehouses, warehouses, and cellars, and the guards who rode around on horseback. These were a jumble of all sorts of people: ex-storekeepers, market-stall owners, brokers, servants in inns. Some were illiterate know-nothings who'd been given these jobs because they were insolent SOBs with hearts of stone; others could just about do fractions, according to rules passed on to them in the utmost secrecy, and used their fingers to multiply, but they could come out with a Russian word when they had to.

There were also ex-*melamdim*, whose bad tempers and quickness to hit were made to order for their new positions. Likewise spongers, nothings, no-goodniks, loafers who had never soiled their hands with labor and were good for absolutely nothing, who stood at their posts like painted dummies. Don't ask *them* what they were supposed to be doing there—they were the poor relatives of highly placed *aktsiznikes* or their wives and friends, or else of rich people, magnates, informers, and big-shots whose goodwill had to be preserved by giving them these jobs.

These compulsory hirees stayed what they had been before and departed not from the proper path, God forbid. They remained exactly the same: the same clothing, the same names—Khatskel stayed Khatskel—and the same language: they spoke *mame-loshn*, Yiddish, loudly and in a singsong, waving their hands. And not only among themselves, but also to their lord and master. When the latter would occasionally make a sudden descent on them in all his glory and ask them anything at all, the answer would be short and to the point: 'We don't know. Reb . . . Reb Somebody or Other put us here and here is where we are."

Nevertheless, a whiff of heresy clung to them, too: they used to comb their beards and *peyes* during the week, and sometimes even on Shabbes. They no longer blew their noses freely in front of everyone; they taught them, the noses, that is, manners, taught them to do their business quietly, off to the side, and actually wiped them with a cloth, instead of their hands or the skirts of their capotes. They would sometimes *daven* very quickly, garbling the words in perfunctory haste. They would doff their hats to their master and stand before him bareheaded. They'd sometimes hear foul language from their *aktsiznik* comrades, and would often enjoy it instead of rebuking them. Those ruffians, horrible illiterates among the *aktsiznikes*, used to befoul their speech and commit sins not, God forbid, on purpose or out of spite, but simply to satisfy their desires. Except, of course, the former *melamdim*—they indeed sinned intentionally, for the sake of the transgression itself. The only difference between them and regular middle-class *aktsiznikes* was that the latter sinned and enjoyed it, while these sinned and got no pleasure. The others would violate the prohibition against *shatnez*, for example, with a suit of linsey-woolsey; these, with a woolen patch on torn linen trousers. If the others mixed milk with meat, they ate a chicken with butter, drank the most expensive gentile wine; these used a dairy spoon to eat a meager gruel cooked in a meat pot, and the wine that they sometimes allowed themselves to drink after making it *treyf* by having it touched by a goy, was made of raisins. And this was nothing— they'd sometimes force themselves to commit a sin, even though it was unpleasant and even contrary to their nature, like eating crabs, for instance.

A rung above the middle-class were the upper-class *aktsiznikes*, the managers, for example, each of whom was virtual monarch of his own particular domain and controlled everything having to do with the *aktsiz* there; also inspectors, recorders, bookkeepers, the secretaries in the regional offices and in the head office of the lord of lords, the monarch of monarchs, the holder of the lease for the liquor-licence monopoly, the great and terrible magnate himself. The better part of these were intelligent, educated, honest, respectable people.

All these types of *aktsiznik*, from small to great, were the fathers of the *Haskole* in the last generation, and their children's situation, the situation of the *maskilim*, was the same as their own. That is, there was also riffraff among the *maskilim*, rabble of every type—*maskilim* with full pockets and empty heads, merchants, entrepreneurs, and so on. Also *melamdim* who became "masters" in the schools, who used to teach their students the beginning of Genesis and a bit of the *Khayey Odem* with a highly Germanized translation—God forbid that *boro*, created, should come out as the plain Yiddish *bashafn;* no, it had to be *schuf.* These were the heretics, the question-askers, the linguists of the time. There were also theoretical scholars who used to turn up their noses at the standard liturgical poems and point out errors in them. They spent all their time banging their heads against difficult verses in the Bible or cruxes in the *Agode,* explaining them for the most part as allegories of the human condition or contemporary politics. The *megile*, The Book of Esther, was *the* place for them to read deep meanings into the words of Haman and Ahasuerus; they laboriously probed every word uttered by Mordechai and Queen Esther, explaining them rationally and according to the science of politics, no less. They didn't go along with *shlogn kapores,* used to skip certain bits of the festival prayers and nod along with those who demanded "reforms" in the *Shulkhan Orekh.*

Nevertheless, the *maskilim* of the last generation should not be dismissed so lightly. We have to remember the time and place in which they were living. They should also be given credit for the fact that if not for them, the wise men of our own times would never have come into the world. And you, evil tongues, instead of reviling and belittling the old-timers, should revile our contemporaries instead. How many ignorant, debauched, idle *maskilim* do you have now in your own times? The earlier ones at least had an excuse. People are like the air in a balloon; once the seal is opened, the air rushes out to the other side. Once the door from the *besmedresh* to the *Haskole* opened a little, the Jews ran like lunatics and went pretty far. But what excuse is there for today's *maskilim,* to whom the door of the *Haskole* was never closed? The earlier generation strayed unwillingly, unknowingly; today's does so deliberately. And, of course, not everybody in the last generation was corrupt. Just as there were a few decent people among the *aktsiznikes,* so, too, among the *maskilim.* Many great scholars, wise and learned men, were numbered among them, famous writers and poets who were an honor to their own generation and to later generations of Jews.

And you, wise men of the new generation, impugn not the honor of your forebears for their failure to deal with a particular issue in the way that the schools of Hillel and Shammai, for instance, dealt with a newborn egg. With the passage of time, new thoughts and needs will be born among your children after you, and it is possible that they, too, will laugh at their fathers, at their objects of study and their dreams. Every age has its own little chicks. And new chicks sing new songs.

5

WHAT HAPPENED WITH SHMULIK the old-clothes man is but one of thousands of excellent proofs that a Jew has to bear every stroke, every blow—not to mention a slap—with equanimity, even if it causes him great pain. He has to believe that there is nothing gratuitous in the slap, that he's been slapped for his own good, if not in the present then in the future. It seems that a Jew can only be born after it has been inscribed above that he is not to get a lick of pleasure in this world without sorrow and pain. Jewish luck is like a nut; it lies inside a hard, many-layered shell and is very difficult to get to without breaking your teeth.

Shmulik suffered terrible pains that night, both heartache and the aches from the blows he had received. Yet if not for the latter, he would surely never have attained to the honor of having Mikhoel Sapir, the chief of all the *aktsiznikes* in Volhynia, attend on him, take him and Moyshele into his carriage and deliver them both to the infirmary. And it really was an honor, a great honor, which can be properly appreciated only by those well acquainted with the way of life of the Jews in this region, their behavior and opinions at the time of which we're writing.

Our grandfathers believed that our entire life in *this* world was only for the sake of the next. "Man is born to perform *mitsves* for the sake of heaven, to die here in order to live there." Hence, everything given man here on earth is not for the sake of bodily preservation or pleasure, but for the sake of being able to fulfil a *mitsve*. Our grandfathers, for instance, ate in order to make *hamoytse* and the post-meal grace during the week, and to fulfil the *mitsve* of "three meals" on Shabbes; they tasted summer fruits in order to make the fruit-blessing with *Shehekheyonu;* drank wine on Peysakh to fulfil the *mitsve* of drinking four cups of wine. They didn't marry the way other peoples do, but in the Jewish way, so that they could fulfil the first of all *mitsves*. When they went to the bath, they didn't go for their own sakes, but in honor of Shabbes or *yontef.* They didn't think so much of cleanliness or appearance when washing their hands, as of the blessings over hand washing and evacuation. And forget about anything that wasn't necessary, that merely looked nice, and other such pleasures—they had no use for them at all. Their whole wardrobe consisted of a pair of socks, some linen underwear, a *tsitsis,* and a capote, one for weekdays and one for Shabbes. They weren't too proud to walk, had no horse-drawn carriages. They managed without expensive furniture, inlaid floors, or marble columns; without doormen in frills and brass buttons, and without doorbells, too. The door stood open, and anybody who needed to could come right in. And if somebody went right in to the master's or the mrs.' bedroom, that was alright too. At the time, there were no Jewish "functionaries," no Rabbiner, no attorneys or jurors, no Jews with medals, decorations, or titles, apart from community officials, who changed every month, and members of the communal assembly: beadles, *khappers,* gravediggers, *melamdim,* yeshiva principals, men who abandoned their wives to study, clergy, *kaptsonim,* welfare cases, and idlers.

Time passed, the Jews sat nice and Jewish, their yarmulkes and caps on their heads, sweating pleasurably—and that's all! What did they care for the world? One Jew gave the other the finger—big or small, it was all the same, all Israel are brothers, each as well-born as the next. At home, among themselves, the Jews really were princes and dignified people, but when they went out into the world they put their dignity, their pride, aside and took on the appearance of slaves, bowing and scraping, lowering themselves before every petty nobleman for a cursed bit of livelihood, standing bareheaded, bowing and flattering all the while, fearing him while looking down on him in their hearts.

And the *aktsiznikes*, the new men at the time, can be said to have been the first Jews to distinguish themselves from their fellows in their lifestyle, their dress, in the whole of their conduct and ways. It was they who began to be "functionaries," higher and lower officials, one standing over the next and each following orders according to his place in the chain of command. The chief, the head of the *aktsiznikes*, was the absolute ruler in his domain, and held everyone in fear. His house was always full of people—one there to beg for a job, another begging not to be fired; one tavern keeper complaining that his supply had been cut off, another begging for mercy, that the fine levied on him be lifted. Each came with his case; all stood without their hats, waiting in the antechamber for the hour when they would be called to the great lord's office, one after the other. Clerks and attendants ran back and forth like demons, passing the waiting crowd in haughty silence, and happy the man who merited a word—a glance!—from them.

These strange new people were considered genuine nobility by the swooning, trembling little Jews. What else could they be, if they had their portion of this world too? They lived in beautiful, palatial apartments with expensive furniture, wore fine clothes even during the week, rode in carriages, and held the keys to prosperity in their hands. It wouldn't do to treat such lords in the plain old Jewish way, without ceremony and without respect, as the Children of Israel do among themselves. It was right to humble oneself to such people, to bow, kiss their hands, remove your hat, and make yourself as dust and ashes—it was OK.

But this great respect was tendered to these *aktsiznikes* only for the sake of money. They were not thought of the way they were spoken to, because, of course, they didn't act like Jews. But things were different with Mikhoel Sapir, a good and pious man who kept a Jewish house—he was sincerely loved and respected. He had a good Jewish as well as secular education, knew Hebrew well, loved his people, and made his love manifest in gifts of money to the needy, to Jewish authors. In those days a Jewish author was generally a pauper who used to abase himself by traveling around to distribute his book. True, some authors today are still *kaptsonim*, perhaps even more so than their predecessors, but their poverty isn't quite so obvious. They don't distribute their books in person, but through great screaming, awkward advertisements in the newspapers. And if they are shamed by the Jews' not buying, being shamed behind one's back is not as mortifying as being shamed to your face. Mikhoel Sapir, however, treated poor authors in a friendly fashion; he was happy to accept their books, he paid them well and often even invited them to his table. He was especially friendly toward *maskilim* and teachers in the state-run Jewish schools, who were not popular in the wider community at the time. He considered it his duty to enroll his only son in the Rabbinical Seminary in Zhitomir, in order to get other wealthy people to follow his example. And he took Rivkin, one of the seminary's best students, an upperclassman, he took Rivkin into his house to teach his son. Rivkin was conscientious in his duties, which led Sapir to take a strong liking to him and keep an eye out for opportunities to give him little treats. On the day of the Shmulik business, Sapir had to go to a nearby village on business. It was a very fine day, so he took Rivkin along for a drive in the fresh air.

Truly, it was a great honor for Shmulik the old-clothes man to have been freed from the *khappers* and transported to the infirmary with Moyshele by a man like Mikhoel Sapir. Still, it was not certain that Shmulik would have agreed beforehand to suffer such bitter torments for the sake of this honor. He might well have said, "No *khappers* and no deliverer, no illness and no recovery, no wounds and no infirmary." Are there not arrogant *kaptsonim* like this among us, who, forgetting the good that has been done them, come out against all our alms-givers and philanthropists with noisy screams: "It would have been better for us and for all of Israel if you'd never been born!" And so honor alone wouldn't have been enough for Shmulik, if something more tangible could not have been squeezed out of it.

SHMULIK'S WOUNDS didn't heal any too quickly. He was still lying dangerously ill when Moyshele left the infirmary in good health, and he didn't leave his bed for a long time after. And at the same time as the doctor, thanks to Mikhoel Sapir, was paying him close attention to heal his broken body, Rivkin the rabbinical student was attending closely on Moyshele, to heal his soul, to educate him; that is, to teach him to read and write Russian. Rivkin was doing it out of pity—he saw a poor, sick boy, and his heart swelled with the looking. He paid him a sick-call every day and didn't let any distance spring up once Moyshele had recovered. The upshot was that Rivkin, finding real qualities in the boy, as well as a good head for study, started to like him very much and praise him to the skies. Mikhoel Sapir was very pleased that a good student had been delivered through his efforts, and he thought to help the boy by enrolling him in the Rabbinical Seminary, whence he would emerge in time as a useful, well-rounded *mentsh*. Rivkin undertook to prepare him, and he did his work with gusto.

This new Torah caused strange new thoughts to ferment and rise in Moyshele. It was the same fermentation as dough or seeds undergo, without which growing and sprouting are simply impossible. Like leaven, the Torah of the *Haskole* caused an upheaval in Moyshele's heart, a complete change in his way of thinking; things that had been perfectly clear weren't so clear anymore. Good and bad, beautiful and ugly, permitted and forbidden—they all came into question. The sages of old couldn't compete with those of today; they were finished. But this didn't last long. His studying in *kheyder* as a child, his later learning in the *bes-medresh* under the supervision of Reb Avrum; his longing for his mother and father, his image of how they lived, how they spent Shabbes and *yontef*—these stood by him at the time of his fermentation and made sure that he kept to the proper path, that his new world was built on the foundation of the old. Luck also played a part, sending him a good teacher like Rivkin and a good friend like Mikhoel Sapir's son; they were both sedate and well-mannered, and this, too, had its influence on Moyshele. Moyshele educated himself, grew more and more with time, until he burst from his shell like a chick that beholds the world for the very first time, as if it has just been created.

Shmulik lay in the infirmary for a considerable time and was still not fully recovered on his release. With the support of good people, he remained in Zhitomir until such time as he should regain his health and be able to work. He was pleased to see his son hanging around with students, and thought, "They must be yeshiva boys that he learns with in the *bes-medresh*. They've for sure realized how well he knows *Gemore*, and everyone considers it an honor to be his friend." This was Shmulik's only comfort in his desperate situation—imagining, as he always did, the good luck awaiting him, with God's help, in the future. He saw his son as a rabbi somewhere, sitting imposingly in his chair, flanked by under-rabbis and a beadle, his door never closing due to the number of people who flocked to him, one with a legal case, another with a question of ritual, one with this, another with that, all blessing themselves in him and saying, "Happy are you, Reb Shmuel, that God has given you the grace to have such a son."

And as Shmulik was comforting himself with hopes for the future, his eye suddenly fell upon some books, unkosher books, which Moyshele had inadvertently forgotten at home. Seeing these books, Shmulik nearly passed out. Master of the Universe, *gevalt!* His Moyshele, for whom he had sacrificed himself so, on whom he had spent his last penny for tuition in Torah—how could it be? How could his Moyshele have been led so far astray as to look into these unkosher null-and-voids, these secular books? He's spent his whole life running around the streets like a dog, looking for a piece of bread, degrading himself—all in the hope that his son would bring him honor, grant him great happiness and pleasure. But now that his son had left the straight and narrow, all his hopes were extinguished—what point did his life, his dog's life, have now? His whole world and all the good things that he'd imagined were coming had been destroyed; the bright star of consolation, which twinkled and shone for him from afar, had fallen, and Shmulik was left in desolation and darkness.

The saying *Odem korev le-atsmoy,* A man is close to himself, or if you prefer, Everyone looks out for number one, also applies to the love of fathers for their children. No matter how great and powerful the father's efforts for the good of his children, he's still doing it, more or less, for his own sake: to have honor from his children's honor, to become famous through their renown, proud and great through their greatness. Thus, when Shmulik the old-clothes man realized that his son had shattered all his hopes and left the paths of righteousness, he felt as if Moyshele had robbed him, taken away everything that Shmulik had meant to have through him later. Nu, his pity departed, and Shmulik fell into a fiery rage.

He was furious. He was waiting for Moyshele to come, so he could vent his wrath on him.

Moyshele came, and Rivkin with him.

"Let's go home to Glupsk," Shmulik screamed at Moyshe, reddening like a turkey with anger.

Moyshele stood confused, not knowing what this scream was supposed to mean.

"To Glupsk," screamed Shmulik, his whole body shaking.

Moyshele withdrew into a corner, speechless with fear and amazement. Rivkin answered in his place. "Reb Shmuel, your son will not go to

Glupsk. He will stay here in this place of Torah, where he will be provided with everything he needs."

"And he'll be provided with books of heresy," said Shmulik bitterly, nodding his head. "You'll give him heretical books to lead him astray."

"Dad, what are you saying?"

"Shut up! You think you can fool me? O, no. Don't worry. I found your books, I saw . . ."

"Saw what?" said Rivkin.

"Saw that they're heretical."

"You're wrong, Reb Shmuel. A Russian-Hebrew grammar and a geography book—that's what you saw."

"And what good are they?"

"What do you mean, what good? He has to know Hebrew, the holy tongue—he's a Jew, isn't he? And he has to know Russian, too; it's the language of the place where he lives. And he has to know what the world's like—he's also a human being, you know. You understand, Reb Shmuel: this is all a must."

"Some must! A new must that isn't in the Ten Commandments. We never heard about this must in Glupsk. The Glupskers, thank God, can live without this commandment. We didn't know it in the old days, and we don't know it now, and we're still fine people, kosher Jews, good businessmen by any standard. And now my Moyshele comes along and takes this must upon himself as a sacred commandment."

"That's right, he must," said Rivkin, smiling. "He must so that he can get into our *bes-medresh*, the Rabbinical Seminary."

"So woe betide such a *bes-medresh*, woe betide its so-called rabbis, and woe betide my son, who has abandoned our *bes-medresh* to enter theirs. Throw away your new habits, Moyshe, and come back to Glupsk!"

"Your son is very weak, though, and proper nourishment is of vital importance to him," Rivkin entreated, to stir up fatherly pity for the son. "Look how much he's suffered in his life: want, suffering, and anguish; look how pale he is, how the recent pains and blows have affected him. You yourself, Reb Shmuel, are a wreck, you still haven't recovered your powers and don't have the strength to do business—so what will you do in your beloved Glupsk, how will you support your wife and children there?"

Shmulik moaned and tears came to his eyes. Rivkin took advantage of the auspicious moment and placed his hand on Shmulik's shoulder. "Calm down, Reb Shmuel, and stay here until you're completely recovered. Raise your hands in praise to Heaven, thank the Lord for having sent you such a good, dear man as Mikhoel Sapir in your hour of need. Don't worry—he won't forsake you. You understand? With God's help, you will merit yet to live in much happiness and pleasure. Your son will graduate, get a good, lucrative post as a Rabbiner—and, with God's help, things will be good for both of you."

May we never be tempted as Shmulik the old-clothes man was in that minute. His good and evil inclinations were struggling within him, each presenting its case. On the right, Shmulik saw an emaciated rabbi, with a pale, wrinkled face, who fasted regularly, sat all day in *tallis* and *tefillin*, lived from pure spirituality, and who was saying to Shmulik, "This is a man, how happy he is." And on his left, Shmulik saw a Rabbiner, fat and pot-bellied, who ate and drank enough for ten, played cards and pursued the pleasures of this world, and who was saying, "This is the kind of man who has it good in this world." One said, "My rabbi is highly respected in his town." The other said, "My Rabbiner has plenty of *shlep* with the elite." One said, "Take your son and go to Glupsk. Be a *shmatte*-man, deal in *shmattes* and keep away from the *maskilim*. What good is their decency, their kindness, if the Master of the Universe is dissatisfied with their *yidishkayt?*" And the other said, "*Feh*, leave Glupsk to the Glupskers and *shmattes* to the *shmatte*-men. Stay here. Here you have some hope of prosperity." The right said, "Happy is my rabbi—he'll have *such* a position in the world to come." And the left, "The hell with your rabbi for my Rabbiner. The young generation won't want to know yours, while mine will have both this world and the next right here on earth." Shmulik hesitated and stood like a golem, neither here nor there.

"Don't be afraid, Daddy," Moyshele begged his father in a trembling voice, choking on his tears. "Don't worry yourself on my account; let me study here. From everything that's happened with us here, it looks like that's how God must want it."

Moyshele's words tilted Shmulik a little toward the left. He took hold of a sidelock and stammered, "And what's going to be with your *yidishkayt?*"

"Not to worry. It will be the same as it was in Glupsk."

"Do you think, Reb Shmuel," said Rivkin, helping Moyshele out, "Do you think that *yidishkayt* was given only to Glupskers, that if not for them it wouldn't exist? You're mistaken, Reb Shmuel, as I live and breathe."

"And what will the Glupskers, the Glupsker Jews, say about you?" said Shmulik to himself, not really listening to Rivkin. The image of a rabbi came into his mind, a dark, angry image.

"Woe betide the *yidishkayt* that has only the Jews of Glupsk to thank for the fact that it's breathing," said Rivkin, shaking his head. "Some *yidishkayt* that would be! And this is really the whole trouble—you and a lot of others like you want only to satisfy your Glupskers in everything you do. You have no interest in whether the thing itself is good or bad, all you care is what Glupsk will say about it. Forget about them, Reb Shmuel, and forget about your *shmattes!* Herr Sapir will give you a job; you'll be an *aktsiznik* and your Moyshele, a Rabbiner."

Shmulik's rabbi burst and vanished like a soap bubble, and a Rabbiner in sacerdotal vestments appeared in his place. Shmulik thought it over and gave in, saying, "Ta."

Book Eight

1

THE VILLAGE OF N. is one of those lovely spots in Volhynia to which the Master of the Universe has done His best to impart a particular godly charm; one of those places through which He wished to express the calm and pleasure that were in His mind, as if in writing. If the high mountains of Switzerland and the Caucasus, looking down proudly, frightening and dangerous to tread upon, express God's might; if the roistering sea with its towering waves tells noisily of God's terrible wonders; the soft hills around this village offer you a friendly greeting, a warm invitation to come over and stretch yourself out on them for as long as you like. The quiet green valleys encourage you: "Come on, old boy, lie down on the grass and let yourself go." The river runs and twists before your eyes, playing hide-and-seek in the meadow, hiding here in the reeds, disappearing, then jumping back out again, appearing before you in all its splendor: diamonds and golden spangles, gifts from its loving relative, the sun, which kisses the water and preens herself in its reflection. The river winks to you, furrows the surface of its brow with a quiet murmur, and you undo your belt and wade in, just as your mother bore you, eager to refresh yourself.

There is a pine forest there before you, the trees reaching up to the sky, their thick-grown crowns knotting together to form an arch. Their smooth trunks are like high, straight pillars set at a little distance from one another. The green grass is like a flowered silken rug at their feet. Looking at the forest, it strikes you as a sort of Temple. The fragrant resin of the trees is the incense, the music of the birds on their branches, the song of the Levites. You feel a certain holiness, soft, sweet repose, a yearning, a longing for a new life; your heart beats with a fervent prayer to Him Who Lives Forever.

And into the divine beauty of these regions comes man, who puts up a distillery to honor the golden calf. This building arrogantly sticks its nose—its chimney, that is—into the air; smoke gushes forth, spreading in every direction, blocking the shine of the sun and blackening everything that gets in its way. The low peasant huts are nothing in comparison with this high building, like poor peasants in comparison with the local squire.

Yes, that's the way it is: Beautiful and ugly, good and bad have stood face to face since the world began. Whatever the Almighty does in His world, Satan also does—satanically. The Master of the Universe once punished the sinful human race with water, so Satan came to them with his own liquid punishments of wine and whiskey. And this punishment was much worse than the first. Water was only a problem for the generation of the Flood; whiskey has been a problem forever. Noah, "the first to till the soil," the most famous peasant of his time, lived in peace and brotherhood, together with his family. Once he developed a taste for drink, once he got drunk, ugly things took place, and instead of peace, friendliness, brotherhood, there was estrangement, quarreling, and hatred among his children. And Ham, the father of the Slavs, became an eternal slave to his brothers.

Serfdom dates from this time, It has been an affliction and a plague for countless generations!

The Lord placed the rainbow in the sky as a sign that there would never come another flood to destroy the world; Satan set up distilleries and taverns to inebriate it. As long as there is drunkenness, there will be no end to poverty, crudeness, ignorance, quarreling, and lasciviousness; and Ham will be a slave to his brothers forever . . .

A long avenue running between two rows of high trees leads from the village of N. to the squire's court with its beautiful buildings, its orchards and other good and pleasant things. Fields, meadows, forests on the mountains and valleys stretch out for a considerable distance, giving the court a full measure of beauty. Squire Jan lives here in peace and contentment.

One beautiful summer evening, a carriage drawn by a pair of expensive horses drove down the avenue from the court, stopping when it reached the highway by the village. There were two people in the carriage, their faces beaming with the afterglow of a tasty lunch; yet it was still easy to read in the face of one that he was subordinate to the other.

"Good thing I remembered," said the senior of the two, taking a sealed letter from his breast pocket. "Dunay's son gave me this letter to give to his father, the supervisor of the distillery here. But I was so mad about the irregularities that I saw there, that it slipped my mind completely."

"I assure you, Herr Inspector," said the other apologetically, "I don't cover up for the people under me. I've warned Dunay more than once. But what do you do with people, with nobodies like that, who only get jobs because they have friends in high places?"

"In general, it looks to me as if Dunay knows what he's doing and is careful to do his duty," the inspector said, frowning to hint at his displeasure with this denunciation.

"Quite right, Mein Herr. Dunay stands well above this rabble, both in intelligence and in honesty, in his entire conduct. And they all respect him for it. Even the squire told me today at lunch, 'Shmool is an honorable Jew.' "

"And what do we do with this letter?"

"Give it to me, I'll deliver it and come right back."

"Thank you very much, Herr Yarkhi."

Yarkhi took a shortcut through the backyards to get to Dunay's more quickly. It was a holiday, and all the local peasants, young and old, were standing in happy circles on the street, some of them a little tipsy, all of them bareheaded, looking respectfully at the carriage from a distance and discussing it quietly among themselves. The leader of the little *shkutsim* pointed at the carriage and put his hand to his mouth, which meant, "Shh! Have respect for the gentlemen."

"If they're cops, then where are their brass buttons?" wondered one of the boys.

"They don't wave their hands or shift their eyes or have voices like cops," said another kid in a high-pitched whisper. "When a cop talks, his voice rises up from his belly, his eyes turn red. He gets madder than hell and bangs his fists. Our Mikita once fell into a fit from a cop's shout. Mikhai's wife was so scared by his screams that she miscarried. But these guys talk quietly and look around like anybody else. Who could they be?"

"*Aktsiznikes*. Shh."

"What?"

"Shh!"

They were trying to quiet each other with deafening whispers.

"Who's more powerful, *aktsiznikes* or the boys with the brass buttons?" The question was put among the adult peasants, many of whom became absorbed in it and wrinkled their brows.

"There is no one greater than the chief cupbearer, who has control over whiskey," ruled an old man with no hatred for a wee drop.

"These *aktsiznikes* had lunch at the court." Someone was helping the old man. "They eat and drink at our squire's. And that ain't hay."

"And they're Jews?"

"You can't tell from their noses?"

"And eat pork?"

"Eat it and like it and lick their fingers."

"And Shmool," mocked one of the local wags, "Shmool says, '*Khazer, feh! Treyfe. Oy vey iz mir, Basye*, gimme kugel. Kugel—good. *Tsimmes*—ay-ay!' I once stuck my finger in his mouth and said, 'Here, *khazer*.' And Shmool started screaming '*Oy-vay*,' like I'd just stuck a knife in him. Wiped his beard, his lips, screaming, '*Oy-vay, oy-vay*.' "

"Shabbes, Friday night, I mean, I go to Shmool's to put out the candles," said Yurke the Shabbes goy. "On his table there's *khale*, goblets, a bottle of whiskey—strong stuff, the real thing—and the smell of fish goes right up into my nose. Shmool was sitting at the table, his face glowing, and he's like singing, muttering, kind of wailing, crying like, begging like a kid. 'Oy, oy, Daddy, Mommy.' Don't ask me what he wanted! There's the *khale*—eat! There's the whiskey—drink! What's there to cry about? But his Basye knew, she went out and brought him *tsimmes*. He ate the whole *tsimmes*, then went on singing and crying. I'm standing there amazed, my heart's bursting with pity for him. Finally he gave himself a shake, gave me a shot of whiskey and a piece of *khale*, and I went away happy."

"Come on, listen to what our town clerk has to say about him and all the Yids of his faith." Nasal Pakhos, a bit of a *makher* in the village, intervened with a word. "The clerk says that they're leeches, that they suck our blood, grow fat off our toil; whatever sucks, that's what they are, he says."

"Aah," said the old experienced peasants. "Guys like the clerk don't prove anything. They lay their own faults on others and think that they can trick us. Devil take them all."

"One devil's not enough for them," said a voice from the crowd. "There's too many of them here for that. So let them go to *all* the devils."

The Shmool, a.k.a. Dunayska, who is being discussed here is Shmulik the old-clothes man, who had had his place at the distillery for four years already. Moyshele his son was studying at the Rabbinical Seminary.

Yarkhi came back, and the carriage started to move. The villagers escorted it with their eyes, standing for a while longer and philosophizing, until the sun had set and the flock had come noisily from the pasture.

At the same time as the carriage was leaving one end of the village, a wagon came in at the other and drove straight to Shmulik's house. An old man with a small bundle in his hand got out of the wagon and entered the fenced-in courtyard through a low door. As soon as Shmulik and Basye noticed him, they ran toward him with joy, both crying at once, "Reb Avrum!"

2

REB AVRUM HAD AGED considerably in the last four years. The wrinkles that had appeared on his brow had been put there by his troubles, many of which had been caused by Moyshele. The Moyshele business had been a long chain of suffering and heartache for Reb Avrum from beginning to end. The tears of Moyshele's mother when she burst into the *bes-medresh* crying, "*Gevalt*, Reb Avrum! Where is my son?", the rumors that had flown about Moyshele afterward, were like knife wounds to Reb Avrum's body. He was constantly blaming himself; all these troubles were his fault. It was he, after all, who had sent Moyshele to look for Hershele. Moyshele left and never came back. When the news that Shmulik the old-clothes man had been murdered spread through town, and that his killers, Mikhai and Gavrilo, were sitting in jail, Reb Avrum was so stricken by grief that he almost went out of his mind.

"*Oy vey*," cried his heart within him. "Mikhai and Gavrilo have killed Shmulik, and I killed Moyshele. They killed the father, and I—the son. They've made Basye the wife into a widow, and I've made Basye the mother a desolate, mourning mother. Together with these murderers, I have laid waste the house of the poor, whose beloved son was their only comfort in their bitter want, their last hope for the future. Now there is neither father nor son; Basye and the children have been set adrift with nothing to grab onto. I don't even have the guts to go to them with a word of consolation—how would I look them in the face?"

When it later became clear that Shmulik and his son had actually fallen into the Jewish hands of Shneur-Wolf and his partner, who were *khappers;* that a series of miracles had got them out of the *khappers'* hands and that both were lying in the infirmary, sick from beatings and wounds, Reb Avrum joyously thanked and praised the Lord that Moyshele and his father were alive. But his sorrow increased in proportion with his joy, when he realized that no one was to blame for this catastrophe—not Mikhai, not Gavrilo—nobody but himself, who had made a fool of himself by putting his trust in some total stranger called Shneur-Wolf, without bothering to find out who he was or where he came from. Praise the Lord indeed, for having freed pure, kosher souls from the hands of the *khappers;* otherwise, Shmulik and Moyshele would assuredly be soldiers by now, learning how to hold rifles and shoot the enemy. And the mere thought that his own stupidity could have brought this about, could have destroyed an entire family, was enough to cause Reb Avrum great grief. And besides all this, it sickened him that there were such horrible people—bandits, *khappers*—among the Jews, and his heartache led him to point an accusing finger at many another of us. Reb Avrum was a poet by nature, and, like a poet whose blood is up, he poured out his bitterness on everyone, lamenting and saying:

"Oy, how low have you fallen, my people, my poor, unhappy people. Not all your hundreds of thousands, slaughtered by the wicked Titus during the great Destruction; killed and burned in the fires of Spain; all the others who were slaughtered and killed; not all of them together embitter my life as much as the noses that Jews themselves tear from one another's faces, as the sorrows and sufferings that you yourselves perpetrate upon each other. For the murdered, those slain by fire and water, there is still consolation: Heroes, they died for their country. Martyrs, they died in Sanctification of the Name. But what shall I say about those who were killed by your evil tongues, about those whom you yourselves have turned into scapegoats? I weep over the blows of strangers and say, 'All right, the good and the weak often suffer in this world. It's still possible that their attackers will reconsider and regret.' But when the scratched scratch, the slapped slap, the captured capture, the tortured torture one another, I weep and have nothing to say . . . Oy, how fallen, how low have you fallen, my people Israel."

And how many wrinkles did the affair with Hershele and Beyle put on Reb Avrum's face? These unfortunate children caused him great grief, as did the presence among us of hoodlums whose foul deeds blacken the face of the Jews. And at times like those, when Reb Avrum really needed to chat with Refoel in order to forget his sorrows for a while, Refoel had to abandon Glupsk forever and move to the famous commercial center of Leipzig. His move there came about entirely unexpectedly, thanks to Reb Asher the middleman.

When Reb Asher saw that Refoel was starting to refrain from making deals and that no urgings or arguments were going to change his mind, he imposed upon his nose to sniff out the reasons for Refoel's unwillingness to take a risk—not so much for the pleasure of knowing as for the sake of his livelihood, because his earnings depended more or less on how much business Refoel was doing. When Refoel cut back, things got tight for Reb Asher, who was suffering want. The new capote, which he'd had made when Refoel was doing a lot of business through him, was worn out, had lost its appeal just as he himself had lost *his* appeal—he was no longer received by the storekeepers with the same respect as before. Should he go into a store, they gave him an equivocal welcome, looking him straight in the face to see if maybe he'd come with some business. But once they'd seen that there was nothing to talk about, there was also no one to talk to— they simply stopped looking at him, as if he weren't even there.

It's true that this gave Reb Asher plenty of time to spend on politics, which he loved as much as life itself. Do-nothings who were dying for news used to gather round him in the market and *bes-medresh* while he reported on what was doing with the government, what was happening in different countries, explaining it all with his smooth and ready tongue. But he didn't get a groschen for any of these lectures. Not even "his France," which was more dear to him than all other countries, which he praised so highly and to which he was so loyal, not even France gave him a single penny toward his needs. And so Reb Asher was forced to put his nose to work to sniff out the reason why Refoel had stopped doing business. He followed a middleman's line of reasoning; he sniffed and he found.

Knocking his head from one particular to the next, Reb Asher came up with the following inference: Refoel is a man who knows what he's doing, a Leviathan among the little local fish. What is Glupsk to someone like him? A small pond. He needs a sea, where he can spread his fins and swim free, and Moscow and Leipzig were the only seas there were. Now, forget about Moscow—the things a Jew needs to do to live there are beneath such a person as Refoel. So it has to be Leipzig; reason demands it. The storekeepers of Glupsk bring goods in from Leipzig, wait eagerly for Leipziger merchandise; further, there's Elye-Leyzer the wagon driver's Leipzig wagon. If things were not so, then what's the meaning of the wagon, what's the meaning of Elye-Leyzer?

But not just any merchant can get there. It's very far, the expenses are considerable, the language is weird, the way of life even weirder, and the stupid Germans are totally weird. So then? Then it follows that Refoel is going to move to Leipzig. And that explains why he's been seen talking to Elye-Leyzer these days. He was even seen looking the wagon over once, paying close attention to the little copper-colored colt wobbling dead-center behind it. Yes, Refoel is for Leipzig, but the question is, why? To what end, that is? We know that a man doesn't just jump up and move out of the blue like some sort of lunatic unless he's doing it for business, for a little money. So what is Refoel up to then? You have to say that he intends to become an expediter or commission agent for foreign merchants; that is, he'll sit in Leipzig and send goods to us here from the factories over there. "If so, if that's really so," he thought for a while, raising his nose, pushing back his hat until a little fire of joy appeared in his eyes, as if he had solved a riddle, "Ha, ha, *that's* the meaning of the biblical verse: Rejoice, Zebulun, in your going out—rejoice, middleman, in *your* going out. Go, Reb Asher, and do—for the good of the storekeepers here and for your own good as well, not to mention your own enjoyment."

And Reb Asher's feet bestirred themselves, the skirts of his capote drew themselves aside, and he ran to reveal his secret to the shopkeepers, to describe with his own holy mouth the great good that was going, God willing, to result for them. During the time when he was running around, there were no more politics in Glupsk. The do-nothings were calling him, pining for news. "Reb Asher, what's going on in the news?" Not a word; he just wagged his finger in the distance and ran. While Reb Asher was running, Refoel was sitting at home and suffering. May you never undergo his torment, Jewish merchants! Sure, going bankrupt is an everyday affair with us. If a merchant should go bankrupt, even more than once—so what? It's nothing. Either he goes away for a little while or else locks himself up in his house, lives it up in his confinement while waiting for the storm to blow over. But not Refoel. No sooner had he noticed a hole in his accounts, still concealed though it was, than he felt a hole in his heart. He was eating himself away with worry over the speed and haste with which he had made deals recently, his abandonment of the careful consideration that he had used before. It was impossible for him to stay in Glupsk, but to run away like a thief was also bad. His situation looked hopeless.

On the day when Refoel had chosen to sit down alone with his books and make a clean accounting, his house was as full of storekeepers as a stock exchange. His door didn't close all day—one came in, one went out, everybody wanted him to do business for them with the Germans, the manufacturers in Leipzig, where he was going to move, and they offered him good terms for his trouble. At first, Refoel denied everything; there was nothing to it at all, he'd never even thought about moving to Leipzig. But the storekeepers saw his denial as a trick to wriggle out of doing business with them, and they were as upset as if he'd doused them with a pail of slops. The insult made them stubborn; they were going to stand on their honor and talk the matter over with him until they talked him into doing it.

When Refoel saw how far they were prepared to go, he started to consider: Maybe it was really a good thing for him. Maybe it was a sign from heaven to get him out of his bind and free him from all his problems. He nodded to the storekeepers, and, stammeringly at first, then with no beating around the bush, said, "Gentlemen, I'll do it for you. But only on condition that you pay off your notes for the goods from Lodz right away, so that we can settle our business here before I go."

This stipulation was a bitter pill to the shopkeepers and gave them a bellyache, but their burning desire to do business with Leipzig led them to accept it with a mask of graciousness. For his part, Reb Asher the middleman pushed them, urged them on, prophesying huge returns. The storekeepers took heart, paid what was owing on their notes, and Refoel left Glupsk in Elye-Leyzer's three-horse wagon, the little bells jingling on the forehorses' bridles while the copper-colored colt swaying behind knocked into the back of the wagon. Refoel departed in high style, hit the road, and came to Leipzig, where he opened his expediting agency.

Parting from such a devoted friend was hard for Reb Avrum, and it was hard for Hershele too. Refoel had taken him into his house, looked after him and helped him as much as he could. Refoel's departure was like having his legs pulled out from under him. Hershele missed him, he suffered so terribly that it showed in his face. He sat in a corner of the *bes-medresh* for hours on end, his *Gemore* open before him, not studying, just sitting quietly, sunk in his thoughts. And he had plenty to think about. He thought about Refoel, dear, good Refoel, whom he missed so badly; about Beyle, his heart and soul, who had gone home to her parents; about the wishing-ring and other such wonderful things that could make a person rich. He poked around in such books as *Mifaloys Eloykim*, The Wonders of God, by Rabbi Yoel Baal-Shem and *Toldos Odem*, The Generations of Adam, by Rabbi Elye Baal Shem, from which you could learn to do neat tricks with kabbala; "to see your predestined bride in a dream, be she maid, widow or divorcée," for instance; "to be one who sees but is not seen," that is, to be invisible, "to tap wine from the wall," and so on. Hershele took the necessary steps to see his bride, and they worked; he really used to see Beyle and pass the time with her very pleasantly in his dreams. But when it came to tapping wine from the wall or making himself invisible, he always did something a little bit wrong and ruined it all before he could finish. Hershele didn't despair, though; he started back at the beginning over and over again because he saw his salvation, his hope of prosperity, in miracles and magic tricks.

He was wrong. His salvation came from Khantse.

3

KHANTSE MISSED REFOEL more than anybody, and his departure worked like oil on the fire of her love. A fire glowed within her, a quiet, hidden fire that scorched her soul. A love that had no tongue. But if the mouth did not speak, the hand yet wrote. She wrote often, sending letters through the mail and receiving them by way of Hershele—all in the utmost silence. Hershele was a standing Shabbes and *yontef* guest at the home of Red-Headed Leybtse. Refoel made the arrangement before he left, and he most likely knew what he was doing. Khantse must have known, too, because she took an immediate liking to the boy. And with Refoel gone, Hershele became even dearer to her—he was her postman, her secret was no secret to him.

Yes, love burned like a fire in Khantse's heart and her father, Leybtse, was an unwittingly good bellows, blowing on the embers of his daughter's love, sparking them to life with his very own mouth. Whenever he spoke of Refoel, he praised him to the skies—Refoel was a one-man brain trust, a blazing talent, a real intellectual who had more insight into business than anybody. And he would always conclude with a moan that business, earnings, were no longer what they had been in Refoel's time. This was Leybtse's opinion of Refoel's relations with his fellow men. With respect to God and *yidishkayt*, however, Leybtse wasn't so pleased. He used to shake his head and say, "It's a shame that he isn't one of 'us,' that he doesn't believe, has no faith in our Rebbes. Why, he doesn't even believe in demons and evil spirits."

The evil that her father found in Refoel bothered Khantse not at all, while his praises penetrated and filled her heart, not leaving a space the size of a pinhead for Bentsye. Bentsye was out, and Khantse still had no children.

Yentl went to the Rebbe to beg intercession for her childless daughter, and he promised Khantse a child. But if Khantse was "rebellious" and didn't want to know from her husband, how was it the *tsaddik*'s fault if his promise was not fulfilled? And if Khantse was "rebellious," what was Bentsye supposed to do? The free board at his in-laws' was the main thing for Bentsye—his wife was only a fringe benefit. He ate and drank like a perpetual eating-and-drinking machine, and didn't worry about anything else, in contrast to Khantse, who was growing thinner, more emaciated, from one day to the next, eaten away by love and hate.

Yentl complained to her friends about the troubles she had from her daughter, and her friends comforted her, all of them—Yentl and the friends—talking at once. Yentl beat her breast and said, "My daughter is green, she's sallow, and she still isn't pregnant. Name me one thing that I haven't tried," and the tenderhearted women made themselves heard, speaking words of comfort with a bit of a sting. "Yentl," said one, "Don't worry, Yentl. A green complexion, what is it? It's nothing. After she has a child, a woman has a glowing complexion." Another one yelled over the others, "Kondriatikhe the goye is the only one who can help with having children." And an even stronger voice piped up, "Bulan the sorcerer is way better. He's got a charm that works." "Hodel, Tsippe, Feyge-Sosse," cried a thin voice, "Listen. Nothing's better for children than foreign hot springs." The biggest mouth of the bunch, with a tongue like a bell, lent her support to this idea, saying, "Shh. Here's a case in point. Esther-Tsviye, a stunning young girl, married an old man, Reb Yisroel the Rich Man, and she also didn't have kids for a long time. So she went to the hot springs and got pregnant. And since then she goes every year, comes back home and has a kid. She's got four now, thank God. And solid, hefty, beautiful—you can't even look at her face, it's like looking into the sun. But what's so special about Esther-Tsviye? She's no different from anyone else, God has other daughters too. I know of plenty of other women who go to the hot springs, get cured, and become pregnant. They say it's because of something in the water that is especially good for barren women."

"Exactly like the rods of our father Jacob, which the Bible says heated the sheep up and made them conceive." Feyge-Brokhe the *khazn's* wife explained the meaning of these things in a voice as low as a man's.

And so all of Yentl's friends decided that Khantse should go to the hot springs, and without any lengthy delay. How, though, could they help Khantse's bitter spirit, when it was love and hate that were making her sick? She bore the hatred within her as quietly as she bore the love. She knew that none of her complaints against Bentsye had registered, that it was very difficult to get rid of such a *shlimazl*. Her father was crazy for Bentsye, because his connection with Bentsye's prominent family had brought him to prominence too; he'd become a leading citizen, an official in the infirmary, the synagogue, the Hebrew school, and he struck fear into the hearts of the poor. When she first told him of her hatred for her husband, he became furious with her and told her off. "Where do you come to say such things? What does it mean, you hate him? A Jewish girl doesn't know from love and hate—she's supposed to be a wife and do her husband's will. Do, I say; you understand? Do, really do—and not take any foolish notions into her head. Love-shmove, hate-shmate, like by the goyim. Hear me well, daughter: Don't be crazy. Be a wife like you're supposed to be, the way all Jewish women are."

Khantse heard her father's reproof and understood that she could no longer complain to him, so she bit her lips and kept her troubles to herself and shh . . . But with time, so many troubles accumulated in her heart that her nerves couldn't bear them anymore; she changed so much that she was scarcely recognizable. God knows what the end would have been if something unexpected hadn't happened, something very common back then in

Haskole times, but over which people today would shake their heads in amazement.

In the beginning when the *Haskole*—education, that is—first hit "the Jewish street," it spread, as described above, like a plague, God preserve us, that seized a Jew all on a sudden. A Jew would spend his life in study and prayer, cut off from the world, knowing nothing but God and *tsitsis*, not even taking a drink of water without a blessing—and suddenly, *oy-vey!* the evil husk grabs hold of him, turns him wrong-side out, and he becomes, so to speak, "edumacated." Or else one of the yeshiva boys, a healthy, strapping young buck who has thrown off the yoke of labor to eat days—eat at a different house every day of the week—and warm a bench, between the pages of whose open *Gemore Haskole*—books are suddenly discovered! Completely corrupted. Or take a modest woman who keeps the three women's *mitsves*, shaves her head the way she's supposed to and keeps it well covered with a cap, makes wicks for memorial candles, and weeps and laments when she says the *tkhines*—all of a sudden the devil gets into her and turns everything upside down. She casts off her veil and goes around in her own hair, like a tramp. And what else? She sticks a cushion under her dress, behind her, excuse me, behind, to make it look fatter, more fashionable, and breaks her poor tongue to try to chatter a kind of Russian. And just as people take care to avoid anything with a hint of contagion during a plague, so they kept their distance from those infected with *Haskole*.

And who would ever have thought that this plague would come to Bentsye, too? Our sages are indeed correct when they say, "At a time of plague, the Angel of Death isn't choosy," and sanctified Bentsye was one of those caught like a bird in a net. He was ruined and so was his life.

Bentsye's executioner, his Angel of Death, came in the form of a Litvak, a *melamed*, who looked like a very pious Jew, a kosher soul with beard and *peyes*. He was a first-rate scholar, knew the Bible inside-out; he spoke quietly, calmly, in a slightly hoarse voice, and he spoke pearls of wisdom. His clothing was immaculate, he never wiped his nose or fingers on it. Everyone respected him, each word from his mouth was a delight. His students were older boys, engaged to be married, who were semi-independent and studied on their own volition, not because they were forced to. When learning Bible with them, he'd mix Mendelssohn's commentary in with Rashi, *Medresh* with philology, and sometimes add sharp drops of scientific inquiry into such miracles as the parting of the sea or pose difficult questions about reward and punishment, predestination and foreknowledge. So, if God knows a person's deeds before they are done, and the person does not thus perform them of his own free will, why then should he be rewarded or punished?

He administered large doses of this prescription to his students, to cleanse their souls of the rot that had taken root in them. The medicine was effective; it fermented and fermented within them until they became fermented themselves.

And because Bentsye used to hate Litvaks and sit with his group of Hasidim and mock them in the synagogue; on account of his sin of gratuitous hatred, Bentsye's evil luck visited him with this *melamed*, this Litvak. Calmly, with smooth, sweet utterances, the *melamed* drew near to Bentsye and confused him, enchanted him with his smooth tongue as if he were charming a snake. Gradually, little by little, his sugar-sweet words dropped poisonous drops of heresy into Bentsye's heart. The poison spread farther and farther until, suddenly, he wasn't Bentsye anymore. Bentsye didn't taste the meat of the *melamed's* Torah, he swallowed only the shell. His friends noticed a change in him—not the same fervor, not the same Bentsye as before; he was skipping his morning dip in the *mikve*, didn't shove for whiskey like he used to on a *yortsayt*. Still, they thought no evil of him. On the contrary, their interpretation was "oh-oh-OH," that is, it was a descent, the kind that great ones make before rising to a higher level. He should go to the Rebbe, who would fix him up. But what good was all this when a man's worst enemy is his tongue? An unguarded tongue will bury its owner.

The Hasidim were once sitting behind the oven in the *bes-medresh*, telling stories about the Baal Shem Tov, about the miracles performed by *rebbes* and *tsaddikim*, when Bentsye suddenly burst out and said it was all lies, there were no miracles. The Hasidim were furious, dumbfounded. "What the hell?" they yelled. "It's blasphemy. How can we listen to such things in silence?" They stood up, slapped his face good and proper, and threw him out of the *bes-medresh*. The story spread all over town, and Red-Headed Leybtse nearly buried himself for shame. Once Bentsye was on people's lips, there was no shortage of good people to hurry and make things worse for him, to broadcast such evil reports of him that he became quite notorious. Things went so far that Bentsye was forced to leave Glupsk.

And Khantse got her divorce.

AND WHEN IT CAME TIME for spasmatic women to travel to the hot springs, Khantse was preparing to go to Vienna on the advice of the doctors of Glupsk, to consult with specialists about her condition and which baths she ought to visit for it. Yentl was very busy making preserves, baking honey cake, butter-cookies, fruitcakes, and fancy *khales* for her daughter to eat on the way. She never stopped talking; she lectured Khantse, warned her for the love of God to look out for herself and her things on the journey, giving her numberless blessings and pieces of advice. Leybtse was silent, frowning sourly as if displeased with everything going on around him.

He was sulking alone in his room one day, when in came Reb Avrum, who, after a brief exchange of obligatory courtesies, said, "I've come to offer a proposal for His Excellency and his daughter, the divorcée."

"You mean a match for her?" asked Leybtse, frowning and waving dismissively, as if washing his hands of something he didn't wish to hear.

"Very like a match," said Reb Avrum with the kind smile of a guileless man.

"Ay, ay—this has nothing to do with me. It isn't up to me, Reb Avrum," said Leybtse, jumping up and shaking his head while holding it in both hands. "It's a new world today, a different world with different customs. Respect for a father is out—what's a father, anyway?—and respect for children is in. Whatever your kids say, just shut up and do it. If not . . ."

"Calm down, Reb Leybtse. There's some truth to what you're saying, but it doesn't have anything to do with what I want. I want to put something different to you. It's like this," said Reb Avrum, running a hand across his face and looking at Leybtse attentively, "It's like this, Reb Leybtse. You know Hershele, of course, the boy, the orphan who eats with you Shabbes and *yontef*, as Refoel asked you to let him. In short, I got a letter from Refoel recently, asking me to send the orphan to him in Leipzig. He sent me the expense money, too. I don't know what to do now. It's a long trip and who knows what can happen? How do you send that kind of pup off on his own? He's still wet behind the ears. His father, RIP, a kosher Jew, the former cantor in the artisans' synagogue here, entrusted his son to me before he died and I gave my solemn promise to look after him. If the boy goes out traveling on his own and something should God forbid befall him, I'll be liable to his father forever. I heard tell that your daughter's going away, so I came here to request that the boy should travel with her, understand? If, as the Bible says, two are everywhere better than one, how much the more so when traveling?"

"In my opinion, it's only just to grant your request, but a father's opinion is of no importance these days. Please, Reb Avrum, go to my daughter and try to present your request to her."

So Reb Avrum went to Khantse, and hardly had he said, "I received a letter," when she cut him off out of impatience and distraction. "Received? Me too, Reb Avrum."

Reb Avrum looked at her in amazement. Excited, carried away, a friendly smile on her face. "I know, Reb Avrum, I know," she blurted out. "I know, Hershele's coming with me."

"You answer before I even ask. I haven't even said it and you already know," said Reb Avrum, regarding her sharply. "Where do you know it from?"

"Where from?" stammered Khantse, turning red from having opened her mouth and trying to correct her mistake. "I know about Hershele . . . received . . . accepted his request. What else is there to talk about? Hershele's coming with me!"

Reb Avrum didn't reply. He stood for a time with his head bent and his brow furrowed, as if considering something that had just occurred to him, then came back to himself and, waving a finger alongside his nose, said "*Shkots*" in an amiable tone.

•   •   •

Several weeks without so much as a note passed after Khantse's first letter from Vienna. Her parents and the rest of the family were terribly upset and asked Reb Avrum whether Hershele might have written him something about her. "No," said Reb Avrum—he had yet to receive any letter from Hershele at all and was getting very worried. Idlers, loafers, the newspapers with feet who provided the city with news, took up the issue on their tongues, interpreted it in frightening ways, and concluded with a moral particularly apropos to parents, that they should not allow their daughters—and that includes widows and divorcées—to go wandering around in the world. Especially not with young men, not even with little boys.

In the middle of all this a letter posted in Leipzig arrived from Khantse. It started with, *"Mazl tov. I am married to Refoel!"*

"Fire take all hot springs," screamed Leybtse in a fury.

"Oy, I'm gonna kill myself. A wedding without her parents!" wept Yentl.

"Everything's come out OK. It looks like they'd settled on Leipzig before, and the *shkots* knew all about it," said Reb Avrum with a satisfied smile.

5

MOYSHELE'S LETTER to his parents, which Yarkhi had delivered, read as follows:

You will soon be receiving a welcome guest, a dear man to whom I owe lasting gratitude for his great love for me and his sterling character, from which I learned as much as I could in my youth and have still plenty more to learn now— I mean good old Reb Avrum, who is here in the city right now for the wedding of one of his grandchildren, a daughter of his daughter, who is married to a typesetter. At our first meeting I said hello to him with joy and gladness, and he—get a load of this!—he answered rather halfheartedly, as if he were angry. This was explained in a long talk we had that lasted around two hours. Dad, it was the same story as you and I had when I enrolled in the Rabbinical Seminary—anger, wrath. Red-hot anger at government schools for Jews in general and at the Seminary in particular because, to begin with, they weren't made in the Jewish tradition, weren't made by Jews themselves but by outsiders; anger at the supervisors, the teachers and the students, especially the Seminary students, whose behavior is not what it should be and who don't let a Hebrew word cross their lips; they don't even want to know it. Some of them go into the school as ignoramuses and come out the same way; those who go in with Hebrew forget it immediately and come out with nothing.

Those were the kinds of sins that Reb Avrum enumerated, shaking his head at me like I was a lost soul who had strayed from the proper path. If I didn't succeed in changing his opinion about some of my colleagues (and really I couldn't, because he was right about many things), I was at least able to prove conclusively that I am the same person as I was before, and haven't let myself be led at all astray. Once he found this out, he gave me a very affectionate kiss and said, as he tends to, 'Shkots!'

Why am I telling you all this? On account of a very important question that came up in our conversation and which it is my duty to report to you, my dear parents.

Since one has to say that the Jewish schools, including the Rabbinical Seminary, are looked down on by our people because they were not instituted and run in the Jewish tradition by the Jews themselves, the question of the point to my studying here and working so hard naturally arose. To be a teacher in some school somewhere? Good God, whom would I teach, when there are hardly any students there? A teacher in the government Jewish schools is subject and subordinate to the gentile supervisor who holds him in terror and does what he pleases, like the goy who directs the Rabbinical Seminary. He rules our Jewish teachers with an iron hand and considers them as nothing. This lowers the teachers in the eyes of their students, which in turn lowers the prestige of the Jewish subjects.

And if I don't become a teacher, maybe I'll be a rabbi, a Rabbiner, that is? Woe to such a rabbinical post, which is not what a rabbinical post is supposed to be and was imposed upon us by force. Something that is nothing more than duress will cause trouble in time—factionalism, quarreling, strife in Jewish cities and towns.

I've thought a lot about this and have finally decided that after graduating from the Seminary, I should enroll in a university to study medicine. Some of the better students, my friends, are also thinking the same thing. Reb Avrum has agreed to it, and now I'm presenting my plan to you and asking for your consent.

Our exams are starting soon, and I'm studying hard for them with my friend Sapir, the son of Herr Mikhoel Sapir. If God helps me to pass, I'll have one more year until I graduate.

My friend Sapir is simply in love with Reb Avrum. Reb Avrum's habit of calling people he likes shkots has become a private joke with us. Herr Sapir invited Reb Avrum for Shabbes; there were other guests there, too, from whom Yiddish and words of Torah were heard. Reb Avrum is absolutely charmed by Herr Sapir, in whom Torah and worldly wisdom, yidishkayt and Haskole are combined. "If we only had lots of people like him!" he says. Reb Avrum's character hasn't changed, he's the same warmhearted, feeling person as before, but his body has been weakened by the great troubles which he has had in recent years. It's vitally important that his health be improved. I've begged him to spend two or three months with you in the village; the fresh, clean air, the savory fragrances of the grass, the fields and the forest will give him health and life. I'm well aware of how much you love Reb Avrum, so he'll surely be a very welcome guest. Reb Avrum has consented to this, and he'll be with you in a few more days.

The letter was delayed in transit and reached Moyshele's parents at the same time as Reb Avrum himself. When Reb Avrum started to talk about

Moyshele, describing each individual detail of his life, and said that Moyshele was going to be a doctor, the pleasure brought a sweet smile to Shmulik's lips.

This smile deserves to be placed in our archives, so that future historians and researchers can use it to prove how far the *Haskole* had penetrated by then. I mean, a little while ago we saw a Jew crying and moaning over the rejection of the study of Torah; there was nothing better or greater to him than a rabbi, an authorized instructor of the Jewish people. Yet the same Jew later turns away from the rabbi; he's pleased by the doctor, delights in him with a sweet smile—and it took no more than four years to go from the weeping to the smile, from the rabbi to the doctor. And who might this Jew be? Shmulik, who from being an old-clothes man became an *aktsiznik!*

Book Nine

Epilogue

THE POGROMS OF THE 1880s—may they never happen again—inflicted terrible sufferings on the Jews of many towns, Kaptsansk among them. Its citizens became *kaptsonim*; one part of these *kaptsonim*, new and old alike, abandoned Kaptsansk to wander the world, while the other stood packed and ready to drag itself off wherever it felt like going.

Pogroms and fires—these are the twin destroyers that afflict the Children of Israel, ravaging them, their houses, and possessions, creating plenty of paupers, widows, and orphans wherever Jews happen to live. Merely mentioning their names makes a Jew behold scenes of terror: doors and windows knocked out; dishes and utensils broken; pillows ripped open, feathers flying—blood, fire, and screaming . . .

Kaptsansk is desolate, its streets silent, wailing and lamentation in its cemetery. And it isn't Elul, the Jewish time for prayer and weeping, the season of mourning for decaying nature. No! It's springtime, with bright days, green fields, and a cloudless sky. The world is blooming, growing, blossoming, living; it's a time when hunting birds and animals is forbidden, and when it's open season on Jews.

And the unfortunate Kaptsanskers, who have no one to comfort them among the living, stretch themselves out on the graves of their parents, weep and beg mercy from the dead. Women weep bitterly and claw at the graves, waking the dead, the martyrs, urging them to go as quickly as possible to implore the Heavenly Father and be spokespeople, good mediators before the Throne of Glory on behalf of the wretched, desolate Children of Israel. Those who are planning to depart across the sea bid farewell to the graves of their loved ones, which they will never see again. They cry and make others cry with them; they all sigh and spill rivers of tears.

Master of the Universe! If your wineskin of tears is still not filled with the tears of your Jews, one could make a mistake and think that it is like that coverless pot in Gehenna that can never be filled. So the question is: Why do you have the wineskin? Why are the tears poured into it? And what possible use does it have?

And while Kaptsansk was weeping thus, a carriage drove up to the cemetery and a richly dressed man of about forty got out. The paupers huddled around the gate made way for him and stretched out their hands; he gave each of them a donation and went into the cemetery. The Jews were astounded to see him there, thinking that he was probably a great lord, an important courtier, and did not know what to do. Some, in their great confusion, held onto their hats and moved slowly backward; others stayed where they were and bowed, but their hats moved back and forth on their heads, and the weeping suddenly ceased all over. Women, female prayer-leaders, and professional mourners, all fell silent immediately. They blew their noses, looked at this newcomer with wet, red eyes, winking to one another and whispering in each other's ears.

The faces of the Kaptsanskers looked very strange at that moment. They expressed fright, abasement, subservience to powerful and exalted aristocrats. They all stood as petrified as Lot's wife when she turned into a pillar of salt.

Shh . . . quiet!

"Where's the *shammes?*" the man asked in Yiddish.

These words penetrated the ears of each individual and all of them were resuscitated on hearing that he was a Jew. Their bowed backs straightened up, they pulled their hats down over their eyes and felt their strength returning.

"Heh, heh. If he's a Jew, then why are we. . . ?" said those who had retreated, coming nearer now and looking the man and his clothing over.

"If he's one of our brother Jews, then we're . . ." said those who had stayed in their places, approaching the man to shake hands.

"He speaks Yiddish, he does," exclaimed the women loudly, pointing with their fingers and staring, their faces half-laughing, half-sad, like the face of a child after it has cried.

"Please," said the man to the *shammes*, who had come up to him immediately, "Please show me where the grave of Leyzer-Yankl is."

"Leyzer-Yankl, Leyzer-Yankl?" wondered the youth of Kaptsansk. "Who is this Leyzer-Yankl?"

"The *bal-tfile?*" said the older people, recalling him for the good. "A kosher Jew, Leyzer-Yankl, a marvelous *davener*. The words came out of his mouth like pearls, each one melted all the way through you. People melted with tears from his *Unesane Toykef*, the way he used to weep at 'who will live and who will die,' quietly, quiet as a child, then give a roar and yell and wring the last syllable out of "who will rest and who will wander"—it could have brought tears to a stone. There's no *bal-tfile* like *him* anymore."

Leyzer-Yankl's grave was long since overgrown with grass, the stone almost completely sunk into the ground, and it had been difficult to find. The *khazn* made a *mole* by the grave, and when he shouted out "the soul of Eliezer-Yaakov," tears came to the visitor's eyes and he turned aside and wept.

From there he went to the grave of "the woman, Malke-Toybe." The *khazn* made a *mole* there too, but it was harder to hear his voice because of the number of people weeping over a newly covered plot beside it. This was the grave of a mother and her two daughters who had been raped and murdered on that black day; part of the *mole* could be heard making its way to heaven through the weeping: "The soul of the martyred woman Beyle the daughter of Ben-Tsiyen and the souls of her two pure and martyred daughters." The voice carried far, frightening birds in the air; crows in the tree-tops were scared to death, and flew off quickly with noise and screaming.

Hearing the name Beyle, the visitor was seized with trembling. He stood for a while, perplexed, his head hung down, then wrung his hands with a deep sigh, went quickly back to his carriage, and drove to his inn.

The next day the visitor went walking through the streets of the city, going into the ruins of the houses, the plundered, empty shops, noting everything down in a little book. It was a great miracle for you, Kaptsansk, that you didn't go out of your mind trying to figure out who this person could be and what he could be doing there.

And I, Mendele, happened to be in Kaptsansk just then. As soon as the visitor came into the synagogue courtyard and saw me standing beside my wagon of books, he recognized me immediately, and after looking for a while I recognized him, too, and we each said hello to the other.

I'd seen him for the first time in Tuneyadevke. We met there, he liked me, and we discussed important issues. His arrival in Tuneyadevke had also caused a clamor. Sleepy Tuneyadevke awoke staring in amazement; how did someone like this pop up all of a sudden in its dreams? Tuneyadevke looked as if someone had suddenly brought a candle into the darkness where chickens doze on their perches; the chickens blink their eyes, half-asleep, and with foolish expressions on their faces groaningly ask each other, "What kind of nut runs around at a time like this?"

All of Tuneyadevke ran out to meet me as I drove into town, all of them crying breathlessly, "Some kind of person, Reb Mendele, some kind of person has turned up here all of a sudden, like he dropped from the sky! He goes around looking at everything, listening, searching, investigating, crawling into every hole: the poorhouse, the *talmud toyre*, the *kheyders*, the big *shuls* and the little ones. What could it be? He's for sure not doing it for nothing. Maybe he's a government spy? Tell us, Reb Mendele! The shop-keepers have disposed of their *khomets*. Who knows what's gonna happen? The flesh on the *melamdim* is creeping. Jews with yarmulkes are trying to keep off the streets."

When I had finished my work, unpacked my bundle of merchandise, given my horse a bit to eat and wanted something to eat myself, I looked around, and into the courtyard of the synagogue came a man in his middle years, dressed in fashionable western clothing, who looked, from a distance, like a clown, as if he'd worn the same clothing into the bathhouse where everyone else is naked. I ask you: Why doll yourself up, for whom, when worn soles, bare shoulders, naked chests and holey elbows are also alright in Tuneyadevke, and are not, God forbid, such a crime? I'd already guessed that this was the newcomer and looked at him in no very friendly way. He came up to my wagon and stopped there, looking silently at me, my horse, my merchandise. And then he asked me, "What kind of books have you got there, *Reb Yid?*"

"Books!" I mumbled just to get rid of him, thinking to myself: "Back off a little, buddy."

"But what?" he asked in a pleasant voice, looking me so kindly and mildly in the eye that he won me over. I stopped my act and answered him like a *mentsh*, in real words.

"Jewish books: regular prayer books, holiday prayer books, penitential prayer books, women's prayer books, and dirges—the usual stuff."

"And that's everything?"

"There's more, but not much. It doesn't pay to carry them—*Haskole* books in Hebrew, they're like stones. The Jews here don't even want to touch them."

"The Jews here," he said sighing, "The Jews here need bread, not books."

"What?" I said, as if to bawl him out. I was a little perturbed with him for dumping on my wares. "You say that the Jews here need bread, not books? Well, I can assure you that there's never been such a good season for my books—dirges, women's prayer books, penitentials, and Psalms—as right now."

"God forbid," the stranger apologized. "I didn't mean *these* books. I meant those full of chastisement, reproof, moral advice; nothing but smoke and mirrors. '*Feh*, you're neglecting your duties. *Feh* on this, *feh* on that.' The books that the Jews here, as you said, don't want to pick up. And they're right. Bread, a livelihood—that's what they need. Sermons and chatter are no cure for an empty stomach: rigmarole and clever sayings, moral counsel and flowers of rhetoric are no compensation. To complain that there are cast-off machines rotting and molding somewhere in a corner is nothing but a joke. Go, lift them up with your own hands, put them to the work that they're meant for, with real raw materials, not with words, and you can bet that instead of moldering they'll take on a whole new appearance. But insofar as I'm familiar with this corner of the world, it seems to me that you don't have too many practical people. You preach very beautifully, you make jokes, you argue, you cook up schemes, drive them forward with your mouths—and you do little, almost nothing."

His words made a real impression on me: Weren't things really the way he described them? The times were very bad, fresh troubles and afflictions by the day. Kaptsansk, Tuneyadevke, and other such Jewish towns lay sunk in troubles like a cow up to its neck in mud, and those masters of rhetoric speak and awaken. "Kaptsansk, awake! Bestir yourself, wake up, Tuneyadevke!" Others reprove, screaming: "*Gevalt, kaptsonim! Gevalt*, idlers! *Gevalt*, depressed, humiliated, beaten, sick, broken—gird yourselves and get up! If you're not for yourselves, then who is for you? Kaptsansk, be not Kaptsansk! Tuneyadevke, be not Tuneyadevke!" And all of them together: "Animal, out of your mud! Free yourself, animal. Stretch out your tail, shake your feet, lift, pull, pull this way and that and get yourself out!"

I stood for a long while, quietly marveling at these utterly different words, this utterly new type of person, so unlike our usual "experts." Have you ever heard that a "German," an "expert," should take the side of the common Jewish crowd, and not God forbid dismiss its books and hold only by those that seemed appropriate to *him?* This was a new style indeed—what should I call it?—German with a hasidic lining, frock-coat, and *tsitsis* in one. Something absolutely brand new, over which we should say *Shehekheyonu!* Still, I was peeved with him in my heart: What right did he have to accuse others of talking but not doing? What did he do? Who was he, where did he come from, how did he come to be here in our corner of the world? I figured that I had no need to be shy—I'd do what I always do, what a Jew always does on first meeting someone, so right away I asked him, "What's your name? What is His Excellency's business? And where does the Jew come from?"

I received no answer to these questions, only a nod of the head and a smile—this person seemed to like me very much. Later, after we knew each other a little better, he invited me to his inn, where he treated me to a glass of punch and detained me for a good couple of hours, questioning me—an expert—on sundry matters. We fell into a deep conversation, in which he told me certain important things in strictest confidence.

His name was Heinrich Cohen. He was one of the delegates, deputies, emissaries, that is, sent by a group of wealthy foreigners to study the Jews who had suffered in the pogroms. Their business was the close observation of Jewish life in those places where the Jews were living, of their occupations and needs, and the consideration of what means could be used to improve their condition, lest they, God forbid, perish. In the meantime, they could give the unfortunate indigent at least some help to keep body and soul together. These emissaries were traveling around among us, holding meetings and consulting with intelligent people. Heinrich Cohen, a learned and distinguished man, was traveling around the entire Glupsker region.

A month passed between our first meeting in Tuneyadevke and our encounter in Kaptsansk, and his face had changed so much in this short time that I only recognized him after a good long look.

"Why are you looking at me like that?" he wondered. "You don't recognize me? So many days have passed since we parted?"

"From the way you've changed, you'd think it was years. You've aged, sir, in these few days." I shook my head as if my heart were breaking for him.

"I've seen enough misery to make these few days into several years. Oy, Reb Mendele, the misery of the Jews—I've seen so much of it in so brief a time!—their misery is terrible, their misfortune is great, their troubles a deep abyss. Please, come see me this evening; we'll talk and have some tea. Right now I have to see the town fathers about helping my poor Kaptsansker brothers in any way I can."

When I came into his room that evening I found him hunched over, deeply absorbed in writing. Papers and open books lay on the table. As soon as he noticed me, he gave me a friendly invitation to sit down across from him.

"I'm glad you came," he said amiably, straightening his back. "It gives me an hour's rest from thinking and writing about Jewish troubles. This work of mine has been depressing me terribly lately. Because now, in these last days, and here in this town, my work has turned into something with no hope of any positive outcome, no practical results for the future—despite what I thought when I started. All the things that my eyes have chanced to see lately have blasted my previous thoughts, sunk them like a foundering ship."

"But still, you can't lose hope," I reassured him with mild words. "Let's assume that everything you thought about us in your country was nothing but dreams. You should know, though, that dreams are also worth a little something to us Jews here, as are the notes of certain types of merchant, and we take them to the Lord along with other dreams of ours when He's occupied with the Priestly Blessing and doesn't have time to look around. We tell them to him quickly, as we rattle off the "May It Be Thy Will" prayer that we say during the priests' blessing: *Khazkeym ve-amtseym,* He should be good enough to make our dreams come true. And if they should require amendment, if they need a little work yet, do it with your good will."

"Right on target," he said with a slight smile, and then turned serious. "What foreigners think about you Russian Jews really is nothing but dreams, and dreams are what their thoughts should be called. Our brothers there think, or dream rather, that the pogroms here are a simple epidemic; that it's more or less possible to improve the bad conditions through intercession with the government and the financial aid that rich Jews here and there will give to the needy; that the Russian Jews are all great boors, terrible spongers, savage, uneducated creatures with no idea of how to behave—and that it's absolutely necessary to educate them. A big millionaire, as rich as Koyrekh, wants to put some tens of millions into the government treasury for the establishment of special schools for Jewish children— that's what they think out there. But the reality shows how deluded they are. From everything I've discovered through my research and seen with my own eyes, it's become clear to me that I, as well as they, have been living in a dream. The pogroms are not merely an epidemic. Intercession with the government will not only not help, it'll make things worse because it reeks of fawning, involves a humiliation, a diminution of respect for the people of Israel. Poverty is increasing, the hosts of paupers swell from day to day. The places where they are allowed to live are too small and 'the gates of prosperity' are locked before them. When they are pressed by need, when there's nothing left to live on, they leave their homes and wander about like lost sheep, beating a path to the doors of the wealthy, the charitable, and begging and mooching—what else should they do?—disgracing themselves in public. Charity alone? What power, what significance does it have against such abysmal poverty, such multitudes of paupers that want is increasing by the day? The charity that our brothers in other countries send here can only be of temporary help—and even that is severely restricted. The Jews here scarcely participate in this charity at all. Some can give but don't want to; some want to but can't. The Jews here are not unfortunate because they're savage and uneducated; on the contrary, they are unfortunate, as our enemies say, because they're better educated than the common people among whom they live. The Jews, they say, are too clever, too educated; they have a finger in every pie—in business, banking, manufacturing, every branch of science, trade and commerce—and they must therefore be kept away from the common people of the land, simple folk who cannot, do not know how to compete with them."

"So, then, what should be done?" I asked.

"Oy, Master of the Universe, help your people, your poor people of Israel!" he sighed.

"This prayer of yours is a desperate measure, and it's useless already, way too late," I said, as if a little offended. "It isn't fitting for a man like you to despair."

"These two big books that you see here," he said, pointing to the table.

"In one I note down everything I've seen and heard in all the Jewish places I've been to. In the other I sum up all my thoughts and propose how and by what means to improve the condition of the Jews here. I can tell you straight out that much of what is in there looks foolish now even to me, and there are many things in need of complete revision in light of the development of *a certain significant thing* which, out of our present confusion and chaos, has begun to dawn in the Jewish world, although it is now no more than the redness that presages the sunrise *in the east.* The work that lies before me is great and very hard, and it is impossible for me to devote myself to it right now. Jewish suffering has sapped all my strength."

"Your sorrow over Jewish suffering," I said, "brings you great honor. Your colleagues, the emissaries, they, as we say, aren't eating their hearts out like you are."

"My colleagues, you say?" he said, standing up. "My colleagues are 'of the Mosaic Persuasion.' You understand? And I am a child of the people, a Jew like all my forebears, a thread woven in with them in the great piece of cloth known as 'Jew' from time immemorial. My colleagues are all foreign born, and I—I was born in Kaptsansk."

"You, a Kaptsansker?" I said in amazement.

"Only one who is flesh of their flesh, bone of their bone, who has suffered the same sorrows and pains, can feel a people's sorrows and pains. I passed my youth in deprivation and want; suffered hunger and cold, slept on every bench in the synagogues, until a good and prominent man had mercy on me and took me out of this country with him. He cared for me like a father, enrolled me in a famous school from which I emerged a learned man with something to offer the world. I have a very respectable occupation. Yes, yes, that's how it is. I am a Kaptsansker and my name is—Hershele!"

We said goodbye the next day, each of us wishing the other well.

With all due respect for myself, I made a bit of a slip while we were wishing. Confidentially, I'm no great master of wishing, just like a lot of other Jews who go to convey their wishes at some festive occasion, thinking that it's their duty. They bleat away for maybe an hour, their faces shining, and say nothing. They tell the host: "May God grant that . . . that . . . that . . ." And the host tells them: "Would that . . . that . . . that . . ." They're at the point of vomiting, throwing up, fainting, each side is wishing to be rid of the other . . .

I usually hold myself back and polish off my wishing duty shortly, muttering into my beard. But this time, out of my love for Reb Hersh, I was seized by a crazy desire to come out with full-fledged good wishes. No sooner had I opened my mouth, though, than it was as if I'd been strangled. I bleated, I that-ed that . . . that—don't ask me what—and found myself in a fix, neither here nor there. Reb Hersh, long may he live, got me out of it with delicacy, saying wisely, "I know, I know, Reb Mendele. You wish me more good than it's possible for your mouth to say. Would that the Master of the Universe should fulfil all your good thoughts for me and for all Israel right away, speedily and in our days."

"Amen!" I answered with all my strength. "Amen, and so may it be His will!"

Glossary

Agode: Classical legendary material.

Akeyde: Binding of Isaac.

Aktsiz: Liquor-license monopoly in Czarist Russia; dominated by Jews.

Aktsiznik (pl. *Aktsiznikes*): Employee of the liquor-license monopoly.

Ato Zoykher: "You Remember," a Rosh Hashana prayer.

Bal-tfile: Prayer leader, cantor.

Bartenura: Commentator on the *Mishne.*

Beheyme: Animal, idiot.

Bentsh goymel: Make the blessing for having been delivered out of danger.

Bes-medresh: Study house; basically, a smallish synagogue.

Bokher: Male youth; unmarried man.

Daven: Pray.

Dreydl: Top played with on Chanukah.

Esreg: Citron for use on Sukkes.

Eyn Yankev: Collection of legendary and narrative material from Talmud.

Farfl: Crumb of dough; a type of noodle.

Feh: Yuck.

Feierabend: Work's over! Time to go home!

Fir kashes: The four questions asked by the youngest son at the Passover *seyder.*

Fleyshik: Pertaining to meat, or one who has recently eaten some.

Gematria: System of numerology in which Hebrew letters represent numbers.

Gemore: Talmud.

Gevalt: Exclamation of surprise or dismay meaning literally, What happened?; drat!; help!; heaven forbid!

Goles: Exile.

Gotenyu: Dear God.

Goye: An old gentile woman.

Groschen: Penny; small coin.

Gut yontef: Happy holiday.

Hamantasch (pl. *hamantaschen*): Triangle-shaped pastry eaten on Purim.

Hamoytse: Blessing over bread.

Haskole: The Jewish Enlightenment.

Havdole: Ceremony to mark the end of the Sabbath or a holiday.

Haydà: Let's go; get moving.

Kaddish: Doxology, recited by mourners or those who have *yortsayt*; also, a son.

Kapores: Chickens used for ritual; in singular, a scapegoat or person who is sacrificed.

Kedushe: The Sanctus; one rises on tiptoe when saying "Holy."

Khale: Fancy bread for Sabbath and holidays.

Khap: Grab, snatch.

Khapper: Kidnapper who took children to make up the quota of Jews in the Czarist army; these kidnapped children were often stand-ins for the children of wealthy or prominent families.

Khayey Odem: An ethical work.

Khazer: Pig.

Khazn: Cantor.

Khes: Eighth letter of Hebrew alphabet.

Kheyder: Elementary Hebrew school.

Khomets: Leaven, possession of which is forbidden on Passover; a symbolic amount is burned on the eve of the holiday. Also, contraband, something you're not supposed to have.

Khumesh: Pentateuch.

Kiddesh: Sanctification recited over wine.

Kiddesh Levone: Blessing of the new moon.

Koyletch: A kind of fancy bread for Sabbath and holidays.

Koyrekh: Korah; according to Agode, so rich that he didn't want to leave Egypt at the time of the Exodus.

Kreplakh: Dumplings.

Lamed-vovnik (pl. *Lamed vovnikes*): One of the thirty-six hidden saints for whose sake God keeps the world going.

Lekhayim: Cheers, skol; also used to mean simply a drink.

Makher: Big shot.

Makhzer: Holiday prayer book.

Maskil (pl. *Maskilim*): Adherent of the *Haskole*.

Mayriv: Evening prayer service.

Mazl tov: Congratulations!

Medresh: Midrash.

Megile: Scroll, history, a long drawn-out story; also, the Book of Esther.

Mekhaye: A pleasure, a delight.

Melamed (pl. *melamdim*): Hebrew school teacher.

Mentsh: Human being; respectable person.

Meylekh Elyoyn: A High Holiday hymn.

Mezoynes: Blessing over baked goods to which *Hamoytse,* the blessing over bread, does not apply.

Mezumen: Company of at least three men, which alters the form of the grace after meals.

Mezuzes: Doorpost amulets.

Mikve: Ritual bath.

Minkhe: Afternoon prayer service.

Minyen (pl. *minyonim*): Quorum of ten males required for certain prayers.

Mishne: Earliest stratum of Talmud.

Mitsve: Commandment, good deed (three women's *mitsves:* throwing a bit from all baking into the fire, going to the *mikve* after menstrual periods, and lighting candles on Sabbath and holidays).

Mole: "God Full of Mercy," prayer for the souls of the dead.

Na'aritsokh: Part of the *Kedushe.*

Nebbish: A hapless jerk, to be pitied rather than scorned.

Oymer: Period of forty days between Passover and Pentecost, a time of semi-mourning.

Oy vey: Woe is me.

Parve: Neither meat nor dairy.

Peyes: Sidelocks.

Peysakh: Passover.

Peysakhdike: Pertaining to or fit for use on Passover.

Phnyeh: No screaming hell.

Pilpul: Subtle argumentation.

Pittum Haketoyres: List of ingredients for the incense used in the temple, the recitation or writing down of which is considered to help drive away sexual thoughts.

Rabbiner: Government Rabbi in Czarist Russia; graduate of seminary rather than yeshiva; more a government official than a religious leader.

Rashi: Preeminent commentator on Bible and Talmud.

Reb Yid: Mister.

Rebbe: Hasidic leader; also, *melamed.*

Rebetsin: Rabbi's wife; also, overly pious, sanctimonious woman.

Seyder: Ritual Passover meal.

Seyfer Ha-Yoshar: Book of Righteousness, popular religious work.

Shabbes: Sabbath, Friday night to Saturday night.

Shabbes goy: Non-Jewish Saturday servant for Jews.

Shakl: Blessing over certain drinks, especially whiskey (and milk).

Shalakh-mones: Gifts exchanged on Purim.

Shammes: Beadle of a synagogue.

Shatnez: Mixture of wool and linen, forbidden by the Bible.

Shehekheyonu: Blessing said over something new or never before seen, or something pleasant (for example, holiday, encounter with a friend) that hasn't happened in a while.

Shekhine: Divine presence.

Sheygets (pl. ***shkotsim***): Under-age gentile male; also, Jewish boy who's either misbehaving or not very religious.

Shikse: Gentile girl; young gentile woman.

Shkots (pl. ***shkotsim***): Scamp, rascal.

Shlep: Influence, pull.

Shlimazl: Incompetent at taking care of business.

Shlogn kapores: To wave a *kapore* (a chicken) thrice around your head and transfer your sins to it on the eve of Yom Kippur.

Shmaltz: Fat for cooking.

Shmattes: Rags; old or cheap clothes.

Shmendrik: Hapless jerk.

Shminesre: Eighteen Benedictions, central prayer at all services, recited standing.

Shofar: Ram's horn, blown on Rosh Hashana and throughout the month of Elul.

Sholem aleykhem: A greeting; equivalent to hello.

Shor ha-Bor: Legendary giant ox to be eaten by the righteous when the Messiah comes.

Shoyshanas Ya'ankoyv: Purim hymn.

Shpil: Line of patter.

Shtetl: Small Jewish town.

Shtrayml: Round fur hat worn by Hasidim.

Shul: Synagogue.

Shulkhan Orekh: Authoritative code of Jewish law.

Shvues: Pentecost.

Simkhes Toyre: Rejoicing of the Law, a holiday.

Slikhes: Penitential prayers recited from the beginning of the month of Elul until Rosh Hashana, a month later. On Saturday before Rosh Hashana, they're recited at midnight.

Spodek: High, round fur hat worn by Jews.

Sukkes: Feast of Tabernacles.

Taf: Last letter of Hebrew alphabet.

Tallis: Prayer shawl.

Talmud-toyre: Charity school, a *kheyder* for the children of those who couldn't afford tuition.

Tanakh: The Bible.

Tanna: Mishnaic sage, rabbi quoted in *Mishne*.

Tefillin: Phylacteries.

Teygelekh: A type of pastry.

Tishe B'Ov: Ninth of Av, fast-day commemorating destruction of both Temples.

Tkhine: Women's prayer, in Yiddish.

Toysfes: Commentary on Talmud; known for being difficult and incomprehensible.

Treyf: Not kosher; make treyf: bribe.

Tsaddik: Holy man, *rebbe*.

Tsholnt: Simmered Sabbath stew.

Tsimmes: Fruit or vegetable stew.

Tsitse: Ritual fringe.

Tsitsis: Ritual fringes or the garment to which the fringes are attached.

Unesane Toykef: High Holiday prayer.

Va-yehi ha-yoym: It was that day.

Vey iz mir: Woe is me; same as *oy vey*.

Vishnick: Cherry brandy.

Vide: Confession before death.

Volekhl: A kind of song.

Yale: Hymn recited on the night of Yom Kippur.

Yidishkayt: Jewishness, Judaism, appropriate Jewish behavior.

Yontef: Holiday; more loosely, celebration.

Yortsayt: Anniversary of someone's death.

Zmires: Sabbath songs.

Zohar: Major Jewish mystical text.